Obligation for Justice

A NOVEL

By
Glenn
Morris

Bainbridge Editions

Boston New York Paris

Published by
Bainbridge Edition
A division of
Eli Bainbridge and Company, Inc.
33 Murray Road
West Newton, Massachusetts 02465
855.556.5561
646.405.5280 (NYC)
33.1.70.38.73.20 (Paris)

www.bainbridgeeditions.com

For Bob, my brother,
who everyone else knew as Momo

1

ANNIE SITS ON THE EDGE OF THE SINGLE BED, THE contents of the shallow drawer strewn about her. The stiff corners of the photographs catch the nubs of the candlewick chenille bedspread, so Annie gets up, gathers the pictures into a jumbled pile and lays them on the night-stand. She folds the spread back, exposing a triangle of sheet. The small Laura Ashley flowers startle her for a moment. She had been meaning to change to the winter sheets since last fall—more for convention than anything else; now it was on the verge of becoming summer again. No one had used this room since Liz had gone back to Baltimore for her senior year at Johns Hopkins. Liz had come home only a week ago. She had gotten a job in Cambridge and an apartment in Boston with two friends, both male.

Annie didn't particularly like Liz's room-mates, but she had resolved not to mention her reservations to Liz. Woodrow was the bigger of the two—football big, steroid big—and seldom expressed more than the occasional grunt. Connie was shorter and skinnier and more than made up for Woodrow's silence.

Annie sits back down on the bed, picks up a bunch of the photos and fans them in her long fingers like an over-sized deck of cards. She sorts them, first separating the Kodaks from the Polaroids, then separating out those with Harold in them, some of which she will offer to the kids. Finally she sorts them into a rough chronology, not

1

so much of years as of her life's events. She spends the fading hours of the afternoon with the photographs, remembering most of the moments and events they chronicle with a clarity that surprises her. She is flooded with emotions, see-sawing between sheer joy and haunting melancholy. She feels torn between an urge to call the kids and the need to finish her journey.

The sun has moved deep into the west now, its thin yellow glow high-lighting the dust motes floating in the air. Annie shifts her attention to the particles, pondering dreamily their sizes and shapes. How much, she thinks, they appear like remnants of lives lived, each one a different shape, a different size, a different weight; each one from its own place in life's fabric. It has been a year to the day since Harold left, and nearly five months since he died.

Annie imagines that the photographs are like enlargements of the specks of dust. It is as if her guardian angel picked the most important specks to be immortalized in a form she could see. Here are the traces of her life and the lives of her husband, her children, her parents, her friends.

Harold had moved out and left her with this house, this museum, to the lives of others. The kids may be grown and gone, but their artifacts remain: the basketball hoop in the driveway and the bikes in the garage. On the dark-stained shelves, her mother's Beleek and bric-a-brac still stand where her mother had arranged them; the Infant of Prague still stands on her mother's sturdy old oak buffet. Everything in her life, it seems, belongs to someone else's story. So little is truly hers. She is, she thinks, the curator of the collected belongings of the dead and the gone.

As she gathers up the photos she will keep, Annie remembers she has two more sets of photographs: one in the box with her wedding album and the other in the old typewriter paper box sealed up in the back corner of her sweater drawer in the old chest that had been in her bedroom before she married Harold. It's a wonder she ever kept it, she thinks, but now it seems as if God had willed it. It has remained taped shut for all of her twenty-three years of marriage. She wonders whether the specks of dust from that box are here in the room too, or if they have been successfully shut away, hermetically sealed against the infection of her memories. When her mother died three years ago and they sold her house, the chest and the sealed box had come here. She'd been tempted to open it then, but that would have been an act of disloyalty toward Harold, and Harold, after all, had been her crutch, had given her the strength to close that chapter in her life. Only now was she struck by the thought that her mother had not thrown it out.

Annie goes into her closet, where the chest resides now, and opens the sweater drawer. She fishes under the sweaters along the drawer bottom until her fingers touch the box. An electric anticipation sweeps up her arms to her chest as she draws the box from its dark lair and sets it upside-down atop the pile of sweaters. She slips her fingernail along the seam of the box top, easily splitting the brown paper tape that has become brittle with age. A cacophony of scents greets her as she lifts the lid: a slight vinegary smell followed by a soft earthiness that reminds her of the wet leaves of fall. She removes the piece of onionskin paper from atop the photos, and Ben's illuminated face appears immediately in his eight-by-ten hand-colored high school graduation picture: smiling at her, but with an intense stare in his eyes that seems to accuse her of betraying him.

Perhaps she had, she thought, although it hadn't felt like it at the time. Lives change, after all. People change. Besides, she may have done him a favor. From all reports, Ben was doing just fine. She often heard about his projects in the news, especially the huge Ocean Park project, and she saw the picture of him in the Globe with his wife and his two sons on the porch of his newest home on some island. She had only been faintly jealous; after all, she had had most of her dreams fulfilled. She had her kids and her nursing career, and she had had Harold.

The question burning inside her now was whether she would betray Ben again. If she did, it wouldn't be out of malice. She had wanted to reach out to him when she'd seen him in the hospital emergency room the night that Don was brought in, but she hadn't. She'd told herself then that she didn't want to intrude, even though she'd known that wasn't entirely the truth. She'd reached out to families before, had offered them solace for their pain. That's how she had been trained. Who knew how many Saturday nights had unfolded with the same scenario? Hadn't she reached out to Clyde Washington's mother after Clyde was delivered, already dead? She might have approached Ben then—might have, but didn't. She had spoken with Ben's wife. Annie had recognized her from the Globe photo, but the newspaper photo failed to capture her full essence. His wife had seemed to make Ben larger, simply by being in her presence.

Annie looks back at the young Ben's face. She hopes the police will work things out for themselves so she won't need to get involved. Perhaps they are being blind—or choosing to be blind. They treated the rich and famous differently from everyone else. She had prayed each morning and evening for the last week-and-a-half, seeking guidance from her patron saint. She had decided to wait until today to see if there was news of any development in the investigation, but there had been nothing since the two-paragraph story on the third page of the Metro section. Now, with Ben's eyes staring back at her, she wonders if she will be able to fulfill the obligation Saint Anne had confirmed. When the story had broken after Clyde Washington's death that Clyde had been a suspect in Don Holt's murder, she'd known Washington's killer had been Ben.

The slamming of the door downstairs startles her. She withdraws her hand instinctively, as though afraid of being caught in a criminal act. She closes the drawer quietly, stands, brushes down her skirt, and turns toward the bedroom door.

A pleading voice reaches her from downstairs, "Mom, Mom, are you here?"

"Coming, Liz."

COMING FROM THE bright light of the street, Ben Holt is blinded by the darkness in the bar. He moves—too carefully, he thinks—toward a stool he can barely make out, but that is close enough to the door to abbreviate his self-conscious movement. The form of a pudgy, pony-tailed woman emerges slowly from the darkness behind the bar.

"What'll it be?"

"Miller, please."

"Lite?"

"No, High-Life."

The woman disappears back into the darkness, but this time she is farther away before Ben loses sight of her. His eyes are getting used to the lack of light. Slowly a dozen figures begin to emerge from the gloom at the far end of the bar, then a dozen faces appear, staring at Ben. A trim man with grey streaking in his black hair approaches him from behind the bar, a bottle in his hand held chest high. Ben recognizes Sallie from Don's stories and knows that he still played baseball in a city league—his dreams of making it to the majors having stalled in a single-A club in upstate New York.

"Want a glass?" Sallie says.

"Please."

Sallie pulls a glass from under the bar and rubs it briskly with a bar towel. He sets it on the bar and slides a Rolling Rock coaster under the bottle as he sets it down. "You're Don's brother, aren't you?"

"Yeah. Ben."

"I'm Sallie. What brings you here?"

"Today is his birthday."

"Yeah, we know, but what brings you here?"

"Just wanted to have a couple of Miller's and visit with him."

"Could have done it when he was here."

"Not really my home any more."

"Was once."

Sallie walks away toward the far end of the bar and stops to talk to the faces. In two's and three's they stop staring at Ben and gather in pools of conversation. One woman— dark and pretty but with an unfortunate nose—smiles at Ben before joining one of the pools.

It would be tempting to think that Sallie's Bar had had a glorious past. Ben, frankly, knew better. The fake barn-board plywood façade, painted a dull, cold tone of gray, is part of the "We don't need anything any better" aesthetic that is far too prevalent in his old hometown. Ben ponders the gray color, trying to recall where he's seen it before. There is a row of small rectangular windows high on the front wall. They are 'licensing board windows'—not placed for allowing light into the dank interior, but the minimum requirement of the alcohol control board; the theory being that they could peer in from the sidewalk to catch any wrongdoing. The beer company signs in the windows had been all anyone had really needed to know about the place. The "Sallie's" sign that Ben had seen above the door in jig-saw-cut wood script almost seemed superfluous.

Ben's wife, Claudine, had once commented that the neighborhood was extraordinarily ugly and depressing. Ben had objected with a wry smile, arguing that nothing could possibly be so ugly by chance and so it was, therefor, a work of art. The area had been very different when he'd been growing up here. Then, Lynn Hospital, with its various specialist departments, medical offices, and the nursing school, had filled most of the city block across from Sallie's. The emergency room had often been the second-home of the Holt boys, and Ben's dad had complained that they should have named the x-ray suite after the Holts since they had spent so much time there for one sports injury or another. The huge multi-building, several-story hospital complex had been torn down, and its site was now covered by a single story big-box supermarket with a few smaller stores attached, all fronted by a huge, undulating field of asphalt sparsely populated by small Japanese cars and a significant scattering of pick-up trucks. The strip of stores where Sallie's stood had once housed a prosperous pharmacy with a marble soda fountain counter fronted by vinyl-covered chrome stools. In those days, the drugstore made soft-drinks from syrup mixed with carbonated water drawn from a pastel-painted, chrome-handled spigot. Ben recalls now how he, Don, and Ron would visit the store and order their own variations of Coke: vanilla Coke, cherry Coke, pineapple Coke made with chunks of pineapple intended for the sundaes, and a decidedly failed attempt at chocolate Coke. It had become a game: "Who could create and drink the grossest Coke." Ben pictures a movie of the three of them and the drugstore clearly in his mind. The movie continues with a flood of scenes with Don in sharp focus: child-Don, man-Don, but, Ben thinks, there will never be an old-Don to laugh with and share those memories with again.

When the hospital had died, the drug store had died with it. Everything is so ephemeral, he thinks, arising and dying. As Ben remembers the old nursing school and Annie, he drains the remnants of the bottle into the smallish glass. The last dribble barely drops into the glass when Sallie appears with another bottle.

"Said you wanted two. The first one's on me, the second's on them." He waves the bottle toward the back of the bar. The brunette steals a moment's glance at Ben, then rejoins a conversation with a tall, pale, balding man wearing mostly-brown coveralls over a grimy once-white t-shirt, a hammer still dangling from a loop at his hip.

"Thanks."

"You're welcome to come back...next year." Ben notices Sallie's emphasis on "next year," separated from "come back" by a momentary pause. An objection arises in him, but he quickly realizes he won't be back before then anyway. There is no reason to be.

Ben finishes the remainder of the first beer and re-fills the glass from the second bottle. He quickly drains the glass, refills it one last time with the last of the second bottle, and finishes the beer with one draw. He slips a couple of bucks under the glass and slides off the stool and out the door. Once again, he is blinded, this time by the sunlight. He pulls the sunglasses from the inner pocket of his linen jacket, places them over his eyes, and looks into the low, hazy red sun. His driver starts the Jag and the engine springs to life with its classic soft whistling from the big engine. Ben moves toward the car and opens the rear door. He stands at the open door, his arms resting on the car's roof, and looks across the street where the hospital and the nursing school once stood. He dreams of the long path that brought him here:

2

October 1953
Roxbury, Massachusetts

B EN STARTLED WHEN THE BEDROOM DOOR HIT THE wall. His father strode into the room, bellowing words—or sounds—Ben couldn't understand. He watched his father's lips quizzically, trying to make out the words, but his father ignored him and marched straight for Don who sat in the corner crying, his little legs splayed out in front of him. He stood looking down at Don for a moment, then turned and stepped back towards Ben, grabbed a handful of his pajama top and lifted him from the floor. Ben hung helplessly as his father marched out through the living room, opened the door from the first floor apartment to the building's front hall, continued out through the wood-framed glass door and set him outside on the landing. Ben heard the click of the doorlock behind him and sat down on the cold front steps, waiting for his father to return with his belt. He listened for noises from the apartment, but heard nothing. A couple walking by looked at him shivering in his thin pajamas and walked off, whispering to each other. At the corner they stopped. The woman looked back for a long moment, but the man took her arm and led her across the street where they disappeared into the darkness.

Ben decided he needed to find someplace warmer. He got up and walked to the corner, then turned down the side street toward the alley behind their apartment building. He tried the latch on the gate to the building's small backyard, but it wouldn't open. He peered through the narrow slot between the wooden fence post and the gate and saw that his mother had threaded a coat-hanger through the small hole in the latch, locking it so the boys couldn't get out while she was busy in the house. He looked around the dark alley for a stick or another coat-hanger to jimmy the obstruction from the lock, but only found a small piece of asphalt siding from the building next door. The siding only broke apart when he tried to slide it against the latch and hanger.

Ben turned and collapsed against the gate. His efforts to jimmy the lock had warmed him a bit, but he now started to shiver again. He thought of going back to the front door and ringing the bell for his father, but fear and pride overrode his need for warmth. He would wait for his mother to come home, though he wasn't quite sure he knew how long it would be. He did know he had to find someplace warmer to wait. He ran through a list of potential places in his head: the front lobby of the doctor's office down Warren Street, which he rejected because he might be found there and returned to his father; the Mishkan Tefila shul or the church at Saint Joseph's, which he rejected because they were too far away from the corner he expected his mother to cross on her way from Dudley Station; the space under the bulkhead to the cellar at Frankie's house where he could watch the corner through a crack in the siding that he'd discovered playing hide-and-seek. The bulkhead would do.

He felt relieved when he tugged on the handle to the bulkhead and it moved. The panel was heavy so he lifted it to his knee first, then slipped under it and lifted it with all of his six-and-a-half year-old strength over his head, his arms fully extended. He stood there for a moment trying to move onto the stairs to the cellar so he could lower the panel quietly. He decided the trick would be to walk down the stairs, moving his hands along the panel until it closed. A small pride welled up in him when the panel settled quietly against the sidewall.

It felt good to be out of the wind and he was warm for a while, but the damp cold under the bulkhead seeped into his body and he felt colder than he'd ever felt in his life. He tried to move around to keep warm, but the space was small and every time he moved he caught spiderwebs on his face and his arms. Even the spiders had abandoned the space for a warmer spot, but they had left their egg casings behind, adding to Ben's discomfort. Either from cold or fear—or both—Ben began to shiver uncontrollably. For the first time, his pride and determination were shaken by the thought that he might die here and be found as a skeleton, his body devoured by bugs.

Ben longed to be at home again with his brothers—even with the baby, Ron, who cried and made his father mad. His mother was always calm around the baby, but his father hated any disturbance when he was home. He would fall asleep in his chair, a lit cigarette dangling from his yellowed fingers and threatening to set the chair on fire until Ben gently removed it and placed it, still lit, in the ashtray on the lamp table. Ben never knew whether Ron's crying would go unheard or would wake his father to a stampede of rage. He and Don tried to keep the baby quiet, amusing him with toy animals or letting him suck on their little fingers. Sometimes Ben would pick him up and, setting Ron's tiny head against his shoulder, march him back and forth through the small apartment until he burped or threw up, then fell back to sleep. Too often, Ron would wake up and start crying as Ben laid him back in his crib, and the fear of his father's rage would rise again. The only relatively peaceful days were Fridays and Sundays when Ben's mother would be home from work. The boys loved those days and fought to survive until the next one.

Ben realized he had to move from his hiding place. As much as he wanted to be home, he didn't want to face his father. He didn't know how to find his mother, but he did know she walked from the Dudley Square subway station on her way home from work. She had shown Ben and Don the station one day when she'd taken them to spend the afternoon with her friend, Betty, while she took the train to the Lying-in to see her doctor just before Ron had been born. Norma and Betty were the only friends of his mother that Ben knew of, and they shared an apartment a few doors from the station. Both of them had taken the boys to the station to wait for their mother when she returned from her doctor visit. They liked Norma and Betty, but they rejoiced when their mother emerged from the dark of the station and the three of them could walk home hand-in-hand.

Ben was sure he could find the station again. It was a bit of a walk, but he remembered the look of the streets and stores and houses along the way. He remembered Betty talking to his mother and Norma about a man in the waiting room at the station, and he imagined it must be warm there. If he couldn't find his mother, he thought he could at least find Norma's and Betty's apartment from his memory of the stores on the first floor.

Ben lifted the panel slowly and peered out. Seeing no one around, he pushed hard against the weight—too hard—and the panel flipped over and slammed hard against the bulkhead wall. Stunned, he stood very still until he saw a light come on in the house. He took off running.

He was almost at Dudley Square when he finally stopped to catch his breath. Ahead he could see the lights of the station. His spirits fell when he saw that the adjacent stores were dark. He might not be able to find Norma's and Betty's apartment, after all. He worried that his plan to find his mother would fail. He crossed to the station and peered around the corner of the huge opening to the well-lit busway. There was a bus running, but no one was in it—not even a driver. He slid against a brick wall to the ground. His mother would have to come this way. He was still warm from his running, but knew he would be cold soon. He didn't want to look for the waiting room, fearing he would miss his mother as she left the station. He was tired, but determined to stay awake.

"Ben?"

Ben opened his eyes and realized he had fallen asleep.

"Ben, what are you doing here at this hour?"

It took his eyes a moment to focus. He looked up and saw Betty and a man in a uniform looking down at him. Her kind face was perfect—nose just right, eyes just right, perfect blonde hair—reminding him of Betty Cooper from the Archie comics that he hid under his bed to keep from his brothers. He looked at her, trying to think of an answer, but said nothing. Betty bent over towards him, her face now close to his.

"Ben, why are you here? Where's your father?"

"Home, I guess."

"Get up. I'll take you home."

"I was waiting for my mother."

"Come. I want to have a talk with your father before your mother gets home. She puts up with his... Well, never mind, *come*."

Betty turned and talked to the man. Ben could only hear snippets of their conversation. "I'll take...his father...wanna come...wait for you...his bullshit...tired...works every night...no more." Betty turned back to Ben, took his hand, and pulled him to his feet. As they walked back towards Ben's house, Betty talked and the man either grunted or agreed. When they got near Ben's apartment house, Betty turned and gave the man a kiss on his lips. The man waited on the corner as Betty and Ben walked past the two buildings from the corner to Ben's. She marched up the stairs with Ben in tow, entered the front vestibule, and rang the first floor doorbell. She rang it again.

Ben's father appeared in the glass in the inner door. He wore an old t-shirt and shorts. As he opened the inner door, Ben noticed the sleep still in his eyes. He looked at Betty, but said nothing.

"I brought your son back. What was he doing out at this time of night? Look at him. Dressed only in pajamas and walking the street in the cold."

"He ran away."

"Don't give me your bullshit. If he ran away, why were you sleeping? Why weren't you out looking for him? Go in the apartment, Ben, and get into bed." Ben slid past his father into the apartment. He stood by the living room window so he could still hear Betty and his father.

"Look. He and his brother were fighting and I took Ben out to the front steps to stop the fighting."

"In this cold? In his thin pajamas? Are you an idiot?"

"Don't talk to me that way," Ben's father said, but without conviction.

"I'll talk to you any way that's necessary to get you to act like a father and not a selfish buffoon."

"I did go looking for him and got a few of the neighbors to help. We couldn't find him."

"You and your stupid temper. You blow up, *then* think. It's going to get you into more trouble in life than you're going to be able to handle. Mark my words. And don't blow up at Binky when she gets home either. I have nothing left to say to you." Betty started back down the stairs toward the sidewalk and the man in the uniform moved from the corner to her side.

Ben couldn't see his father, but heard the inner door of the vestibule close. He scooted into the bedroom he shared with his brothers, then slid into bed next to Don and pretended to be asleep. He cocked one eye open to look across the small room to Ron's crib. Ron was gurgling rhythmically, fast asleep. Ben's father opened the door, then closed it after a long moment. The apartment was quiet.

Don stirred. "Don't ever run away again. I thought you were gone forever and I was so scared."

"I probably will," Ben said. "But if I do, I'll always come back for you."

ROBERT POLISHED THE brass escutcheon on the front entry door for the third or fourth time in the last half-hour. He wanted to see Claudine off on her first day at *Premiére Année*, but knew that Madame would not tolerate loitering. He heard steps on the grand staircase and peered from the vestibule to see Madame descending. She was a serious and severely beautiful woman—marble-white shin and perfect jet-black hair, green irises punctuating almond-shaped eyes. Robert had never seen a smile though her thin, rose-red lips.

"Robert, Robert."

"Yes, Madame."

"Where is Claudine? We'll be late. I don't know why she insists on walking, anyway."

"Yes, Madame. I believe that she is still upstairs."

Bernadine stopped at the bottom of the staircase, turned and climbed back up. She strode down the long hall to her daughter Claudine's door, knocked twice and entered without waiting for a response. "Claudine, we must..." Her eyes widened, and her face froze as she took in the scene before her. "What have you done?" she cried, then lowered her voice and repeated, "What have you done?"

Claudine was sitting on the floor, her back against her bed, wearing her blue school jumper and a starched white blouse. She had a pair of scissors in her right hand. Spread neatly out before her were the dismembered parts of her school blazer. "I won't wear this, Bernadine. It's not right. See?" She pointed the scissors at the sections of stiff horsehair lining arranged on the floor as if they were freshly cut from the bolt and waiting to be sewn. "And feel this *horrible* fabric."

Her father entered the room and immediately covered his mouth with his hand, but failed to stifle a hearty laugh.

"It's not funny, Marcel. Don't encourage her."

"My love, it is indeed funny. It's hilarious."

"Then *you* deal with this." Bernadine pushed past Marcel and disappeared through the door.

"Come, Claudine, leave that, and let's walk to school."

Claudine stood, then sat on her bed to put on her shoes before rising again and taking Marcel's hand. She was tall for her age and her long neck was made to look even longer by her short, bronzed-red hair.

They walked the hall without talking. As they descended the stairs, Robert looked up at them and clapped very quietly. "Ah, you've forgotten your blazer, Mademoiselle."

"Robert, will you please call my tailor? Claudine and I will be by this afternoon to have him make a new blazer."

"Yes, sir."

"And we'll tell him 'no horse-hair,' Marcel," Claudine said.

"Yes, we will, Claudine, and perhaps a cashmere fabric."

"Cashmere *and* wool, Marcel."

3

THE MORNING SUN SHONE THROUGH THE ALMOST-closed blinds in the large window on Ben's side of the bed. It illuminated the small dots and threads of dust and cast yellow stripes across the green-blue cowboys and brown bucking broncos on the wallpaper of the boys' bedroom. Ben lay in bed, his eyes open, running through the plans for the upcoming day. The weather had been cool and rainy for late June and the boys had been confined to their porch or the cellar of Jimmy's house. Jimmy had set up a clubhouse in an old coal bin. It had a dingy sofa, a few wooden chairs in various states of disrepair, and makeshift shelves laden with Jimmy's comic book collection. Jimmy's clubhouse was their hideaway.

"Don. Wake up." Ben reached over and nudged his brother, then swung out of bed and looked through the narrow slot of the blind. His father's car was gone. He looked through the hole where the string threaded through the blind slats and confirmed that the usual location of the car was empty, then lifted a wooden slat to make sure it was gone. Today was going to be a baseball day.

"How's this? Do you think this will work?" Ben held the ball up for Don, who took it in his hands, rotating and pressing it, confirming its firmness.

"Yeah. Pretty good job."

The baseball had had a dingy grey-brown stained cover when they'd found it in the monkey-weeds against the outfield fence. There had been only a few stitches missing in the cover then. Now, a week-and-a-half and a dozen games later, the leather cover was gone and some of the string windings had been lost near the end of the last game. Now, the ball had a shiny new cover of black electrical tape. Ron grabbed the ball from Don's upturned hand and headed down the driveway toward the street, flipping the ball into the air and catching it in his bare right hand. Don followed, punching the pocket of his worn glove. Ben carried their one bat and their only other glove—a Ted Williams model fielder's glove from Sears that had been his birthday gift a few weeks earlier.

"Hey! Wait up!" The three boys turned to see Jimmy and Richie running towards them. Jimmy had a bat stretched across his arms, held in place by his left, gloved hand. Richie was wearing his glove on his head. It almost slipped off as he ran, so he had to raise a hand to steady it.

"Gotta ball?" Jimmy said. Ron held up the shiny black ball.

"Lemme see." Jimmy reached for the ball, but Ron clutched it to his chest.

"Tell him lemmee see."

"Give him the ball," Don demanded.

Ron held out the ball at arm's length, staring at Don, and Jimmy grabbed it. "Not much of a ball," Jimmy said. "Didn't you have white tape?"

"Yeah, but it's cloth tape and it's not sticky enough and the ball would have lumps," Ben said.

"Fuck. I didn't ask for the fuckin' Encyclopedia Britannica version."

"Don't say fuck in my yard."

Jimmy glared at Ben for a moment. He was known for his explosive temper and the stare between the two boys was full of electric tension. Nobody talked back to Jimmy.

"Well, maybe someone else will bring a *real* ball," Richie offered.

Jimmy blinked and turned towards Richie. He reached up and flicked the glove off of the taller boy's head. They all looked at the fallen glove as if their silence would resurrect it. Then, one by one, all of the boys except Ben laughed—Jimmy last.

"Let's go. We need to get a field before they're all taken," Don called over his shoulder as he set out down Shepard Street.

Fifty feet before the railroad bridge, which spanned over the road between two concrete walls, Don turned to Ben and took the bat from his hand. Neither boy spoke. Don walked on, dropping the fat end of the bat onto the sidewalk. *Bung. Bung. Bung.* Don drummed their marching cadence—one beat for every two steps—dropping the bat on the right footfall. Right foot. Right foot. *Bung* foot. *Bung* foot. At the underpass, the echo amplified and returned the beat—*bungung, bungung.* As they reached the corner of Harbor Street, the view opened to the ballfields. To their disappointment, both of the fields were being used.

"I'll see where the games are." Richie took off running, pausing at the fence to thread his long, skinny body through a slim, vertical break in the chain link, ignoring the gate some hundred yards away. By the time the rest of the boys had gotten to the fence and squeezed through the hole in turn, Richie had headed to the farther field, having stopped for a moment to talk to a couple of kids sitting along the fence. The kids turned out to be Artie and Mike. When Don, Ron, Jimmy and Ben got to where the two boys were sitting, they slid to the grass-pocked gravel beside them.

"This is our best bet. I think the other game just started," Artie said.

Richie ran up and dropped to the ground facing them. "This is our best bet. The other game just started," he panted. The other boys nodded.

"These guys are in the bottom of the seventh," Artie said, more to himself that to anyone else.

"How many are they playing?" Ben asked.

"Nine."

"*Nine?* Who plays nine?"

"They're putting up a team for the Summer League that starts after the Fourth."

"Hmmm. If we could get enough players, *we* could put up a team."

"Yeah."

Ben watched the older kids play. They were not very good. The first baseman dropped a couple of balls that were in his glove. Stiff new glove, Ben thought. The second baseman closed his eyes whenever a grounder was about to hit his glove.

"We could beat these guys," Ben said.

"Yeah, if we had nine players," said Don wistfully.

"*Sometimes* we have nine players," Richie said defensively.

"Yeah, but *sometimes* doesn't count. Besides, when did we ever have nine, except when our cousins were here from Hartford? We'd forfeit more games than we'd win. Might not lose any though. If we don't have more than nine we can't do it. Look, we've only got seven today."

"Stevie's coming."

"Yeah, well, so's Christmas."

The boys resumed their watching of the game, now in silence, each dreaming their own dreams of their Summer League team. Jimmy threw small pieces of gravel at the remains of a beer bottle no more than ten feet beyond his outstretched legs. Ron piled gravel in the pocket of his glove, then dumped it and started again. Ben stared across the field, past the game and the players in motion, toward the houses arranged in the sun on the far side of Harbor Street. The building at the corner was a triple-decker with a single-story front porch facing Shepard Street. It was a large cube with straight sides and cut-out windows and rear porches stacked one upon the other attached to identical apartments for each of its three stories. The only break from the perfect cube was the three-story bay that extended for all three stories at the far side of the front porch. Ben knew the room layout well. The neighborhood was full of triple-deckers. Richie, Artie, Stevie and Mike lived in triple-deckers. The Holts had bought one when they'd moved out of Roxbury two years ago.

The houses along Harbor Street were smaller, with pitched roofs and sunny, flowered gardens. Most were clapboard, a few shingled—small wooden houses adjacent to much larger, asphalt-clad triple-deckers.

Ben noticed that the sun made the windows of the apartment buildings appear opaque, while the smaller, mullioned windows of the houses
revealed patterns in lace curtains and the folded drape of heavier fabric. The bright light created a painting in shade and shadow, revealing
lines and blocks of decoration on the smaller houses while bleaching the
nearly-flat façade of the apartment buildings.

Ben was watching the way the sun played on the porch of one of
the houses when he noticed a gang of six or seven boys and a couple
of girls walk through the gate. They headed for the far diamond,
stopped at the bench, and picked up a couple of balls, tossing them
back and forth. They gathered around one of the players, who was
standing with a bat in hand, twenty feet to the left of the batter.
The player stiffened and stretched to his full height. Several of the
other players left their positions on the field and moved in behind
him. The two groups stood face-to-face for a few minutes, then the
newcomers straggled away behind the backstop and headed down the
left-field line towards Ben and his friends. The players moved back
to their positions, but watched the newcomers until they had passed
the left-fielder. Then they resumed the game. Ben noticed one of the
newcomers, who was quite a bit shorter than the others, walked with
a pronounced limp.

"Clyde Washington." Jimmy answered to Ben's unasked question. "Trouble."

Clyde was followed by the biggest kid Ben had ever seen—a kid
whose neck was thicker than Ben's waist *Holy fuck*, Ben thought.

"We've got this field reserved," Clyde announced when he was
two dozen feet away.

"Can't reserve a field until after the Fourth, and then you have to
be in a league," Jimmy retorted as he moved towards Clyde.

Clyde's friends quickly gathered around him, facing Jimmy.
Jimmy was taller than Clyde, but not by a lot. The rest of the gang
was taller than Jimmy, including the two girls.

"Well, those're old rules. These're *new* rules."

"Yeah? Whose rules?"

"Woodrow's rules," Clyde said, jerking his thumb toward the mountain of a kid. "Right, Woodrow?"

"Yep, these're Woodrow's rules," the mountain rumbled.

"Wanna play against us?" Richie offered.

"We'd kick ya ass." One of the girls laughed, and the others, except Clyde and Woodrow, joined in.

"No. We're taking the field," Clyde ordered, and the laughter died.

"Sorry, but that isn't going to happen." Ben pushed through the circle to Jimmy's side. He was taller than everyone there but Woodrow, but he was certainly no match for the mountain.

"You lookin' for a hurtin?" Clyde asked. He moved half a step towards Ben and stared into his face—but he stared at Ben's chin, avoiding his eyes.

"Look me in the eyes if you've got a question," Ben demanded quietly, so that only Clyde, and perhaps Woodrow, could hear him.

"You guys need help?"

Clyde broke his stare first and looked toward the approaching voice. Ben looked up and saw that he and Clyde were now surrounded by the players from the contested field. He noticed for the first time that emblems were sewn on their left sleeves with the letters P-A-L underneath.

"Do we?" Ben asked Clyde.

"Just having a conversation," Clyde said. He backed away from Ben, stumbling into Woodrow. "Get out of my fuckin' way," he yelled at the mountain and moved past him. He slapped one of the girls. "Who're you lookin' at?" His gang turned and followed him. They marched back the way that they had come, back toward the far field, around the backstop and toward the street. The players on the far field stopped and watched the procession. Clyde stopped when he was even with the pitcher and whipped the ball he had taken earlier at the kid's head. The pitcher instinctively raised his glove, and the ball glanced off it toward third.

"That guy's bad news," said the player who had spoken earlier.

"Thanks," said Ben. "What's the P-A-L stand for?"

22

"Police Athletic League"

"You're *cops?*" Ron exclaimed, surprised that kids could be cops.

"Nah. They have a league with teams from around the city. We're the Connery team."

"Can we come watch you?"

"Sure. Games're Tuesday nights."

"You play at night?"

"When it gets dark they turn the lights on. Listen, gotta go."

"Thanks again."

"Yeah, thanks," Jimmy added.

"Just watch out for them. They'll be back, but not today."

The game lasted until the sun fell low into the sky and a salty sea breeze chilled the players' fingers. Nobody really wanted to continue; the other ball field was long empty and the ball was now losing more tape and bits of string whenever it was hit. So they called the game, argued a bit about the score, picked up the bat and headed for home—back up Shepard Street with the sun setting just over the scrap yard fence, setting out beyond the huge buildings of the Riverworks plant that loomed over the landscape almost a half-mile away. The Riverworks buildings were so massive and menacing that their night-time glow was fearsome and depressing—pools of yellow, orange and red light amidst dull cold-gray blocks that became blackish behemoths in the silhouette created by the security lights behind them. Clouds of black smoke underlined in orange belched from several smokestacks, blown horizontally by strong land breezes toward the sea. Ben thought that Hell must resemble that plant.

Don started up his baseball bat drumming again as they approached the railroad underpass. Ahead of them, one of the girls who had been with Clyde and Woodrow, the girl that Clyde had slapped, stepped from behind the bridge abutment. She was facing them, her shirt open to her waist. Her eyes darted occasionally to her left, her head tilting slightly as if she was listening to a hidden voice.

"Hi boys." The girl swung her hips slightly and slid her left hand through her open shirt and into the band of her shorts.

23

Trouble, Ben thought. When they were directly under the bridge, less than a dozen feet from the girl, two more girls stepped from behind the abutment. One was wearing a man's bowling shirt and apparently nothing else—at least nothing Ben could see. Jimmy was almost giddy as he walked up to the first girl and slipped a hand into her open shirt and around her back.

The girl shrieked.

"Wha'choo doing to my girl?" demanded a voice from behind them. Clyde, Woodrow, and three other boys stepped from the monkeyweeds that Ben and the other boys had just passed. Ron had been straggling behind as usual, so Clyde and Woodrow were almost upon him. Ben moved quickly and got between them and Ron, facing Clyde and Woodrow.

"Ready for your whuppin'?" Clyde raised his hands to Ben's chest and pushed him. Ben grabbed Clyde's forearms and pushed him back. The two boys stood face to face for several seconds—it seemed much longer to Ben—their hands clamped on each other's forearms, pushing and twisting in a small dance. Then Woodrow moved behind Ben and was about to wrap his arms around Ben's neck when Don moved in and blocked him, swiftly hitting Woodrow just below his left eye, sending the mountain crumbling to the ground. He quickly turned on Clyde with a four- or five-punch flurry that sent him sprawling back into the abutment wall where he slid to the ground. Ben moved around Don and the grounded attackers to face their backup. Don moved in behind him and all but one of the boys took off back into the monkey-weeds.

The remaining boy stood, dumbfounded, his arms hanging loosely at his sides. From behind him, Ben heard girlish screams and boyish grunts. He turned and saw that one of the girls was tying to hit Richie in the head with a Coke bottle, but Jimmy had his arms enclosing hers. The other girls were hitting Jimmy about his head and shoulders, trying to make him let go. When Ben and Don moved towards them, they stopped their attack and ran back behind the abutment and up to the tracks. They turned back to where Clyde and Woodrow had fallen, but the two boys were gone.

"Jeezus, Don. What did you do to Woodrow?" Jimmy slipped his right arm over Don's shoulder. "You, like, sucker-punched him."

"What did you *want* me to do...*hug* him? Or dance with him like Ben was dancin' with Clyde?"

"You were ice. You cold-cocked him."

"Yeah, take 'em when they don't see it coming," Richie chimed in.

"Where's Ron?" Ben was suddenly aware of his brother's absence. All of the boys turned around. Ron was sitting on the ground with his back against the abutment wall.

"Get up." Don yelled. "You're sitting in pigeon shit."

Ron rolled onto his right hand and rose from the sidewalk. He bent to pick up the baseball glove.

"Don't touch that!" Don screamed. "Now you've got pigeon shit on your hands!"

Ron wiped his hands on his shirt, reached and picked up the glove, slipped his hand into it and grinned at Don.

"I'm never touchin' that fuckin' glove again." Don said.

"That's exactly what he wants." Ben said, shaking his head. He bent to pick up his own glove and noticed his hand was trembling. He quickly stuck it into the glove, tucked his glove under his right arm and headed for home.

"*Ba dump, ba dump,*" the bat sang.

"Thanks, Don."

"Brothers got to stick together."

4

"UP AND AT 'EM." THE BOYS' FATHER SLAPPED HIS open hand against the door of their bedroom just as the door slammed against the wall. Ron, lying in the lower bunk, pulled the blanket over his head. Don swung his legs over the edge of the upper bunk and sat silently, gazing into space. Ben's single bed was empty, the covers drawn up and folded down at the top, six inches of sheet showing just below the pillow.

"Where's Ben?" Ron grumbled under the covers. Don sat still, staring aimlessly.

"Better be downstairs in ten minutes if you're gonna eat. We start work in thirty."

Ben was just coming through the back door when his father entered the kitchen, the screen door slap-slapping into the latch. The boys' dog, Rinty, sat at his feet, staring up at him with his eyes locked onto the Milk Bone in Ben's hand.

"You'd better make some breakfast for your brothers. I don't want them dawdling when they have work to do. Then load the wheelbarrow with two buckets of sand and bring it around the back."

SPENDING A SATURDAY during summer vacation working with the Old Man wasn't pleasant, but wasting a precious Saturday like this at the end of a school week seemed worse to the Holt brothers. It wasn't as if they were doing anything interesting, just waiting for the Old Man's command to fill the wheelbarrow or bring him a stone for the retaining wall he was building to level off the backyard. The Old Man would spend the day sitting on an over-turned bucket, barking orders.

Once the wall was laid up to its planned height, the Old Man decided to top it with a cap of concrete. "Ben, get a dozen two-by-sixes out of the garage. Ron, get a can of eight-penny nails in the workshop. Don, hold this rod and I'll shoot the grade."

Don held the rod as straight as any surveyor's helper, although he was barely eleven. Ben carried the long two-by-sixes four at a time, as many as any construction laborer, although he was just twelve. Then they stood waiting for Ron to return with the nails.

"Ron, move your ass," the Old Man bellowed.

Ron emerged from the workshop a few moments later, the can of nails clutched to his chest. The Old Man grabbed the can and withdrew a few nails, pushing them into Ron's face.

"Jesus Christ, almighty Jesus, you're useless. Do these look like eight-penny nails?"

Ron stood staring silently at the can.

"Get in the house. You're useless to me."

Ron walked slowly toward the house, his head and shoulders hanging.

"Don, take these back and bring me eight-penny nails."

AFTER A LONG day of wrenching boredom, Don and Ben walked into the house to find Ron sitting in the reclining chair, a plate of Crispy Treats and a sweating glass of milk at his left hand, watching basketball on TV.

Ben shook his head. "You did that on purpose, didn't you?"

"Yup."

Don whacked Ron on the back of his head. "Yeah, but now Dad thinks you're stupid."

"Stupid enough to sit in here watching TV while you guys waste an entire Saturday mostly standing around watching him. Yeah, *I'm* stupid."

Don scowled. "I don't care. I'm never gonna let him think *I'm* stupid. I'm the *smart* one in this family. You'll see; you'll *all* see, but especially him."

The following summer, Don wrote book reports on thirty-nine books and received an academic award for his effort. The next closest kid had written twenty-two. Ben admired Don, knowing there was no way he had actually read the books, but had instead figured out the pattern for writing believable reviews.

5

May 1962

ALICE MCCULLEY CARRIED HER BOOKS HIGH ACROSS her chest with her arms folded around them. They were held together with a leather strap that had been her father's when he was at Holy Cross.

The day had started a sullen gray, but the afternoon sun was warm on her face. Alice usually got a ride home from her father who was finishing his day at *The Shore Press* ("News That's Right"). Recently, she'd started getting a ride in the morning as well, when he'd been heading to the office and she'd wanted to get to school in time for the seven a.m. Mass. She loved the early morning time with her father when he was bright and smiling, unsullied by the weight of the day's news. It was the one time of day when she shared him with no one—not her mother, not his reporters and editors, not the subjects and suspects that populated the stories he ran.

This morning Alice had told her father she needed to spend some time at the library after school and that she'd take the bus home. Now, as she walked from the Girls' High building, past the Annex where the Freshman homerooms were, she turned from the path that would lead to the library across the Common and headed over to the parking lot where the boys' track team practiced.

Alice was on a mission.

DON SAT ON the last stool on the far end of the soda fountain at Angelo's Spa, sipping slowly from the cone-shaped paper cup inserted in the brown plastic base. His eyes followed Toni, the fifteen-year-old daughter of Tony Angelo. Most guys, man or boy, wouldn't dare to cast their eyes on the beautiful Toni, lest they incur the wrath and retribution of Tony the Father. Don respected Tony's power, but he admired Toni's already ample breasts and long black hair even more.

Don nursed the nickel Coke as long as he could, sat quietly on the stool for a moment savoring one last look, then dropped from the stool and headed for the glass candy cases at the rear of the store. Tony's had less penny candy, but more nickel bars, than Reitman's. Tony didn't like to have a lot of kids hanging around the Spa. He wanted to get the adult business when those adults weren't hanging around the bar at the Hi-Hat Café across the street. Tony owned the Hi-Hat too, as well as the liquor store that sat kitty-corner from the Spa. The only corner that he didn't own was Stone's Bakery.

When Don stepped up to the candy counter, he found the view of the candy in the double-wide glass case blocked by a big, open book that sat on the glass top. The book had columns of names and numbers that Don knew contained the names, bets, pay-offs and debts of the people who played the daily numbers. Don had come in with his mother one day when she wanted to play her number on her birthday. She placed a bet on special numbers commemorating the birthdays of each of her children, her mother and father, each of her dozen sisters and brothers, her husband and herself. She also played on the feast day of Saint Anthony, the patron saint of lost causes whose feast day she would announce to everyone each time it came around. Each year, Don wondered who or what the lost cause was, and the unanswered question made him try to be especially good for a few days before and after.

Don's head bobbed back and forth as he attempted to survey the bars in the case. A large policeman appeared, closed the book, stuck it under his arm and walked through a double curtain into a back room. As soon as the cop left, one of the ladies who worked at the soda fountain came over and stood silently behind the case. Don pointed to the box of Chunky bars and laid a nickel on the glass. The woman slid open the door at the rear of the case, withdrew a Chunky and placed it on the glass next to the nickel. As she withdrew her hand, the nickel disappeared and she silently walked back to her station and started up a lively conversation with a man and woman sitting there. Don felt uncomfortable, but was fascinated by the magic disappearance of his nickel. As he walked from the store, conversations paused, and he felt that the eyes of each of the patrons and the ladies behind the counter were following him. They'd stare at him again, he vowed, but then it would be with respect when they all knew Toni was his. He would find a way, he thought, to win Toni and the admiration of everyone who would see them together.

BANG!

Alice heard the shot as she came around the corner and saw Ben leaning against a low granite wall, watching two boys running the hurdles. As the first two boys crossed the finish line at the far end of the track, Ben and another boy got up and took their places in the starting blocks. As soon as Ben was set, he looked to the side where the coach was standing and saw Alice standing directly behind the coach. Ben shot her a wry smile, then turned his head and his attention straight down the track.

Bang!

The shot startled Alice and Alice's scream startled the coach who hadn't known that Alice was so close behind him. She repeatedly assured the coach she was fine, but her ears rang terribly. It hurt to talk, and it hurt to hear him talking.

Ben walked toward Alice and opened his mouth to speak. "Please don't ask me if I'm okay," she said. "Here." She handed Ben a small envelope. "You don't need to open it now. It's an invitation to my house. I'm having a party Saturday and I want you there."

Ben smiled and stuck the envelope in the front band of his track shorts. He nodded and turned away, trotting back to his teammates.

Alice watched his long, slender back for a moment and admired the way his butt branched into his thin hard legs. She sighed involuntarily, then headed for the library to meet Annie.

One more stop and her mission would be accomplished.

DON PERCHED ON the edge of the bed, dressed only in his almost-white jockeys. He had been up for half-an-hour, but he wasn't really awake. It was the same routine every morning. Ben and Ron had learned long ago not to disturb Don during his morning ritual. His mother believed that Don was praying during his "spell." He had God in his heart, she insisted, and she allowed him his "prayer time." His father was not at all convinced that this was so; he was still dreaming, he said—dreaming with the sun coming up and work to do. On Saturdays when he wanted Don and Ben to help him with whatever construction job he had going on, he would goad Don into moving, yelling, "Get your ass in gear!"

Whenever he was asked about his morning reveries, Don remained silent, looking at his inquisitor as if they were demented. Ben believed that Don's brain and his body hadn't connected yet and Don was waiting for his motors to warm up. Ron believed Don was planning his day—running through schoolwork, writing the course of the day's events before they happened. Through it all, Don remained silent. He wasn't praying, he wasn't thinking about today or tomorrow, next week or next month. Don was dreaming his life.

ANNIE SAT AT the long oak table with her books on the chair next to her. The seats in the large reading room were about half-full. She had taken two facing the door so that she could see Alice when she walked in, although the thought occurred to Annie that you could be blind and deaf and you'd still know when Alice entered a room. Alice was a force of her own.

Alice had called the evening before and commanded Annie's presence at the library this afternoon—no small talk, no explanation, just, "Be there," and then she was gone. Alice had always been that way, from their first days in kindergarten. "Play this. Do that. Wear your cream sweater." It wasn't that Annie objected to either the command or Alice's choice of activity; it was Alice's assumption that Annie would comply that occasionally grated on her, but comply was what Annie did well.

Annie turned to look at the large clock built in to the high wall behind her. It was ten past four. Alice had said she would be there by four, but it wasn't yet late by Alice-time. Alice never apologized for being late. She would simply arrive and start telling you the story of her day from which you just might glean the reason for her tardiness, if indeed there was one. Annie chastised herself for being such a pushover for Alice. She chastised herself for being so controlled by her mother, and she thought of her father—how he could let her mother believe he was doing exactly what she wanted while fostering his own invisible rebellion. That was what truly connected them: Annie and her father and their underground resistance.

"Good afternoon, Sunshine." All the faces in the room turned as Alice strode to Annie's table. The librarian gave Alice a stern glare as she passed, but Alice just smiled and shrugged, and the librarian silently turned away. Annie pulled out the chair next to her for Alice, but Alice chose a chair opposite her.

"What a day I had. Good though. I just finished my composition for English in Mass this morning. That was hard because Ben was there, right in front of me, and I just wanted to look at him. Oh, Annie. You and he are going to make such a great couple. You're going to have such *beautiful* babies. So, anyway, *then* I get to homeroom and I find out that the assignment isn't due until tomorrow. So I figure that's okay, it could have been due yesterday. Well, yesterday was Sunday, so Friday—but you know what I mean. So, anyway, then I get to the cafeteria—wait, that was before the homeroom thing— then I get to the cafeteria and Ben's not there so I can't tell him about the party, so all day I'm carrying around the invitation. So, anyway,

I think maybe Ben will have track practice after school and I'll invite him then. So this afternoon I have Geography and guess what, *that* was the paper that was due today. So I had to stay after school and see Sister Mary Patrick and I tell her that I forgot and could I give her the paper before school tomorrow and she said okay. I think it helped that I'm at the top of her class. I also think she likes my father, you know, like in a man-woman way, which is just *so* scandalous for a nun. So, anyway, I head over to track practice and Ben is jumping hurdles and I walk right up to him and I give him the invitation and he sticks it down the front of his shorts. You'll be *such* a great couple. He's beautiful *and* dangerous—although he doesn't act it which means he *knows* he's dangerous—don't you think? So, anyway, his dad is something in the construction unions or something and you know what *that* means. My dad knows all this stuff but he doesn't say much about it, but I read his paper. So, anyway, what are you going to wear? You're going to be a *great* couple, like one of THE great couples. I just *love* looking at him and I love the way he talks. I could listen to him forever. *So?*"

It took Annie a moment to realize Alice had stopped talking and was looking at her quizzically.

"So, *what?*"

"So, what are you going to *wear?*"

"Oh." Annie realized that, in fact, she hadn't been thinking, especially not about what she was going to wear to Alice's party. "I was thinking…"

"Wear your new Villager skirt and that beige sweater. No, better make it the black sweater. It is an evening affair."

"I'm not sure that I like the black sweater with that skirt."

"The black will be perfect. There's a black line in the plaid. Besides black goes with everything and it will set off the color of your hair."

"Black? The skirt is blue and green and beige." Annie smiled. She was proud of the deep red color of her hair. It had gold highlights that became brighter in the summer sun. Alice was right about the black sweater, but Annie was unconvinced about the skirt.

"There is a black line in the plaid. Look closely at it. It will be perfect. Come over to my house Saturday afternoon and we'll do each other's hair before the party."

"I'm Candy Striping until one."

"Okay, come over after and you can stay over Saturday night."

"I'll have to see if it's okay."

"My mom will call your mom. It's okay."

DON STOOD AT the head of the triangle with "Mutt" and "Jeff" forming the base. Mutt and Jeff were the derisive names that the Brickyard Vampires gave to Woodrow and Clyde. When the three boys started their clockwise waltz, Ben knew that the dance would soon be over. Never move clockwise on Don, Ben knew; it moved you right into his fast right fist and, besides, Don hated to dance.

One, two, three times around. *Bam!* Don's right flashed and Woodrow was sitting on his butt, dazed. Woodrow was a little stupid—something like this happened every time Woodrow fought Don. Maybe Clyde hadn't learned to stay away from Don; maybe the honor of his gang required that he fight him again, but Clyde had learned one thing at least—don't stand in range of Don's fists.

Clyde dropped his head and charged Don, butting him in the stomach. He missed the spot he'd been aiming for that would have knocked the breath from Don, so Clyde wrapped his arms around Don's waist and held on. Don seemed confused for a moment, wondering what Clyde was up to. He looked across the court to Ben and Ron and half-a-dozen friends sitting on the porch stairs of the house behind Reitman's. He shrugged at them, then brought his two hands together in a joined fist, raised them above his head, and brought them down with a dull thud on the base of Clyde's neck. Clyde groaned and slipped to the ground.

The cluster of boys that was Clyde's and Woodrow's Alley Street gang had been standing at the corner, blocking the view of Shepard Court from Shepard Street. As Woodrow, then Clyde, went down, they began to move on Don. Ben and the Brickyard Vampires rose together, and the advancing cluster stopped. Bert, one of Clyde's and Woodrow's brothers, raised his right arm, and Ben saw a railroad ballast stone as it started its arc toward Don. He yelled out to Don, but the stone fell harmlessly at Don's feet. The steps cleared, and the Vampires rushed the Alley Street gang, pairing off randomly. Jimmy attacked with fists flying. Richie and Stevie wrestled their opponents to the ground. Several of the boys danced and pushed back and forth, talking tough.

Ben hit Bert several times in the face. It had been a while since he'd felt his fist hitting flesh, and he liked it. His opponent didn't put up much of a fight—the one punch to Ben's chest had fallen without effect. Bert seemed dazed and ready to fall, but he just stood there wobbling, his hands by his side as Ben repeatedly tested him with left jabs.

An arm swung around Ben's neck from behind and a chest pressed into his back. He arced his right fist over his shoulder and his cheekbone. Ben couldn't see who was holding him. The boy was trying to leverage Ben onto his back, but Ben kept punching, trying to hit higher into the socket of the boy's eye. Ben's arm was getting tired. After a dozen or so punches, the boy let go, and Ben swung around to face him. He began a long swing of his left arm and was about to hit flesh when he came face-to-face with Don—the boy had crumpled to the ground between them.

"Look out behind you!" Don screamed, and Ben turned to see Clyde walking towards them with a large knife in his hand.

"Shit!" Ben ripped off his shirt and wrapped it around his left hand. Don did the same.

"*Cheez-it.*" Clyde stopped in his tracks as he heard the slang for police and looked toward Shepard Street. His hand dropped to his side as the patrol car pulled into the end of the court and two cops jumped out. The knife clanged as it hit the ground, and Ben stared at a huge kitchen knife. One cop charged Clyde with his gun in one hand and handcuffs in the other. His partner duck-walked towards Clyde with both hands on his raised gun. They cuffed Clyde and stuffed him in the back of the car. It was then Ben realized that the other members of the Alley Street gang had vanished.

The cops left Clyde in the back of the patrol car and walked across Shepard Street to a Ford Skyliner parked there. They talked through a half-open window to the driver, then walked back to their car and backed out of the court. Everyone in the Court knew who that car belonged to. The driver was Tony Angelo.

After the cops left, Tony lowered the window, stuck his arm out, pointed to Don and crooked his index finger, indicating for Don to approach. No one had ever been asked to approach Tony's car before. Don walked to the car, listened for a few moments nodding his head, then watched the window close. He stood there in the street as Tony drove away. The Vampires soon surrounded Don.

"What did he say?"

"He said he liked my style and wants me to come see him on Saturday." Don cocked his head and and blew a short whistle from between his pursed lips.

"Wow, man." They took turns slapping Don on the back.

"He's going to give you a *job*."

"That's as good as a job at the *Riverworks*, man."

"Shit, you'll be *untouchable*."

"Yeah, and *we'll* be untouchable too.'

"You'll be under Tony's protection."

"Can you put in a good word for me?"

Ben slipped away from the giddy celebration. He saw Ron still sitting on the steps; he hadn't moved during the melée. Ben was relieved Ron hadn't joined the fight, but annoyed he hadn't defended Don. Brothers stick together.

"C'mon, let's go home." Ben headed through the backyards to home, Ron trailing behind. Ben flipped over the chain-link fence around his yard, then waited as Ron climbed the fence, placing each foot carefully in the diamond-shaped spaces formed by the wire. He wasn't sure what would happen next, but he was sure that, for him, it didn't include Tony Angelo.

It didn't take long for word to spread that Don was going to work for Tony. There was even speculation on the street, fostered by the Vampires, that Don was going to be a hit man. When Richie mentioned this to Ben, Ben turned on Richie and chastised him. "Don't be a fucking idiot. Don's *fourteen*; he's not going to be a fucking hitman. He's probably going to sweep floors or stack returns."

"You're just jealous," Richie said. "That's ugly."

DON SHOWED UP at Tony's office in the back of the Spa on Saturday as instructed. He'd hoped to catch a glimpse of Toni, but she was nowhere to be seen. Too bad, Don thought, she would have been impressed with Don, her dad's new associate. Oh, well. There would be time for that later.

"Sit." Tony pointed to a chair beside his desk, extending his hugely muscled arm—larger, Don thought, than even his father's.

Don sat.

"I've got a job for you if you want it. You're going to be a runner."

"Sure."

"You want to know what that is?"

"I know. I run between you and the bookies."

"Not me...one of my associates."

"Right."

"Now, I have to talk to you, man-to-man." Tony thumped his fist to his chest.

Don suppressed a smile, repeating the words "man-to-man" to himself.

"I seen you looking at my daughter. You can *look* all you want, but you don't even smile, because if I think you are enjoying it too much, you *won't*."

"Yes, sir."

"She says 'good morning' to you, you nod."

"Yes, sir."

"You talk to her without my permission, you hurt. You touch her without my permission, you're dead. I won't talk to you about this again."

"Yes, sir."

"One more thing. I don't like guys with independent ideas. This ain't no democracy. *Capeesh?*"

BEN LOOKED AT the knuckles on his right hand. It had been five days since the fight and most of the cuts and scratches were slowly disappearing, but the middle joints in his fingers were still swollen. It still hurt to close his hand.

The only clothes he had that he could wear to Alice's party were school clothes. He hated the blazer, and other than his jeans, he had only two pairs of pants—one black and one brown. He chose the black, because they were newer. He pulled his tan sweater from the drawer, but noticed a small hole in the armpit. He put it on, hoping the hole wouldn't be noticeable, but he found it when he reached over his shoulder and felt around the back of his shoulder blade. He went through Don's drawers and found Don's maroon sweater. He inspected it and found no holes. Ben wondered whether he should wear a tie or not. He tried to recall what the TV kids wore—Wally, Eddie, Ricky, even Timmy—but it was a mixed bag. He decided to wear a tie.

An hour before he was supposed to be at the party, he dressed. He stood in his stocking feet and looked at himself in the bathroom mirror. Then he sat on the toilet with the lid down and memorized two more jokes from the *Reader's Digest* he'd taken from the pile in the wicker basket beside the toilet. He chose an older issue so the jokes wouldn't be fresh in people's minds and they might forget that they knew them. He went back into his room and took the black snapjack shoes he had polished that morning from underneath his bed. He was glad he had convinced his mother to let him get them. They were slick. They hurt his feet when he snapped them shut, but they were slick.

He took off the shoes and stuck them in the cloth bag that came with them and put on his worn sneakers. He went back to the bathroom for one last look and decided to take off the tie and go with the open collar. He looked in the mirror again and decided that the open collar made his neck look too long and weak, so the tie went back on. Ben headed downstairs. Don and Ron were sitting on the floor with their backs resting against the couch, watching TV.

"Oh, where's the pretty Bennie going?" Don teased.

Ron laughed.

"Out."

"Is Bennie going to see a *girlie?*"

Ben scowled at Don, even though he knew this might just egg him on.

Ben's dad was sitting in his chair, his head pitched to the right, sleeping. Ben stood in front of his father and called out, "Dad." His father didn't stir, but kept on sleeping—a soft snore and a thin line of drool flowing from his open mouth—oblivious to the noise from the television. Ben moved to his father's side and touched his arm.

"Dad." Still nothing. Ben noticed his father's upper dentures had dropped. He shook his father lightly and said, "Dad," more insistently.

"Whah. I'm awake, I'm awake. Just resting my eyes."

"I'm leaving now."

"Where're you going?"

"To that party I told you about."

"You didn't tell me about a party."

"Yes, I did, at the McCulley's. Remember?"

Ben's dad closed his eyes again and settled his head to the left. Ben looked at Don and Ron and shrugged. He headed for the front door and reached for the doorknob.

Without opening his eyes or moving his head—without stirring at all—Ben's dad said, "Be home by ten."

IT TOOK ALMOST half an hour for Ben to walk the mile and a half to Alice's house. Usually, he'd walk much faster and be there sooner, but he didn't want to work up a sweat before the party and his shoes hurt his feet. He had never been to Alice's house, but the property—and the street that it stood on—was well-known and storied. It had been the home of the Brahmin publishing baron who founded The Shore Press and its family of newspapers and craft magazines. The house was included in the publishing business property when the McCulley brothers bought it at auction. The legend was that the last act of the Brahmin was to blow his brains out in his library. Ben had been wondering ever since he got Alice's invitation if he would get to see the infamous room.

When he found the house, he thought it must be at least three times as big as his own. Its backyard bordered Sluice Pond, which Ben glimpsed through the trees in the back yard. The house was shingled on the upper floor and at the dormers, and the lower floor was clapboard—all of which was painted a soft yellow. The window trim and sash were painted white. A large curved wall on the side of the house at the lower level was covered in ivy and matched the stone of the foundation and the base of the front porch. The front porch, itself, ran the length of the front of the house and disappeared around the side. As impressive as the size of the house was, Ben was struck by its feeling of calm comfort. He wasn't quite sure why, but the house felt "right." Ben walked up the stairs to the porch and rang the doorbell. Alice's father answered, and Ben introduced himself. He told Mr. McCulley he had been invited to Alice's party.

"Oh yes, I *know*. I've heard quite a lot about you. It's nice to meet the boy who has succeeded in getting Alice to attend Mass every morning."

Ben looked at Mr. McCulley quizzically for a moment, not sure he had heard him correctly, but quickly recovered. "Yes, I think that's a good way to start each day." Obviously, Alice and her dad had spoken about Ben, and he liked that.

"They're downstairs in the rec room. I'll show you the way." Alice's dad laid his hand lightly on Ben's shoulder and steered him down a hall to the cellar door. He was about to reach for the knob when the door burst open and two giggling girls came rushing through. It was all Ben could do to move his face out of the way of the swinging door, and it hit him squarely in the chest.

"Oops." A tall, red-headed girl with the grayest-green eyes Ben had ever seen came from behind the door.

Ben just stood, his arms limp by his side, staring at her.

"Are you *okay*? I'm sorry, but Alice was pushing me."

"Hi, Ben." Alice peeked out from behind the red-headed girl's hair. "Did we hurt you?"

"Ummm, no, no, I don't think so." He felt a small, but sharp pain in his chest where the door had hit him.

"We were going up to my room to get an album I left there. We can get it later." Alice was smiling at Ben, but Ben didn't notice—he was staring at the red-head, staring at her eyes, really, and the freckles that surrounded them—and her smallish nose—and her pinkish lips. Ben was instantly smitten.

"Hi," she said. "I'm Annie."

"Hi, I'm Alice."

"I think my work is done here." Alice's father walked back down the hall toward the front of the house.

"Hi, I'm Ben."

"So I gather," Annie said. "Are you sure you're okay?"

"His eyes seem to be focusing just fine," Alice giggled, and Ben turned a quite bright red—not just his face, but all over. He could feel the tingling heat course down from the top of his head through his body and into his legs.

"Do you need anything?" Alice said.

Ben turned and shot a warning glance at Alice—no more commentary. He managed a raspy, "I think I could use some water." Alice slipped out from behind Annie and held Ben's hand. She led him down the hall to the kitchen and took a half-gallon glass jug of water with ice in it from the refrigerator. She by-passed the paper cups on the counter and took a glass from the cupboard, filled it, and handed it to Ben, watching him drink it to the bottom without stopping for air.

"More?"

"No thanks."

"Better?"

"Yes ma'am."

"I'm not 'madam', I'm *'mademoiselle'*."

"Yes, *Mill*."

The two girls hesitated a moment, got the pun, then laughed uncomfortably. Ben was embarrassed and vowed never to use that pun again. They spent the rest of the evening talking and dancing and—for Ben—staring at Annie. They ate hot dogs and chips and elbow pasta in a mayonnaise dressing and drank Coke. There were eight or nine other kids at the party, all of them from Ben's school. Ben knew the boys because they were in class together, or on the track team together, but he didn't know the girls, except maybe a couple on sight. He never could recall later which girls had been there, except Annie and—of course—Alice.

Two days later, he called Annie to invite her to his next track meet. She came.

6

October 21, 1963
Dearest Ben,

I hope that you find this note before anyone else does, especially that jani-tor. I'd even rather have the nuns find it. Anyway, I just wanted to tell you that I love you. Diane thinks that I love you because you are dangerous, but I told her that is not true. You are not dangerous to me. You make me feel safe.

I want you to meet her. I'll be at the library at 4. Can you be there?
Love Annie
  XXOOXX

THE NOTE HAD been in a small, scented envelope, slipped behind the mimeographed notice of the Chi Rho dance that had been tacked to one of the two framed cork bulletin boards in the vestibule at the back of the church. Although Annie and Ben talked on the telephone almost every day—sometimes twice—Ben felt an especially warm con-nection to Annie through their secret notes. The notes had started only a few weeks ago and up to now consisted of "I love you. **XXX**" written on an index card or on the back of one of the small prayer cards. Ben's collection of these notes already filled a couple of inches of the shoebox where he hid them among his baseball cards. He was going to need to find another place to store them if this kept up.

The reading room where Annie would be waiting was on the second floor of the large white stone library. There were two public entrances: one directly into the Children's Library at the ground level—actually the basement—and one at the top of a dozen wide outdoor steps. The latter sat behind a tall portico and led through pairs of tall, heavy, intricately-patterned doors to the first floor and the large round circulation desk. The main part of the first floor was an open room that stretched nearly the width and breadth of the building. Beyond the circulation desk, the room was full of thick oak tables, leather armchairs, newspaper racks and shelves that lined the walls. This room was usually full. Older people read newspapers, high-school kids studied in small groups at the tables, parents—who's children were restricted to the downstairs library—browsed the shelves.

Ben turned to the right and headed up the staircase that led to the second floor. The reading room there was smaller and less populated and had the added advantage of often being empty of library staff.

Upstairs, high windows lined the walls above the stacks. The falling sun streamed through one of them directly into Ben's eyes. He looked away for a moment to try to clear his eyes and stepped out of the sunbeam. As his eyes readjusted to the ambient light of the room, he saw Annie and a girl with dark, wild hair and heavily-rimmed glasses facing him from a nearby table.

Annie pushed her chair from the table, making a loud scraping noise on the travertine floor. Both girls grimaced, looked at each other, then broke into giggles. Annie rose from her chair and moved quickly and gracefully to him as if she had wheels for feet. She pecked Ben on the lips, then grabbed his left hand, slipped it around her waist, tucked it under her left arm and led him back to the table. Ben could feel the firm mound of her breast beneath his hand and momentarily thought of closing his fingers.

"Diane, this is Ben. Ben, Diane."

Diane spoke first. "It's nice to meet you. You are *all* she ever talks about. It was getting quite boring, but now that I've met you..."

Ben interrupted Diane. "It's nice to meet you, too. I've been hearing a lot about you, as well." Ben looked through Diane's strong glasses into her dark, strangely magnified eyes. It struck him she was not especially beautiful—not the same way that *Annie* was beautiful—but there was an extraordinarily powerful sexuality that hung about her. They stood there facing each other for a moment, and, when it was obvious to Diane that Ben wasn't about to do it, she moved into him, raised herself on her toes and kissed him lightly on the check. She whispered into his ear, "I know what you're thinking, you dirty boy."

"OK, you two," Annie said. "If you're done, let's sit."

As Diane drew away, Ben noticed the smile on her face and the dancing light in her eyes.

Annie had already moved back to the table, and Ben walked around behind her to hold her chair. As he reached for the chair beside hers, Annie put her hand on top of his and caught his eye. She swept her head towards the other side of the table where Diane stood. Ben got the message and moved to the other side of the table, drew the chair out for Diane, and waited for her to sit. He then moved back around the table to Annie's side and sat. Annie shot a smiling glance at Diane.

As Diane opened her book, she looked at Ben's empty hands and his long fingers splayed out on the table. She thought, Don't flaunt those big hands and long fingers in front of me, but she said instead, "You didn't bring a book?"

"No. I'm going to quiz Annie on her math. Then we're going to do some Latin together."

"*Wow*. That's *really* romantic." Diane shook her head. "Why don't you read something sexy together? We *are* in a library, aren't we?"

"You seem to know so much, what would *you* suggest?" Ben said.

"Old Testament. Song of Songs. *If* you think you can handle it."

"Oh, I can handle it alright."

"I've got to study," Annie broke in, looking sternly at Diane, "and I need Ben's help with my math. If you two want to read smut, go off and do it, but leave me alone."

Diane smiled at Ben and raised her eyebrows in invitation.

"I think I'll pass," Ben said quietly.

"Maybe I misjudged you," Diane said. "Too bad."

Ben could smell and feel the force of Diane's sexuality. He flushed from the heat she radiated. Diane got up and moved away, leaving Annie and Ben at the table. Ben made up algebra problems for Annie who would work through them hesitantly, looking for a message in Ben's face and hoping for approval each step she took. Each time she finished a problem successfully, she would kiss Ben lightly on the lips. Ben started making the problems easier.

7

May 20, 1964

Dearest Ben,
Can you meet me at the library after school? I can be there by 4 or 4:30
if I get the early bus. I need to talk to you. Nothing terrible.
Love Annie
XXOOXX
ps Sorry that I couldn't talk to you yesterday. I'll explain.

BEN FOUND THE letter early in the morning, almost an hour before school started. His heart sank to his stomach as he folded the
letter and envelope separately and stuck them into his inside jacket
pocket. She did say, "Nothing terrible," but the tone worried him.
This was going to be a very bad day. His ears buzzed through the
first two periods. He couldn't pay attention. His eyes wandered to
the large, bright windows. He stared at the passing wispy clouds.
He searched his mind for events, for incidents. He worried he had
upset her. He looked for signs she'd lost interest in him. He tried to
convince himself not to worry. Each time he began to feel better, each
time his mood would start to lift, worry would sweep back over him
like the passing clouds.

The third period was French. French was easy for Ben since he often spoke it with his father and brothers at home. His vocabulary was limited, but he understood the structure and the quirks of pronunciation. Don was more proficient than Ben and had a better ear for language, but the nuns assumed that Ben shared Don's acumen and credited him with his brother's skill, which worked to Ben's advantage.

His mom didn't like them speaking French around her, so they only spoke it when she was working in the restaurant at night or when they wanted to irritate her. In Maine, where she had grown up on a dairy farm, the French-speakers were all *Canucks*—French-speaking Canadians mostly from eastern Quebec—day laborers and summer help. Ben's dad was proud that his family came from France, not from Canada, and insisted that meant he was from a better class, somehow. Ben's mom had bought that story when she'd met the handsome, lean, and muscular man at a church social in Portland. Now, she wasn't so sure.

Ben had hoped the French class would take his mind off of Annie and the letter. He was amused by the teacher, Mr. Cherry. That he was a layman among a faculty of nuns might have been enough, but the stiff, elegant bearing in an extraordinarily tall, barrel-chested man whose huge head was topped with wild silver hair and matching bushy eyebrows was too iconic not to be comical. Today, even that was not enough.

Ben searched for something to divert his thoughts from Annie. His worries were making him crazier and he wasn't paying attention to the lesson anyway. If he went to the bathroom, that would only buy a few minutes at best. Lunch was a long time away. This would be a wonderful time for a fire drill. They hadn't practiced their duck-and-cover routine for a nuclear attack since Junior High; it was high time they did that.

Ah yes, thought Ben. He reached under his desk and slowly unzipped his bookbag. He slipped his hand in and felt around for the thick, hardcover book inside. He almost whacked the desk with his chin as he reached to the far end of the bag, but at last he found the book he wanted. He withdrew it slowly and—he hoped—quietly, and set it on his lap. When Mr. Cherry walked past Ben's seat to a student three desks behind him, Ben opened the book to a page that he'd marked with one of Annie's scented envelopes. He moved close to the desk so the book was hidden beneath it atop his thighs. After Mr. Cherry passed him on his way back to the front of the room and mounted the raised platform to the teacher's desk, Ben moved back and exposed the open book.

Several minutes passed. Ben had read a dozen pages before Mr. Cherry boomed out Ben's name. "Mister Holt, is that a French book that you are reading?"

"No, Mr. Cherry, I am translating it," Ben retorted, mimicking the tone and cadence of the teacher's voice.

"May we share your learn-ed work?"

Ben withdrew the book from his lap and held it out to Mr. Cherry, who had descended from his platform and now towered over Ben's desk. The book was *Seven Days in May.* Ben expected laughter—or at least a few giggles—from his classmates, but there was only silence—ominous silence.

"Mister Holt, please go to my office *immediately.*"

Ben spun in his chair to face the voice that came from behind, but he'd already recognized it. It belonged to Sister Eustelle, "Mother," the Principal.

"*Crap,*" he thought, and rose from his chair. He looked at the nun, then back at Mr. Cherry, and started for the classroom door.

"You can *leave* the book," Mr. Cherry said, archly.

Ben felt strangely peaceful and calm as he waited in the office for Sister Eustelle. The sun was shining warmly on the back of his neck and he had forgotten his anxiety over Annie's note. Maybe he had been a bit of a smart-ass with Mr. Cherry, but he hadn't been foul-mouthed or directly disrespectful—both capital crimes in a Catholic high school. Sister Eustelle had enjoyed his and Don's antics in the past, enjoyed the "spirit of two real boys," which Ben took to mean *public school* boys who hadn't had the spirit beaten out of them by that other, stricter order of nuns who ran the grammar school.

Ben's and Don's antics had never been particularly destructive, but they danced along the boundary between funny and real trouble. When they got a bit too close to the edge, a well-placed word or two would bring them back. When Ben rebelled against the jacket-and-tie rule by wearing his jacket inside-out, exposing the colorful paisley lining, he noticed Sister Eustelle and more than a few of the other nuns hiding their amused faces behind folded hankies or palms. When he noisily ate popcorn during film strips, he could see their laughing eyes in the beam of light that leaked from the side of the projector.

So it was that the stern look on Sister Eustelle's face surprised him. She walked past him to the front of her desk, her back towards him, shuffled through a few papers, then turned to him. Her stern face had softened a little and was almost compassionate. This worried him more than the stern look. He didn't see himself as a candidate for compassion.

"Look, I know that things aren't great at home and that probably affects your behavior and your ability to pay attention…" Sister Eustelle paused as if seeking confirmation from Ben, but Ben was confused and silent. He thought that things were okay at home.

"How is your mother?"

"She seems fine. The baby's due in the next week or so, I guess."

"Well, I'm sure that you are worried about her, but we're all praying for her." Then she added, "And the baby." She paused again. "I'm sure she'll be fine."

Of course she'll be fine, he thought. She's only having a baby. That's what she *does*, has babies. Sure, it's been a while since Jen was born, but so what? She seemed perfectly fine. Sure, she soaked her feet in Epson-salted water every night, but that just seemed to be part of her routine. He couldn't remember if she had done that for Ron or Don.

"I suppose that I blame myself partly for encouraging your behavior, but I must put my foot down this time. Mr. Cherry, you know, is *not* one of us."

Again, she paused for confirmation that Ben knew this. Ben had to stifle the urge to yell out, "Oh my god, he's an alien creature come to suck the brains from our cranial cavities with his foreign-sounding gibberish. He's not teaching French, he's liquefying our brains with his Neptunian vibrating war tongue." Not today.

"Mr. Cherry is a Huguenot, a protestant. He's Christian, of course—we'd have to demand that—but he's not Catholic and we want to make sure that he carries away with him a good impression of Catholic young men." She looked at Ben.

Ben tried to think of the right thing to say, but he was thinking, "Yeah, he's Protestant, so he's different, like Mikey's Greek Orthodox, Stevie's Jewish and Richie's Episcopalian. Or was he Presbyterian—who cares—since you and the rest of the Catholic church think they're going to Limbo 'cause they're not Catholic? What a bunch of *crap.*" He didn't think Sister Eustelle wanted to hear this right now, so he just stared at her as blankly as he could.

"So, when he comes up here after school, I want you to apologize to him like a gentleman."

'Yes, Sister."

"I've had one of the other boys bring your book bag up. It's across the hall in the library. You can spend the rest of the day there and wait for Mr. Cherry."

'Yes, Sister."

"You know, all the other boys look to you for leadership. Don't let them down."

"Yes, Sister. Thank you, Sister." Ben was surprised that a teacher of boys had so little understanding of them. Maybe Catholic school boys looked to other boys for leadership. Real boys didn't. He shuddered in disgust at the very idea. Ben recalled his short Boy Scout experience. One of the boys with all the patches and badges and the perfect uniform with the bandana and the golden clasp had tried to bring his troop to order so that the Scoutmaster—his Dad—could speak. The kid had held up three fingers on his right hand and the troop had fallen into their ranked order—all except Ben, who'd offered to break the kid's fingers if he ever held them up to Ben again.

Ben's mother had been very angry when she'd gotten the call from the Scoutmaster informing her Ben had been kicked out of Boy Scouts.

"I UNDERSTAND YOU have something to say to me, Mr. Holt?" Mister Cherry said.

"Yes, Mr. Cherry."

Mr. Cherry's frame filled the doorway. "Well, get on with it." He stepped into the room and folded his arms across his chest.

"I'm sorry that I was disrespectful and inattentive in your class. It won't happen again."

"Thank you, Mister Holt. I will accept your apology as genuine. As long as you keep your nose clean in class, I will forget this unfortunate incident."

Ben looked at the man, fighting back a smirk.

"Do you have any questions?"

Ben couldn't believe it. Here was a hanging curve ball as big as a melon, begging to be slammed out of the park. "Just one."

"Please?"

"Are you giving me permission to pick my nose in class?"

Cherry stood there as if he had been stunned, beaned by a line drive slammed back to the mound. He silently turned and walked from the room.

Ben quickly packed his book bag and hurried out of the school, through the parking lot, past the church, across the common and into the front door of the library. He half-expected to turn and see the forms of Sister Eustelle and Mr. Cherry chasing after him, carrying baseball bats, very *big* baseball bats.

He was only a few minutes late, at worst. When he got to the top of the stairs, he instinctively dodged the sunbeam, looked around, and saw Annie sitting at one of the tables in the far corner. She was sitting in the middle of the long side of the table facing him. Her large pocketbook lay open with its strap extended to her right. Her books were spread out on her left. The arrangement made it clear she didn't want anyone else sitting at her table. Ben walked over and sat in the chair opposite Annie.

"I don't get a *kiss*?" she pouted.

Ben stood and leaned over the table, pursing his lips, but she moved back.

"I want a proper kiss."

Ben pushed back his chair and walked around the table to Annie. She raised her face toward his, but remained seated. Ben bent to kiss her. As their lips touched, Annie exposed her teeth and bit Ben's upper lip firmly.

"*Owww.*"

"Next time I don't expect to have to ask for a proper kiss." Annie's lips were stern, but her eyes were glossy and smiling. "Sit; I have to talk to you."

"Serious?"

"Hmmm. *Possibly* serious."

Annie paused, looking to Ben for further conversation that could delay her having to deliver her message. She feared Ben's reaction. She felt as though she really knew him, knew she could get him to listen, but her confidence had waned each time she'd rehearsed her speech over the last two days. It had been a hard day full of recurring doubts. Ben thought that "possibly serious" sounded a whole lot better than "serious," but Annie's long pause worried him. Just get it over with, he screamed to himself. He had known three or four guys who'd gotten dumped or done the dumping as school had drawn to a close. Maybe this was dumping season.

"My mother wants me to see other boys, but..."

"*Shit!*"

"Ben, don't. Let me finish."

"*Shit!*"

"Ben. I don't want to see other boys. I want *you.*"

"Did you tell her that?" he said.

"Yes, but she said that if I saw other boys, I'd know if I really wanted *you.*"

"*Shit, shit, shit.*"

"*Wait*, will you?" She grabbed his arm. "I went and talked to my dad and we came up with a plan."

"What's that?"

"You're going to come over to my house on Saturday and help my dad repoint the foundation. My mother has been after him to do it since spring started. I told him how you helped your dad build the wall in your backyard. He thinks that if my mother sees how hard you work and how you have a useful skill, she'll love you like I do."

"Hmmm. You're dad's pretty tricky. I never saw that in him."

"My dad wants his girls to be happy. It can get pretty moody and unpleasant at home when one of his girls is unhappy."

"I'll have to remember that. So it's all set then?"

"Yeah. My mother and dad argued about it a bit, but then my dad said, 'Mary, it's all set. Be pleasant to the boy,' and hid behind his paper. That means 'discussion over'."

"It's hard to imagine your parents arguing. They always act like June and Ward."

"Oh, they don't yell." Annie was about to say, "like *your* parents," but she stopped herself. Ben knew that she had.

"What do they *do* when they argue?"

"They become all formal-like, and my dad listens to my mother, then issues his verdict."

"I always thought that your mother never loses."

"She never does. Is there anywhere we can go to be alone? Just for a few minutes before my mother comes to pick me up?"

"Yeah, let's go."

BEN REACHED OUT and pulled the latch handle of the huge, heavy oaken door, putting his weight into the pulling, extending his legs to leverage the force against the strong late-afternoon breeze. He placed his back against the open door and motioned for Annie to enter. As she walked into the vestibule, he reached for her hand and entwined his fingers in hers.

"We're going to make out in a *church*?" Annie exclaimed. "Isn't that a sin?"

"It would be a sin *not* to," Ben smiled. He led Annie through the vestibule and up the stairs that led to the choir loft. Half-way up was a metal lattice door with a large lock on it, but Ben leaned on the door and it swung open.

"How'd you know it would be unlocked? Did you plan this? Annie thought Ben might have been romantic—or bad. Either worked.

"I'd put a piece of black electrical tape over the latch bolt." Ben didn't mention he'd actually done this the last time his father had thrown him out of the house.

"Ohhhh, you're *so* bad." Annie wrapped her arms around Ben's neck, placed her open mouth over his lips, and pushed her tongue between them—into the space between his teeth and his upper lip. After a few moments of dallying there, she pushed her tongue hard against his teeth, and he relented, separating his teeth and letting her tongue find his. Their tongues danced, and Ben wrapped his arm around Annie, pulling her hard to him. He could feel the mound between her legs press into his belly. He could feel the rising between his own legs.

"Whoa, wait a minute. Where'd you learn to kiss like that?" Ben pulled away. "Have you been making out with other guys?"

"No. Of course not. Diane and I practice on each other."

The rising between Ben's legs immediately became a granite boulder. His whole body became hot and weak at the same time. He pulled Annie to him again. "Well, practice makes perfect," he mumbled, with his mouth on hers. He started to reach up inside the back of her white blouse, but she pushed his hand down.

"Hold on, sailor. Not here, not now."

Ben felt like he was burning up. He slipped one arm, then another, from the sleeves of his jacket, always keeping one arm around Annie's waist. He let the jacket slip to the floor. With all of the twisting and turning, Annie opened her eyes momentarily and Ben read the message, "What the hell are you doing?" in them, but she closed them again and her lashes fluttered.

"What's going on here?" The small cranky voice came from above them, and Ben looked over Annie's shoulder to see one of the elderly nuns who cleaned and primped the church. "Take your *disgusting* activities away from here. This is *God's* house. Shame on you. Heathens! *Heathens!*"

Annie nearly knocked Ben down, running down the stairs. He hurried after her. Annie noticed that the double center doors were open, and she rushed through them, nearly knocking down a man dressed in black carrying two large urns of flowers. A line of black cars was pulling into the drive that led to the front of the church. She was across the street on the Common when she finally stopped and bent from the waist, trying to catch her breath. As Ben pulled up even with her, she looked up at him and laughed.

He smiled at her. "Yeah, I guess that was pretty funny."

"No," she gasped, amid her laughing."No, that's...not it."

"*What,* then?"

"You left your jacket in there." Annie jerked her right thumb back towards the church.

"*Shit.*"

8

"IT COULDN'T POSSIBLY BE A BETTER DAY," BEN thought. "Well, it *could* be if I had more money in my pocket." The sun was shining in a perfectly blue sky and he was sitting close beside Annie as she drove slowly along Pleasant Street looking for a place to park. Ben could smell the pungent salty-sweet mix of sea air and fried food. Lynn Beach had the sea air and fried food smell, too, especially if you were near the Halfway House or Christie's, but this was a crisper smell, without the added coconut of suntan oil. The light was different too—somehow less brutal, less harsh. The faded old-green of the leaves of the aged trees lent a deeper, golden-green tone to the sunlight.

Taking Route 127 north from the end of 128 would have put Annie and Ben right at Bearskin Neck, but Annie had taken a right at the sign for the old railroad station and driven further to the east to drive along the water. She'd said she was more likely to find parking at this end of town. She had clearly been here before.

Annie found a spot below Cove Hill Lane and backed the Buick expertly into it. She hadn't had her license for long, but she was already a confident driver. Her mother's car was a 1959 Invicta "Hard-top Convertible," which really wasn't a convertible at all, not like the Ford Skyliner that Tony Angelo drove, but it had no post between the front and rear windows so when the windows were down it was open from the windshield to the back sweep of the roof. Ben had never been in a real convertible, but he thought this was pretty close.

"Do you want to close the windows?"

"No," Annie said. "The car will get too hot."

As they walked the few hundred yards down the hill to Dock Square, they passed art galleries and an art supply store. Ben noticed a display of drafting tools in the window of the art supply store, including a huge lead-holder, thicker than any he had ever seen. It had "KOH-I-NOOR" stamped in silver block letters on its side.

Annie wore a short-sleeved white blouse and "madras" Villager shorts. It wasn't the Indian madras that faded when you washed it several times, but the American version—guaranteed not to fade.

Ben loved Annie. He loved just *being* with Annie. He loved how Annie loved him, but he wished he could break through the shell and find a way that would let him inside—let him into the center of the heart of the Annie he knew was in there somewhere. He wondered whether she, herself, had ever gotten inside.

"You're so quiet. What are you thinking?" Annie said.

"I was thinking how much I love being with you."

"Yes, it's particularly beautiful today."

"No. Just *being* with you. It wouldn't matter where."

Annie stopped and squeezed Ben's arm. She turned around in front of him and kissed him, her soft lips just inside his. She slipped her arms over his and squeezed him tightly. Ben raised his arms from his elbows and wrapped them around her lower back. He felt a warm rising in his pants and didn't want to pull her too closely, so he left his arms softly wrapped around her waist. Annie knew the rising mound would be there and pressed her hips hard against him.

"Ummmm. Let's go," Annie said, as she unwrapped herself from Ben.

"Great work, if you can get it," came a voice from behind Ben. He turned to the voice and noticed that seven or eight people had been waiting on the narrow sidewalk behind them. Several smiled; the others looked as though they were annoyed at having to wait. Ben smiled back. Annie pulled on his hand as she walked on, yanking him into motion.

"I want to go to Tuck's, but let's do Bearskin Neck first," Annie said. They walked past the candy-maker and turned the corner to head out along the peninsula. Bearskin Neck was chock-a-block with people and tumble-down shacks. The odd amalgam of kitsch and art amazed Ben. Painters and crafters, restaurants; Roy Moore's lobster shack, which was no bigger than a small garage; the Bearskin Neck Country Store with an old nickelodeon constantly playing piano-like tunes. It was more than a street fair, more than art; it was a *performance*.

As Annie pulled Ben through the crowds, he felt like he was constantly in danger of trampling a small child or an old lady. As they got to the end of the main road, the narrow space opened and the sea reappeared. They made their way to a jetty constructed of huge quarried granite and stepped carefully along the stones for a short distance. There, they sat, looking back on the harbor.

"Wow! *That* was an experience!" Ben was nearly breathless.

"Yes. My father used to bring me here a couple of times each summer. Usually it would be just the two of us. A few times my mother came, but usually it was my time to have him to myself."

Ben was struck by how she became quieter, more thoughtful, when she spoke of her father. She looked away across the harbor as if she was seeing him there.

"Did you know," she spoke again in an animated voice. "That the most painted building in the world is on a little side wharf back near the square?"

"No."

"It's called 'Motif No. 1.' We can stop and see it on the way back. We can stop in some of the stores, too. I just wanted to get you out here to see how beautiful it is before we went shopping."

Ben fingered the eleven dollars in his pocket. He had planned to buy gas for the car and something for them to eat. He wouldn't be doing much shopping.

"Great," he said. Ben leaped to his feet and offered his hand to help Annie up. As her eyes met his, she smiled. She stretched on her toes and kissed him lightly on the lips, then started past him on the stones. Ben slipped his left hand around her waist, then let it drop as she picked her way across the slippery rock.

For the next hour-and-a-half, they stopped into galleries and stores, looking at everything and talking the fantasy talk that teen-age lovers talk.

"Wouldn't that look great in our living room?" Annie said, looking at a painting of sailboats at rest in the harbor.

"Ummm, yes; but then where would we put the Rockwell?"

"Yes, well, let's think about it then."

At a small silversmith, Ben looked at charms, while Annie looked at earrings. He couldn't afford the silver, but the pewter charms were almost the same color. He looked at a nice little sea-shell and a tiny Motif No. 1.

"What do you think of this?" Annie said, holding up a silver leaf.

"Not bad."

"But you don't really *love* it?"

"No, it's not that. You don't have pierced ears."

"No, but I have adapters than convert them."

"Oh. Well, sure, I love them then."

Annie bought the tiny leaves and three other pairs of earrings. Ben plotted ways to get back to the store to get her a charm. Maybe he could stop at the marine hardware store and, if she wasn't interested in going in, he could slip back to the silversmith while she was looking in the ladies' lingerie store. Maybe, maybe not. He would have to look for an opening.

On they went. No store was too small or too tacky for at least a few minutes of their time. Ben mostly stood silently, his arms across his chest, while Annie looked through trinkets, gifts, toys, clothes several sizes too large, good art, ugly art. Nothing was too small or too unusable for her attention. She bought a bag of penny candy, a can of Finnan Haddie for her father and some Boston Baked Beans in a box—the candy beans, not the bean beans.

"Come down this way," Annie said, as she started down a side road. "This is Tuna Wharf and you can see Motif No. 1 from here."

Ben followed, but stopped in front of the Portside Chowder House. He could see that it was a two-story restaurant with a dining room on the lower floor and a covered semi-enclosed deck above. He'd love to be able to take Annie to dinner here. He looked at the menu in the glass-enclosed case as his hands nervously worked the folded bills in his pocket. They'd have to eat somewhere else.

"Coming?"

"Yeah. I just wanted to see what they had."

"Come see this." Annie slipped into an alley that separated two blocks of stores.

Ben followed and saw her standing at the edge of the wharf looking at a deep-red fishing shack across a narrow channel of water.

"That's it. *That's* Motif No. 1."

"Hmmm. Interesting." Ben had expected something a lot more impressive that a small, weather-beaten fishing shack. After all, this was supposed to be the most painted building in the world. He thought that maybe its setting would be more interesting in the morning light, with the boats bobbing in the silver water. Perhaps fog would change its personality. He wondered what he was missing. Obviously, many artists were drawn to it. He had to admit he just didn't get it. "Do you stand here with your father?"

"Yes. He gets misty-eyed when we stand here. He'll stare at it for fifteen or twenty minutes—probably longer if I didn't drag him away."

"He doesn't paint, does he? Is that a secret side of him that I don't know about?"

"Oh, no. There isn't an artistic bone in his body. I think he expects my mother to take care of that. She doesn't paint or anything, of course, but she does think that art should be a part of your life, and she *does* take him to galleries. And she has her Beleek."

"Does she like the view, too?"

"Now that you mention it, I don't think I've ever seen her stand here with him."

"Maybe she's seen it so many times she feels like she doesn't need to stand here staring at it. Besides, she can look at the artists' rendering of it in all of the galleries. She may enjoy the interpretation of it more than the building itself. Maybe it just means more to your father than it does to her. Sometimes people see something different in the things that they're looking at."

"Yes, but in the end it's really just a garishly painted little shack, isn't it?"

Ben looked across the water and thought about Annie's comment. He felt that it said something about Annie's relationship with her father and her mother. It felt like she was walking a tight-rope between the two of them. He turned to Annie, but she was gone. He hurried to catch up and found her waiting for him at the busy end of the wharf.

"Let's walk up Main Street. There's a few stores I want to stop in. If you're hungry, we can stop and get something to eat."

"I'm okay for now, "Ben said. He just wanted to get away from the Portside. "Some day," he thought. "Some day, I'll be able to afford to bring her back here for a nice dinner."

Ben hated being poor. He was embarrassed by it. It made him feel small and insignificant. He hated the clothes that his mother bought him at Sears. He hated his family's small and insignificant life. His dad made good money when he worked, but he often worked less than half of the year. When he wasn't working, he'd be at the union hall or at the airport, trying to pick up someone needing a flying lesson or two—all the time dreaming of his scheme to fly lobsters from Maine down to restaurants in Boston. The trouble was he only dreamed about it. There was no apparent effort to actually make it happen, except to talk about it to his buddies at the airport or at the Hi-Hat. The fact that they didn't own either a lobster boat or a restaurant seemed lost on Ben's dad.

Annie stopped at the Madras Shop and waited for a couple and their kids to come through the door before heading into the store. Most of the clothes in the store were women's clothes, but there was one wooden table with men's shirts on it and another with cotton sweaters. Ben walked over and fingered the brightly colored plaid shirts. They were real madras: Indian Madras.

"The colors fade and get softer when you wash the shirts," Annie said. "I think you'd look good in one." Annie held a few of the shirts up to Ben's chest, looking at the colors against his summer-tanned skin.

"Are you going to be here for a while?" Ben was anxious to get away from the shirt table. No madras in *his* budget—genuine or otherwise. Besides, he wanted to get back down to the silversmith to buy the charm for Annie. "I need to find a boys' room."

"Go back down to the Portside. The restrooms are supposed to be only for customers, but just walk in like you own the place and they won't bother you. I'll be here."

"I'll be right back," he said, and headed out the door.

"Did you forget something?" Ben turned and saw that Annie was pointing at her lips. He blushed and kissed her.

"That's supposed to hold me while you're gone?" She wrapped her arms around his neck and kissed him, holding him until he opened his eyes and looked into hers. "Now...go do your business." She turned and riffled through the thin sweaters on the table.

Ben walked to the door, self-consciously keeping his eyes straight ahead. As the screen door slapped behind him, the air slipped audibly from his lungs. He stood for a moment on the wood-decked door recess to wait for an opening in the flow of people on the crowded sidewalk, then slid into the stream. As he reached Dock Square and the foot of Bearskin Neck, the river of people fanned out and Ben was able to slide away and head for the silversmith. The neck was still crowded and he had to pick his way around the human obstacles in the road—families gathered around a baby carriage to wipe an ice cream-splattered face, an older couple confused about where they were going, a group of kids looking at a purchase one of them had made.

He entered the store and saw there was only one couple looking at jewelry at the far end. Two sales clerks—an older man and a young woman—were chatting with them. Ben was nervous that he only had a few minutes before Annie would start wondering where he'd really gone and was relieved when one of the clerks broke away from the conversation to head towards him.

"Can I help you?" said the young woman. She was a couple of years older than Ben with a deep, mellow tan and light brown hair softly streaked by hours in the sun. Ben noticed that she was extraordinarily pretty, nearly as pretty as Annie. He almost wished that it had been the man who had come to help him. He wasn't going to spend much, and he wouldn't care as much if the man thought he was poor or cheap—or both.

"Yes, I'm looking for a charm."

The clerk smiled, and Ben blurted, "For a bracelet."

She smiled again. "Are you thinking gold, silver, or pewter?"

"Well, I like the Motif No. 1. I only saw that in gold. And I like a shell that I saw in pewter. I guess that I'd like to see them both."

"We do have the Motif No.1 in silver too, so let me pull the silver out for you, as well." She bent and took three trays from the glass case. Each had six rows of charms. Ben noticed other charms and began to wonder whether one of them might be better. He wanted something to remind Annie of this day. Then, thinking of his limited time, he decided he had to keep it to the two charms he'd been considering.

"The gold are five dollars, the silver four dollars, and the pewter are three dollars."

Ben quickly disposed of the idea of the gold. That would break the bank. He thought that the Motif No. 1 was more symbolic of their day, but he was worried about Annie's shack comment. "No time, gotta decide," he whispered to himself.

"What's that?"

"Sorry, nothing. Just thinking out loud."

The clerk smiled again.

Ben was out of time; he had to make a decision. "I'll take the pewter shell."

"I'll get you a fresh one," the clerk said, and she headed down the row of cases through a bead curtain and into a back room.

"I don't have *time* for a fresh one," Ben screamed silently to himself. Then a sickness welled up from his stomach. Annie's charms were all silver, although one—a horse—had a touch of gold on its mane and another had a little glass orb. The pewter was going to stick out as the cheapest charm on her wrist. Maybe he should get the silver Motif No. 1. No time. God, *why* had he made such a bad decision?

Too late, the clerk emerged from the back room with a small square box in hand and headed for the cash register. "Would you like this wrapped?"

"No, that'll be fine," Ben said. I haven't got time, he screamed to himself.

"Three dollars."

Ben handed her the three bills.

"Is this for the pretty red-head?"

Ben was surprised. Obviously, Annie was so pretty that she stood out even among the throngs of pretty women who must come into this store. He felt quite proud he was with her. "I'm surprised that you noticed...with the crowds and all."

"I noticed she was with *you*." She smiled, and Ben noticed her eyes were smiling, too. "Thank you; I hope you come back soon."

Ben smiled, and his face burned. He slipped the box into his pocket. As he walked from the store he felt a tingle in the back of his head. What did the clerk mean? Was she flirting with him? Ben hoped that she was. Not that he'd do anything about it. It was more likely she was wondering why a high-class girl like Annie was with such a loser like him. "Be positive," he thought. "Yeah, right. Look at the facts. You had to hit up your little brother for money. You've got nothing. You are a loser."

"Be positive," a deep voice in his head said.

"That was fast." Annie was waiting in the door recess at the Madras Shop with two shopping bags in hand.

"I didn't wear a watch, so I was worried I was taking too much time. The neck is crowded."

"Always is. Do you want to get something to eat?"

"Sure. There's a clam shop down at the corner. Let's eat there. It's more genuine than a sit-down place." Ben was impressed he'd come up with such a rational argument on the spur of the moment.

"Okay."

The clam shack turned out to be much more. It had self-service and open tables and a range of seafood on the menu. Ben's heart jumped into his throat when Annie ordered the lobster roll and a Coke. Ben scanned the menu on the overhead board and saw that the lobster roll was a full three dollars. *Crap*, he thought. He ordered the foot-long hot dog and a Coke. The dog was only a dollar, so he'd be back on track.

"Do you want chips with that?"

Ben scanned the menu to see if he could afford the chips, but didn't find them listed. "Of course," he thought. "Why would they list chips?"

"They come with it."

"Sure."

'That'll be four-fifty."

Three dollars and fifty-cents left. Enough for gas and an ice-cream cone. Ben's spirits were lifted.

Annie and Ben stepped aside to wait for their food. They held hands silently and watched the crowds out on the square, although somewhat thinner now. It struck Ben that, even with all the galleries, no one was apparently carrying a package that looked like a painting.

"Lobster roll and a dog," the middle-aged woman at the counter yelled out.

Ben stepped forward and took the tray from the counter. As he turned, he noticed Annie had taken a table by the open windows near the street. He moved to her and placed her plate, the little cups of tartar sauce and cup of Coke in front of her, then placed his own plate and cup on his side. He headed back to the counter and returned the tray. It would be easier not to have the tray on the small table. He grabbed a couple of napkins from the dispenser and headed back to the table.

As he sat down, Annie said, "I bought you a little something," and handed him one of the bags. He pulled out the tissue-wrapped object and knew immediately it was the madras shirt which she had held up to him in the store.

"Thank you. Thank you very much."

"Do you really like it?"

"Absolutely. I'd put it on now, but I don't want to make hearts swoon when I take my shirt off."

"Yeah, well. Anyway, you have to wash it before you wear it. It you sweat in it before you wash it your body might become permanently plaid."

"Then I wouldn't have to wear a shirt." Ben stuck the shirt back in the bag and stuffed the tissue paper in after it.

"I bought you something too," Ben said, as he stood up to take the box out of his pants pocket. The edges had gotten slightly crushed, but it still looked more elegant than any present Ben had ever bought for a girl. He handed Annie the box.

"Don't you think it's too soon for an engagement ring?" Annie opened the box. "Wow!" She seemed truly delighted.

Ben's anxiety disappeared. She seemed really impressed.

Annie took the charm from the box and Ben saw that it was not the pewter shell, but a beautiful silver shell, finely detailed, and gleaming like a bright summer star.

"I love it. I love you. Thank you." She pulled his face to hers and kissed him. Her soft lips parted. Ben could feel her teeth with his lips. They parted, too, and her tongue pressed between Ben's lips and into his mouth. He felt the blood rushing to his head. He quickly sat down.

"So, you bought me a cheap dinner so you could spend all your money on jewelry for me. I *like* that in a man."

Ben still didn't feel entirely like a worthy man for Annie, but he was glad she had said so.

9

B EN SAT ON THE LOW STONE WALL THAT SEPARATED
the Holt's front yard from the sidewalk and street. The box that
held his graduation gown lay beside him, his mortarboard and cap
sat on his head. He blew at the tassel, thinking of the day to come
and the life that lay beyond. He was looking forward to a long, gold-
en summer with Annie before they had to start college. She would
be starting nursing school here and Ben would be attending night
school at the Boston Institute of Architecture. He had been accepted
at Miami and Cincinnati, but he wanted to stay in Boston to be close
to Annie. Annie was starting to talk about their life after they married. Ben had grown to love her sunny picture of a coupled future,
but there was still a remaining stone of doubt in his gut.

Ben thought of the events of the night past and the party at
Mike Murray's house in Nahant. Mike lived at the end of Swallow
Cove Road in a large house overlooking the ocean and the path to the
caves in the cliffs below. The afternoon had been warm and Annie
had worn a sundress that exposed her freckle-dappled shoulders and
accentuated her long, slim legs.

As the sun set over the house, he was gathered with Annie, Mike,
Mike's girlfriend Kate and a dozen or so of their friends on the stone
patio. The voices were happy and the boys were even more animated
than usual, back-slapping and embracing each other, while the girls

gathered in small, quiet groups. Beneath it all he felt the tender edge of melancholy. He looked around the patio and knew that he would not see many of these familiar faces —faces that had been part of each day —again.

"Penny for your thoughts," Annie whispered as she stood behind him nuzzling his ear.

Ben turned and kissed her. He wrapped his arms around her and pulled her close.

"Let's go down to the water, Annie."

"I promised to bring Diane something to eat. I'll meet you inside. Talk to your friends for a while. After tomorrow, many of the people you've cared about will be gone."

Ben made a point to talk mostly to the guys he knew would be leaving right after graduation. Some had enlisted, mostly in the Navy, but one guy was headed for West Point. They all promised to keep in touch. He knew that most wouldn't.

Suddenly he realized he had lost track of time. He headed to the house to look for Annie.

"Hey. Where have you been?" Diane stood at a table near the door, piling food onto a paper plate that was collapsing under the load.

"Talking to my friends." Ben looked at Diane's plate. "More food?"

"I haven't eaten yet. Annie was going to bring me a plate but she never showed. Have you eaten?"

"No."

"Grab a plate and come sit on the wall with me."

Ben and Diane sat silently on the wall, eating and watching the stars. "I guess I'd better go find Annie." Ben got up and started for the house.

"Ben."

"Yes?" He turned toward Diane.

"She's still a virgin."

Ben said nothing, but turned for the house again.

"You'd better fuck her or you'll wake up some day and she'll be with someone who will."

BEN SLID THE screen aside and walked into the house. The living room was dark and crowded with dancers clinging to each other. Ben had difficulty navigating the room, apologizing more than a few times for bumping into people. He made his way to the kitchen where there was a small pool of light from a dozen candles burning on the table in the breakfast nook. There were two distinct gatherings in the long, narrow room. A half-dozen of the school's athletes were clustered next to the refrigerator, half of them sitting on the counter. Dennis, a huge guy who threw the shot put, turned and nodded to Ben. Four girls sat on the benches in the breakfast nook. None of them were Annie.

Ben headed downstairs to the rumpus room. The jukebox was lit up and playing "Hookah Tookah." Two couples were shooting pool while another couple made out on the sofa.

Ben checked out the girl on the sofa, then chided himself for even thinking it might be Annie. He headed back upstairs by the stairway that lead to the garage. There were low voices and moans coming from the back of the van that Mike's dad used for his importing business. Ben slid past the van and walked quickly and quietly through the open garage door. Annie's car, which had been parked in front of the closed gate in the high wall, was gone. The gate was open.

Ben's heart dropped. He sat on the ground just outside the open gate. He was stunned. Where could she have gone? Why had she left? Maybe she's still here and someone had just taken her car. He thought of getting up to go look for her again, but didn't move. He sat on the ground for almost an hour-and-a-half. A few couples came out to the driveway. Cars were shuffled and a few drove away. Ben thought of going inside and asking someone for a ride, but he decided he didn't want to talk to anyone right now, didn't want to explain, didn't want to appear foolishly worried, didn't want to make up some covering story and didn't know the true story either. He got up and started walking home. He wasn't sure how far it was—five miles, maybe six.

When he got to Short Beach, he left the road and walked along the water. The surf that usually comforted him had no calming words tonight. He rejoined the road after the Coast Guard station and walked into the parking lot that ran along the beach into Lynn. There seemed to be an unusual number of cars parked on the beach tonight. Most had steamed windows; a few revealed the profiles of young couples whose windows would be steamed soon enough.

It suddenly occurred to Ben that he might find Annie's car parked there, her windows steamed, too. If she was there, he was sure he didn't want to know it. He cut over the low concrete retaining wall and headed toward the surf that had denied him comfort back on Short Beach. The full moon was high and small now, but its light was a bright and cool white.

Just after the Beach Police station, Ben turned and headed up to the road. He cut across the Shore drive at the traffic circle and stopped in the grass median. He noticed that the parking lot at Christie's was busy and could hear the radios blaring Arnie Ginsburg's show. He wondered whether he should take his regular route down the Lynnway, then up Market and Franklin, or if he should cut over the hill, which might be shorter, although he didn't know those streets as well.

From behind him near the beach came the sound of screeching brakes and blaring horns. Ben turned toward the sound and saw Annie's car with Annie standing by the open driver's side door, her arms crossed over her chest.

"Get in the car!" She screamed to Ben, oblivious to the traffic snarled behind her.

Ben trotted towards the car, cut in front of it and turned along the passenger side, reaching for the door handle just as Annie pushed it open from inside.

"What are you doing?" Annie screamed. "Are you crazy? Are you drunk? Why did you leave Mike's? What's wrong with you?"

"I could ask *you* the same thing."

"I was dealing with your drunken brother. He showed up at Mike's stinking of beer and his hands were a bloody, swollen mess."

"*Shit!*"

"Don't say 'shit' in front of me."

"Sorry."

"I drove Don to the hospital. Anne-Marie's friend Harold came with me. He just finished his first year of nursing school, so he offered to help. Anne-Marie was supposed to tell you all of this, but she couldn't find you."

"I was out on the patio talking to Diane."

"I know—she told me." Annie was calmer now.

"Why didn't you come tell *me?*"

"Because I was coming out of the kitchen when Don came through the front door. I could tell from that far away he was already drunk. He was flirting with Anne-Marie and Harold was getting pissed. You know how Don looks for a fight when he gets like that. I went over to head him off and send him home. He put his arm over my shoulder and that's when I noticed his hands. I didn't want him to stay. I didn't want anyone to see him. I wanted him out of there. Harold offered to help, even though Don kept threatening to beat him up. He was very belligerent one moment, then apologetic for acting badly in front of me, then back to being belligerent again. It was a struggle, but as soon as we got him into the back seat of my car, he fell asleep."

"Where is he now?"

"In the emergency room, unless they've already x-rayed and bandaged his hands. Harold stayed with him."

"I'll have to thank Harold. Thank you for taking care of him. I wish that I'd known though."

"Well, Anne-Marie didn't do a great job of looking for you. I found her with two guys in the back of Mike's father's van. It's a good thing that Harold stayed at the hospital. Not good...not good." She shook her head.

"I couldn't find you and then I saw your car was gone. I didn't know what to think."

"So you thought the worst. How do you think that makes *me* feel? You know that I love you."

"I know. I know."

"Don't ever do that again. You worry me when you act crazy."

"Okay."

Ben laid his head in Annie's lap as she drove. He inhaled the soft scent of her. She stroked his head with her right hand, driving with her left hand, her left arm through the open window. She liked it when he inhaled her scent. It confirmed her power over him.

"Do you want to go up to Den Rock?"

"I'd love to, but I need to check on Don. Can you drop me at the hospital?"

"Tonight?"

"I'm sorry, but I've gotta. He's my brother."

AFTER AN HOUR-AND-A-HALF at the hospital, Ben walked home with Don. The emergency room staff had wanted Don to be admitted, but he'd refused. They walked home in silence, but as they drew close to their house, both knew that Don would have to face their father and explain his condition. Both expected the worst and Ben was worried for his brother.

But it wasn't Don who drew their father's ire, it was Ben. After sending Don to bed with his mother attending to him, their father turned on Ben and accused him of abandoning his brother and palming him off on a stranger, Harold, while Ben partied. Once again, after a long, angry tirade that had his mother cowering in Don's room while Don slept, Ben found himself on the street.

Ben tried to hate his father for throwing him out on the street. He tried, but couldn't. It was in his father's nature as surely as the yellow-jacket's sting. He may not have hated him, but he was sorely embarrassed by his thuggishness—a trait keenly seen by Annie's mother and used by her to try to drive Annie away from him.

Ben had told Annie only one time, about a year ago, that his father had tossed him to the street. He had expected some sympathy, some support, but had only seen fear in her eyes and felt her instinct to flee from him. He never told her about his occasional exiles again.

Tonight, Ben walked across the lonely coal yard of the power plant and settled on the edge of the dock, his feet dangling over the water. He looked across the moonless bay to the lights of Boston. The hulking form of the crane stood silently behind him and he imagined its great steel boom settling its dark fingers on his shoulder, comforting him.

Soon he would be free to flee, to be in the world on his own, but there was the problem of Annie. He knew it was in her nature to stick close to home, to be near her parents, and his life was entwined with hers.

10

Late Summer 1965

TIME IS CAPRICIOUS. WHEN WE ARE YOUNG, DAYS stretch on before us—a week is forever. There is time to dream many dreams—dreams splashed happily with the summer's golden sun and dreams as clear as the summer's blue sky. When we are young, summer vacations are not measured in days or weeks or months, but exist separately from time. The summer of 1965 passed well for Annie, Ben, Diane, Alice and their friends. When it passed, it passed quietly and alone, abandoned to new life and new dreams—and new fears.

Ben and Annie were inseparable. They spent long days on the beach, nights swimming in the dark at the reservoir jumping into the water from the large rock about fifty feet offshore. Ben would accompany Annie on her shopping trips—usually to Salem, which Ben found to be more exotic than the shopping in Lynn. They would often talk about their dreams of their future home in a large, dark-red colonial on a couple of acres of land, probably in Lynnfield to be close to her parents, but maybe Pride's Crossing. They looked in stores and magazines at the furniture they would buy. They went to the Hawthorne Hotel to have tea and look at their antique furniture—European, Annie pointed out, was the best. At the fabric store on Essex Street, Annie picked out wedding dress patterns and talked about their wedding day—the flowers in the church, which priest would marry them, the food at the reception, their going-away clothes, who would be there and who would not.

When he went home at night, Ben would sketch Annie's dream house and draw dream furniture in ballpoint pen on a leftover lined school notebook and present his sketches the next day for approval, making revisions to them as Annie suggested. Some days he would sketch old buildings they'd seen on their trips to Marblehead and Rockport, casting dramatic shadows and capturing the sunlight.

On one trip to Rockport, Annie bought Ben an Aquabee CoMo sketchbook and the Koh-i-noor thick-lead sketch pencil that he had wanted for so long. He started sketching while they were out and his sketches became softer, the shades and shadows more varied, the lines more suggestive. Ben liked the feel of the soft lead on the texture of the paper. He loved Annie's gift; he loved Annie, and life was warm and bright.

Annie's mother and father stopped suggesting to her that she see other boys. They seemed to accept that Ben was—and would forever be—a part of their family. They included Ben in family dinners and assigned him the salad-making duties. After dinner he and Annie's dad would retreat to the living room to discuss the affairs of the day—"men's talk," Annie's mother called it.

Annie's dad arranged for Ben to meet architects who he knew from his work at the Housing Authority. Ben liked meeting "real architects" and enjoyed the tours of their offices, but was dismayed by their suggestions that he drop his intention to attend the Boston Institute for Architecture. One suggested an undergraduate education in Fine Arts at CCNY before graduate school in architecture. Several others suggested architecture schools in London or Berkeley or Cincinnati. Ben thought it a bit odd that none suggested any of the Boston or Cambridge schools. Ben was determined to attend the BIA and be close to Annie.

As he was leaving the office of the architect who had suggested Cincinnati, he noticed a wall covered in framed certificates. There were architectural licenses from several states, awards for projects that the firm had done and, bearing the name of the architect whom he had just left, a graduation certificate from the BIA. A chill ran down Ben's spine, but he smiled as he heard Sister Eustelle's voice, "Knowing what no one else knows you know is real power. Keep your own counsel."

DON FLIPPED THE cap of the Miller High Life bottle into the trashcan using his thumb against the middle joint of his forefinger. He still had it, he thought. His hands had healed since the fight almost three months ago, but his thumb had remained deformed. X-rays revealed that his thumb had been broken and was healing improperly, so they'd had to break it again and set it in a cast. The cast had been off for a couple of weeks, but his thumb was weak. He thought that the exercise the physical therapist had given him to strengthen it was silly—twiddling his thumbs—but it did seem to work.

The night that Don hurt his hand he had been freelancing. He'd beaten up a guy who'd been seeing the girlfriend of one of his associates. He'd found them sitting on a concrete wall at the beach, making out in full view of passersby and other couples who had the sense to make out in a parked car. Don remembered Tony's ban on freelancing, but this had been a matter of honor. The guy was bigger than Don and wore a large motorcycle chain around his neck. It was the chain that he must have hit when he'd broken his thumb. The guy had been trying to take it off to use as a weapon, but Don had pummeled him to the ground first and had kept hitting him while the girl had just stood there beside him, crying uncontrollably.

As Don walked away, he felt the throbbing in his hand and looked at it for the first time. The combination of the beers he'd been drinking all afternoon and the adrenaline rush of the fight may have dulled the pain for a while, but it had become excruciating. He decided to head for the party at Mike Murray's.

When Tony Angelo found out about the beating Don had given to a biker from a gang trying to move in, he called Don to his office and reminded him of his prohibition against freelancing. It seemed to Don to be a half-hearted lecture. After Tony dismissed him, he walked from the office and was greeted by smiles and back slaps from the cops and associates hanging around the Spa. As Tony emerged from the office, however, everyone turned quiet and serious until he had passed through the front door.

Don wished that Toni had been there to see his triumph, but she hadn't been around in a couple of weeks. She'd gone up to a lake in New Hampshire with her mother and sisters and kid brother. Don hoped that her cousin, the jilted associate, would pass on the story of his gallant work and perhaps start talking around the Spa that maybe Don was ready to move up—to become a collector. He may have broken one of Tony's rules, but he had proven himself.

He was convinced that his plan for getting Toni had advanced.

11

THE FALL OF 1965 WAS FULL OF NEW LIFE FOR BEN, Annie, Don and their friends. Ben had started architecture school at the BIA and taken a job as the overnight watchman at the huge America's Park development project along the formerly industrial shoreline that ran along Lynn harbor. The construction company had assigned him a trailer on-site to live in and he used the plan tables in the project engineer's trailer for working on school projects. Ben's schedule allowed him to see Annie on those few afternoons when she could get away from nursing school and those nights—Friday through Monday—when he didn't have class.

Annie couldn't remember a time when she hadn't wanted to be a nurse, and the deep immersion that nursing school required thrilled her. Some of her classmates were overwhelmed and some dropped out in the first semester, but Annie blossomed amidst the storm and the angst. Classmates came to her for advice and counsel or just for a little dose of comfort. It seemed to Ben that Annie's happiness made her even more beautiful than ever.

Ben found the first year of architecture school trite and boring. It felt like kindergarten art class; some of the design exercises involved assignments like moving shapes of colored paper around on large black or white backgrounds, then noting the differences in perceived space and mass in a notebook. In drafting class, the assignments included drawing the unfolded shape of a shipping box, which could be made from one sheet of corrugated cardboard, then constructing the actual box from the drawing. He was quite sure he had done this in junior high. Ben chafed at the simple exercises. He wanted to design *buildings*, not construction-paper compositions. He wanted to draw great structures, not boxes. He was more than a bit embarrassed that Annie was giving shots and caring for patients while he was bringing home "refrigerator art." To make matters worse, he became defensive when he had to explain to people why the BIA's night classes were really as good as any other college's daytime program.

Just after Thanksgiving, Annie told Ben she would have to be away in Connecticut for six weeks for her psych rotation. Ben offered to travel to Hartford on the weekend, but Annie told him it was unlikely she'd have time to see him and that she'd often have to work on weekends.

"The separation will only make me love you more," Annie claimed. Ben thought her words sounded as if they'd come directly from her mother's mouth. He looked at Annie, but saw her mother standing before him.

"I understand you need to do this and that it's part of what you love to do, but you can't ask me to like it."

"I don't like it either, but I have to do it."

After that, they didn't talk about the rotation or her upcoming absence all through the weeks leading up to Christmas. It lurked behind every conversation, every look, every kiss, every quiet moment, but its presence was never acknowledged. They stopped talking about what she was doing in nursing school and what he was doing in architecture school. Their silence felt strange and uncomfortable. The joy they had both anticipated around the holidays was absent.

They spent Christmas at Annie's house. Ben gave Annie a Parker Duofold pen—gold-trimmed with a mother-of-pearl and black barrel. "For writing notes in charts," he said. Annie bought Ben a long wool scarf. She said that it made him look artistic—like an architect. The spirit in the house was dull and stale. Ben felt uncomfortable and filled with a heavy sense of dread. Nothing in the demeanor of Annie or her parents made him feel as though he was over-reacting. Her father avoided him. It felt as though someone was dying and nobody wanted to talk about it.

Annie went back to school the day before New Year's Eve. She said that she wanted to get packed and be ready to leave for Hartford on the second. It was the first New Year's Eve that they had spent apart in four years—since they'd been kids. Ben spent New Year's Eve in the trailer. Just before midnight he took a walk along the ocean, accompanied only by the stars in the clear, cold night sky.

DON DECIDED TO put off college so he could work with Richie on his father's political campaign. Richie's dad, Ezekiel Samuel—"call me Sam"—McGonigle, had served two terms on the City Council and had run a successful newspaper distribution company that delivered Boston and local papers throughout the North Shore. He had worked in the warehouse while attending law school at night, then had taken over the family business when his father had suffered a heart attack. At first he'd thought he might run the business for a short time until his father recovered, but when his father showed no signs of wishing to return to the business, Sam thought he would just run it for a short time to get it ready for sale. In the end, however, Sam never left, never pursued the promising law career. Now he was running for an soon-to-be open State Rep seat against a half-dozen other candidates. Richie, Sam and his dad had come out of the Brickyards. That was enough qualification for Don.

Don seemed born to campaign. He made friends easily and quickly earned their respect and loyalty. His family name made him welcome in labor circles and he used his connections to Tony Angelo to organize neighborhoods for the campaign. Don worked in Sam's unofficial campaign office in the basement of the warehouse during the midday, did Tony's business early each morning, went back to it later each afternoon, then attended campaign events at night. He was busy and happy.

Sam liked Don's quick wit, admired his street-smarts and cherished his connections to Tony Angelo. He thought of Don as his envoy to Tony and as the buffer who kept the two men from being seen together. Sam, in fact, had never met Tony—not one on one—although he had seen Tony's daughter at a campaign fund-raiser. She was an amazingly beautiful young woman and Sam made a mental note to offer her a job when the campaign staffed up in the months before the coming election.

Don loved the energy of the campaign, loved being an insider. At the end of each long day, the senior staff and a small cadre of committed volunteers would get together over beer and pizza and talk through the day's successes. Though Don was underage, nobody seemed to care that he could tear into the beer with the best of them.

The pace of the campaign slowed between Thanksgiving and Christmas, but the week between Christmas and New Year's was a time of renewed activity. They were about to start hiring a full campaign staff and there were lists of positions to be filled and potential candidates for those positions to be identified. Don's work for Tony was also picking up— the week after Christmas was particularly busy for collections. Don left his room early each morning, headed to the home of that day's first name on the list, waited for the joker to leave for work, then moved in to corner him. By ten a.m. he was in the campaign office where he worked until the factories started letting out at three. He finished another wave of collections for Tony when the white-collars guys started getting off at five. By eight he was at a campaign event or back at Sam's for more work, more beer, more pizza until two a.m. or so. In the morning, he'd heat up a slice or two of the left-over pizza he had grabbed the night before, then head out the door to start it all over again.

On New Year's Eve, Don left the empty office just before midnight. He walked to his room at the Oxford Hotel, counting his steps between each crack in the sidewalk. Life, Don thought, couldn't be better.

12

Winter 1966

HAROLD SUGGESTED HE AND ANNIE LEAVE FOR Hartford early to settle into the nurses' residence before the big rush began the week after New Year's. Annie agreed. She had missed him over the Christmas break when he'd gone to his mother's home in Juan-les-Pins in the south of France. Harold hadn't visited his mother in almost three years, not since she'd divorced his father and re-married her first husband. Harold saw his father at the Hotel Edison downtown every Tuesday for dinner and spent his off-weekends with him in his childhood home in the central Massachusetts town of Oxford.

Annie and Harold had become close over the last several months. She had talked him through the difficult time after his girlfriend, Amy, had left him for a college classmate, Dan, a guy they'd known in high school and who'd been on the gymnastics team with Harold. Diane attended the same college as Amy and Dan—Aquinas—and told Annie that Amy was pregnant and would have to leave Aquinas after the first semester to go away to have the baby, unless she married the father. Annie decided not to mention Diane's news to Harold. She felt as though her secret knowledge connected her even more closely to him. She began to notice there were days when all of her idle thoughts were of Harold.

Annie decided to tell Ben she wanted to take a break. She'd tell Ben that it wasn't fair to him and that she was so immersed in her nursing education she didn't have much time left for him. She'd assure him that she still loved him and still planned to marry him when she got out of school. She'd understand if he saw other women during the break, but she wouldn't date anyone else. She didn't have time for dating anyway. She'd only be a phone call away—that is, if the pay phone in the common area wasn't tied up. She had her "little talk" all worked out in her mind. Instead, she said nothing.

Harold had swept into Annie's life like the first crisp breeze of fall. He'd swept away all the restraining ties that bound her to her past life. He brought to her a new light that shone with life's possibilities. His light infected Annie and excited her. It made her feel as though she was living in a newly-detailed world, a world she hadn't seen before, even though it had been right there in front of her all along. She felt as though she saw everything and everyone around her with a new clarity. She understood the continuing dance of her father around her mother—like a moth flirting with a flame, barely avoiding being consumed. She saw Ben and his family and understood he was really, in the end, more like them, even as he strode away from them. She pictured Ben as being attached to his family by some huge rubber band: as soon as soon as he got to the limits of the band, he would be snapped back.

Annie loved Ben, but she wanted Harold. Over the holidays, she decided to let go, to enjoy the thrill of free-fall and see where she would land. Anticipation energized her. Ben did not. He had been her transition from childhood. Harold offered an opening to new life and she was now ready to step though it.

13

April 1966

"**I** KNOW THAT I PROMISED, BUT I CAN'T SEE YOU tonight," Annie said. "I've really got to study."

"Really? Didn't you get to study this weekend? I haven't seen you in almost six weeks."

"I couldn't study this weekend…I had clinic."

"Was it that bad?"

"Well you know what Saturday nights are like. It's the worst night of the week and I took the overnight rotation so that Kathy could take some time off with Steve."

"But that gave you all day…"

"I *slept* all day."

"When is Kathy going to cover for you so you can take some time off with me?"

There was a long silence.

"It just seems you work too hard and have no time to do anything."

More silence.

"It just seems that I care a lot more than you do."

"Ben, you know how important this is to me. I've got to do well. I don't want to just be a floor nurse, I want to be in a specialty. Surgery or anesthesiology maybe. This is very important and you should want this for me too. Don't be so selfish."

"Sorry. I just miss you, that's all. You know how much I love you."

Silence.

"Tell me you love me, too."

"The phone's in the corridor. There's a lot of people around."

"Everyone knows I'm your boyfriend."

Silence.

"Well, when can I see you?"

"I'm not sure of my schedule yet."

"When do you get your schedule?"

"I don't know...at the end of the week. I've got to go."

"Did you go to the parade with your dad yesterday?"

"No, I couldn't. Why are you giving me the third degree? No, I really don't want to know. I have to go."

"Okay, bye. I do love you." Ben smooched into the receiver. Then he heard a click and the dial tone.

Harold knocked lightly on the half-open door. "Are you decent?"

"Yes, come in."

Harold plopped down on the single bed, the only piece of furniture in the room not fully covered by books, paper or clothes. As he leaned back on the bed, he felt the phone under his back and pulled it out, setting it on the pillow.

"Did you already make your call?"

"Yes, all taken care of."

"How is everything at home?"

"Pretty good. My dad's still not eating the way he should and my mother is fretting over him, which drives him crazy and probably makes his stomach worse, which means he doesn't eat, and so the cycle goes."

"Classic."

"Yeah."

"Are you ready to go? I got us a six-o'clock reservation so I could get some studying in later. I'm not ready for the test tomorrow and I still haven't started the psych paper. Did you finish yours?"

"Yeah, I finished it last Friday. I didn't want it hanging over me over the weekend. We won't be seeing many four-day weekends anytime soon."

"I liked hanging over you this weekend."

"You certainly did, but I wouldn't exactly have called it 'hanging'."

Harold smiled and twisted his lips. "No, and my boys could barely hang yesterday."

"It's your own fault."

"Yeah, like you had no part in it!"

"Good girls like me *never* have a part in it."

It struck Harold she was quite serious.

Annie smiled and reached across Harold to pick up her sweater. He grabbed her and pulled her down on top of him and kissed her hard. Annie's lips were still sore and felt swollen, although they had looked fine when Annie checked them—first the outside, then the inside—in the mirror this morning. Her mouth and cheek muscles still felt strained from the weekend. She lifted her head several inches above Harold's face.

"I thought you wanted to get going."

"That was before I knew you were going to attack me, but yes, we *do* have to go. Ready?" Annie grabbed her pocketbook and slung it over her head with the strap cutting a line across her chest.

Harold liked her breasts—not terribly large, but firm with nice nipples. Harold sighed, recalling his visit with those breasts a few days earlier. He sighed again. "Ready."

BEN FELT A hollow sucking in his chest and a soft tingling in his head. Was it his disappointment over Annie's unavailability? Was it a feeling that things were changing with Annie and that school was becoming more important than he was? Was it because he hadn't eaten much all day? Hard to know, he thought. Only one treatment for this condition: a ham and cheese sub at Angelina's. The thought made him smile. The ham, the cheese and the onions were standard sub shop fare and didn't justify a special trip, but the bread—Oh, the bread! *That* was what made it special. The sub rolls at Angelina's were wider and flatter than at other shops—soft, and topped with sesame seeds. Angelina's was just a short ride from the trailer where Ben lived.

Ben was proud he'd gotten promoted to assistant project engineer himself, without help from his father or Annie's father. He like the "project engineer" title, although it involved little more than copying the red pen mark-ups from the "shop drawings" that the project manager marked up so they could ultimately be returned to the subcontractors. He was still, for all intents and purposes, just the night watchman.

Ben thought of Annie working away in the nursing school library, concentrating so hard that she twisted her lips. He remembered their nights together at the library, upstairs in the reading room, the movement of her lips a testament to her concentration. He folded up the grid paper he'd been working on and stuck it under the last page of the grid pad, just inside the heavy cardboard backer. I suppose the good part is that I really should be working too, he thought. His boss called it "found time" when someone cancelled a meeting at the last minute. Ben thought he could always finish his structures homework when he got back and leave the design assignment for the morning.

He grabbed his old brown leather jacket and started out the door. The jacket had been Jack Wall's, the older kid from next door. After he'd died, and the army had sent his body back in a sealed coffin, his mother, Dottie, had given all of his clothes, his sports equipment and most of his 33 RPM records to the Holt boys. Being the oldest, Ben had gotten the jacket and the records—all of the records except "A White Sports Coat and a Pink Carnation," a record that Ron had asked for.

"Keys," Ben said aloud and patted his jacket pockets. He found them in his right pocket. The phone rang and Ben picked it up before it could ring a second time. "Ah, so you changed your mind."

"Huh, about what?" It was Jen.

"Oh, nothing…I thought you were someone else."

"Annie?"

"Yeah."

"Well, we've got another problem here. Don and Dad are fighting again. Don's drunk and pissed…Dad's just pissed. He knows he should leave Don alone when he gets like this, but he has to keep egging him on. How soon can you be here?"

"Fuck, this is what I need right now."

"What?"

"Sorry…fifteen to twenty minutes. I was about to head out, anyway."

Ben checked the lock on the tool locker, turned off the light and locked the door of the trailer. As he got to the chain-link fence, he turned to look around the site. All, he thought, looked fine. He closed the gate, wrapped the heavy chain around the fence post and gate frame and locked the big Master lock.

He hopped into his Olds Super 88. It had been his father's before he'd gotten the 98. The 88 was big and powerful, with long sweeping lines. Jade green. At nineteen feet long, it offered plenty of room inside for fooling around. He thought of the nights at the beach with Annie, parked along the sea wall and making out. It had been this time last year when the cop had rapped on the window just as Annie had gotten his pants open. After that, they'd never gone back to the beach, preferring the cemetery instead.

Ben sighed. The "innocent" days of making out at the beach— or in the church balcony—were gone. He could bring Annie to his trailer, he thought, although she hadn't stayed there yet.

DINNER HAD BEEN a bit disappointing. The food was fine. Anthony's was as good as ever and a welcome break from hospital food. Harold was attentive, even dashing, and she loved how he said "escargot" with a perfect French accent.

Annie was feeling unhappy about her phone call with Ben and she didn't like to feel unhappy. Why couldn't Ben understand she was not a high-school girl any more? Why couldn't he let her be the independent adult with a bright future that she was now? He said that he loved her, but all he wanted to do was to hold her back in his world.

He had once planned to be an engineer—*that* might have been a good job for her husband—but then he'd thrown it all away and decided to study architecture. His father had "studied architecture" in a correspondence course and look at him—out of work most of the year. She couldn't, she *wouldn't*, live like that. Her mother had said he'd be lucky to get a drafting job somewhere, but it wouldn't have been the kind of job he could have gotten at GE. There was no reason she should support him while he hung out at the coffee shop or the track, like his father. And to make matters worse, he had become so needy: constantly making demands on her time. She had outgrown him and his silly dreams; why couldn't he see that? Why couldn't he let her live a better life?

Her mother had warned her this would happen, had urged her to see other boys. If Ben really cared about her, he'd be happy for her. He wouldn't mind a little competition if he was good enough for her. Her mother had smiled when Annie had told her she was now seeing Harold. "These things work out the way God has planned."

Ben should know that.

As he drove up to the house, it struck Ben that Larch Road had completely and surreptitiously changed its character. It was a quiet tree-lined street—now that the guys who always hung around to play two-hand touch and whiffle ball in the street with the Holt boys had gone off either to college or to the Army. He parked the car at the end of the narrow driveway, behind the other three cars already there.

The day had been warm, a harbinger of the spring to come, but the evening dark brought a chill with it. The maple trees were still barren, their trunks standing as sentinels to the waning day. A few twinkling lights were visible in the flatlands below and the steady blue light on the spire of the John Hancock building in the far distance signaled a clear night.

As he walked up the stairs to the front door, he could hear muffled sounds of arguing inside. He reached for the door latch and depressed the tongue with his right thumb. It didn't move. It either wasn't working right—again—or was locked. He fished in his pocket for his keys.

As he opened the heavy wood and glass door into the vestibule, the thunder of the arguing inside struck him full in the chest. Trying to place the location of the people inside, he squinted to see through the gauzy curtains covering the glass of the inner door. Ron and Louise were sitting on the sofa under the set of casement windows. Jen stood by the entrance to the dining room, her hands on her hips, her body moving as though she were yelling—although Ben couldn't even hear her voice over the unintelligible bellowing of the two men, bellowing that seemed to him like the deep animalistic sound of fighting bulls. He opened the door into the living room.

"Hey, what's up?" Ben said, in as normal a tone as he could muster.

"None of your fuckin' business. D'you call him?" Don screamed at Jen.

"Yeah, I called him. I don't want you two killin' each other."

"Then tell him to stay off my back," Don screamed, jerking his thumb towards his father who was now slumped in his chair.

"You don't come in my house all belligerent and doped up and expect me to just sit here!" his father said.

"Yeah, well what are you going to do about it, old man?"

"I can still kick your ass," the old man bellowed as he sprang from his seat and stood eye to eye with his son.

"Ben!" Jen pleaded.

Ben pushed between the two men, separating them with his forearms. His father, Lewis, still had the chest and arms of a carpenter—solid, even though it had been six years since he'd last swung a hammer full-time. Don was thinner, not as thickly-muscled, but with an ominous physical presence. Ben could feel the adrenaline coursing through his body, his leg muscles tightened almost to the point of cramping, his stomach knotted.

Breathe, he told himself. Breathe. Then he turned and faced his father. "Go sit down," he said as gently as he could and turned to his brother. "I'm going to Angelina's. We haven't been there together in a long time. Come with me?"

"I've got my beer here."

"Bring it, come on."

"It's downstairs in my refrigerator."

"We'll go out the back way."

"I'm not gonna take his shit."

"Well I'm *dealing* shit." His father started to rise again from his chair. Ben stared him straight in the eye and bellowed, "Sit down now!" The older man relaxed his grip in the arms of the chair and sat.

"I'm not gonna take his shit," Don repeated, louder this time.

"We *know* that. *He* knows that. Come on, let's blow this joint."

"Who's driving?"

"I think I am."

Harold was worried that Annie was worried about her father. She had been so quiet at dinner, so quiet since he'd picked her up at her dorm.

He tried to jostle her out of her mood, joking with her and commenting on the bravery—or insanity—of the first person who'd eaten a lobster. He tried a light patter about the Celtics and the Bruins. He tried asking her about her psych paper. He held her fingers across the table while they waited for dessert to come. Her responses were joyless, short and efficient.

Her father had always been skinny—since the war, anyway. He had been buried when a trench collapsed. Four or five guys on either side of him had died; her father had been buried up to his mouth in silty dirt, his nose drawing in the dirt with every difficult breath. He'd felt like he was drowning. After they dug him out they found that his only apparent injury was a broken foot, but there were other unseen injuries. After he returned home, he got a job in the Chelsea VA hospital processing paperwork for the soldiers and sailors who had been severely injured and needed long periods of recuperation and rehabilitation. When the veteran's affairs position came open in Lynn, he got the job.

He had met Annie's mom at the VA hospital where she worked in the admissions office. They married and bought a house near Flax

Pond in a middle-class neighborhood. Lynn was a bustling community, with lots of job opportunities for engineers, skilled machinists, shoe craftsmen and construction workers. It had two hospitals: Union Hospital, a small cottage hospital for the better off—or those who expected to be—and Lynn Hospital, a large and comprehensive general hospital that was widely considered one of the best of its kind. Annie's mom and dad would never think of going to Lynn Hospital. In fact, Harold thought, he had never seen them visit her at the nursing school. She always went home to visit them. A dutiful daughter, he thought, then smiled thinking that that was something her father would say.

"What are you smiling about?" she said.

"Just you."

"Oh."

"Are you worried about your father?"

"Not especially right now…Oh…Well, yes, I guess that I am. Why would that make you smile? Do you always smile when people are hurting?"

"*Schadenfreude.*"

"What?"

"That's what they call it when someone smiles at another's pain, but, no, I was smiling because I was thinking of how good you are to your parents. How considerate you are. I didn't mean that I was taking your concern lightly. I wouldn't do that. I know that you worry about your father. I would never make fun of that. I hope that you know that. At least, I hope that you learn to know that. I'm sorry."

Annie laughed for the first time that night.

"Are you laughing at me?"

"It's that shah den thing," Annie said.

"Shah-den-froy-duh." Harold squeezed Annie's fingers. "Ready?"

"Oh, yes."

Annie's eyes were smiling, too. Harold felt hot and a surge of blood filled his groin.

"Do you need to sit here for a minute?"

"It might be good," Harold said, struck by Annie's understanding.

"You know that they're all against me…especially him," Don complained, the aggression still in his voice.

"Don, the fact is that Jen is your best friend in this world. She called me for you. And Dad has always been your biggest fan…all I've ever heard is how good Don is at everything. School, sports… whatever. You two are just too much alike. Neither of you will back down from anything. I'll bet you don't even remember what started the fight."

Don was silent.

"Do you?"

Ben turned his head towards Don. His brother was asleep.

Harold pulled the car up to the curb in front of Annie's dorm. The curb was mostly open except for a few cars in front of Angelina's Subs up at the corner. Annie was sitting close to him. He could smell the sweet fruitiness of her hair and sweet tartness of her perfume. He wanted to bring her back to his dorm, but he really had to get his psych paper done. Annie might have been able to put hers off, if she hadn't done it already, but Harold's grades weren't good enough to let it slide just now.

He let the car engine run and turned in the seat to kiss her. Her lips were soft and moist and parted easily to his kiss. Annie pushed herself up onto Harold's lap and reached through the spokes of the steering wheel to turn the ignition off. His tongue was exploring the space between her upper lip and her teeth. Annie sighed and melted into him. She tried to reach inside the front of his pants with her right hand, but the belt was too tight and she was pressed too hard against him. He sucked in his tightly-muscled stomach and sucked in her upper lips at the same time. Blood rushed into Annie's head and her scalp tingled. She drove her hand deeper into Harold's pants and found his hard penis. Harold arched backwards in the seat, pulling Annie with him.

At the same time, an odd, calm voice in his head said, "We have ignition."

Harold stifled a laugh. His tongue was far too deeply into Annie's mouth, her tongue darting around the tip of his. Annie moaned lightly and Harold felt a warm wetness spreading on his thigh. He reached up inside Annie's skirt and found her wet hair. He pressed two fingers through the wetness and into her. Her head jerked backward and her pelvis pressed into his hand. He looked into her face and noticed the glistening black streams staining her cheeks. Annie was crying.

Harold thought, Damn, I'm good! I can get 'em wet from both ends at the same time. He worked his fingers atop the soft ledge inside the front of Annie's vagina. She opened her eyes and smiled at him. His fingers moved deeper inside her. Suddenly, her eyes widened with a strange fear-of-death look and she lurched from his lap.

Ben parked the car along the curb. There was one car in front of him and a couple of open spaces up the street a bit closer to Angelina's, but with Don asleep in the car, he didn't want to park too close to the brighter lights at the corner. Don, asleep, was benign. When Ben woke him later to have his sandwich, the complaints and recriminations would start anew. Ben was perfectly happy to put that off for a while.

He slid from the car and closed the door quietly so that the latch would hold the door closed, though still not fully engaged. He walked around the front of the car and peered through the window to make sure he had not disturbed Don's sleep. As he reached the curb and turned up the street, the brake lights on the car in front of him flashed for an instant and Ben noticed through the lightly-steamed windows that a woman in the front seat had startled and jumped from the arms of her companion.

Oops, sorry! he thought, and smiled to himself before a pinge of sadness overcame him. That should be Annie and me tonight, he thought. He turned and looked at the lights in the nursing school windows and wondered which one of them might be Annie's.

As he reached the sub shop, Ben was relieved to see that there were only two customers inside looking at the menu on the wall above the back counter. He wanted to be quick and get back to the car before Don awoke and wandered off. He walked into the shop and stood a few paces behind the two women, students from the nursing school dressed in scrubs.

"Oh, go ahead. We're still thinking," said one.

Ben ordered two ham and cheese subs: one with just lettuce and oil, the other with everything including "hots." He grabbed a couple of Cokes and two bags of chips and paid the kid behind the counter. Ben recognized him as one of the JV football players who'd been at Classical when Ben had been a senior at St. Mary's. He could tell from the mood in the room that all three of the occupants were glad to see him go so quickly. Flirtation was in the air. For everyone but me, Ben thought.

Ben exited the store and turned the corner to head back to his car. He looked down the street to see if he could still see Don in the car. It was too dark to see clearly inside, but the headlights of a passing car gave a moment of light and Ben could detect the form of Don's head and shoulders slumped against the passenger side window.

The couple in the car in front of his were still at it, but they had turned the engine on and the air from the defrost had cleared the steam of their passion from most of the windshield. As Ben got closer, a passing car on the other side of the street lit up the parked cars in its high-beams. Stupid driver, Ben thought, but as it passed the lights caught the faces of the lovers in a snapshot that burned in Ben's eyes. He dropped the bag.

"Annie!" he called out involuntarily, blood draining from the top of his head down and out of his arms and his legs. The couple instantly broke apart, and the man at the steering wheel pulled the car sharply to the left and away from the curb, missing by inches a car that had just passed. He accellerated hard, his tires screaming. Ben could see the action in front of him and was acutely aware of the scene, but could hear nothing. Suddenly he awoke and ran to his car, jumped in, and inserted the key in his badly-trembling hand into the ignition. The engine roared to life. He floored the accelerator and felt the powerful engine pushing his back against the seat as he gave chase.

The blue Buick was a full block ahead of him and the light at the corner was yellow, but Ben roared through the intersection. Impending death was the least of his worries. His brain burned, his eyes burned, too, but there were no tears—just a strange, overwhelming animal emotion, like the nameless adrenaline rush before a big fight.

The two cars sped down Western Avenue towards Salem, Ben gaining on the Buick. At Eastern Avenue, the two cars were almost bumper to bumper. The Buick took the turn onto Eastern too fast and fish-tailed as it struggled to regain its track. Ben was not as quick and shot through the intersection, but made a sharp turn into the gas station at the corner and headed back out onto Eastern, barely avoiding a head-on crash with a stake-body truck. The Buick was now a full two blocks ahead. Ben squinted to keep sight of the other car's tail lights.

He lost sight of them, but knew they must have taken a right on Lewis Street. They were probably headed for Chestnut to loop back to the dorm. Ben took the right at Marianna, figuring he'd cut them off near English High School. He slowed down in the residential neighborhood. He knew he'd be driving a shorter distance and hitting fewer lights anyway. He worried that Annie might guess his ploy, but she didn't know the streets in this part of the city that well. God, make them think they got away, he thought.

As he pulled up to the Chestnut Street corner, the Buick drove by, moving slower now. His headlights caught Annie and the driver full in profile and Annie yanked her head to the right and looked Ben in the eye for a fleeting moment. She yanked her head back towards the driver and the Buick accelerated, its tires squealing. Ben turned the corner and floored the gas pedal. The big Olds responded.

Ben could see the light at Western Avenue turn yellow. Annie and the driver had completed a large loop and were headed back to the dorm. He wondered whether they would stop for the red light. What would he do if they did? Would he jump from the car and pull Annie from the Buick? Reclaim her? Would he pull the driver from the car? What then? Watch while Don beat the crap out of him, while he held Annie is his arms? Beat up the guy himself? Didn't he have the right? Wasn't Annie his?

The brake lights of the Buick glowed red. They *would* stop. Ben pulled up close behind the car, his lights exposing them in a harsh, bright glare. He slipped the transmission into park and reached for the door handle. Annie grabbed the rear view mirror and re-aimed it so she could see Ben. In the mirror, Ben's eyes met hers. He could tell she was crying by the black streaks that ran down her cheeks. He paused, the door ajar. He looked away. The light changed. The driver of the Buick gunned the engine, turned left, and roared away.

Ben sat back deeper into the driver's seat and rested his head against the top of the seatback. The driver behind him leaned on his horn. Ben straightened up, pulled the door shut, and drove straight ahead. He made his way back towards Central Square, took a right at Anthony's Hawthorne and pulled up in front of Don's rooming house on Oxford Street.

Dark fluid filled Ben's brain. Despair held his stomach in a vise-grip. He could not breathe. He wretched and threw up on his pants. He could only cry a tearless cry. Despair was drowning him.

Don was still asleep.

14

BEN SAT AT A PLYWOOD CUBE IN THE LARGE, OPEN
room. The cold, pulsing, fluorescent light made the gray board-
formed concrete beams, gray tile floors and Tectum ceiling all the
more emotionally crushing. Three of the walls were cold gray concrete block, punctured only by oak doors in black frames and black
double-sliding doors to a single elevator. The fourth wall was made
almost entirely of glass in black steel frames. In the sunlight these
would light the room with a warming sunlight, but it was just after
seven thirty, and it was dark and raining. The reflected image of the
austerely lit gray hulk of a room hung like a billboard in the glass.

Ben thought that even a sunny personality would be sad in this
room, and he was anything but sunny these days.

It was an award-winning building. The architects had won an international competition to design it. The design that had been built
was remarkably similar to the design that had won the competition—
which didn't happen very often. Building committees had an almost
visceral need to change the buildings that won design competitions,
and few of the competition-winning architects had the power to challenge them. The designers taking part in competitions were usually
young architects or college professors who hadn't yet built much more
than a house.

It was the first new building in the long history of the Boston
Institute for Architecture and the building committee was inclined

to give the designers some leeway in order to acquire an iconic building. The massing of the exterior had become more important and more expensive than anyone had anticipated. There was little money left for the interiors and for furniture. The result was, in part, this industrial shell of a design studio—cold and hard.

Ben's cube was identical to the eighty or so other cubes in the room. Most were occupied by men hunched over desk surfaces, drawing furiously, stopping only to rip pieces of yellow tracing paper off their rolls, then drawing furiously again. Few ever erased the yellow trace. If they didn't like something they had drawn, they would rip off another piece, lay it over the previous drawing and redraw their work, changing only the offending parts.

Ben's work was never as detailed as the drawings of the other students. His drawings were spare—heavy dark lines drawn with a soft, thick-leaded pencil. He used the softness of the pencil to vary the blackness of the lines, using the variations to create a sense of depth and texture in his sketches. He worked less frenetically than the others. He didn't need to draw complex stairs, elevators, and toilet rooms in plan view. Where the other students designed and sketched in plan view, Ben designed all of his assigned projects in three dimensions, capturing the space created by the structure and by its relationship to the surrounding environment. His plans were few and less detailed than the others, showing quickly the organization of his plan, but eliminating the stair railings and the door casings.

As the time approached eight p.m., the hands in the room drew more furiously, the backs hunched themselves even lower over the cubes, and the faces came so close to the drawings that occasionally a cheek got smudged with graphite. The critics—the design studio professors—usually arrived to begin reviewing the projects at eight o'clock. Everyone was supposed to stop drawing then, in part to pay attention to the critics' evisceration of another student's project, and in part to keep students from redrawing elements in their projects that the critics had blasted in their earlier reviews.

Ben finished his work and stood beside the stool, arching his body backward to stretch out his shoulders, then up and forward to stretch out his lower back.

As he stood quietly at the side of his cube, the overwhelming sense of loss descended on him again as it had done in all the quiet times of the last few weeks. The dark liquid of his grief rose through his body, filling first his groin, then his abdomen, forcing the air from his lungs. He could not feel his legs and grabbed for the cube. It began to flip over under his weight, then settled back down with a loud thud.

"You okay?"

Ben couldn't see the source of the voice, but recognized it as Hezekiah Wilson's. He didn't think to answer.

"Hey Ben, you okay?" Wilson asked again.

The fog in Ben's head dissipated and he could see Wilson leaning on the opposite side of the cube. "Yeah."

"Did you eat today?"

"Not yet." It was a half-lie. Ben had eaten little since the night Annie left him, and there was a better than even chance that he wouldn't eat much tonight. He tried from time to time, but dry toast and some flat Coke was usually the best he could do.

"Do you want me to get you something?"

"No, I'm okay for now. Thanks."

"I grabbed a sandwich on the way in—it's just ham and cheese on white bread—you can have half."

"No, you go ahead and eat it." Ben wondered if ham and cheese might ever be in his diet again.

"C'mon. I insist." Wilson pushed the half sandwich towards him. "Do you want some of my Coke?"

Ben took the half sandwich. "I'll just grab some water."

"Okay, but have some chips too. I got a coupla bags."

"Thanks."

"No problem. I know how this place can get to you. Too much work, too little rest, then they beat the crap out of you."

"True."

"Mind if I look at your work?"

"Sure. Go ahead." Ben often thought he learned more from the crits from other students than he did from the professors. He knew that other students felt the same way. They held it up as an indictment of the studio system.

Ben bit into the thin soft bread of the sandwich and his teeth hit resistance at the ham. A burst of vinegary yellow mustard hit his mouth and ran up into his nose. The simple sandwich tasted extraordinarily good. It was the kind of sandwich his mother might have made him for lunch in elementary school.

Hezekiah Wilson had come to the BIA directly from high school as had Ben. They— and a few others—were the exception though. Most of the students had gone to other schools. Some had an Associate's degree in Architectural Technology from Wentworth Institute, some had Bachelor's degrees in everything from engineering to physical therapy. Many worked as draftsmen in architectural offices, a few as job captains managing the work of other draftsmen, fewer still as designers. One still worked as a physical therapist.

"Jeez! How do you get these lines? They look like charcoal!"

Ben unwrapped a canvas roll and showed Wilson his tools. There were a half-dozen or so 314 Draughting pencils of varying lengths, three Caran d'Ache number 3 lead-holders, each with a different color push-button on top, a well-worn Koh-I-Noor lead-holder with a hugely thick lead, and a standard drafting lead-holder that looked brand new.

"What do you have in these things?"

"Mostly B and 2B leads. One has an HB, I think. The drafting pencil has an H or 2H lead in it, so it's not really useful for drawing on trace."

"Not useful? I'll bet everyone else here is drawing with that pencil. You can tell by the little tear holes in their trace from sharpening the pencil too often."

Ben shrugged.

Wilson looked at the sketches with their powerful dark lines tracing the sweep of the roof and anchoring the walls to the solid topography of the site. Softer lines filled in the outlines of the glass wall facing the street, the texture of the brick and granite walls, and the play of light and shadow across the building face and entry court-yard. He studied the drawing intently, promising himself he'd re-member the texture of the lines, the unusual representation of light amidst the shadows. "Where's your plan?"

"I've still got to draw that."

"You did the sketches without drawing the plan? How do you know that the design will work? They're not going to like it if the plan and the sketches don't come together."

"I have the plan...I just haven't drawn it yet."

"D'you mean that you have a little sketch somewhere and you need to redraw it? Okay, let me see it."

"No, it's up here," Ben said, pointing to his head.

"So you have an idea of what it might look like. Don't you think that you should draw it and work out the kinks? When you draw a plan it never quite works the way you think it might. You have to draw it to see it."

"No, I actually *see* the plan. I *see* the details. It's very real. It exists physically. I just haven't drawn it yet."

"How in hell do you do that?"

"I don't know. I've never thought about it. It just happens."

"Does it work the other way around, too?"

"What do you mean?"

"If you draw a plan, do you see the rendering?"

"No, I see the building. I see people moving through it."

"Hah! Do you talk to them?"

"Sometimes. Just small talk, really."

Ben smiled and Wilson wondered whether he was serious or just pulling his leg.

Wilson smiled back—just enough of a smile to let Ben know he was in on the joke.

"I'm not sure I'd tell the critics that. It'd freak 'em out. You'd better make up a better story."

"I'll try."

"I'd better leave you alone so you can get your plan done. You've only got ten minutes before they show up."

"I'm on it."

Ben quickly, but unhurriedly, completed the plan sketch, making a small change to the 3D sketch to reflect the plan he had drawn. As he finished, he looked at his watch. The critics were late, probably still in the small bar farther on up the street where they gathered almost every night. Only the more advanced students, mostly those finishing their theses, ever ventured into the Webster House. There was a sort of unwritten rule that it was reserved for the professors, a sort of BIA version of the Harvard Faculty Club, but without its amenities or its history.

At twenty past eight, the elevator doors slid open and nine critics entered the studio, spilling from the elevator cab and forming a rough wedge-shaped mass behind the Head Critic, M. O. Sather— Munroe Owen Sather. As they moved through the room, they peeled off from the back of the wedge and spread out until only Sather was left to move to the head of the room directly in front of the windows.

Ben could only think of the opening scene of the *Tales of the Texas Rangers* and the show's theme song played in his head, "These are tales of Texas Rangers..." to the tune of "I've been working on the railroad...". It was hard to take these guys seriously.

Sather stood patiently for a few moments—not a long time, but uncomfortably long. The room was dead quiet and all eyes were on him. He scanned the room as if he were a general on a ridge scanning the battlefield below him. When he was satisfied that he had sufficiently reconnoitered the field, he turned his head slightly to the left and nodded almost imperceptibly.

An assistant critic along the concrete block wall to Ben's right bellowed, "Gentlemen, may we have your attention."

Sather paused. He stood for a few more moments, then said, "Gentlemen...*and both ladies*..." He paused again. When he felt that the impact of his correction had been duly absorbed, he started up again. "We have been together for seven weeks now and you have been getting desk crits from my esteemed fellow critics. Tonight some of you will present to me. Your assignment is to show me why I shouldn't fail you. Good luck—you'll need it."

The groan in the room was like a wave, moving from the back and ebbing as it got to Sather's feet. Sather relished it and barely stifled a smile.

Each of the dozen or so assistant critics had a half-dozen students who they worked with every week. This week, one of the students from each group was to make a presentation to the assembly of Senior Critics and Sather. A few students had volunteered to present. Ben's critic, Frank Fisher, had chosen to pick names from a hat. That had struck Ben at the time as particularly odd, since the perception of the students was that the assistant critics were being judged along *with* their students. Why hadn't Fisher simply picked his best student? Ben won/lost the draw. He would present last.

A large mobile tack-board was rolled to the head of the room for the students to use to pin up their yellow tracing paper sketches. A crescent of five chairs was placed facing it. Sather and his four senior critics sat in the chairs and waited for the first victim to enter their makeshift lair.

The assigned project was for a branch library in Newton. The site was in a working-class village known as Newton Upper Falls. It was adjacent to a railroad branch line used for moving freight to the warehouses and factories along Needham Street and along the outskirts of the village center. On the opposite side of the site, along Oak Street, were the tiny houses that had been built to house the workers in the paper and bowling ball factories that occupied the old red-brick five and six-story buildings standing along the far end of the street. A small train station, now used mostly for storage, sat alone between the façades of factories like a broken tooth in a blood-stained grin. The lot where the library was to be placed sloped about ten feet from the street to the back. It was mostly weed-strewn, except for an almost-bare patch of stony gravel and broken glass.

One by one the chosen students entered the semi-circle, pinned up their few drawings—usually two or three plans and sheet of elevations—and turned tentatively to face the jury.

Ben was not surprised that most of the designs looked so similar. It was widely discussed among the students that you didn't want to present anything outside of a narrow range of acceptable, understandable, and rather mundane buildings. Brick walls, flat roofs, an entry door with a sidelight or two, simple slot windows—this was the vocabulary of the day. No colonial, no Wright, no Corbu. Nothing freaky. You were a draftsman learning some design. You had to know your place. Never give them anything that they had to try to understand. Never give them anything to think about. Show them that you knew the style and could draft it properly.

The first student pinned up drawings showing a circular floor plan. He had barely started to speak before Sather summarily dismissed him with a broad backhand wave of his hand and the comment, "Mr. Warren, I'd suggest that you seriously consider insurance sales. Good night." Warren took down his drawings and left the room by the stairway that emptied into the alley behind the building. Ben imagined that Warren had simply chosen to end it all right there and to descend the stairway into the fires of hell. It would probably be a relief for the poor guy.

Wilson presented next. His plans, elevations, and a single isometric perspective were meticulously and crisply drawn. His design also showed the brick walls, the slotted windows, the flat roof, and the glazed entry door with two sidelights, but he had raised the roof to get a clerestory of glass between the top of the walls and the roof. The glass was set back a foot-and-a-half from the fascia of the roof and two-thirds of a foot back from the brick façade. He had set the building back on the site and placed parking on either side of a tree-shaded walkway that ran from the street to the front door.

The criticisms from the jury were fairly mild. One critic decried Wilson's "use of gymnastics," referring to the clerestory. Another wondered whether the design was "too Cambridge" to be located in Newton. Sather was silent.

Ben clapped Wilson on the back as he returned to his cube. So far, his presentation had been the highlight of the evening. Wilson had fared rather well with the critics, Ben thought. However, if Ben had hoped this to be the start of a run of more interesting designs, he was soon to be disillusioned. The presentations slid back into the mundane. The presenters used more "uh's" and "um's" than enlightening prose.

During the more boring presentations, Ben's attention waned, his thoughts returning to Annie, and the dark, crushing weight returned. He searched his memories, trying to recall the moments in their relationship that would inform him when it had happened, how it had happened, and why. He looked for the small details of a glance or a word that should have told him Annie was leaving him. How could he have missed the clues? What *were* the clues? Had there even been any clues? His mind, his heart, his lungs—even his eyes—were filled with the dark fluid. He couldn't find the answer.

"Ben, you're up!" Wilson's voice came from somewhere in the darkness.

Ben rose, as if from a sleep, grabbed his sketches, and walked carefully down the aisle between the cubes. At first he felt for the floor with his feet, not able to see more than shadowy shapes. As the light returned, he walked more briskly, more assuredly to the head of the room and the vertical slab of cork tack-board.

Ben pinned his drawings to the slab with the sketch rendering placed at the top. It was on crème trace paper at least twice the size of the other drawings. Below it, he tacked a colored site plan as wide as the rendering, but half as tall, and below that, his three floor plans marked *"Lower Level," "Street Level,"* and *"Upper Level."*

He twirled like a dancer—on the ball of his right foot—with his left foot lifted slightly off the floor and turned to face the critics.

"Ah, Mr. Holt. So you chose to go last. Was it fear? Were you hoping to learn from the misfortune of your predecessors? Or, did you think that we would tire and give you a pass just to get out of here?"

"Respect."

"Ah, so you expect to influence us with your pleading of respect for your jury? You will find that I am not so easily bought."

"No. It is my respect for my work."

"Mr. Holt, *I* will judge whether there is any reason to respect your work. Proceed."

Ben's sketch rendering showed a building with three distinct parts. The portion of the lower façade that was exposed in the rear of the building, gradually disappearing as the slope rose along the sides toward the street, was clad in a gray granite which extended to three feet above the elevation of the street-level floor. It was capped with a sloped water table coping. Above that sat a story-and-a-half of red brick which ran to six feet above the upper level floor and was also topped with a granite coping. Above the brick, the exterior walls were glass, set in two feet from the line of the lower façade. The brick walls had few windows except for the two-story glass façade facing the street that wrapped a dozen feet around both sides. The building was topped with a shallow-arched metal roof.

"Good evening," Ben said, looking directly into Sather's eyes for a response. He found nothing there, the near-black of Sather's pupils disappearing into the espresso black-brown of his irises. Sather was silent, and a few mumbled responses came from the other critics. At least one glanced at Sather as if to beg his forgiveness for breaking the silence.

"Good evening!" called Wilson in a strong voice from the middle of the pack of students. It was followed by a chorus of "Good evenings," random mumblings and a stray "Yo!"

Sather sat silently, looking first at the drawings, then directly at Ben.

Ben spoke. "A library is more than a warehouse for storing books. It is more than a dispensary for circulating printed materials. It must do more than represent the government that...marginally... owns it. Sure, it does all of those and it must function well, must do its work well, must represent its owners well. A library is a temple and a refuge. Its products are inspiration, insight, and solace.

"The building of a library is a great community event, bringing with it the pride and hopes of those who really own it. It is an icon for that pride and those hopes. It is a symbol of the spirit—the true unalloyed, unpoliticized spirit of American democracy."

The room erupted in a rumbling sound, growing louder until it broke out into spikes of "yeah, man!" and loud whistles. From the back of the room came a chant of "Ben, Ben, Ben!" Sather leaned over and whispered to the critic sitting to his left. The critic raised his large, beefy arm straight up and the noise in the room subsided.

Ben didn't wait for any comments from Sather. He launched into his description of his plans, pointing out the front entry courtyard and the three-story atrium behind the two-story entry façade. He had included the lower level in his entry, making it an integral part of the building, rather than the service area shown in other designs.

The lower level held the children's books area and could be entered from a small park at the rear of the building. The street level had a circulation desk, periodicals, reference books, gondolas with some of the most popular books, and the card catalog. The upper level held stacks set into recesses under the windows and a large open area with tables and several sofas and club chairs. Ben explained his reasoning behind his zoning of library functions. He described how he'd placed the most often sought items on the street floor so that he could have space on the upper level for comfortable seating—the "refuge" that he had spoken of earlier.

Ben then spoke of his site plan. He had placed parking for only a half-dozen cars at the rear-most portion of the site so that he could place a park with sitting areas along a meandering walk and a fenced-in play area accessible only by the children's reading room in the lower level of the library. He explained that his few parking spaces were for the library staff and the few people who might have to drive to the library.

Having finished his presentation, Ben turned from his drawings, looked again into Sather's eyes (again finding nothing there) and simply said, "Thank you."

Jay Cummings, the critic on the left end of the crescent farthest from Sather, leaped to his feet. "I'm impressed."

Sather leered at him. Cummings stood for a moment, staggered back like a drunk looking for a place to collapse and sat heavily into his seat. He seemed to shrink into half the man he'd been a few moments before. He spent the rest of the evening slumped over and silent in his chair. One by one, the other critics took turns asking questions, alternating sides of the crescent from its far ends towards its center.

"How can you justify having only six parking spaces on the site?"

"Since this is a branch library—a village library—most people will walk. Most of those who *do* drive will park on the street any-way...there's plenty of parking there, *and* it's more convenient."

"Don't you that people will be upset when they can't find space in the lot?"

"Since the parking lot is behind the building, many people won't even know that it's there."

"Why do you show a park when we didn't ask for one?"

"Because I really do see the library as a community building, not just a warehouse. The park extends the building outward. It makes the building less self-centered, less smug."

"How do you control circulation from the children's area? Won't this second access point simply be an invitation for children to steal books?"

"I suppose I could think of worse things." Ben smiled. "I do have a small work desk adjacent to the exit for a librarian to work and check out books."

"What if the librarian is away from her desk, or busy with some-one? Isn't that a security problem?"

"Sure. But books are stolen from libraries every day...libraries that have large circulation control desks, one way in and out, and some-times even guards. This is a village library. I want it to feel neighborly. I think most people don't want to steal from their neighbors. Those that do, will. I don't think you can absolutely control that."

"Don't you think that most librarians would disagree with you?"

"I assume they would. But all of this discussion misses the point. I have a circulation control desk in the children's area. It does all of the things that you want a circulation control desk to do. The only thing that it is *not* is a wall between the librarian and the children that says 'I'm in control here, you will fear me.'"

"Why do you show an elevator in your plans? It's not in the program."

"I want mothers with babies in carriages to be able to access the lower level children's area from the street level. I want older people to be able to easily get to the refuge on the upper level. Crippled veterans can use it to get to all of the library's materials. The staff can use it to move heavy loads between floors."

"All of the other presentations showed drafted plans. You show us freehand sketches. I'm appalled by your disrespect. Can't you draft properly?"

"You will find that the drawings have all of the detail of the drafted plans…are as true to scale as any of the drafted plans. These freehand drawings communicate the flow of the design…the *spirit* of the design…better than a drafted plan could."

"Your design doesn't say library to me. It doesn't speak of the solidity, the permanence of government. It is far too small a program to justify bejeweling it the way that you have. How can you possibly believe that this is an appropriate response to the program? How can you believe that this small building deserves these baubles, these flourishes?"

"Some of the greatest temples are small buildings. They deserve as much of our attention as a cathedral."

It was Sather's turn. He closed his eyes for several moments—for an eternity, it seemed. He opened his eyes, the fire now burning in them. He leaned forward and spoke. "Mr. Holt, let me educate you. Architecture is not theatrics. You can spin and twirl all you want, you can obfuscate your lack of a coherent design with chiaroscuro flourishes, but you cannot snow me. You have presented a building that is bigger than its program, and I'm not referring to the floor area of your sad plans. Leave religion to the clergy, Mr. Holt, you are not so qualified. Good night."

Sather stood and the other critics stood with him. They turned and marched to the elevator, reforming the Texas Ranger wedge as they left. When the elevator doors finally slid closed behind them, the room erupted into a frenzy of clapping. Ben knew Sather could hear the racket and wondered what he might be thinking.

Wilson slapped him on the shoulder, "Unbelievable! You shot them down big time."

Ben wondered what Wilson had missed.

15

B EN LEFT THE BIA AND HEADED OUT OF THE CITY,
across the Mystic River Bridge, got off Route 1 at Route 16 and
headed east. He pulled the Olds into the dark parking lot of a shopping center, turned off the engine, and cried. He sucked at the air,
trying to breathe. He found no bottom to the depths of his despair.
For the first time, he truly understood the words that had been running around in his head, orphaned; there, but without connection.
Annie was gone.

16

B EN SAT AT THE TABLE IN HIS TRAILER STARING AT the plans spread out before him. They seemed remote and disconnected from him. He hadn't been able to concentrate on his work for almost five months now and this project would count for half of the semester's design studio grade. Each time he started assembling the myriad sketches that represented vignettes of his design thoughts, his mind would wander, and Annie and Harold would shove his attempts at concentration aside.

He had progressed from his diet of dry toast, but still lived on saltines and Coke—and an occasional slice of American cheese—because anything more sickened him. His stomach was bundled in painful knots and his weight had dropped by twenty-two pounds. His long hair was dirty and matted. He hadn't slept a full night since Annie had left.

No use trying to do this right now, Ben thought; maybe a walk will help. He pushed the chair from the table and started to rise from his seat. As he did, his brain objected to the movement, his eyes lost focus, and the floor moved beneath him. He struggled against the oncoming dizziness, but his last conscious vision was the light on the ceiling as his head dropped back, his knees slipped forward, and his body collapsed.

AT TEN A.M. the alarm clock jangled Don's unconscious and he erupted from his shallow sleep. His lips were dry and cracked and his mouth felt wooly and the fucking alarm wouldn't shut up. He whipped his arm out from under the covers and sent the alarm clock slamming into the wall. It fell to the floor, undeterred.

Don swung his feet over the edge of the narrow bed and lifted his body laterally, sitting with his eyes closed and wondering whether it was really possible to learn Russian while you slept. He'd be good at Russian, he thought, and he could get a job in the Foreign Service. He'd always been good at languages in high school. Maybe he'd study Russian. He stood slowly and edged his way, his eyes still closed, to the dresser just five feet away. When he got there he opened his eyes slowly and painfully; he had always been sensitive to light, especially in the morning.

He surveyed the top of the dresser. The pizza box from last night—it *was* last night, wasn't it?—hung precariously over the front edge of the dresser with the toaster oven (door open) and his hot plate arranged along the dresser's back edge. An old, cracked coffee cup and a new glass purloined from Sallie's sat bottom-end-up on his meager supply of Dunkin' Donuts napkins. Next to the napkins, a coral-colored melamine bowl held several pop-tops. Four cans of Miller High-Life remained from the second six-pack he had taken from the bottom drawer last night. An open jar of instant coffee was empty, save for a teaspoon. The saucepan he used for water and soup was nowhere to be seen.

He took a slice of cheese pizza from the side of the box that still sat on the dresser-top, and the box tipped over the edge and landed upside down on the floor. Stepping around the box, he slid the slice of pizza inside the toaster oven and closed the glass door. He turned the little knob to somewhere close to where he thought three hundred and fifty degrees was and watched the bottom elements glow red. He reached for a can of beer, popped it open and tossed the top into the bowl. Filling his mouth with beer, he swished the bitter liquid around his mouth and swallowed, thinking that the advantage beer had over Listerine was that it could be swallowed. No waste. Taking one more mouthful of beer, he headed from his room down the corridor to the bathroom he shared with the other men on his floor.

Don sat on the toilet and thought he might get in touch with Helena again. He hadn't seen her in a couple of years. They had gone to the same high school, but had never even talked until the night she'd come here. She had disappeared early the next morning before he'd woken up and he hadn't seen her since—but, she *did* speak Russian. She was studying it in college, he vaguely recalled.

As he was heading back to his room, he noticed smoke seeping from the open transom above his door. He opened the door slowly and peered into the room, seeing a plume of smoke rising from the back of the toaster oven and spreading across the ceiling. At least the *room* wasn't on fire, he thought. He walked to the dresser and turned the knob of the oven to "off," then walked to the only window and opened it from both the top and bottom about a foot. He went back to the dresser, picked up the pizza box from the floor, tore off a piece of the box-top and used it as a spatula to remove the shrunken and blackened wedge from the oven. He backed towards the window, turned, and threw the wedge and the cardboard through the window into the alley below. He removed the pillowcase from his pillow and used it as a cape to fan the smoke from the room. After several ineffective minutes of fanning, he threw the pillowcase on the bed, took another piece of pizza—sausage this time—and slipped it into the oven.

Don sat on the edge of the bed, stared at the toaster oven, and wondered how Russian might sound. Had they spoken Russian in *Doctor Zhivago?*

IT WAS DARK when Ben awoke and he felt an urgent need to pee. Leery of standing up and passing out again, he crawled on his hands and knees to the bathroom door. Realizing he'd have to stand at the toilet, he drew himself up slowly, clutching the metal frame of the bathroom door. He still felt a little woozy, so he moved gingerly, letting go of the door frame and grabbing the edge of the bathroom sink. He would need both hands to unzip his pants, so he wedged himself between the side of the toilet and the sink, half-sitting on the sink. As he stood there watching the urine flow from his body, he imagined it draining the poison of Annie and Harold from him. He would write a letter to Harold to tell him who he was and why he loved Annie so. He would be magnanimous and exhort Harold to be good to Annie. Bobby Vee singing "Take Good Care of My Baby" played in his head.

Ben moved from door frame to table to chair to desk to the little kitchenette and took the saltines from the cabinet and four slices of American cheese from the refrigerator. He sat on the fold-down sofa that doubled as his bed and turned on the TV. He saw Jack Chase and Don Kent flicker on the tube for a moment, then fell into a deep sleep.

17

October 21, 1966

Dear Harold,

Hopefully you realize by now what a special woman you have in Annie, so I won't bother to try to sell you on her, but I do want you to know that I miss her very much.

Despite the fact that her mother never liked me very much, I was always good to her and I think that I actually won her father over.

I grew up in a tough neighborhood and most of the guys that I grew up with are still stuck in that neighborhood. Annie's love helped me to want more and I will always thank her for that. While my high-school grades weren't stellar, I did test out at genius level. I'm not bragging, or maybe I am a little, but I wanted you to know who I am. I played several sports in high school and my team-mates called me "boom-boom" because of my aggressiveness. I was never a dirty player but I played hard, although our opponents were a bit afraid of me.

As for my life from here on out, I intend to be one of the world's greatest and most famous architects and rebuild the city I came from. I won't do it to make Annie want me again but just because she made me want it for us.

I suppose that I should have known that something was happening. The last time we made out she mistakenly called me Harold. I didn't think much of it at the time, but you know how they say that love is blind. Deaf too, I guess.

Anyway, you should know that my tears are falling because you've taken her away and though it hurts me so there is something that I've got to say.

125

Take good care of my baby. Be just as kind as you can be, but if you should discover that you don't really love her, send Annie back home to me.
Sincerely,
Ben Holt

Ben rushed down to the Post Office as soon as the letter was done, the envelope sealed and addressed. He feared that he wouldn't send it if he thought about it too much. He hoped that Annie would see it and...

He wrote a second letter:

Annie-
   Sorry.
Ben

He walked over to St. Mary's and left this letter behind the Chi Rho announcements at the back of the church.

18

January 1967

WHEN THE PHONE RANG IN BEN'S TRAILER, A second ringer on the outside wall announced it loudly for all the site to hear. If the wind was right and the traffic noise was low you could hear it all the way over to the General Edwards bridge. Perhaps it wasn't quite as bad as the loudspeaker at the car dealership a quarter-mile away calling errant salesmen—often drinking in a used car in the remotest part of the lot—to the phone, but Ben hated it anyway and thought of rigging a switch to turn it off during the day.

"Watchman," he answered. He hated having to answer "watchman," too. It was demeaning.

"Mister Holt? This is Emma Pittsfield, the Dean's secretary."

"Hello, Missus Pittsfield."

"The Dean would like to see you this afternoon. You can be here at five forty."

"Yes, Missus Pittsfield."

There was a click and the line went dead. Ben wondered whether she was just being taciturn or whether the line had gone dead. He looked out the window and didn't see any interruption in activity among the back-hoes and the large steam shovel, so he assumed Mrs. Pittsfield had considered the task complete.

"*Shit,*" Ben said. "*Shit, shit, shit.*" He could only think of one reason that Dean Piscara would want to see him. Admittedly he was late turning in his design projects and perhaps he had skipped too many of his drawing classes. He should have seen this coming. No one had said anything to him, no one had seemed to notice. The semester had ended a couple of weeks ago, but he hadn't seen his grades yet.

"No need for grades," he said out loud. "Just the old *heave-ho*. *Fuck*. This is *just* what I need right now." Ben felt he was holding on to his sanity by a thread. He fought the surging river in his head that threatened to sweep him away.

Breathe, he thought. Breathe.

By three thirty the site was quiet and nearly empty, the last few pick-up trucks and the carpenters' cars filing off of the site along the dirt road. Most of the laborers came by the bus that ran into Central Square, so they had left work by three ten to catch it up by the motel near the bridge. Ben decided to take the bus into Boston early and walk from Haymarket to the BIA though the Common and Public Garden.

He slipped on his camel wool sweater with the worn-leather elbow patches and left the trailer, headed along the bulkhead, and let the sound of the incoming tide lapping against the timber wall wash his mind clean. A chain-link fence separated the America's Park site from the adjacent Gas Wharf so when Ben got to the fence, he grabbed the vertical pipe that extended a foot-and-a-half over the bulkhead and swung himself to the other side—over the surging water below and onto the heavy plank floor of the wharf. Ben, his brothers and their friends had always called it the "Gas Wharf" because of the three huge natural gas tanks on the adjacent land, but it was really an old coal wharf from the days when the site housed an electricity-generating plant. The old hulking gantry crane that was used to off-load coal from freighters docked at the wharf remained— apparently immobile now—watching over the young intruders who fished from the wharf below. One of Ben's cousins had won the *Boston Globe* fishing tournament with a pollock caught from the wharf. Ben and his brothers had wondered aloud whether it was legal to win a legitimate fishing tournament with a fish caught while trespassing on forbidden property.

As Ben walked along the wharf, he noticed a bright yellow truck parked between two of the huge piles of coal sitting beyond the crane. It was dwarfed by the coal mountains and made the scene seem almost picturesque. The rain-washed channels which striped the coal from top to bottom and the little deltas of coal at their base looked like alpine mountains—flat-black alpine mountains—no snow, no green below a tree line; in fact, no trees for a tree line at all.

Ever since he'd been a kid, the scale of the site—the crane, the mountains of coal, the tanks, the long wharf and the abandoned power plant with the massive broken-glass windows—had always been overwhelming. It had all seemed so monstrous, so inhuman. It was a feeling that had always struck him deeply, plucking an off-tune chord that reverberated within him.

BEN GOT TO the bus station in Central Square just in time to catch the four-o'clock bus for Boston. He calculated that the bus should reach Haymarket just after four-thirty, which would give him plenty of time to walk down Tremont and across the Common and the Public Garden where he'd then have a choice of routes through the Back Bay up to the BIA: Boylston Street with more stores; Newbury Street with a mix of townhouses and the Ritz; and Comm Ave with the green mall and townhouses once owned by Boston's wealthiest families.

"Today I'll do Boylston," he whispered to himself, though loudly enough for a fat woman sitting beside him to turn and say, "What?"

If Ben had planned his walk through the Common and Public Garden as a salve for his loneliness, he was sorely let down. Wherever he looked, couples held hands, laughed together or listened intently to each other. He looked for Annie's face in the face of each girl, knowing it would not be there, that it would never be there. The pit in his stomach returned.

It was just after five-thirty when Ben walked in the door of the BIA. He headed to the Dean's office and saw Mrs. Pittsfield sitting at one of a half-dozen desks in the space behind an oak-faced counter outside the four offices that were occupied by the Dean, the Bursar, the head of admissions, and the head of administration. Mrs. Pittsfield's desk was immediately outside the Dean's door, which was open.

A young woman, probably only a year or two older than Ben, looked up from one of the front desks and said, "May I help you?"

"I'm here to see the Dean."

"Put your name on the sign-in sheet and take a seat in the lobby and we'll come get you."

Ben pulled the clipboard with the sign-in sheet toward him and was looking for a pen when Mrs. Pittsfield looked up and said, "Oh, Mr. Holt doesn't need to sign in. You're a little early, but let me see if the Dean can see you now."

Ben flashed a smile at the young woman as Mrs. Pittsfield disappeared into the Dean's office. Mrs. Pittsfield was gone two or three minutes when she walked to her desk, picked up a small pile of papers and looked up at Ben.

"Please come in."

Ben walked to the opening at the end of the counter and followed Mrs. Pittsfield as she walked back into the office. The office was quite long and stretched to the left of the door to the window line. The left-hand wall was lined with books old and new. Ben recognized a number of the authors as architects he'd been reading about for the past several months. One book was lying open with a note card sticking in the spine extending above the top. The writing on the card was in fountain pen ink and Ben recognized the signature, Josep Lluis Sert. The text seemed to be in either Italian or Spanish—Ben couldn't tell which. The top of the bookcase held several busts and a fragment of a classical building element. Ben wondered whether these were the work of the Dean, perhaps from his own school years. He had once seen a fully-rendered Beaux Arts floor plan from the Dean's architecture school thesis, pen drawn and water-color washed.

Mrs. Pittsfield was standing at the Dean's right shoulder, waiting as he signed some papers. When he was done she took the papers from his desk and placed another set of papers in front of him. She looked up at Ben, motioned him towards a chair in front of the desk, pulled one paper from the pile that the Dean had now shuffled and placed it on top of the pile. Then she walked out of the room.

Ben was still standing by the chair when the Dean said, "Please sit, Holt," without looking up from the papers. Ben watched him read, his comically-thick silver eyebrows dancing as he read. His deep-set eyes were dark and foreboding and Ben remembered that his visit was not a social call. He waited for the words to come, but the old man didn't seem about to deliver them any time soon. After several minutes he stood up, walked around the desk and headed through the door. Ben remained frozen to his seat, not knowing whether the Dean was getting something else from Mrs. Pittsfield or if the meeting was over. Mrs. Pittsfield stuck her head through the doorway.

"Mr. Holt, would you accompany the Dean please?"

Ben sprang from his chair, nearly knocking it over, then inadvertently caused it to fall into the wall as he reached to grab it. He took a deep breath, placed the chair gingerly in front of the desk, and looked at Mrs. Pittsfield apologetically.

"Don't worry, the chair will be fine. Now go."

Ben hurried to catch up to the Dean and found him standing in front of the elevator just as the doors opened. He followed the Dean into the cab and stood silently next to him as the doors closed and the cab didn't move.

"Six, Holt."

Ben pushed the button for the sixth floor and the cab began to move. He would have wished for a swift non-stop ride, but the elevator stopped at the third floor and opened to two students and a design instructor vigorously discussing a baseball game. When they saw the Dean they fell quiet, mouthing "Good evening, Dean" almost in unison. On the fourth floor, the cab stopped again and opened to the figure of Sather standing alone.

"Good evening, Dean." Sather looked at the Dean, then Ben, then turned his back to the other three occupants. At the fifth floor, he was the first one out, quickly followed by the others. Ben looked to the Dean for any message in his face, but found none. When the elevator stopped at the sixth floor, its doors opened to a crowd of people waiting to get on. They had just started to push into the elevator when they recognized the Dean, and all but one of them retreated. A hand emerged from the cluster and pulled the lone intruder back onto the landing. The Dean then moved through the doors to the chorus of "Good evening, Dean." Ben followed, barely avoiding the resurgent rush of the masses into the elevator.

The Dean opened a pair of doors to an old oak-paneled room with book-shelves that lined two of its walls. Three huge heavy dark-oak tables with turned legs and carving along their aprons dominated the room. The room had once been part of the original school property and had moved to this new building when the old school had been demolished for an urban renewal project. It was not often used, but Ben was familiar with it because he had snuck up here on weekends to work on his sketches on the tables amidst the spores of the place—spores of discussions and arguments, timeless art, and some mold from the deteriorating, aged books.

Ben could hear the voices beyond the room's walls, voices from the new library that surrounded this room. Despite the voices, he felt apart; apart in time and place whenever he was here. The presence of the old man reinforced that feeling, and he felt strangely calm.

"You are in the wrong place." The Dean said.

His words confused Ben. Was he in the wrong room, standing where he shouldn't, in the wrong school?

"I have found a place for you. You will need to give your notice, of course."

Ben stared at the Dean's face, waiting for more, but Piscara reached into his jacket pocket, produced a slip of paper and offered it to Ben. Ben looked at the paper, which bore on it just the word "Nivola" and a telephone number.

"Tomorrow, Holt."

"Dean?"

"Call him tomorrow. You will work with him until you leave for Paris."

"Dean?"

"Tomorrow, Holt."

Piscara walked from the room and was gone. Ben stood alone in the room, confused. He had fully expected to be told to leave the school. Was that what this was? But what was the name and the phone number? He had heard of a Vincent Nivola who had studied under Corbusier with Sert, Jackson and Zalewsky. Was this the same guy? He must have misheard "Paris." Did Sather know about the conversation?

IT WAS FIVE-FIFTEEN a.m. when Ben awoke. He looked at the clock and slid from the cot. He would call the number on the piece of paper just after nine.

The paper! he thought, wondering what he had done with the piece of paper. Was it real or had he dreamed it during the night? He grabbed his pants from the back of the chair and rummaged through the pockets, throwing his wallet, his keys, and his meager cash on the cot. There was no paper. He almost ripped the shirt as he pulled it from the chair, but there was no paper in the shirt-pocket, either. Maybe he really *had* dreamed it. He felt groggy and confused. He scooped up his keys from the cot and headed toward the trailer door to see if he'd left it in his car. As he opened the door he saw it—a quarter-folded scrap of Aquabee Co-Mo sketchbook paper—sitting on the table. He unfolded it slowly, afraid to see that there was no number there, but sure enough, written on the paper in smudged soft pencil, Ben read "Nivola. AL 7-1225."

He let the air escape from his lungs. Now he had the paper, the name and the number, but what was it really? Was this a brush-off from Piscara? Had Sather been involved in this? Maybe he should just forget about it, not call the number and get on with his life. He could call his father and try to get into the union. The thought of admitting defeat, especially after the loss of Annie, roiled him. Perhaps it would be best to just stay where he was. The job wasn't so bad and gave him time to do school work. Maybe he should just take a semester or two off from the BIA, get his feet under himself and try again, but Piscara had been so direct. He had to go through Piscara if he wanted to get back into the BIA in a year or so.

Ben realized he was already starting down the slippery slope that allowed a person to defer their dreams—the beginning of the long drawn-out death of hope. He thought of the kids he grew up with. He thought of Don and recognized the head of the slope.

I suppose it can't hurt to call the number, he thought. Just don't expect much.

19

IT WAS THREE PAST NINE WHEN BEN PICKED UP THE phone to make the call. A chirpy voice answered "Nivola and Capizzi" and identified itself as Leslie.

"Hello, my name is Ben Holt and..."

"Yes, Ben, Vincent said that you'd call. Can you come tomorrow? He's away today."

"Sure, what time?"

"The office is usually open by eight thirty, but I don't get here until nine. Vincent usually shows up around ten thirty. Come around at nine thirty and that will give me a bit of time to clean up for you."

"Okay."

"Oh and you'll meet Tom too, he's the head of the drafting room, and Joe, Vincent's partner, although he may be out at a construction site."

"Okay"

"We can make a list of what you need when you get here, if that's okay."

"Sure."

"Okay then. See you tomorrow." Before Ben could respond, he heard a click. He stared at the dead phone in his hand for a few moments. When he heard the dial tone he set the handset back on its cradle.

That was strange, he thought.

The next morning Ben stood across the street from 419 Boylston Street, looking up and down the white artstone facade. He entered the small, ornate lobby and, bypassing the elevator, climbed the six flights of stairs to the seventh floor. The seventh floor landing was clad in a white marble wainscoting with brightly-painted white plaster above. The corridor to the left was decorated with unframed, glossy photographs of buildings set in universally sunny landscapes with mere wisps of clouds against azure skies. The photos were bonded to a dark brown board—probably masonite, Ben thought—and raised a quarter inch or so from the wall. Ben laid his head against the wall and tried to peer along the wall behind the mounted photos to see how they were attached, but he couldn't get close enough.

"It's foam double-faced tape."

Ben turned and met the liquid blue eyes of a man with thin, wild, sandy blonde hair.

"Thanks."

"Frank McLellan." He held out his hand to Ben. "Photographer."

"Oh, did you take these?"

"Only one...Vincent takes most of his own, but I did the photo of the chapel from his hometown in Italy and he's got another of my pieces in his office that was taken in Beirut."

"Wow. Do you travel a lot?"

"Who wants to know?" Frank's eyes turned icy.

"Sorry, I just..."

"You didn't tell me *your* name," Frank interrupted.

Ben noticed that the ice had melted and the blue eyes were smiling. He was struck by the man's abrupt change of demeanor.

"Oh, Ben Holt." Ben started to raise his right hand from his side, then remembered that they had already shaken hands. He awkwardly moved his hand into his pocket and stood before Frank, one hand in his right pocket and the other by his left side.

Frank let a small laugh escape his lips and said, "See you around, Ben Holt." He turned and opened the door to an office identified only with the number "776" in small black numbers edged in gold on the milk-white glass.

Ben stared at the door for a moment and chastised himself for being so socially clumsy, then turned and headed down the hall to the double doors at the end that were mostly made of clear glass with a heavy frame of oak. On the door were the same style numbers reading "785" with "Nivola and Capizzi, Architects" arranged underneath in a simple, black sans-serif font. Ben opened the right-hand leaf of the door and walked into the small office reception area. No one sat at the white desk with the light wood top, and Ben couldn't see anyone around when he peered through the door openings to the right and the left. He could, however, hear Buffalo Springfield's "Broken Arrow" coming from the far reaches of the large room on the left. He stuck his head through the door opening and called out "Hello?"—to no response.

He walked a few steps into the room. Again he called out, "Hello?"

A large, dark face with olive-shaped eyes poked out from behind a low partition. The face disappeared again, but an extended arm clad in a rolled-up white sleeve still beckoned him closer. Ben walked toward the arm. When he reached the partition, he saw the arm was attached to a short man standing at a drafting table who alternated between holding the phone at arm's length and bringing it in again to his left ear. A deep red tie was knotted loosely around his neck and the tails of the tie were tossed over his left shoulder. Occasionally the man would speak short sentences into the phone in a language that sounded vaguely Middle Eastern. After ten minutes or so of the arm-stretching performance, the man set the phone down gently and turned to Ben.

"Sorry...my wife. She's not happy this morning. I'm Ilhan."

"Ben. Ben Holt. Leslie told me to be here at nine-thirty, but I'm a bit early, I guess."

"No, you are on time. It is Leslie who is late. One of her habits, I'm afraid."

"Oh."

"You are to work with Vincent, am I right?"

"Honestly, I'm not really sure what I'm doing, or, umm, *supposed* to be doing, anyway."

"Would you like some coffee? I can make some."

"Oh, don't bother for me."

"I'm going to make some for me anyway. I can make more."

"Okay..."

"A double?"

"Okay..."

Ilhan was gone for almost ten minutes before Ben started to wonder if he'd disappeared completely and left him in the office alone. While he was waiting he sensed movement behind him. He turned to see a thin man—whose height made him appear all the more a beanstalk—walk through the doorway from the reception area.

A shorter, barrel-chested man with unruly red hair followed behind. "Leslie in yet?" he said. His voice seemed to bellow, although its volume was normal.

"No. I haven't seen her. Ilhan's making me a coffee."

Both men laughed just as Ilhan walked through the doorway with two smallish white cups in hand. He offered one to Ben, who peered at the dark, black almost-liquid.

The redhead said, "That which doesn't kill us makes us stronger," and moved to a drafting stool at the table closest to the doorway. The beanpole moved to a chair that backed up to the redhead's chair and slipped his jacket off and over the back of the chair.

Ilhan spoke next. "Ned and Johnny, this is Ben who is going to be working with Vincent."

"If you haven't killed him with your poisonous slurry before Vincent even gets in," the beanpole joked and looked to the redhead for affirmation.

"Come, Ben. Let me give you a tour of the office while you are waiting for Leslie. We can leave these infidels to stew in their jealousy while they drink their thin swill."

Ben followed Ilhan and sipped gingerly from the small cup as they moved through the office, smiling whenever Ilhan looked at him. They walked through the conference room, the library, and the small kitchenette which had no sink, but which did have an electric percolator and an espresso machine—the instrument of Ben's current torture. The partners' office was about half the size of the drafting room and had two smaller spaces carved out of it, defined by a thin ceiling-high partition that stretched half-way across the room. Each side of the wall had very different papers pinned to it. Vincent's side was covered with thick-lined sketches that reminded Ben of his own drawing style. They were tacked helter-skelter with no apparent composition. Joe's side was neater, with typewritten sheets arranged in a grid, except for one piece of a blue-print the same size as the type-written sheets.

Just off the partners' office was a small room with a large window that framed a view of the steeple of the Arlington Street Church. The room was empty except for a door on two sawhorses and three boxes stacked akimbo in a single pile. It looked as though it had been freshly painted—the same color as the corridor—and the black tile floor had been freshly cleaned and waxed. Ben wondered whether he would be able to smell the paint, the cleaner, and the wax once his sense of smell—now overpowered by the taste of the espresso in his throat—returned.

"I think they're going to stick you in here. We'll get Bob, the office boy, to move the boxes. You can grab a chair from the conference room for now. Leslie probably ordered you a chair from Charrette. So settle in and she'll be here soon."

Ilhan walked away, leaving Ben to stare out the window at the steeple and the hint of a view of the Public Garden and the Common beyond. He raised the cup of espresso to his lips but found it was cold and even less drinkable than it had been when it was hot. His mouth and throat were now coated in a soft clay mud that seemed like it would prevent him from talking when the time came. He hadn't seen any source of water on his tour, and he desperately wanted—no, *needed*—to wash out his mouth. He walked out of the small office, through the partners' office, through the reception area, and stuck his head through the doorway into the drafting room. The redhead—he still wasn't sure whether it was Ned or Johnny—looked up from his drafting board.

"It's down the corridor beyond the elevator, on the right. Do you need a piece of gum?"

Ben just nodded and took the gum. It was a piece of Dentyne. Ben stared at it for a moment wondering how this tiny piece of gum was going to clear the mud from his mouth. He could chew a whole pack and still need more. He looked up and met the redhead's eyes and mouthed, "Thank you."

As Ben started down the corridor, he felt pressure growing in the lowest part of his abdomen, followed by a gurgling. He knew he had to move fast. He clenched his stomach muscles and walked as quickly as he could without running. He hoped no one would appear who he'd need to talk to. He threw open the door to the men's room and ran—no time for decorum now—into the first stall as the pain in his stomach surged. He was barely seated when the flow came, a surging flood that emptied his bowels, and Ben let out a loud sigh of relief. No sooner had the sigh escape his lips when Ben heard the door open and heels clacking on the tile floor. He clenched his bowels and tried to breathe quietly. He heard water running in the sink followed by the retreating clacking of the heels and the opening and closing of the door. He started to breathe normally again and prepared to leave the room, wiping his hands on a small white cloth towel from the pile that was stacked on a small table by the sink—a nice touch, he thought, not the paper he would have expected—and looked around for a receptacle in which to dispose of the towel, finally finding a basket near the back of the door.

When Ben re-entered the reception area he found Leslie sitting at the desk, her coat still on, counting money and putting it into a divided tray in a rectangular grey steel box.

"I was wondering where you had gotten off to. Then Ned told me you'd had some of Ilhan's espresso." Leslie's entire face beamed at Ben.

He stood there silently, red-faced, just grimacing.

"Well, enough of your sparkling conversation. Let's get you settled before Vincent gets in. I have some forms for you to fill out and we can put together a list of supplies. Oh, and your chair will be here in a half-hour or so. Would you like to start with a tour of the office?"

"Ilhan already took care of that."

"Oh, yes. Well you can count on Ilhan to take care of things." She looked to Ben for a response, but Ben only grimaced again. Leslie opened a file drawer behind her, took out a file and walked around her desk, through the partners' office, and stopped at the door to the small room. She turned and looked at Ben who was still standing at the doorway between the reception area and the partners' office. "Coming?"

Ben followed Leslie into the room and stood at the table with her. They both looked at the chair. Ben was waiting for her to sit and she was wondering whether to sit. She set the file on the table and turned to Ben.

"We're going to need a second chair in here," she said. "I'll call Charrette, maybe they haven't left yet. Fill these out," she said as she flipped the file open, "and I'll be back."

As she walked from the room, Ben took in the shape of her body. She was skinny, with almost no hips. At five-foot-six or so, she looked like a boy, but the long shape of her neck accentuated by her shortish hair made her surprisingly attractive. He smiled, then realized it had been several hours since he had worried the bone of Annie. His mood plummeted. Despite this new adventure, which he still didn't understand, Annie was still gone, and the hollow remained in the space she had occupied.

20

IT WAS ALMOST NOON WHEN BEN FELT THE CHANGE in the sound and feeling of the office. A thin, ascetic-looking man with dancing amber eyes and thinning grey hair stuck his head into Ben's room. His hair still had a hint of blonde in it.

"Ben. I'm Vincent. Vincent Nivola."

"I'm Ben Holt."

"Yes. I know," Vincent said, and Ben noted the gentleness in his voice. "Can we meet in the conference room in five minutes?"

"Of course."

Vincent seemed to evaporate from the doorway. Ben sat staring at the empty opening for a few moments, then grabbed a pencil and the white paper pad he had found on the bookshelf in the library and headed for the conference room. The pad was made from old memos and project reports, stapled together blank-side up in one corner and Ben started to read one of the memos about a church in Millinocket, Maine as he walked. No sooner had he cleared the doorway from his office when he walked into Leslie carrying a box with the word "Charrette" in the same sans-serif lettering as the firm's name on the front door. The box slipped from her hands and as she lurched toward the falling box, Ben lurched to grab it, too. There was an audible crack as their heads collided, and they both stumbled backwards, hands to foreheads, as the box hit the floor.

"Oh, I see you two have met."

Ben looked up to see a large man, barrel-chested and black-haired, laughing at his own joke.

"Funny, Joe," Leslie said.

The man held out a large ham of a hand. "Joe Capizzi. You must be Ben."

"Yes. Sorry," Ben said, looking into Joe's face as he shook his hand.

"Oh, it didn't hurt me much, except the laughing maybe... might have bust a gut."

"Funny, Joe," Leslie said again.

"I'm sorry," Ben said. "I wasn't looking. Are you okay?"

"I'm fine, but only *one* of us should bend over to pick up that box."

Ben stood still, looking at the growing red patch on Leslie's forehead just above her right eye.

"Ben."

"Yes, Leslie?"

"I think that it should be you."

"Oh, I'm sorry...of course." Ben bent and picked up the box and looked at Leslie again. The red spot was growing. He felt a burning on his own forehead, but couldn't reach up to feel it with the box in his hand.

"The box is for you, Ben."

"Yes, of course."

Leslie turned and walked away from Ben, and he took the opportunity to enjoy her again. As she walked through the doorway into the reception area she gave her hips an exaggerated double-wiggle. Ben felt his whole face burning, then smiled and looked around to see if Joe had seen the show, but he was gone. Ben could see part of Joe's back moving back-and-forth in his chair and realized by the cadence of Joe's movement that he was talking on the phone. Ben went back into his room and set the box on the table, the rushed off to the conference room to meet Vincent.

Vincent was sitting at the conference table with a cup of coffee in front of him and another cup in his hand. Steam rose from the second cup as he poured first one, then another dollop of water into the coffee.

"I'd like you to go over to the Carpenter Center and meet with Witold Grabowski. He'll have a maquette of the sculpture for the garden of the Millinocket church. He'll expect you to have lunch with him so stop at Elsie's on the way over. He'll want a dry tongue on seeded rye. Leslie can give you the details. He won't eat until one, so don't go too early. Do you have a sketchbook?"

"Yes."

"Good. A couple of sketches should be fine. He'll probably take up your time for the rest of the afternoon, but leave whenever you need to. He won't notice that you've gone."

"Okay."

"Bill Jordan from Cabot Stains will be here in the morning. Nine, I think. Meet with him and get the samples of the stain for the cedar cladding."

"Okay."

"When I get in I'll want to get together with you to go over the library. The library consultant will be in for lunch. We will need to make our own list before she gets here."

"Okay."

"Any questions?"

"No, not for now."

"Wow! Four words in a row! Amazing." Vincent pushed his chair back, and Ben did the same and followed Vincent out of the room. As they passed Leslie's desk, Ben dawdled and waited for Vincent to sit down at his drawing table.

"Can I go over this with you?" Ben held out his pad of paper and motioned back toward the conference room with his head. As he walked into the room, he resisted looking over his shoulder to make sure Leslie was following him.

By the time Leslie had walked into the room a couple of minutes after Ben, he had poised himself against the edge of the conference table, his legs stretched out to buttress his weight. Leslie looked at his long, lean form appreciatively before noticing the fear in his eyes. He seemed so child-like and yet his body was sinewy and powerful.

She made a note to check his age when he gave her back the employment application.

"Leslie?"

Ben's voice broke her thoughts and she looked at him for a moment before realizing he had spoken her name. She liked the way it sounded in his mouth.

"Yoo-hoo, Leslie." Ben was looking straight into her eyes now, and she returned the gaze, noticing how stormy the sea of hazel and brown appeared, like the swirling tides in a cup of coffee if you poured the coffee over the cream. The thought of coffee made her think of Ilhan and she resolved not to let him see her eyeing Ben.

"Go on, Ben. I'm listening." She wanted to sound irritated to cover her thoughts.

"Where the hell is Elsie's? Should I take the trolley? Am I going to have to carry the maquette back and how big do you think it is? Do you have any idea what Vincent is expecting of me?"

"Elsie's is on Mount Auburn Street near Harvard Square. It's a sandwich shop that the Harvard kids and professors and a lot of the architects who have offices in the Square go to. It's quite small but they have a lot of different sandwiches and lunch stuff there. It's kinda cool, really. What was the other question?"

"Am I supposed to bring the maquette back and how big is it if I am?"

"Grabowski will never let maquettes out of his studio unless he's with them. Did Vincent mention anything about a sketchpad?"

"Yeah."

"Okay. He wants you to do some sketches so that you can bring them back. I got you a couple of sizes of Aquabee Co-Mo pads and some 314 soft pencils. I'd take a smaller pad with you. It's easier to carry and Vincent likes vignettes. You've never worked in an architect's office, have you?"

"No. I have a job as the night watchman on a construction site."

"*Had* a job, you mean."

"No, *have* a job. I haven't quit the other job yet. This was so sudden and so unreal that I didn't want to assume anything."

"You're going to the other job tonight?"

"Yes."

"Well your stomach better get used to Ilhan's coffee. You're going to need it."

"Leslie, do me a big favor? Don't mention the night job to anyone just yet."

Leslie smiled and walked from the room. Ben gathered his papers and headed back to his office. He noticed that Leslie hadn't stopped at her desk, but had walked into the partners' office and was talking to Joe. The only words he could make out were "Ben...Holt...Piscara."

Ben grabbed a couple of the sketch pads—four-inch by six-inch size—and a box of 314 pencils. As he walked through the partners' office he could see that Leslie was still with Joe and could hear the sound of two men laughing. He turned red at the thought of Leslie telling the men about his night job and he rushed from the office, out the front door and down the corridor where he almost crashed into Frank.

"Where are *you* going in such a hurry?"

"No hurry really, I just move fast."

"Well, slow down and enjoy life. Besides if you don't hurt yourself, you'll kill someone else rushing around like that. If you promised not to run or anything, I'll walk with you to the subway."

"Sure. That'll be good."

As they walked and talked, Ben told Frank of his conversation with Dean Piscara and his morning at Nivola and Capizzi. Frank told Ben that his photography often took him to the far reaches of the world and mentioned that it was he who'd brought Ilhan to Vincent and Joe's attention. Frank had known Ilhan's family in Turkey and they had asked Frank to look out for him when he came to Boston to study at Harvard. Frank told Ben that Ilhan had inflicted his coffee on his housemates when he was an undergraduate and had continued to do so through his years of architecture school. Ilhan's mother sent him the coffee and he never seemed to run out.

"Well, why doesn't anyone just get coffee somewhere else?"

"Mostly because it would hurt Ilhan's feelings."

"For *coffee?*"

"Ilhan and his father and five brothers used to start every morning with that coffee. Then, after he came here, all the males in his family, including a baby nephew, were killed in a terrible attack."

"Oh."

"So now he attacks *us* with his coffee."

"You, too?"

"I actually *like* the stuff."

"Hmm."

They walked in silence for a few minutes until Ben noticed they had walked past the Arlington Station, which was half a block from the office and through the Public Garden, and were now headed through the Common to Park Street, bypassing the Boylston Street station. As they approached the door into the Park Street headhouse, Frank stopped and held out his hand, "Enjoy your afternoon."

"I thought you were headed to the trolley too," Ben said as he took the offered hand.

"I need to go on a bit further. The trolley here goes directly to the Square."

"Thanks."

Frank said nothing, but crossed Tremont and walked on down Bromfield Street.

Ben descended the stairs into the subway station. He was familiar with the layout of the trolley station, had ridden through it almost every day for the past couple of years. He knew that the train station was somewhere below it, but he was unsure of which stairway and which track would take him to Harvard Square. He was about to ask a man standing near one of the stairs when he noticed a sign with black letters on a white enamel-on-steel background with "HARVARD SQ" and an arrow pointing down.

21

January 1969

A LMOST TWO YEARS LATER, BEN CONTINUED TO
work in the offices of Nivola and Capizzi. After a month there,
he had quit his job at America's Park. There had been no construction work going on at the site anyway, so Ben's work had consisted
mostly of filing equipment maintenance reports. By the time he'd
left, at least half of the heavy equipment was gone, too.

The dream of America's Park died from rising costs, mixed agen-
das and too many people grabbing for a piece of the supposed golden
egg. For the first time, Ben realized that great ideas don't ensure a
good result or, necessarily, any result at all. The unions pointed at the
greed of the developers and the corporate owners of the old power
plant who saw one more chance to make money, the political candidates who were looking to get elected to office pointed at the intran-
sigence of the bureaucracy, and the *Globe* pointed at the involvement
of organized crime.

Ben's frustration with the death of the America's Park project
was tempered by his excitement with his work on the church and the
library. He loved working in the city where he could walk down the
stairs from his office to the shops of the Back Bay and to school. He
could take a trolley to Harvard Square and browse the magazines at
the newsstand, buy a sandwich at Elsie's, and visit with Grabowski in
his studio. He loved being immersed in the intellectual and artistic

vigor of architecture, even if his professors at the BIA had been less than enthusiastic about his design work.

Although Tom and Ilhan would ask to see his design school projects, neither Nivola nor Capizzi ever expressed an interest in his school work. However, they did treat him with respect as a colleague in the office. Ben appreciated that and worked hard to repay them for their thoughtfulness. He often worked late into the night and on weekends, sketching elements of the new church or making massing models of the library and its attached student union. Late one Sunday night Ben struggled to complete three massing models that were to be used for a design review meeting with the partners early Monday and a meeting with the client later that morning. The client was to choose between the three, but Ben, Vincent and Ilhan already knew which of the three they wanted to build. They preferred the design that enclosed a courtyard with the library askance at the open end and that included a student union attached by an L-shaped addition to an administration building roughly parallel to the library. The resulting U-shape ensemble neatly defined the courtyard.

BEN STARTED CUTTING pieces of the gray chipboard with a matte knife, changing blades frequently as they dulled quickly in the tough material. As his right hand tired, he would gather up the cut pieces and glue them together in arrangements of walls and roofs before picking up the knife again to continue his work. As the night grew late, Ben became bleary-eyed and found himself occasionally cutting dangerously close to the left hand as it steadied the metal straight edge guiding the blade. He used the last blade in the box and went looking for another. He searched all the cabinets, but came up empty-handed. He searched the drawers at all of the drafting stations, but found only two half-used blades. He searched the coffee cups that had been enlisted as tool holders, but only found two X-Acto knives—not very useful for cutting chipboard. He realized that he absolutely needed the models for the next morning's meeting so he went back to work with the few mostly-dull blades he had left. As he worked, the blades half-cut, half-tore at the material. This would never do, he thought and resolved to get to Charrette first thing in the morning to get new blades to trim the edges of the blocks before the meeting. Just after two a.m., he locked the doors and walked home.

Ben arose early the next morning and walked across the Public Garden and the Common to Park Street to catch the train to Cambridge. The Cambridge store was always open early. He bought two boxes of the blades he needed then headed back down Church Street to Mass Ave to hop the train back to Boston. At Park Street he pondered taking the trolley back to the office, but seeing the crowded platform, decided he would run across the parks to the Back Bay. As he crossed Charles Street he heard a slapping sound and looked down at his right shoe to see that the front half of the leather sole had separated from the base. He slowed momentarily, but decided he had to keep up his pace. He ran across the Public Garden, across Arlington Street and Boylston, his right shoe slapping all the way. As he walked into the office, his face glowed red, half from the exertion, half from the embarrassment of his flapping sole. Not stopping to give Leslie more than a passing wave, he headed for the models. Ben arrived at the worktable to find the models gone. He looked in the drafting room, but no one was there.

"Leslie?" He called out as he headed to her desk. "Leslie?" He almost ran into her at the entry to the reception area.

"Vincent took them into the conference room," Leslie said without waiting for Ben to speak.

"I needed to finish them," he panted, as if pleading an explanation for their condition.

Leslie stepped aside. Ben started for the conference room and his shoe began its loud slapping again.

"Give me your shoe."

"What...?"

"Give me your shoe and I'll glue the sole back on."

Ben slipped off the shoe and, holding it with two fingers in the back of the heel, clumsily transferred it to Leslie's two waiting fingers. He walked a few steps in one shoe, stopped and took it off, set it beside a file cabinet and walked into the conference room with the large toe of his right foot beginning to peek through his sock.

Vincent looked up before Ben had a chance to speak.

"Corbu would have *loved* these. They are so raw, so expressive, so full of emotion. *Perfect.*"

"I wanted to trim the rough edges before the meeting."

"No, we'll present these as they are."

Vincent explained that the models were like sketches. They communicated a design idea but left an opening for the final interpretation of the design. Clients liked sketches because they felt that the design still offered an opportunity for their input.

Ben heard only a few words of Vincent's explanation. His mind dwelled on Vincent's words, "Corbu would have *loved* these," and he felt as if he'd grown two inches, even in his stocking feet.

Vincent had mounted the drawings of the three design schemes on the long wall of the conference room and placed the three models on low tables in front of them—each model corresponding to the design scheme above. Each of the schemes included floor plans, elevations and two cross-sections, but the middle scheme, the design that Vincent and Ben preferred, had a charcoal rendering Ben had drawn tacked to the wall above the other drawings.

The rendering showed the building from a pedestrian's perspective standing at the corner of two streets with the low four-story student union building on the left and the eight-story library building on the right. A sliver of a view into the courtyard separated the two buildings from an existing administration building. The shadows shown on the rendering were long and moody, creating the image of a late afternoon. This visual trick allowed them to show the interior of the lower floors of the library illuminated, with visible activity apparent.

The student union building rose vertically from its foundation, its brick panels modulated by a vertical pattern of windows on the upper floor. Exposed brick columns flanked the full-story glazing of the ground floor. This was to be a background building; the library was to be the star. The library would be an assemblage of finely-defined space and mass. The building was placed on a raised base with steps on three sides. The steps on the side facing the interior of the courtyard rose, then descended into a sunken area that would serve as a stage for lectures or performances. The fourth side of the base, on the corner farthest from the courtyard, contained loading docks from which to access the storage and service areas housed below the base.

A grid of large, square columns rose five stories to a block three stories high that would house the library stacks. Each floor stepped slightly forward from the floor below. The sixth and seventh floors were faced with full-story fins that broke the direct rays of the sun, but allowed light to enter the building. The eighth floor was almost windowless and would house some of the library's oldest collections of prints and photographs chronicling the city's industrial heritage.

The magic of the building was expressed on the first five floors. The view from the street and the courtyard offered a soaring space punctuated by square and half-round boxes suspended from the sixth and fifth floors. The boxes contained performance spaces, lecture rooms and galleries and were solid except for the recessed ribbon of clerestory windows between each box and the floor above.

From the point of view of Ben's rendering, the portico on the first floor of the courtyard side of the student union was faintly visible. Vincent had added the portico late in the design process in response to Ben's offhand observation that the student union building seemed to turn its back on the library. Ben was proud that Vincent had taken his comment seriously enough to add the portico. The spatial effect that the portico had on the composition felt just right. It may have substantially been Vincent's design, but Ben felt that he had made important contributions.

If Annie could only see him now...

22

April 1970

"**B**EN, VINCENT WANTS TO SEE YOU."

Ben turned to see Leslie standing in the doorway of his office.

"In the conference room?"

"Yes."

Ben laid the soft sketch pencil on the piece of sketch paper taped to his drawing table. He noticed that the edge of his hand was black with pencil carbon and went into the men's room to wash up. He wiped his hands on several paper towels, then headed for the conference room.

"You wanted to see me, Vincent?"

"Oh, yes." Vincent motioned Ben in

"An old friend of mine, Pascal Satart, is arriving in town on Friday. We worked together in Corbu's atelier. I'd like you to meet him at the airport and bring him back here. Leslie will make a reservation at Dini's and we can walk across the park for lunch. I'd like you to join us if you aren't busy."

Ben had never been out to lunch with Vincent or Joe. They had shared the occasional lunch in the conference room, usually tied to a project or staff meeting. If it was a staff meeting, Joe would run it and lunch would be pizza. If it was a design meeting, Vincent would run it and there would be a selection of sandwiches from Patisserie C'est si Bon around the corner. Ben particularly liked the ham and boursin or the ham with a mustard that could take your breath away. He liked the mustard because it was French, not French's, and it made him feel a little more sophisticated.

"I can join you. Thank you. But let me make the reservation. I know the maître d'."

"You know Peter? I'm impressed."

"My mother works there, but she works nights so she can be home during the day with the kids." Ben was instantly sorry he had mentioned his mother was a waitress. It had always been a source of embarrassment for him when he'd been with Annie.

"You'll make the reservation then." Vincent had already turned away and pulled out a pad of sketch paper.

23

BEN FELT RELIEVED WHEN HE WAS ABLE TO FIND A parking space in the small lot in front of the building that served as the temporary Eastern Airlines shuttle terminal. The new terminal was under construction to its right. The arches of its facade were fully visible behind the construction barricade and workers were installing the glass curtain wall some distance back from the front edge of the roof. Ben thought that it gave the building the impression of having a front porch.

Having asked a porter where the shuttle from New York would be arriving, Ben stood at a window near the door to the tarmac and waited for the plane to arrive. He didn't have to wait long as three men—one with two red-banded white batons—guided a Lockheed Electra into its parking space a short distance from the building.

As the propellers slowed and came to a stop, two men rolled a stairway from somewhere around the end of the building to within a few feet of the fuselage. One man climbed to the top of the stairs, reached over and slapped the door, then waited for it to swing partly open. He reached over and swung the door fully open, then signaled down to his partner to push the stairs against the body of the plane.

Pascal was the fourth passenger to emerge and was instantly recognizable by the black beret that Vincent had told Ben was permanently sewn to Pascal's head. As Pascal descended the stairs, workers lined up luggage to the left of the stairway. Ben approached him just as he was reaching for the larger of two black leather cases.

Pascal stood up, case in hand, and turned to Ben. "You must be Ben. Vincent described you well. Please take this and I'll grab my other case."

Ben took the case, slipping his hand into the handle just as Pascal let it go. It dropped a few inches into his hand and Ben was relieved it hadn't fallen to the ground.

Pascal straightened up with a smaller case in hand and turned towards Ben. "Can we take the drive through Charlestown? The tunnel is so ugly and the Mystic River Bridge is not much better."

Ben tried to remember how to get to the Back Bay through Charlestown. He clearly remembered the last half of the route, but was blanking on how to get there from the airport.

"And can we make one stop on Meridian Street? I *desperately* need an espresso."

Meridian Street. The route flashed into Ben's mind: down Meridian to Chelsea, out Beauchamp, into Sullivan Square and over the little bridge into the North End. "Sure," he said. "No problem."

They arrived at Ben's car just as a cop was marking Ben's back tire with a white stripe from a piece of chalk attached to a wooden stick. Ben had to wait for the cop to back out from the space before he could slip in to unlock the door for Pascal. Ben smiled; the cop didn't. Ben let Pascal slip down the aisle to the open door then opened the back door on Pascal's side and slipped the two cases onto the back seat. Ben drove out of the airport past the tunnel entrance and onto Meridian Street. Pascal pointed out a pastry shop and Ben pulled over.

The car had barely stopped when Pascal bounded out and called back to Ben through the door he had left open. "Espresso? *Allongé?*"

Ben had no idea what "*lingerie*" meant so he weakly replied, "Espresso, please."

Pascal was gone for several minutes. When he returned he had two cups in hand, one larger than the other. "I got you an *allongé*. I assumed you'd prefer it. It's a bit more like American coffee. Espresso with extra water."

"Thanks. I wasn't sure what you meant by *lingerie*. Sorry." The color rose in Ben's face.

"Now you do," Pascal said. "Enjoy."

Ben started the car and drove on, holding the cup in one hand and shifting it occasionally to the other as the hot coffee burned his hand. He tried placing it on the seat between his legs, but that made two mistakes: one, the cup was hot and two, the gesture was embarrassing.

BEN WAS HAVING a lucky parking day. He congratulated himself on finding a spot immediately in front of the office. Leaving Pascal in the car, he avoided the slow elevator and bounded up the stairs to the office. As he burst through the doors, Leslie pointed back out to the corridor and said Vincent had just taken the elevator down. Back down the stairs Ben bounded, skipping every other tread, sometimes two. As he got to the first floor lobby, he slowed to a walk, hoping to appear more calm and sophisticated than he really felt. A chilling trickle of sweat ran down his right side, followed by another. He was glad he'd worn a sport jacket and lifted it to see if the sweat showed on the exposed sliver of shirt. Not yet, anyway.

As Ben was about to walk through the glass lobby doors, he noticed that Pascal had slipped into the driver's seat and that Vincent now occupied the front passenger seat. The driver's side windows were open and Pascal's arm stretched out the window.

"I hope you don't mind. I love big American cars," Pascal said.

"No, it's fine." Ben said, and climbed into the back seat behind Vincent.

"Off we go then." Pascal pulled the Oldsmobile into the travel lane without looking for oncoming traffic. Ben cringed and wondered if he'd have a car left by the time they got to the restaurant. As they drove, Vincent talked to Pascal about family and friends, calling out directions to him almost after they had already passed the turns. Dini's was not far from the office, but Boston's one-way streets meant that they had to go between the parks and over Beacon Hill to get there. As they approached the restaurant, Ben directed Pascal to an alley on the near side, and they left the car there, parking half on the sidewalk, half on the road.

AFTER THE HARROWING ride, Dini's was a great success. Peter Cinelli spoke Italian to Vincent and French to Pascal. He addressed Ben when inquiring about the needs and desires of the table: more bread, butter, water, and the like. When lunch came and the waitress laid a large bowl of fried clams and a plate of fries in front of Ben, Peter followed almost immediately by passing him the ketchup bowl. Ben watch Vincent's and Pascal's reactions and thought he saw a smile on each of their faces. He dipped the clams in the ketchup, but ate the fries with only salt.

After coffee, Vincent announced that he and Pascal would ride the subway into Harvard Square. They stood on the sidewalk in front of the restaurant and said their goodbyes. The two older men set off arm-in-arm towards Park Street. Ben headed down the alley to his car feeling high and excited. Pascal had talked of his work in Paris, teaching and designing. Ben was struck by Pascal's comfortable self-assurance and his appealing description of Parisian life. Vincent and Pascal recalled stories of their Paris days studying and working with Corbu. Ben resolved to find a way to go to Paris himself some day and be a part of the city's art and excitement.

Three days later, Vincent and his wife hosted a country dinner for Pascal at their farm in Carlisle. The entire office was invited and all but Leslie were there. Much of the time, Vincent held Ben and Pascal lightly by their elbows and guided both of them from conversation to conversation. Ben was mostly quiet, other than a short answer to a question from one or the other of them. Halfway through the night, Vincent began talking about Ben's work in glowing terms to anyone who would listen. Ben felt uncomfortable and a bit sorry for Pascal who had to hear it all, but he had to admit he liked the attention. It was after midnight when the others drifted away, said their goodbyes and headed home. Vincent announced he was heading to bed and simply walked up the stairs without another word.

"I should probably head out, too," Ben said and extended his hand to Pascal. Pascal ignored the hand. He leaned in and gave Ben a firm hug and moved his head toward each of Ben's cheeks.

"It has been nice spending some time with you, Ben, though I suspect that you were a bit embarrassed by all of Vincent's attention..."

"Yes." Ben looked at the floor.

"He likes you very much and sees something in you. I respect that he has a special sensibility."

Ben smiled. He wanted to say more, but he couldn't comfortably think of the right words. "Goodnight then," Ben said, and was about to offer his hand, but thought better of it.

"Goodnight," Pascal said. "I'll see you in the fall, Ben."

"In the fall." Ben turned and walked from the kitchen and out through the back door. He headed around the house and out towards the barn where he had left his car. The yard was dark and Ben was aware of animal noises and smells and the amazing light of the stars. When he was half way across the yard, the lights to the house came on and the stars disappeared. Ben turned and saw Pascal standing in the back door, waving.

24

August 1970

B EN LIKED WORKING ON SATURDAY MORNINGS. The office was usually abandoned until early afternoon and the morning sun that slipped through his office window had a different feel than the weekday sun. It was quieter, more gentle, and infinitely less judgmental.

Ben seldom produced any new work on Saturday mornings. It was a time of reflection on the work of the week past. He would look through his drawings, feeling his way through the floor plans, wandering through the sections and elevations, taking down the miniature study models from the shelf, populating them with friends, strangers and conversations. He would mark building elements on the drawings that he felt didn't quite fit, using a large dark circle in soft pencil notated with a big question mark and perhaps a curt note. He was a tough critic of his own work and often chastised himself in his notes. When something fit just right, he might mark it with an exclamation point and a longer note.

Around eleven o'clock every Saturday the mailman would come, flopping the mail noisily on Leslie's desk to signal that the mail had arrived. Ben could tell by the sound of the *flop* whether the day's mail was comprised merely of letters and bills or if it included more interesting deliveries like the thick architectural magazines he liked to read. Ben usually finished his review before heading out to extract the magazines from the rubber band wrapped around the mail. Today, the *flop* had an odd quality to it which distracted him. He set aside the drawings and headed to the reception area.

The mail lay askew atop Leslie's desk. A few of the smaller envelopes had slid from the pile and hung precariously over the back edge. A large envelope of thin, semi-gloss brown paper sat at the bottom of the pile. As Ben reached across the desk to retrieve the errant pieces he noticed Pascal's printed return address on one of the shiny envelopes. Partially atop this envelope was *Architectural Forum*. Ben lifted the *Forum* from the pile and took it back to his office. Looking at his drawings, he decided to let them sit until Monday. He picked up the soft pencils strewn around his table and set them in the "to be sharpened" cup and headed home.

That afternoon, he read *Forum* on the roof of his apartment building. Afterwards, feeling drowsy in the heat of the afternoon sun, he went downstairs, stripped off his clothes and took a long, sweet nap.

ON MONDAY MORNING Ben arrived at the office just before seven-thirty. He dropped the *Forum* on Leslie's desk and went to his office where he found the envelope from Pascal sitting squarely on his drawing table. He noticed for the first time that it was addressed to him. When he picked it up, he noticed it felt heavy, as if there might be a magazine inside, so he set aside to read later.

By nine o'clock, the majority of the office staff had arrived and Ben felt the hum of activity in the office. Joe stuck his head through Ben's door and asked whether he had seen the envelope from Pascal.

"I have. I need to finish these sketches before Vincent gets in. I'm saving the magazine until lunch."

"I don't think it's a magazine."

Vincent pried his tall thin frame past Joe and through the doorway. "Do you want to talk about Pascal's letter?"

"Vincent, I haven't opened it yet." Ben was instantly sorry for his defensive tone.

"Well, open the damned thing!" Joe said.

Ben was taken back by Joe's bark. He reached for the envelope, opened it and drew out several pages that had been torn from a magazine. He looked at Joe and Vincent and smiled as though he had been vindicated. It *was* a magazine, after all.

Joe reached over and grabbed the envelope and extracted a single sheet of thin paper. He pushed it towards Ben's face. Ben took the sheet and began to read. As he read, the top of his head began to tingle and confusion swirled like a cloud in his brain. He looked at Vincent, then Joe, then Vincent again. He couldn't make himself speak. Joe turned and walked away, shaking his head.

"Vincent. I—I don't know what to say. There must be some mistake."

"And what would that mistake be?"

"Pascal has asked me to come to Paris and work with him."

"You haven't answered my question."

"I never applied to work with him. I never..."

"Pascal doesn't accept applications. You only work with Pascal if you are invited."

"I only spoke with him twice."

"Ah, but I spoke with him many times."

"About this?"

"No, mostly about the lack of a proper baguette in America, but once or twice about you."

"But I have school and my work here."

"And he has work all around the world and people in his office who will challenge you."

"I don't think I can do this. I've got too many commitments here."

"Ben, you are barely twenty-three. What are you doing here that is so important at that you can't accept an offer to work in Paris?"

"I have my work, the housing project and the planning for the old arsenal site."

"The design for both of those projects is nearly done. You can finish it before you leave. Joe will be taking over the construction documents anyway. You can go."

"Vincent, I just don't know."

"Ben, accept Pascal's offer or I will fire you."

"You won't fire me."

"If that's what it takes to get you to go to Paris, I will."

"I…"

"The issue is resolved. Come, let's look at those sketches."

OVER THE NEXT two months Ben worked harder than ever to complete the design for his few remaining projects. As the time drew close for Ben to leave, he found he had growing gaps in his schedule that he could use for making arrangements on both sides of the Atlantic. Vincent and Lydia still had an apartment in Neuilly and he could stay there until he found a place of his own. He obtained a passport and a work visa. He regularly visited Out-of-Town news in Harvard Square to buy French newspapers and magazines. He read of the student strikes and the labor strikes in France and wondered whether they would quash his trip. In his mind, he still saw it as a trip. In his heart, he knew he was a fraud who would soon be discovered and sent home.

A few days before he was scheduled to leave for Paris, Ben went to the BIA to see Dean Piscara.

"You know, Holt, that this is your best chance."

"You know about my trip to Paris, don't you? I should have known that the three of you were co-conspirators."

"Satart is an old friend. I talked to him about you many times. You don't belong here. They'll beat you."

"I don't think so," Ben said. His back stiffened.

"They always select one to beat down, to use as an example for the rest. This year *you're* it."

"If you know that, why don't you stop them?"

"I did. *We* did. Make the most of Paris." Piscara stared directly into Ben's eyes. "I suppose I did it as much for them as for you."

"What do you mean?"

"*You* were winning."

Ben looked for a smile, but there was none.

25

September 1970

BOUT AN HOUR AFTER THE BOEING 707 TOOK OFF,
Ben's thoughts turned to his family, especially to Don. He
thought of their childhood and the promise he'd made to Don to
always return after their father had thrown him out of the house one
more time. He had told Don and his mom that he was going to
Paris, but he hadn't mentioned that he might be there for quite a
while. Working with Pascal still felt more like a dream than a reality.
Ben wanted to see how things would go, to see how he would like
Paris. He felt some anxiety about moving away from the places he
had called home. If he was still working with Pascal in a couple of
weeks, certainly within a month or so, he would call them both.

The steward appeared and asked if he would like some wine. Ben
hesitated, thinking of the small amount of cash in his pocket, cash he
might need when he got to Paris. Before he could decline the wine,
the steward mentioned that it was "complimentary."

"Yes, please. *Oui, s'il vous plaît.*"

The steward smiled.

"*Rouge ou blanc?*" He saw Ben's confusion. "Red or white wine?"

"Red, please."

The steward poured an inch-and-a-half of wine into a stemmed
glass and handed it to Ben with a small napkin. It was Ben's first glass
of French wine and he looked at it for a moment. He noticed that the
woman across the aisle raised the glass and nearly stuck her nose into

it. Tempted to do the same, he thought he might look foolish, so he lifted the glass to his lips and tasted the wine. It wasn't as sweet as the red wines he had occasionally tasted at home. It was interesting, he thought, but he wasn't sure he liked it and wished for a moment that it was a Miller High Life. He raised the glass to his lips again, deciding it was time to start developing a taste for French wine.

DON HAD JIMMIE pull the car up to the front walk of the small house. He got out of the front passenger side. Richie and Roger slipped from the back seats and moved behind him. They walked briskly to the front door without talking. Don ignored the glowing doorbell and rapped five times on the front door. A light came on just inside the door and Don recognized Harold as the door swung slowly open. Don pushed it wider and stuck his right foot against it. The three men were on Harold before he could retreat.

"JE VOUDRAIS ALLER à un Rue Saint Thomas D'Aquin, s'il vous plait." Ben had written this phrase in his notebook and read it nervously.

"Certainment, monsieur." The taxi pulled away from the Orly terminal and into the light traffic. "You are American?"

"Oui."

"A student?"

"Of sorts. I'm going to be working with Pascal Satart, an architect."

"So you are an American architect?"

"I'm working on it."

"Très bon. This Satart, he designed every few buildings in France, no?"

"I don't know. I know that we'll be working on the design of a new capital city in Yemen."

"Yemen is not in France."

"No."

The taxi pulled up to the curb and the truck driver behind him gave a long pull on his horn. The cabbie signaled back to the truck driver, shoving his right arm into the air and pulling Ben's bags to the sidewalk with his left. Ben paid the driver with some of the francs which he had exchanged for half his dollars at the airport as Vincent had suggested. As the taxi driver pulled away, the truck driver followed, cursing through his open window.

Ben stood in front of a huge pair of green-painted wood doors, the number "1" on a porcelainized metal square to its upper left. There was no bell, and the doors looked like the entryway to a garage or stable. He looked around for another door, but the others only led to shops. Thoroughly confused, he stood wondering what to do next when a young man walked up to the right-hand door and pushed against it. As the door swung open, the man looked at Ben, then at the bags.

"You must be Ben." The man spoke in a vaguely English accent and offered his hand. "I'm Paul. Paul Hogan."

"I'm Ben. Holt. Uh...Ben Holt." He shook Paul's hand.

"Yes. Let me help you."

"Thanks."

They pushed through into a small, dark vestibule, then passed through a second pair of doors into a sunlit courtyard.

"We can store your large bag in here." Paul opened the door into a large storeroom on the left and pulled the bag inside. "No reason to drag it up the stairs. You'll be rooming with me and Jared Whiting. We have a large...by Paris standards anyways...flat over in the sixth."

"Actually, an architect I worked for in Boston gave me the use of his apartment in Neuilly for a while, until I get settled."

"Vincent's apartment. Yes, it certainly is nice, but you'll be better off if you aren't living alone. And the office owns the apartment so it is free...sort of, anyway."

They walked across the courtyard and up three narrow flights of stairs to the fourth floor. They entered a long, high, narrow space under the roof rafters. Just about everything in the space was painted white—walls, ceiling, doors and furniture. Only the chairs, the drawings and the few people in the room added some color, and the people were mostly dressed in black. The room was bright, although the windows Ben saw were low on the opposite wall, so low that the head of the windows only came up to a man's chest. As they stepped farther into the room Ben noticed a large set of clerestory windows above and behind him. From the small sliver of sun splashed on the wall at the end of the space, Ben surmised that the clerestory faced north.

"Since you're the new boy, you get the rookie space." Paul led Ben to a long table near the narrow end farthest from the door. Between the table and the wall at the far end were two large workspaces, the closest with two tables separated by a stool space and the second space beyond with three tables—one high and two lower—in a u-shaped arrangement with a swivel chair in the middle of the u. This last table was at the end of the space and Ben assumed it must be Pascal's. Pulling an envelope from his jacket, he started for the u-shaped desk.

Paul followed. "Who's the envelope for?" he said.

"It's a note for Pascal thanking him for bringing me here."

"Oh, *that's* not Pascal's table. His is right here." Paul put a hand on the closer table.

"That's Josep's area. He is the head draftsman and runs the office for Pascal."

Ben was a little surprised, but thought of Vincent and Joe. Josep was Pascal's Joe.

Paul led Ben on a tour of the office. It was on two floors with a lower floor containing two meeting rooms, a supply room, toilets and the kitchen. In the kitchen, Paul made two small cups of coffee in a glass pot with a plunger. Ben took a small sip, grimaced and saw Paul smile. Ben added some hot water from a glass pot and mouthed the word, "*allongé.*"

As they walked on, Paul told Ben that he was an engineer and was born in London to an American engineer-father and an English engineer-mother. They'd moved to Philadelphia when he was almost eleven. He had one brother and a sister who had died at nine and three, respectively. As they climbed the stairs to the upper floor, Ben told Paul of his own family, the BIA and Nivolo and Capizzi. Paul told him about his Dutch girlfriend. She and Paul liked each other, but Paul didn't think it would get more serious. She was, after all, just a student.

"You'll meet her," he said. "She stays with me a lot. Do *you* have a girlfriend?"

Ben told Paul most of the story of Annie, but left out the ending.

"This is Lucio, Ben. He's our model maker and right now he's terribly jealous of you. Pascal showed photos of your study models and Josep abused Lucio with them for days."

"Sorry."

Lucio glared at Ben. "Do not make any of your models here. *I* make models."

Ben looked for the crack of a smile from Lucio, but there was none. The man was at least a foot shorter than him, but had amazing, almost cartoonishly-thick upper arms over sticks for forearms. Ben resolved to keep conflict with this man to a minimum.

DON SAT AT one of the tables along the back wall of Sallie's bar. As always, he faced the door and leaned his chair on its back legs against the wall.

"Do you do that at home?" Sallie said.

"No, my mom won't let me." Don didn't move. Sallie shook his head and walked away.

Two cops walked in the front door, spoke to Sallie for a moment, then walked directly towards Don. The shorter of the two spoke first.

"Sorry, Don."

The taller cop spoke next. "Don Holt, we have a signed assault complaint against you. You'll have to come with us."

"Let me finish my beer." Don stared straight ahead. His left hand held the glass, his right hand lay in his lap.

The taller cop moved toward Don and reached out to grab him by the arm. Don's body uncoiled and his right fist flashed at the policeman's face. The cop fell back, the table fell at his feet, and the contents of the beer glass stained his pants. As the shorter cop bent over his partner, Don stood, walked calmly from the bar, got into his car and headed to his mother's house.

He walked into the house and ordered his mother and sister to go upstairs. He parted the curtains to look out the front window. The street was empty and quiet, verdant in the dappled shade of the maples along the curbside berm. Don knew that the peaceful, verdant scene wouldn't last for long.

"Now what have you done?" Don's mother reached for him, but his sister pulled her away and aimed her up the stairs.

Don hadn't been in the house ten minutes when four police cars arrived silently, blocking the ends of the street and the driveway. A fifth car arrived with its siren blaring. Don watched as the cops poured from the cars and gathered on the front sidewalk. He searched their uniforms and noted that none of them ranked sergeant or higher. If the superior officer arrived before they came up the stairs, it was going to be an arrest. If not, it was going to be a beating.

He went into the kitchen and made a phone call to Sam McGonigle. He noticed that four cops had moved to the back of the house—two near the back steps to the kitchen, two at the cellar door. He went back to the living room, sat in his father's chair and waited. He could hear his mother crying upstairs and his sister trying to comfort her.

He heard another siren and stood to look out the window again, this time without parting the curtains. There were now a dozen or more police cars in the street and at least one wagon. A captain, his gold bars gleaming in the low afternoon sun, emerged from an all-black car and walked to the bottom of the stairs. He turned his back to the house and spread his arms. Slowly the cops dispersed, moving away and into their cars. One young cop who Don recognized from high school—though he couldn't remember his name—abruptly turned and shot his fist into the sky, delivering a one-finger salute to the window where Don stood.

JOSEP ARRIVED AT the office just before ten and barely had his outdoor jacket off and a black cloth draftsman's coat on when Lucio slipped a tiny, steaming cup into his left hand. Josep walked to the far end of the office, stopping for several minutes at each table on his way. It was almost eleven and Josep was one table away when Pascal walked in, waved gaily at everyone, but at no one in particular, and headed towards his own table. He arrived at Ben's table at the same time as Josep and made the introductions.

"You will be working with Pascal and Jared on the Yemeni project. We have heard much talk about you. Now all we shall see what you are." Josep was as stone-faced as Lucio had been.

Ben felt a barely-camouflaged resentment from the two of them. He thought of his father and his clearly uncamouflaged anger and relaxed. He could deal with this.

"Come. Take a walk with me. We'll get some coffee."

Ben follow Pascal out the door and down the stairs. Pascal didn't stop at the floor below but continued down the stairs through the courtyard and the large double doors into the street. He took Ben's arm and led him to the corner where they sat at a café table with both seats facing the street.

"There is a gathering and a small performance that I'd like you to attend tonight. It's in the eighth at the British Embassy. I'll give you the address."

"I was going to take my things to the apartment."

"We're having them sent them over in a taxi."

"Okay, I guess." Ben wondered who would be paying for the taxi.

Pascal then talked about the classes he was teaching at the École des Beaux Arts and told Ben that he'd like him to help in the studio class. They finished their coffee and Jared joined them. They ate lunch and talked about Yemen and the new capital city project there. Just after two, Pascal paid the bill and they walked back to the office. They were about to head to the door when a man came through the other way carrying Ben's bags.

"Wait a minute. I need a few things from my bag." The man set the bag down and Ben opened it, extracting a blue jacket that almost matched his pants and a black polyester tie that sparkled dimly, an effect Ben had hoped would be less apparent under the jacket. It hadn't sparkled quite so much in the dim light at Kennedy's on Washington Street across from Filene's. He closed the bag and thanked the man.

"That cabbie seems awfully well-dressed," Ben said.

"He's not a cabbie. He's our valet."

"Oh." Ben realized he had a lot to learn and thought he should just be quiet until he did.

"Ben, lose the tie." Jared said.

Pascal laughed. "Yes, *definitely* lose the tie."

Ben rolled it up, walked into the storeroom and made a show of stuffing it—like a basketball into a hoop—into a galvanized steel barrel he had noticed there earlier.

Pascal laughed. "The trash man will have a nice surprise." He took Ben's arm again and they headed back across the courtyard.

26

BEN WALKED ACROSS THE PONT ROYALE, THROUGH the Tuileries Gardens and up Rue des Pyramides to Rue Faubourg St. Honoré. He stopped to check his small book of maps and turned left expecting to find the British Embassy there. Somehow he had expected a sign that stated "British Embassy" or the like but found nothing. He tried to remember whether Pascal had given him a street number but couldn't recall one. He looked up the street to see if there were people going into one of the buildings, but realized he had hurried over early, anxious as he'd been about losing his way or being late. Eight o'clock was nearly an hour away.

It struck him that a British embassy must have a British flag flying somewhere. He crossed the street and scanned the rooftops. Sure enough, he saw the Union Jack fluttering in the brisk breeze atop a building set back behind a gate. It was flanked by a couple of almost-matching buildings just a few doors down from where he stood. He crossed the street and noticed the small enameled sign with the number "39." It was the only signage on the building. Since he had already found the building and was still very early, he decided to take a walk and explore the surrounding streets He noticed several clusters of trim, uniformed men in flat-topped hats a block away, turned, and headed in the other direction.

TWO TUXEDOED MEN checked guests' names against a list. One wore a small French flag pin on his lapel, the other a British flag pin. Ben approached the man who wore the British flag and offered him his name. He noticed a bulge under the man's jacket just above the base of the clipboard the man held against his left chest.

"Welcome, Mr. Holt. You'll find Monsieur Satart in the lobby at the head of the stairs to your right."

"Thank you." Ben took the program offered by the man with the French flag and walked into the ground floor lobby, turning to climb the stairs. The stairway was mirrored above the wainscoting and Ben watched himself emerge in the mirror at the intermediate landing.

"Oh God," he thought, looking at the way the bright light from the chandeliers and the sconces accentuated the difference in the textures of his pants and his jacket. The mismatch was jarring and he felt overwhelmingly embarrassed.

"Ben!" Jared and Paul stood just off to the right of the head of the stairway, each with a long, thin-stemmed glass in hand, both glasses empty. Jared spoke first.

"We thought you might have gotten lost. You should have come back to the flat with us. We'd have all come together."

"I wanted to take a walk and get my bearings."

"Yes, we can see the dust of the Tuileries on your shoes." Ben looked down to see that his black shoes and the hem of his pants were mottled with a fine, gray-brown dust.

"You just missed the Aubrey's grand entrance. Money, power, and beauty...they do seem to flock together."

"Who are the Aubreys?"

"They host these soirées, usually here. *Monsieur* is French, *Madame,* British and the daughter, delectable."

"Pascal knows them?"

"*Monsieur* is a client. I think they are related somehow."

The lights dimmed and rose three times, three sets of double doors swung open, and the gathering began to move into an adjacent room. As they moved to the middle pair of dual doors, Ben noticed a thin man with a black eyepatch and a white dinner jacket looking at him. Ben blinked and the man was gone, leaving only a glimpse of his jacket as it disappeared from the room.

"Who is the man with the eyepatch?"

"William Button. He works for the American Embassy. Some sort of cultural attaché. We think he's a spy."

"Really?"

"Paul makes up histories for a lot of people we meet, especially those who reappear often. You can usually find Button at one of the cafés in the sixth near the École des Beaux-Arts or in the seventh near the Finance Ministry. The first suggests that he is a cultural attaché, the second..."

"A spy?"

"*Mad* for Claudine Aubrey. She lives nearby."

THE SEATS AT the back of the room were full, so Ben, Jared and Paul found three seats about a third of the way down the aisle in the middle of the left-hand row. The room was clad in paneling that had been painted a uniform white, but the flush panels had been covered with a loose fabric on some kind of backing. Ben would have guessed that it was Homasote, but he wasn't sure they even had Homasote in France. From the placement of the chandeliers, noticeably unsymmetrical, Ben surmised that the room had once been two rooms. The floor was flat except for a small, raised platform on which the musicians were slowly gathering. Two small rooms, one on either side of the platform, looked like they'd been built sometime after the two rooms had been combined into this larger space. The musicians entered from a door from the left-hand room. A podium stood in the center.

One of the violinists, seated immediately to the left of the podium, stopped his tuning and laid his violin on his lap. The other musicians took their seats; those who had been tuning their instruments became silent and assumed their performance postures. They sat there, their hands on their instruments or in their laps, until the door to the right-hand room opened and most of them stood.

A diminutive man walked briskly to the podium, tapped his baton twice, then raised it above his head, holding it there for what seemed like several minutes. He lowered his baton, looked down at the podium, raised his baton again, and the baton and the beat of the music became one.

At the end of the first piece, a momentary silence fell in the room. Suddenly, a young woman seated diagonally across the room from Ben rose and began clapping. She was thin and elegantly dressed, clad in a tight, black dress suspended from her bare shoulders by thin straps. She had short, chestnut-colored hair that emphasized her long, sleek neck, and when she turned toward the violinists, Ben saw a glimpse of her high cheekbones, wide mouth and trim nose. He was instantly smitten. He rose and applauded, looking intently at her until she finally glared back at him with a look that meant "*stop it.*"

Ben sank back into his seat.

"*That's* Claudine," Paul whispered into Ben's left ear.

THE RECEPTION ON the lower floor was as lively as the performance had been sedate. Ben stayed close to Paul and Jared as the other guests gathered in groups of friends and acquaintances.

A half-hour into the party, Pascal approached the trio, apologized to Paul and Jared, and led Ben away by the elbow. "I want you to meet my cousin, his wife and their daughter."

As they approached the partiers clustered around the Aubrey family, a space opened up in the crowd for Pascal and Ben. Claudine stood at the center, her father and mother directly to her left, and two men, one in his mid-fifties with ample black hair, the other, the "spy" William Button. Pascal introduced Marcel and Bernadine Aubrey, Claudine, the British ambassador and Button. Monsieur Aubrey smiled and said something to Pascal in French.

"He says that it is nice to meet the young man who honored his daughter with a standing ovation."

Ben felt the heat rising in his cheeks. "I'm sorry. *Desolé.*"

"Oh don't be," said Madame Aubrey in a distinctly British accent. "You were honest enough to do what all of the men secretly wanted to do." She turned to her husband, "Come, Darling, let's leave the young people to themselves." The senior Aubreys and the ambassador moved away. Pascal followed.

"*Bonjour. Il fait beau de vous recontrer. J'ai entendu beaucoup au sujet de vous.*" The phrase was one of two dozen that Ben had written down in a notebook and memorized over the last two weeks.

Claudine glared at him, unsmiling, fixing Ben in her super blue eyes. A corolla of gold marked the upper perimeter of her left iris. "If you can't speak French without a New England accent, you shouldn't be trying to speak French at all."

"Oh, I speak *English* with a New England accent, as well."

Claudine blew through her pursed lips, turned and walked away.

"Well done." Button stood next to Ben and watched Claudine glide through the crowd and all but disappear, her red-brown hair bobbing above the sea of gray and freshly-dyed blonde hair.

BEN CAME ACROSS Paul and Jared near the door to the reception room. They were planning to go to a bistro in the Marais and wanted Ben to join them. Though he protested that he should go to the apartment and unpack, he ended up in the Marais sitting at a small table outside the Café des Musées drinking pastis and beer late into the crisp night. When Jared suggested they go to a nightclub in the eighth, Ben thought of protesting again, but surrendered. As they were rising from the table, a black Citroen pulled alongside the curb. The rear passenger-side window slid down to reveal Claudine's face framed in its opening.

"Join me?" she said, gesturing towards Ben. This was somewhat less than a command, but more than a request. Ben stood motionless until he felt a firm hand pushing him in the small of his back. He moved towards the door that opened to receive him, and Claudine slid further into the car. He closed the door behind him and looked back through the open window for his friends, but they had already walked away. As the window rose, controlled from elsewhere in the car, he noticed a familiar figure sitting at the bar inside the café, his jacketed back to the street. Just as the window closed, Ben noticed Button's eyepatch in the mirror behind the bar, his good eye unblinking.

27

WHEN BEN AWOKE, THE SUN ON THE BACK OF HIS neck felt soothing, but it failed to block the pain of his throbbing head. He tried to move, but movement made him feel dizzy. He moved back into the sun's warming rays and buried his face in the pillow. After a few minutes he realized that he had no idea where he was. Had he made it back to the apartment? Apparently not. The pillows smelled softly of flowers. He needed to find out where he was, but his need to remain in this heavenly shaft of sunlight was even stronger. He quickly fell back into sleep.

When he awoke again the sunlight had moved away and was now lighting the wall several feet away. Ben turned onto his back, opened his eyes and saw that the sun was entering the room through a pair of windows opposite the bed. The room had been decorated in tones of gray and maroon. There was a small sofa and two chairs arranged around a low table near a second set of windows. A chest occupied the wall across from the foot of the bed, with a door on either side. A tall mirror leaned against an adjacent wall and faced the open windows, offering a skewed view of the trees outside. Another door was set to the left of the mirror in the corner of the room furthest from the bed. It was this door from which the faint knocking came. It was a long time before Ben realized he should respond to the knocking.

"Yes?"

The door opened and a man in a black suit and white shirt entered carrying a tray with a gleaming pot and several plates. He set the tray on the low table.

"Where am I?"

"Mademoiselle Aubrey will return at four."

"What time is it now?"

"Just after midday. I am Robert. You may not remember, but we met last night. I was driving *Mademoiselle.*"

"Oh, yes." Ben thought *maybe* he remembered Robert.

"There is a dressing gown at the foot of the bed. *Mademoiselle* has arranged to have some clothes delivered for you. I will bring them up when they arrive."

Ben realized he was naked under the sheets except for his shorts. "What happened to my clothes?"

"They were, unfortunately, destroyed."

"What, in God's name, did I do last night?"

"Nothing. You fell asleep in the car."

Robert moved through the door and was gone. Ben noticed that he had opened one of the doors on the opposite wall, revealing a bathroom. He thought that he might make it to the bathroom if he could just grab the edge of the open door and rest there before venturing on. He moved slowly across the room and grabbed the open bathroom door. He leaned against the open edge of the leaf until he could gather the strength to move on. Then he moved into the bathroom where, using the sink to support himself, he stood before the toilet.

After relieving himself, he decided it was now or never and set out back into the bedroom. When he arrived, he dropped heavily into a chair in front of the low table and surveyed the breakfast before him. A tray had been arranged with baguette, butter, jam and a small round bowl of plump, fresh figs. He poured a dark black coffee from the larger of two pots into a cup and, finding that the smaller pot contained hot water, thinned the coffee and lifted the cup to his lips.

"BUT, *WHY*, CLAUDINE?"

Claudine said nothing, but snapped her handbag shut, the clap punctuating her silence.

"For that American *child*?"

Claudine opened the door and slipped into the darkness beyond, leaving the door open. Étienne sat in the high-back chair for several minutes, watching the empty darkness. Finally, he arose, walked to the door and closed it.

The fact that Claudine had been born rich and beautiful burdened her. She had always been the object of male attention—either for her beauty, her money, or both. Not one of her suitors had ever wanted to know who she really was. Not one of them had asked, not one of them had ever listened.

She'd had her share of companions and lovers. The younger men—her age—were fast talkers and fast lovers, braggarts in and out of bed. The older men were more subtle and spent more time with her—reciting the resumés of their business or sporting successes as a prelude to the bedroom. A few had asked about her design business, but none had ever listened to her answers and usually veered off into another story about how their accountancy or law firm was as innovative as any design business.

Claudine and Ben had spent much of the night sitting in her courtyard, talking sparely, enjoying the night sky. She had been disappointed when Pascal stopped by, thinking that he would absorb all of Ben's attention. Both men had seemed more interested in listening to her until Ben had fallen asleep in the garden and Pascal had excused himself.

"Be kind to him, Claudine. I am very fond of him. He is a magical soul."

Pascal had walked home, and Claudine had watched Ben's face as he slept, bathed in the soft light of a lace-covered moon.

"YOU WERE WITH the most desirable woman in Paris, perhaps in all of France, and you were *asleep*?"

"Apparently."

"And what did you do all day yesterday?"

"Claudine was out most of the day. After breakfast, lunch, or whatever it was, I sat out in the courtyard. That's about it until she came home and we talked, had some dinner and talked some more."

"Did you sleep with her?"

"I don't think so."

Jared shook his head. "What now?"

"Robert is waiting downstairs. I'm grabbing some things. Then I'm going to meet Claudine at her parents' house."

Jared noticed that Ben wasn't packing any clothes.

Ben anticipated his unspoken question. "Claudine brought me some clothes."

"Ah. So you're not her lover...you're a project."

"Maybe."

"You do know she's a fashion designer?"

"Yes. Women's clothes. She's not bringing dresses."

Jared held up both hands, framing Ben between his thumb and index finger. He smiled, shook his head and left the room.

28

BEN WALKED THE SHORT DISTANCE FROM CLAUDINE'S home at 11 Sebastian Bottin to the office on Rue Saint Thomas D'Aquin each day, stopping at the Le Saint-Germain café at the corner of Rue de Bac and Boulevard Raspail to meet Pascal if he was in town. Claudine's poodle, Marguerite, would accompany him unless it was raining. While Ben and Pascal sipped coffee, Marguerite would eat her plate of ham, a treat strictly forbidden by Claudine, strictly ignored by Ben. One morning the energy at the table was more charged than normal. Pascal fidgeted and Ben kept looking down to check Marguerite's plate and inspect the passers-by. Each had something to say and was waiting for the right moment to say it. Pascal broke the uneasy silence first.

"Ben, I have a new project for you. Two really. We need to talk about them."

"Sure, but..."

"The first is an apartment building, the other an office building. You'll have to give up most of your work on the new city project, of course, but these are real projects that will be built."

Ben recalled the atrocious, inhuman concrete apartment slabs he had seen on his trips to Orly. He felt the designers had taken the concept of the apartments Corbu had created in Marseille and bastardized them. His anxiety must have shown on his face.

"Where?"

"New York. You'll have to spend a lot of time there. I'm sorry, I know that you and Claudine have grown very close."

"Pascal, Claudine is pregnant."

"I don't know what to say. Congratulations, of course. It *is* congratulations, *n'est ce pas?*"

"We're happy about it. It wasn't planned, but..."

"You'll get married, of course."

"We haven't talked about that yet. You know how she is. She certainly won't get married because she's expected to."

"No."

"It does complicate things."

"I could send Jared. He's very competent, but you have a special insight that brings a comfort and joy to your designs that is very appealing."

"Did Corbu have that?"

Pascal thought for a moment. "Corbu was sure of his designs, but he was Swiss. His intellect often ruled his heart. They fought. With you, they seem to enjoy each other."

"That's good, I hope."

"We'll see, we'll see. But, Claudine, the baby, this changes everything."

"Don't decide yet. We're going to Cannes for the summer holidays. I can start some work on the New York projects and we can make the decision on who goes to New York *à la retournée.* In September."

"Agreed."

"COME, TAKE A walk with me."

Tony Angelo had been waiting for Don outside his rooming house. He was leaning against the right fender of his Lincoln when Don approached. Don realized that this was not likely to be a friendly chat.

"You've been a good boy, a good lieutenant, and I'm adding that to your account."

"Thanks, Tony."

"No speaking, just listening." Tony wasn't smiling. "What did I tell you when I took you on?"

Don stood silently.

"*Now* you speak."

"No coming on to your daughter?"

"That, too. No *free-lancing*."

"Sorry, Tony...it happened only that once."

Tony Angelo grabbed the hair at the back of Don's head and pulled his face close to his own. "And don't lie to me. I hate liars."

"Sorry, Tony." Don was shaking. Tony pushed him away.

"And I know about your drinking. I can't have you drinking. It's a weakness of character I can't afford."

"Sorry, Tony...I can stop. I don't need it."

"Sorry, kid...I've heard that so many times I think half the world are drunks. I'm cutting you loose."

"But Tony..."

"That's my final answer, kid. Be happy that's all. You're smart. *Be* somebody."

"But Tony..."

"And I don't wanna see you or talk to you again. *Capeesh?* If you see me on the street, turn around and go the other way. We're done."

"But Tony..."

THEY SPOKE LITTLE on the flight to Nice. Marcel had stayed behind, but would join them in a few days. Ben assumed Marcel had made excuses so as to avoid the uncomfortable necessity of supporting his wife in her campaign for a wedding.

The cabin of the Learjet 24 was tight and the arrangement of the five passenger seats, coupled with the noise of the engines, discouraged long conversations. Before they'd departed, Marcel had showed off this new acquisition, reciting specifications and noting for Ben's benefit that the jet's engines were made by General Electric, though he wasn't sure whether they were made at the Lynn jet engine plant. Ben was impressed that Marcel had gone to the effort to make the connection between the engines, details of GE's operations, and Ben's hometown.

After the plane landed, the pilot taxied to an area of the field beyond the terminal and parked near an ivory Cadillac convertible that Ben immediately identified as a 1958 El Dorado Biarritz, distinguished from the '57 by its quad headlights and the vertical chrome strips on its lower, rear-side panels. He knew there had been only eight hundred or so of these cars made and that they were the last of those he considered truly elegant. By 1959, the cars had sported more chrome, more severe tailfins, and taillights mounted high on the fins. Don had always argued for the 1959, but Ben had been strongly in the 1958 camp.

Ben thought of Don and their silly arguments, arguments like Ben's championing of the 1956 Ford Sunliner versus Don's Chevrolet Bel Air of the same year. Don had argued for the Beatles versus Ben's Beach boys, although Ben had secretly switched to the Beatles after the release of the Revolver album. Standing in the Riviera sun, the private jet behind him, this beautiful car in front of him, Ben thought of how much he missed his brother and wished he could share all of this with him.

"Why don't you sit in front, Ben?" Berrnadine Aubrey was in charge, as usual, supervising the loading of the trunk and the seating arrangements. Ben opened the door and pulled the seat back so Claudine could slip into the rear seat. As she slid by him she kissed him on the cheek and grabbed his left arm, a sign of encouragement, he thought, for the days—actually weeks—ahead. He looked for a sign that she was beginning to show, but saw none. He could see the low mounding of her belly when they lay together in bed, but she chose her wardrobe carefully to delay revealing her pregnancy to others.

Ben stood by the open passenger door with Arturo, who ran the Cannes household with his wife Magrita, and ushered Bernadine into her seat beside Claudine. Arturo waited until Ben was seated before moving into the driver's seat and starting the car. As they drove along the coast to Cannes, Ben thought of his rides with Annie to

Rockport. They seemed so long ago. So much had happened in those few years he could never have imagined: Harold, the BIA, Vincent, Pascal, Claudine, Paris, and Cannes. The sun, the breeze, this car, and the smells of the plants and the sea all added to the sense that this was but a dream. Ben's reverie was broken when the car turned through a pair of Art Deco gates onto a pebble drive and into a courtyard before a stone and stucco-faced house.

Arturo barely had the trunk open before a short, round woman with gray hair and laughing eyes bounced from the house and wrapped her arms around Claudine, kissing her on both cheeks. She began rubbing Claudine's belly in gentle circles, talking to it first in what sounded like Spanish, then French. Ben had never seen Claudine so openly animated. Ben looked over at the grimacing Bernadine. She never allowed the familiar form "*tu*" with the staff in Paris, nor did Claudine. Ben liked this change in Claudine.

There were four buildings on the half-hectare of land that was the Aubrey's southern home. There was the main house, a guest house where Ben and Claudine would stay, the caretakers' cottage, and a four-car garage that also housed the pool house on the lower side which faced two pools and the Mediterranean. The two larger houses were in the art deco style, the guesthouse more ostentatiously so. The caretakers' house was more simple, in the same fieldstone and stucco, but without decoration. Ben thought it might be his favorite of the buildings.

From the guest house, large wood and glass doors opened from the salon and the bedroom onto a stone courtyard overlooking the beaches and the group of islands beyond. To the lower right sat the main house separated from the guest house by more stone terraces, dotted with huge pots of rosemary. The hillsides were landscaped with a profusion of bright flowers set before backgrounds of lavender and a bay hedge.

As Ben looked out across the sea, he could make out the spire of a small church on one of the islands. The spire was surrounded by blank stone walls and at the far end of the island stood a stone structure that Ben thought must be a fort. He asked Claudine about the structures in the distance and she explained that the church and its surrounding buildings made up a monastery. The monks there produced honey, she said, as well as the wines her father loved to drink when he was here—wines he loved so much he would sneak them by the case to his office in Paris. Claudine told Ben that her mother would only tolerate the wine at the dinner table in Cannes, but would not do so in the Paris home. Ben envisioned Marcel opening the bottle in his office after a particularly demanding day, enjoying the memory of Cannes and the sea.

STANDING OUTSIDE THEIR bedroom as the sun set, Ben bent over and ran his hands over the rosemary in one of the pots. He raised his scented palms to his face, then offered them to Claudine. She rubbed her cheeks in Ben's open palms.

"*Mercî*, my dear Ben, for your gift."

"You're welcome, but it is only a very tiny gift."

"But no, it is a most wonderful gift." Ben's heart swooned in the sparkle from Claudine's eyes. "A small gesture, perhaps, but a great gift. Rosemary is the herb of remembrance and it brings to me wonderful memories of this place and the happiness and peace I have always found here. Now it will bring me memories of you."

"I love you, Claudine." Ben wrapped his arm around Claudine and she leaned into his embrace.

"Come. Let's sit and watch the moon rise." Claudine took Ben's hand and led him to the low stone wall.

EACH TUESDAY, CLAUDINE and Marcel would fly to Paris, returning in time for dinner on Thursday. Claudine was working on several new pieces—mostly dresses and the new shirt line for her Spring Collection. Though she didn't have a runway show during fashion week, her tradition was to have spring designs ready so that her clients could be part of the excitement surrounding the week-long schedule of shows and parties. On cne of these return trips from Paris, Bill Button flew with them. He was headed to Monaco and the Cinque Terra, then to Milan, Florence and Venice. He stayed for dinner and was joined at the Aubrey's by an arresting, dark-haired woman who struck Ben as extraordinarily quiet. Her eyes were so dark as to be almost black. They showed no emotion, no reaction, no light as they swept the room or stared intently at each person in turn. Her name was Rachel.

After dinner, as Bill and Rachel prepared to leave on the motorcycle that Rachel had arrived on, Bill invited Ben to meet them in Italy during one of Claudine's absences. Ben promised he would, but had no intention of following through. He was intrigued by Bill, but disliked the easy way he related to the Aubreys—and especially to Claudine.

BEN AND CLAUDINE lay in bed, the large window open to admit the moonlight. Ben was propped on his left elbow, his right hand lightly caressing Claudine's belly.

"You really should go to Italy to meet Bill and Rachel," Claudine said. "Meet them in Venice. You've wanted to go see the Piazza."

"I'd rather go with *you*."

"Meet them in Venice, then come to meet me in Milan Friday morning. I have some things I need to do there and I need to visit Carlo Barbera's mill in the Piedmont. We can drive back together from Milan.. It'll be nice for us to be away from my mother."

"I'm not sure about Rachel…She's kind of spooky."

Claudine laughed. "Of course she is. She works for the Agency for International Development. She is a spy."

"How do you know that?"

"Everyone knows that. Everyone knows that Bill Button's credentials as cultural attaché are a cover. He's CIA, too."

"And you want me to visit them?"

"They are no threat to you. They have jobs, that's all. Besides, you *like* Bill."

"Yes. I do like Bill, although I think he likes *you* a bit too much, and sometimes I wonder if likable is his profession."

"Bill is not having our baby. *We* are. Isn't that enough for you? When I dream of our baby growing up, you are there. When I dream of our family, you are there. Isn't that enough? When I come home, I come home to *you*."

Ben couldn't find the words to answer. He lay back and his head sank into the pillow. He closed his eyes and hoped that Claudine couldn't see the moisture beginning to fill the corners.

DON HAD PICKED up the cab from the garage at four o'clock the previous afternoon and it was now almost three in the morning. He was cold and tired. He had to turn the heat off because the heater blew exhaust fumes back into the car when it was parked. His few fares the evening before had complained about the open windows, but Don figured the fresh air was better than killing them with carbon monoxide.

It would be a few more hours before the morning traffic to the airport began. He turned down the volume of the two-way radio, opened another can of beer, and lit up a cigarette. Within a few minutes, he was sound asleep, his head dangling backwards over the seatback and his mouth hanging wide open. Drool crept slowly from the corners of his mouth and pooled just above the "Central Square Taxi" logo on his shirt.

"Hey, hey, get out of there. Unlock the door!"

Don was awoken by a hand being slapped repeatedly on the windshield. He couldn't see the face that the hand belonged to, but he was immediately, intensely aware of smoke choking his lungs and heat coming from his right. He grabbed the door handle and fell from the cab onto the street. When he stood up, he saw that the passenger seat of the car was bright with flames. Within moments, the entire cab was engulfed.

He felt an arm slide beneath him and drag him to the opposite sidewalk. He could hear approaching sirens somewhere deep in his near-consciousness. He looked at the cab, stood shakily, shrugged, turned, and walked away down the street.

WHEN BEN ARRIVED at Marco Polo airport, a porter was waiting for him. Ben was glad he didn't have to find his own way to the hotel. The flight had been longer than Ben had hoped and the itinerary from Nice to Lyons and then to Venice had been taxing. The porter gathered Ben's luggage and they headed to the water taxi that was already waiting at the dock. The trip along the Grand Canal to the Lagoon was a revelation for Ben. Never had he seen such a layering of color and texture in buildings. The variety of open spaces to the right and left alongside the canals fascinated him. He took out his sketchbook and drew furiously; a view—followed by a vision—followed by an idea.

He was met at the Hotel Metropole dock by the hotel's general manager who arranged to have the bellboy take Ben's luggage while he led Ben on a tour of the hotel's facilities—including the kitchen, which Ben found particularly interesting. He then escorted Ben to his rooms.

The suite was spacious with high ceilings and somewhat more decoration than Ben would've liked. Walking through the large entry foyer that Ben would have been happy to have as a hotel room, the manager led Ben into the sitting room and on into the bedroom through a door inlaid with gold. Three tall windows in the sitting room and two in the bedroom opened onto the lagoon. Both the sitting room and the bedroom had ornately carved fireplaces. The suite also had two bathrooms and a large walk-in closet.

"I hope this will do."

The statement struck Ben as hilarious, but he stifled the laugh that struggled to break free. "Yes. It will be very nice."

"Will Mademoiselle Aubrey be joining you?"

"No. We're meeting later in Milan."

"Ah. Well, Milan's gain is our loss."

The manager bowed slightly from the waist and left Ben wondering how well he knew Claudine. Everyone seemed to know Claudine. Despite his fathering their child, despite the fact that they lived together, Ben felt like a relative stranger to her. Maybe, he thought, it was just the pain that remained from Annie's dumping him. As he was pondering this, several phones rang and he looked around the room for one of them. He found one on a table beside the sofa. After a short conversation that was strangely workman-like, he and Bill Button agreed to meet in an hour-and-a-half not far from the Rialto bridge. Ending the call, Ben lifted the receiver again and arranged for a water taxi.

BEN ALIGHTED FROM the water taxi at the dock at the base of the Rialto bridge. He stood and looked at the bridge for a few moments, watching people walk up and down the steps, peer over into the canal then disappear as they moved around couples and groups posing for hidden photographers. He resolved to walk back to the Metropole over the bridge, then headed up the narrow streets to meet Bill and Rachel.

As he entered the Cantina do Mori, he saw them standing near the back of the small bar. Bill held a tumbler of red wine, which he raised upon noticing Ben.

"Glad you came." Bill slipped his right hand over Ben's right shoulder and drew him closer to the bar. He raised his left hand, index finger extended, to signal the bartender and pointed to his glass. The bartender soon arrived and laid another tumbler of red wine on the zinc counter.

"Thank Claudine for that. She encouraged me to come to see the Piazza before I meet her in Milan." Ben reached past Button and picked up the glass. He raised it to his nose, then took a sip before setting the glass back on the bar.

"So it's a working trip for both of you."

"I suppose it is."

Rachel was quiet as usual, staring rather intently at Ben's face, as usual, without making eye contact. Ben leaned in and kissed her on each cheek. When he lightly touched her hip with his right hand while withdrawing from his second kiss, he noticed her eyes widen noticeably. He detected a hint of a smile before her face shut down again.

"Nice to see you, too, Rachel."

Bill slid two plates of small appetizers towards Ben.

"Cicchetti?"

Ben took a piece of squid first and ate the salty, grilled seafood, washing it down with a good-sized gulp of red wine. He would never have eaten squid—or an awful lot of other unfamiliar foods—before he'd left home. He had learned that unfamiliar foreign foods wouldn't kill him. The squid tasted appealingly of seawater, but the texture was something he would have to get used to. He slid a piece of grilled eggplant into his mouth, erasing the texture of the squid, and sipped gently on the wine.

The three of them spent the next hour in small talk. They talked of their hometowns, parents and siblings, Paris and Cannes. Bill mentioned that Rachel's agency was funding part of the Yemen project in the Satart office. Rachel acknowledged this with a nod. They ate several more small dishes, mostly seafood and tiny sandwiches. Bill and Ben drank three more tumblers of wine while Rachel drank sparkling water.

"It has been nice getting to know you a bit better," Bill said. Ben noticed his tone had changed, had become more serious. "This is a working trip for us, too. Let's take a walk."

Rachel didn't take her eyes off Ben's face as Bill spoke. She waited until the two men had headed for the door before slipping some paper money and a few coins onto the table and following them. They walked for several minutes before Bill spoke again.

"We've noticed that you've avoided the demonstrations and the antiwar groups while you been here. Why is that?"

"Don't make the mistake of thinking that means I support the war. I don't. I am not comfortable with zealots of any stripe and the demonstrations feel as if they are produced by interests as unappealing to me as those who execute this war."

"Is that *you* speaking," Bill said, "or Claudine?"

"We share many things, including politics, and I can't deny that some of her views influence mine, but this comes from me. I suppose that being with her encourages me to be comfortable with my feelings, whether political, moral or creative."

"You *do* know that her father makes great profit from the war… or don't you?"

"Yes. I don't know the details because his businesses are so varied, but yes…I do."

"That doesn't bother you?"

"No, it doesn't. Maybe it should, but it doesn't."

"Do you talk with him about that?"

"No. No, not really." Ben stopped for a couple of steps, then walked on.

"You're lying." Rachel turned and looked him intensely in the eyes. He couldn't read anything in her eyes or in her facial expression. Bill touched her lightly on the arm and she turned away from Ben. The three of them walked on silently for a few moments.

"Do you know that Jared and Paul are planning to leave and go to work for a Vietnamese architect they met at a demonstration?"

"No." Ben was shaken by Bill's pronouncement. He looked towards Rachel for confirmation of Bill's story, but she was watching Bill's face.

"We'd like you to start going to the demonstrations." Rachel turned to face Ben. "We'd like you to get involved with the planners. We'll give you cover and a credible backstory. Jared and Paul may only be small players, but there are others they know who we need to know more about."

"You want me to spy on Paul and Jared for you?"

"We want you to step up and serve your country."

"I'm no snitch."

"There are bad people involved in the so-called peace movement who aren't looking to create a peaceful world. They're looking to destroy peace and to destroy America. Your friends are dupes. Guys like you piss me off. You want freedom, but you are not willing to get your hands dirty." Rachel prodded Ben in the chest with a closed fist.

Bill stepped between Ben and Rachel. "Don't say no. Think about it, we'll talk when you and Claudine return to Paris." Bill offered his right hand to Ben and held Ben's right shoulder in his left hand. They shook hands. Then Ben turned and walked back towards the Rialto bridge.

"Why did you lie to him about Jared and Paul?" Rachel demanded to Bill's turned back.

29

"IT WILL BE A TRICKY MOVE."

"I know, but you would agree that I need to expand my market and there are more wealthy women in New York than in Paris."

Claudine and Marcel sat facing each other as the private jet taxied to the end of the runway. The co-pilot turned and called into the cabin that they were taking off. Claudine and Marcel leaned back in their seats, Claudine closing her eyes, her father watching her and admiring the woman she had become. He was happy that she had been spared the constant fear of growing up under the double cloud of depression and war as he had. He had watched her contemporaries and lamented their squandering their lives. They were, he thought, untested and unprepared for responsibility. He admired his daughter's gravitas, yet worried about her decision to carry her baby and marry Ben. She seemed so sure about both decisions and he knew that she would never make a decision, big or small, without being sure. Her confidence comforted him. Still, she was his only child, his daughter, and any man would remain an interloper in his heart.

As the plane reached cruising altitude, Claudine released her seat belt. Marcel left his on and gave Claudine an inquiring look.

"The baby," she said.

"Ah."

"I told Bernadine that we can have a reception in Paris when we return, but I think she's worried that the baby will make me look like a hausfrau."

"Why not wait until June, after the baby is born, and we can celebrate your baby *and* your marriage? A June wedding wouldn't be so bad..."

"Marcel, we've talked about this. Ben and I will be married as soon as we get back to Cannes...just Ben and I, you and Bernadine."

"I'm not surprised that Ben agreed to this, but I thought you'd want something bigger... maybe use it as a marketing event. It would be *very* big, you know."

"I don't want a circus wedding. Besides, Ben doesn't even know yet."

Marcel shrugged, his palms turned towards the ceiling. *"Bien sur."*

BEN SPENT MOST of two days studying the Piazza. He sketched the church, the belltower and the view out to the lagoon, but he spent most of his time wandering the approaches to the Piazza from several streets. Some of the streets were not much wider than paths and some of the canals no wider. He began to think of each approach as a different narrative and wrote lists of phrases in his sketchbook that described his procession. To save time, he created a shorthand of symbols to replace words.

ON FRIDAY MORNING, Ben flew to Milan and met Adamo, a young man who worked in one of Marcel's automobile parts factories, at the gate. Adamo led Ben to a red Opel GT, handed him the keys, and reviewed with him a street map marked with the location of Ben's hotel. Adamo wished him a good stay and got into the passenger side of a waiting black Fiat. The Fiat disappeared into the heavy airport traffic made up of small cars and large trucks.

Ben thought it must be getting close to the time for Claudine's plane to land. He wondered if he should try to meet her here or go on to the hotel. It would be nice to wait for her, to see her here, but he wasn't sure he'd be able to find her. He decided to drive on to the hotel.

After a couple of missed turns and refiguring his route from the map, Ben finally arrived at the Principe de Savoia about a half hour later than Adamo had suggested he would. At the front desk he was told that Claudine had already checked in and was in the spa. She had asked that Ben join her.

"I should go to the room and change first."

"No need, sir, they'll take care of you at the spa," the clerk said. "Giselle, can you take Mr. Holt to the spa?"

A dark-haired woman looked up from the book she was writing in. Instantly, Ben felt a jolt of electricity shoot through his body. It was Rachel. Only after the woman had stood and come around the long desk to greet him did Ben begin to realize it wasn't Rachel after all, although the resemblance *was* uncanny. When they got to the door to the spa, the woman opened the door and stood aside for Ben to enter. "Have a good day."

Ben didn't respond, but watched the woman's face and realized the facial movements were all wrong; she definitely was not Rachel. Probably not.

Ben and Claudine lay naked under white towels on adjacent tables. Two masseuses straightened sheets, arranged towels, and heated oils. Two of the walls were painted a light cream; the two remaining walls were made of floor-to-ceiling glass which overlooked a large garden. The windows were covered by sheer white fabric stretched out over clear-finished maple frames, which hung from a track at the ceiling. Soft music played from under the tables. The sun brought a golden warmth to the room, and Ben found the whole effect to be crisply calming.

He tried to carry on a light conversation with Claudine. She only grunted in response, so he lay silently and drifted off into a half-sleep. He thought hazily of Bill and Rachel, Jared and Paul, the woman at the front desk, Yemen, his notebooks. He looked across to the other table to Claudine's serene face, her eyes closed softly, and thought how much she and the baby had come to mean to him. He felt togetherness even in the separateness of their lives. For the first time, he realized he had never been to her studio, nor her to Pascal's atelier. He realized how much he truly, completely loved her.

They spent three days in Milan, shopping and walking, eating and laughing, talking. Claudine brought Ben with her to visit a few workshops that she called *"petit mains"*: embroiderers, jewelers, and small suppliers of feathers and buttons. They ate breakfasts of fruit, pastries, and coffee. They enjoyed long sunny lunches and dinners of olives, nuts, cheese and bread. Each day Ben awoke and realized that he loved her more than the day before. Each day he resolved to ask her to marry him, but by the end of the day he worried his proposal might break the spell. Why, he reasoned, change something that worked so wonderfully as it was? He wondered what he would do if she said no. *Would* she say no?

On Monday they drove to the Barbera factory and spent most of the day with Carlo and his son, Luciano. They looked at fabric until Ben's eyes burned from staring at the small differences in texture and color. Finally, about two o'clock, they broke for lunch and spent the next five hours eating from small plates and drinking large tumblers of wine.

They slept late on Tuesday, gently and repeatedly excusing themselves from invitations to lunch, and accepted the Barbera's offer to have a picnic packed for their drive to Genoa. It struck them that taking a picnic to Genoa was akin to taking coals to Newcastle, but once they were on the road Ben was happy to have something to nibble on from the basket. Claudine drove the Opel—a little too fast and a bit too close to the shoulder on the curves, Ben thought. She seemed to enjoy the car's handling and crisp acceleration. She was quiet for the first half hour, but then slowed down and cruised along the straight country roads.

"We should be back in Cannes by noon on Friday," she said.

"Will Bernadine and Marcel be there, or are they already back in Paris?"

"They'll be there if you love me as much as you think you do."

"Huh? What does that...?"

"Ben, I want to marry you on Saturday."

Ben fell silent and they drove on for several minutes.

"Ben?"

"Yes, of course I'll marry you, but why Saturday? Why so soon? I haven't bought you a ring. I haven't even told my family you are pregnant."

"First, some rules: no rings, no wedding gown, no guests, no announcements...at least not yet. Just you, me, Bernadine and Marcel and the local priest...and Arturo and Magrita, of course. On Sunday night, Marcel and I are flying back to Paris. Now that the summer is over I need to finish my work for Fashion Week. When we go to New York, we can get married again for your family if you wish."

"Why the rush and why the secrecy?"

I'll introduce my new husband and announce my pregnancy at a party during Fashion Week. Until then it's secret. You can tell your family, of course."

"That may not be a good idea if you want it to be kept a secret for a month."

"As you wish."

"Can I ask you something?" Ben didn't wait for Claudine to respond. "Are you introducing some maternity wear?"

"I hate that term. I hate that idea. I have designed haute couture that my clients will love. *Some* of them may be pregnant."

"Can I see the collection?"

"You'll see it at the party when I introduce the collection...and you."

"One more question," Ben paused. "Do you love me?"

"I'm not sure what that has to do with anything...but yes, Ben, I love you. And before you start interrogating my belly, our baby loves you, too."

BEN LAY IN bed, listening to Claudine's breathing as he watched strings of clouds drift across the full moon, creating soft, dancing shadows on the patio. The wedding had been as uneventful as after-dinner drinks. The priest's ministrations had been minimal and he had been whisked off to have a glass of wine with the staff before being sent on his way with a box of food and a few good bottles. Ben had snuck down to the caretakers' courtyard to shake the priest's hand and see him off with an envelope containing five hundred francs.

"Oh, I've already been paid. They were very generous." The priest held up the box.

"I know. Use this as you will."

"You're very kind. God bless you."

"Goodnight."

THE BREEZE PICKED up and Ben could smell the humidity that was building for tomorrow. He drew in a large breath of the fine, fragrant air, full of the smell of the rosemary that Claudine loved, closed his eyes, and drifted off to sleep.

SUNDAY NIGHT CLAUDINE and Marcel flew back to Paris. Ben planned to stay until Tuesday when he would go to Marseille to pick up Claudine's new Lotus and drive it back to Paris. He had promised Pascal that he would visit Corbu 's housing project in Marseille before returning to Paris by the end of the week. Bernadine planned to stay in Cannes until the end of February, a week before the Paris fashion shows. It was an odd time, a sort of limbo. The marriage was to remain a secret for four weeks, so they were all trying, too hard it seemed to Ben, to be apart. He doubted that anyone cared.

30

WHEN BEN ARRIVED AT THE MARSEILLE AIRPORT HE was met by Laurent, the representative from the Rover "nego-ciant." Claudine's Lotus was waiting, its polished yellow fiberglass body gleaming in the Côte d'Azur sun. To call the car "low-slung" failed to describe it accurately. The roof barely rose to Ben's waist. Its rear window was a mere sliver of glass. Ben hesitated to try to get into the car, but Laurent reached into the driver's side and adjusted the seat, declaring the car ready to fit Ben's long body. It took some twisting and sliding to fit his legs beneath the steering wheel, but once that was accomplished he was surprised at how well it fit him. Laurent got into the passenger seat, demonstrated the controls and recited the car's specs and the modifications to the S2 that Claudine had ordered. The specs included a larger engine and nickel rims. Laurent reached over and started the engine. A throaty, well-tuned rumble sang a deep bass from behind them. Laurent's last task was to hand Ben a clipboard and ask him to sign for delivery. He then slipped from the car, wished Ben well, and rode away in the black Rover sedan that had been waiting for him.

Ben depressed the clutch, slipped into first gear and headed out to the autoroute, comfortable that his shifting produced only a barely-perceptible bucking. As he got used to the engine and transmission, he played at downshifting at turns and in traffic to hear and to share the sound of the engine. Once on the autoroute, he settled in for the drive to Lyons.

"I DON'T THINK we're on the same page on this."

"Why do you say that?"

Rachel could never read Bill's face, at least not as well as she could read others. That disturbed her, in part because Bill seemed to intuit her every thought. When she did read something in his face, she had the distinct feeling that Bill was playing her. In self-defense, she stared at his blank left eye to avoid giving herself away to his good right eye.

"I don't sense any enthusiasm for this project and I think you've been trying to subvert it. What I can't figure out is whether you're going solo or the company has you working another angle."

"What makes you think that I am not one hundred percent in?"

"First, the way you lied to Holt. You had to *know* he could find out that you lied. The power would shift and we'd lose him."

"That's all you've got?"

"Second, you seem to have gone native on the Aubreys. You're supposed to be tracking the more extreme elements of their labor unions—not putting yourself up for adoption to be the son they never had."

"Claudine is more than capable of being both their son *and* their daughter. Her father is about to name her to the board of the bank. In a year she'll be appointed to the board of MAE, the controlling company for all of his interests."

"What? How do you know this?"

"Sometimes adoption is only a minor goal."

After Bill left, a sense of panic overcame Rachel. She was losing control of the project she had hoped would finally move her up from Ops. If Bill was into the Aubreys through the front door, she would have to get in another way. That way would have to be through Ben.

RACHEL UNDERSTOOD THE rivalry between her chief and Bill's chief. Bill's chief was based at Langley. She had gamed her chief to get out of the domestic contact service and into Ops, but that was only the first gambit in her plan to move up in the Directorate of Plans. She had a sense that Ben would provide her with the next move. There was no way Bill was going to keep her from turning him.

The message she had sent her chief had been coded. She looked at her watch, noting that she had just over three hours before he would arrive at her apartment. She decided to get a massage and facial. It was Tuesday, so Marcia could probably fit her in. She slipped a bill and coins beneath the clasp on the plastic tray and rose from her chair. It was sunny and the bistro was busy. A couple slipped into the chairs behind her table as soon as she stepped away—German tourists extending their holidays.

It was a short walk home. As she climbed the stairs to the rooms on the floor below her apartment which Marcia had fitted out as a spa, she pondered Ben's likely route from the auto dealer to Paris. Ben had worked for Vincent Nivola before coming to Paris. Nivola and Pascal Satart had both worked with Le Corbusier and Ben had already visited the Unité project in Marseille. It was unlikely that he would pass up Ronchamp, even if it *was* a detour from the obvious route back to Paris. After her chief's visit tonight she could be in Belfort tomorrow morning, ready for the pilgrim's walk to Ronchamp.

She shed more than her clothes to lie on the table. She had developed the ability to shed any thoughts or anxieties, to concentrate on her breathing, the penetrating pleasure of Marcia's fingers, and the deep pressure from the heel of her palms. Her last thoughts were all of Claudine, how she had taught Rachel the sanguine pleasure of massage and how Rachel had loved her so deeply. Her thoughts were interrupted when Marcia lifted her hair and the warm oil spread across her shoulders like an incoming tide.

CHARLES ROSE THAT evening just before seven, dressing quickly after noticing the time on Rachel's bedside clock. His wife and children would be waiting for him, the children already fed and squealing for his attention, his wife readying the dinner to be shared after the children were in bed.

Rachel didn't begrudge her chief's domestic ritual. This was a business transaction, though not without its own enjoyment. Rachel knew that their arrangement offered her two routes to the execution of her plan—trading her attention for his acquiescence to her demands or blackmailing him if he balked. She knew that ultimately she'd need to implement the second option to arrange for her promotion to Plans and out of his department. For now, she only needed his cooperation.

"Will I see you tomorrow?"

"No, I'll be visiting Ronchamp."

"Ben Holt? Will you be taking Bill Button?"

"No."

JOHN GRAHAM HAD worked with Pascal and Vincent when they had worked in Corbu's atelier. He was the outside man, the construction manager who worked with the contractors to ensure the faithful execution of Corbu's designs. He had come to love Lyon while managing the La Tourette and Ronchamp projects and he'd retired to the city after the Master's death. He still hoped to see the church at St.-Pierre de Firminy built. His wife loved their small trips around the south of France and through much of Italy. Both had been born in England, though Marjorie intended to live out her life "in exile" as she told anyone who would listen. She was a charming and comfortable woman whose demeanor exposed the amiability lying hidden below her husband's gruff exterior.

Ben arrived mid-afternoon and sat with John in the garden, exploring the older man's memories of working with Corbu, Pascal and Vincent. Marjorie offered Ben a bed for the night, with an invitation to dinner and a declaration that he *must* have a good breakfast before setting out on the road again. The dinner was simple and perfectly tuned to the season and the region—rabbit with root vegetables that had been steamed over a bed of fresh herbs. The red table wine was pleasant and unobtrusive, allowing the herbs to shine and complementing the rabbit. Ben guessed Pinot Noir.

John and Ben talked well into the night, John regaling Ben with often humorous and always disarming stories about Corbu. There were stories of dinners interrupted by serendipitous moments when Corbu would be struck with an idea that required his immediate departure. One recollection involved a young acolyte who discovered an element in a Corbu design that did not conform to the Modulor. Corbu had peered over his heavy-rimmed glasses, studied the offending element briefly, then declared *"Tant pis pour Le Modulor!"*

The stories might have continued until morning, but Marjorie intervened and called John to bed with the suggestion that they continue the next morning. She offered John as a guide to the Latourette monastery. John extracted an agreement from Ben to join him for an early breakfast and a visit to the shrine. He headed off to join Marjorie, and the house fell silent for the first time in the hours.

RACHEL'S PLAN REQUIRED confirmation that Ben was en route to Ronchamp. She stayed one night at the Relais du Abergment-la-Ronce and flirted with the owner's son, Guy, who tended bar in the lodging's cafe and boasted that the motel, restaurant and gift shop would soon be his. She told the young Bibendum that she had made a horrible mistake and taken up with an angry and abusive American who was chasing her after she'd left him sleeping off another of his drunken nights. He would have forced her to have sex with him if he hadn't fallen into an alcoholic sleep. She should never have left him a note and regretted that she hadn't taken along her little dog, but she had to make a pilgrimage to Ronchamp and pray for guidance and for what she should do with her life. Abergment-la-Ronce seemed so peaceful, she mused.

The next morning, after a simple breakfast, she embarked on her pilgrimage with a promise from Guy to call her hotel in Belfort if he saw Ben and the Lotus.

IT STRUCK BEN that he was unlikely to have such an opportunity again any time soon, so he decided that side trips to a few wineries would be a pleasant diversion. He dawdled at wineries near Mâcon, in the hilly landscape not far from Beaune and along the spine of hills around Nuits Saint-George. The farmers and vintners were celebrating. The harvest was in, the grapes were crushed, and it was time to party. The feasts reminded Ben of the harvest fairs at home, but here it included a lot more wine—really *good* wine.

After three days of wine and bread and cheese, Ben thought it might be time to get back on the road. He thought about giving up his plans to go to Ronchamp, but decided he had to keep his promise to Pascal and Vincent. He missed Claudine and thought of calling her, but decided she would be busy with her own harvest and that it would be unfair—and probably unwise—to bother her. As he drove along the A36, he came across a motel and restaurant near Abergment-la-Ronce and pulled into its parking lot to look at his small book of maps. He thought of stopping for lunch, but instead decided he would drive to Besançon, have a late lunch, and rest for the night.

GUY COULD BARELY contain his excitement as he dialed the number for Rachel's hotel. He promised himself that he would use his gravest voice when speaking to her and he practiced it in his head while the telephone rang. Sadly, there was no opportunity to express his grave concerns for her safety: The clerk reported that Madame Hudson was out, but that he would be happy to take a message. Guy was crestfallen. He left the coded message that he and Rachel had agreed upon, "Tell her that the Lotus is in bloom."

"Of course, *Monsieur.*"

"Sign it, 'Love, Guy.'"

"Will that be all?"

Guy wanted to tell the clerk that that was not all at all, that he would be coming to Belfort to protect her, to save her from *"La Bête."*

"Yes," he said sadly and set the receiver in its cradle.

RACHEL READ THE message, noted the un-agreed upon addition, crumpled the message, dropped it in an ashtray, and smiled. "Hicks are the same everywhere."

31

"EXCUSE ME, MY CHILD, BUT I FEAR THAT YOU ARE lost."

Rachel had joined the group of pilgrims, all older women, at the visitors' center at the bottom of the road that climbed the hill to the chapel at Ronchamp. She wore the black mantilla that all the women wore, but her shapeless black dress and cloth coat failed to hide her long, slender, unwrinkled hands, and the low, black boots she wore only accentuated the sleek rise of her calves.

"Yes, Father. I got separated from my group. I stopped at the gift store to buy a prayer card for my sick mother and they headed up the road without me." As Rachel looked into the face of the priest, a tear fell from her left eye and descended her cheek.

As the priest lay his eyes on hers, she demurred and looked away.

"Then of course you must join us." He took her hand and led her to the front of his flock as they began the climb up the hill. They were nearing the crest when the crowd could hear the throaty gurgle of a sports car. All heads but Rachel's turned like a flock of curious doves as the Lotus slipped by.

"You weren't curious about the car?" the priest asked Rachel.

"I am weary of worldly things, Father."

"Ah, my lovely child, so beautiful inside and out." He pulled her arm beneath his and they continued their climb.

BEN AVOIDED THE gravel lot and parked the car on the road just below the chapel and almost at the feet of an older cleric draped in a white habit with black cincture. "Brother Francis?"

"You could only be Ben."

Ben looked confused.

"We don't get many yellow Lotuses up here."

"Yes, I guess you wouldn't. It's my wife's… I mean, my girl-friend's car. She's working so I'm driving it back to Paris. Anyway, both Vincent and Pascal asked me to deliver their greeting and to ask for your blessing."

"Please bring God's blessing to them, and to your bride. And you *must* tell me about the baby, but first let's take a walk and observe God's work, delivered through Corbu and his disciples."

Ben decided there was no reason to be surprised at the priest's knowing of the wedding and the baby—it could only be divine in-tervention in the form of Pascal Satart, aided by his cousin Marcel's loose tongue.

They walked first around the outside and Ben took out his sketch-book and captured the spirit of the massing and form in a few deft strokes. Using the side and the point of the pencil he described the light and shadow on the façade and in the window recesses. Brother Francis delighted in the sketches and noted Ben's use of a single dark stroke with the side of the lead to delineate the separation between the roof and the walls that had been Corbu's master stroke, greater even than the more famous detail of the windows.

As the sun cowered in the sky, they entered the chapel to observe the light strewn around the space. Ben slipped his sketchbook back into his pocket, let the sap drain from his muscles and drank in the spirit of the place. After several minutes they slipped silently out into the gaggle of pilgrims and tourists. A priest and a black-clad woman were climbing the hill when Ben noticed a familiar form crossing towards them from the parking lot. Bill Button was almost on top of the couple before they noticed him. Ben watched as Bill appeared to speak to them . The woman's hands shot to her sides, her upper body moving forward and back towards Bill in a staccato motion which Ben thought looked remarkably like a hen pecking grain. The woman turned back towards the priest and pecked a few moments more, then stomped off towards the parking lot.

The priest climbed the remainder of the hill and stopped briefly to address Brother Francis. "A troubled child, I fear."

32

IT WAS ALMOST NOON WHEN BEN APPROACHED PARIS. The sky was laced with woven clouds, pills of sun spotting the fabric. He decided to drop the car at home before meeting Pascal at Le Saint-Germaine. If traffic in the seventh wasn't bad, he'd take a shower and change his shirt. He thought it unlikely that Claudine would be home. He hadn't talked to her since he left Lyon although they exchanged short messages delivered by Robert or hotel clerks. Ben pulled the Lotus close to the large doors that separated the courtyard from the street, got out of the car to unlock the door, only to have Robert swing the doors aside for him.

"*Bonjour*, Robert."

"Good morning, sir. It's good to have you back."

"I'm glad someone missed me. Claudine was probably too busy to notice."

"It's that way twice a year, isn't it, sir? At least you were away and busy yourself this time."

Ben smiled and nodded. Robert looked up and down the street, then, stepping closer to Ben, took the keys to the Lotus and offered his hand. He spoke softly. "Let me be the first to offer my congratulations, sir, on your marriage."

"Thank you, Robert. I hope you approve."

"It's not my place to approve, sir, but I must say that we are all happy to see the changes in *Madame*."

"Oh, I doubt she'll change much."

"Of course, sir."

Ben walked through the service court toward the kitchen door. Claudine would not have approved of his route, but she would be working and wouldn't be aware of his transgression. Last spring, when she was working on the fall show, he would surreptitiously visit the kitchen staff. He loved to be there when the suppliers made deliveries and would often look through their wares and listen to their detailed descriptions of mushrooms and meats, fish and produce.

As he opened the door, Babette, her back turned to him, told him to leave the boxes in the pantry and to make sure that the tender vegetables weren't stacked under the root vegetables. "Don't leave any mushrooms," she ordered, "until I inspect them."

"Yes, ma'am."

Babette turned and looked, a broad smile growing. "You listen to me or I'm getting another vegetable man. Now get out of my kitchen before someone sees you."

"Are you glad to have me back?"

"Out!"

Ben retreated through the door to the huge dining room, skirted around the table that was already set for dinner, and headed through the stair hall. He stopped at the foot of the stairs. The walls of the stair hall had always been populated by paintings of Aubrey relatives. Ben had a few favorites, but had a hard time remembering all but a half-dozen by name. Marcel and Bernadine were there together, and there were two paintings of Claudine, at four and at fifteen. Next to them now hung a sheet of ivory muslin, apparently covering the latest addition. Ben smiled. Claudine hadn't told him that she had sat for a new portrait. He lifted the corner of the muslin and saw a man's booted foot. He lifted the muslin further and saw that the portrait was of Claudine and himself sitting in the garden at Cannes, Claudine holding a sprig of rosemary.

THE CLOCK IN the hall struck one note and Ben realized he was late to meet Pascal. He raced up the stairs, two at a time, through the bedroom and into his dressing room where he grabbed a green silk shirt, stripped off the T-shirt and sweater he had been wearing, and struggled in his haste to button the shirt, finishing only as he left through the front door out to the courtyard. When he got to Le Saint-Germaine, Pascal was sitting at their favorite table, sipping a glass of red wine and reading a folded-over magazine.

"Sorry I'm late." Ben slid into the chair next to Pascal who kept reading for a few moments.

Finally, Pascal looked up from his magazine and lowered his glasses. "Oh. You're here. Sorry, I was reading."

"Not a problem."

"Are you having lunch?"

"Yes, I'm starving. Did you order?"

"No, I haven't decided whether I'm going to eat."

"What's wrong?"

"Eat first, then we'll talk."

Ben ordered his usual lunch: a carafe of anonymous, though creditable, red wine, a bottle of Perrier, ham and sliced tomatoes dressed with balsamic, and a nod of olive oil. He barely touched the bread, but Pascal ate nothing else. Ben knew Pascal was a light eater at lunch, but this, and his demeanor, worried Ben. Still, he respected Pascal's ethic of enjoying the meal, even if it was only bread and wine.

After the plates were taken away, Ben offered Pascal some wine and, when Pascal nodded, split the remaining wine between two glasses. The sky had turned sunny and the day warm, which seemed to brighten Pascal's mood. He held up his glass towards Ben and they tapped glasses. Both then finished their wine and Pascal set his glass in front of him, staring into it.

"It's not so bad that we can't survive it, but it is a blow to the ego."

"Tell me about it."

"AID has withdrawn their support for the North Yemen project and the UN can't appropriate the money needed on their own."

Ben wondered whether this had anything to do with Rachel.

"Since the British withdrew from Aden two years ago, there has been a hope that North and South Yemen would unite, but progress has been slow. AID is moving its money to other projects that are developing more quickly."

Ben felt relieved. At least he hadn't screwed things up by rejecting Rachel's advances on behalf of the CIA. He thought of Paul and Jared.

"How does that affect Paul and Jared?"

"Not at all, really. They've been working on the New York project in your absence. They've been traveling back and forth, even during the holidays. America doesn't do holidays like we do. They seem to work all the time. I barely got away at all."

"I'm sorry. I probably could have been more helpful. At least I understand them."

"No, we always knew you'd be in Cannes, but I'm going to have to press you for an answer about New York."

"Ah, well there is a bit of a complication with the baby."

"I don't see how that's a complication since Claudine will be opening her show room in New York in the spring."

"What?"

"You didn't know?"

Ben took a long while before answering. He considered bluffing instead of admitting his ignorance of Claudine's plans. He reviewed their conversations in his mind for snippets of any mention of a new showroom in New York, but could find none. "No. I don't think I did. How did *you* know?"

"A broker who is working on the New York project asked if I knew her and said that her father's lawyer had inquired about space. That Claudine was the client was supposed to be secret, but evidently his lips loosen when he drinks. By the way, he thinks your wife is quite attractive."

"Pascal! Remember, I don't have a wife until Monday."

"Of course."

"Have you told Claudine that you know this?"

"No."

"Then don't. I don't want her knowing that I knew before she told me."

"Agreed. Now what about New York?"

"I'll let you know by Tuesday."

"Okay. Now, do you want to show me your sketchbooks?"

33

B EN HAD DECIDEDLY MIXED FEELINGS ABOUT FASHION
shows. He liked seeing Claudine's work on display in the comfortable atmosphere of the private showings that Claudine put on, but found
the few fashion shows that he attended, mostly charity events, to be unappealing, boring, and catty. They were charged with a thin energy that
he likened to façade-ism in architecture. There was nothing of substance
below the shallow skin.

This night would be different. It was Claudine's first runway
show and was to be the venue for the announcement of their marriage
and Claudine's pregnancy, as well as for the unveiling of Claudine's
plans for a New York studio and retail shop. The preparations for
the showing of her spring collection were more intense than usual.
She had brought on additional staff for the show but still insisted on
producing it herself. The pressure would have toppled most, but she
continued to be calm and unfluttered as the storm raged around her.
The coterie of staff, light and sound technicians, best-boys and grips,
the stage director, the model wrangler, makeup artist and publicist
all wrestled for bits of her attention.

In the waning days just before the show, she took to joining Ben
and Pascal for their usual lunch, arriving only minutes after them
but staying only twenty minutes. Ben would insist that he not go to
bed until she had come home and had eaten a light dinner with him,
no matter what time, and she acquiesced to letting him cook for her.

He offered her the bed alone, but she would not hear of it and settled each night into the warm curve of his body. He would place his hand over the baby's beating heart, breathing her scent and noting the soft changes that had occurred during her pregnancy—more fig and walnut now, less citrus, less floral.

She would fall asleep quickly, her breathing soft, and he would lie awake, unwilling to move, unwilling to break the physical connection between the three of them, lest they be lost. He felt that if he lost them, he would not die—he would simply cease to be.

THERE WERE MORE than three hundred people in the ballroom, far more than the usual thirty or so women who had attended one of Claudine's two showings during each of the semiannual fashion weeks. There was a scattering of men, mostly there to carry the wallets, and a few of them sat in the front row of the section at the end of the elevated T-shaped runway. This was the area reserved for press and photographers. Claudine's best clients were seated along the front rows on either side of the long stem of the T, interspersed with the most important of the fashion editors and writers who, it was hoped, would be infected by the enthusiasm of Claudine's regulars.

Ben was seated at the base of the T, alongside Marcel and Bernadine. Claudine had made a suit for him out of a cashmere and silk fabric he had selected at the Barbera mill. He wore the jacket open over a black turtleneck, hating as he did the "tyranny of a buttoned jacket." While Marcel and Bernadine chatted with the people sitting around them, Ben sat silently watching the production staff go about their chores.

At the end of the show, Claudine emerged from the dark of the backstage into a pool of light that followed her as she walked the length of the runway to be greeted by the models gathered at the head of the T. The band was supplemented by the music of a standing ovation and calls and whistles from the crowd. She stood at the far end, away from Ben, hugging each model and acknowledging the audience with waves and smiles. As the models walked back down the runway, the music softened and a black-sleeved arm reached up and handed Claudine a microphone. She stood and waited for the crowd to quieten down.

"Most of you know that this is my first runway show."

Applause and calls of "Bravo!" erupted again.

"... and it is a very special night for us..."

Applause.

"... even more so because I want to share some things with you."

Lighter applause.

"Some of you, especially my American friends, have asked when I would be bringing my work to the US."

Enthusiastic applause from parts of the crowd.

"The time has come and we will be opening a studio, and my first retail store, on Madison Avenue next January, so it will be Bon Année in New York for us."

Extended applause and more "Bravos!"

"Thank you. I have two more announcements that are even larger for me personally and even closer to my heart."

A single spotlight came up on Ben and he arose and climbed the stairs beside him. One of the models met him at the end of the runway and placed a pair of doves on his left forearm. One fluttered briefly, then settled down as Ben walked the length of the runway. The single light followed him. As he approached Claudine, he saw tears welling up in her eyes.

"I didn't know you were going to do this." She turned to the crowd, "I didn't know he was going to do this." She buried her head in Ben's right shoulder. The crowd erupted into extended applause. Ben worried that the noise would disturb the doves, but Claudine caressed the back of their necks and they stayed calm.

Claudine lifted the microphone again. "This is my husband, Ben. I had memorized more that I wanted to say, but I can't remember any of that now."

Applause, bravos, and bits of conversation filled the room. The black-sleeved man who had delivered the microphone rose to the runway and took the doves. Claudine and Ben kissed warmly and

Ben held her tightly in his arms. He felt that she didn't want to let go. Taking the microphone from her, he whispered in her ear and she whispered a response.

"I'm sure that most of you have noticed that Claudine is pregnant. Claudine wants me to thank all of you again and to tell you we will be joined by a third—a boy—in January."

Ben motioned to the lighting man to cut the light, then they walked the length of the runway to applause and calls of "We love you, Claudine!" "Congratulations, Claudine!" "Wonderful, wonderful!" Just before they exited the runway, Ben stopped in the single remaining pool of light and turned to the seats which Marcel and Bernadine were sitting in. He extended his arm to them in invitation and they rose from their seats, climbed the steps, and embraced first Claudine, then Ben.

As they all moved from the runway, Ben noticed a face at the back of the ballroom in the light of an exit sign—a face with a single eyepatch.

34

THE DAYS HEADING INTO SPRING WERE BRUTALLY busy for Ben. He started April by flying to New York on Monday night and returning to Paris on Thursday night. By early May, he was leaving Paris Sunday night and returning early Saturday morning. One benefit of the May schedule was the chance to spend Mother's Day afternoon in Lynn, having dinner with his family, playing touch football in the street with his brothers and trying to explain to his family and the neighbors why his work with Pascal in Paris was *not* spending time in the minor leagues until he got the opportunity to come back to do real work in the United States.

Ben's mother was disappointed Claudine hadn't come. She worried about their baby and especially about him growing up French. Why couldn't the baby be an American citizen, she wondered. Ben tried to assure her that the baby would have dual citizenship—would be both French and American. Ben's father said that meant the child wouldn't be either—he would grow up to be a man without a country.

Finally, after hours of this frustrating conversation, the doorbell rang. Ben's driver had arrived. Ben said his goodbyes and promised to be back by the end of the summer.

"Aren't you going to be here before then?"

"No, Mom, I'll be really busy this summer."

"When will I see the baby?"

"At the end of the summer."

"But what about the baptism?"

"We'll talk when we come in the fall."

He decided not to mention that Claudine was a Taoist and that he, too, was practicing Taoism. He didn't want to get mired in that conversation, but he realized for the first time that the subject of the baby's baptism would be another disappointment for her. He walked toward the waiting car with Don who said he was headed out anyway. Don's car was parked across the street from the black Cadillac, whose driver stood beside the open rear door.

"Must be nice," Don said. He gestured with his eyes toward the car and driver.

"Don, you're more the Cadillac man than me."

Ben smiled, then stepped forward and hugged his brother. He stepped back to look into Don's alcohol-puffed face, looking for the brother he'd always thought was going to light the world on fire.

"Yup, well, for now I'm a Dodge station wagon man, but I'll be a Cadillac man soon enough. I've got things in the works."

"Make it happen," Ben said. He slipped into the rear seat of the Cadillac and the door closed. He watched Don standing beside the car until it pulled away, then turned to see out the rear window as Don crossed to the Dodge and yanked on the door handle. The door opened reluctantly.

35

TIME WAS GROWING SHORT. BEN WAS DETERMINED
to get Claudine's studio and their apartment renovated by New
Year's. He knew that little would get done by the contractors in the
week after Christmas and that Christmas week itself would barely be
a half-week of work. He thought that he might spend a few days between Christmas and New Year's cleaning up and arranging things,
but Claudine objected and Bernadine declared it unthinkable. Marcel
quietly advised surrender.

The building at the corner of Madison and East 71st was long
and narrow. Its main advantage was that the long façade fronted
Madison—perfect for Claudine's first retail store. It sat diagonally
across from St. James Church and was only a block from Central
Park and ten short blocks from the Metropolitan Museum. The retail
façades along Madison were populated with mostly marginal businesses, but the residential properties along the street were slowly being renovated into expensive townhouses and apartments.

The building had been a surprisingly robust example of French
Beaux Arts architecture. The first two floors had been bastardized with
a standard aluminum and glass storefront, but the rest of the building was mostly intact. It had about twenty-five hundred square feet
on each of its five floors, perfect floor sizes for Claudine and Ben's use.

Ben's design removed the storefront and replaced it with a bronze
and glass façade. The shine of the new brass bothered him, but he had

rejected an artificially-aged bronze finish and hoped that the shine would diminish over the next couple of seasons. He replaced the upper windows with similar windows crafted by an upstate millworker. They looked the same as the original, but had better weatherstripping and insulated glass. He found one of the original window locks and had it replicated.

The floor plans that Ben designed provided for the retail shop on the first floor with a private showroom and fitting rooms on the second floor. The third floor housed the workroom with Claudine's office and a conference room on the fourth floor. The space on the fourth floor was shared by the lower floor of their apartment and was where the master bedroom was placed. Claudine could walk from the bedroom, through her dressing room to her office. The fifth floor housed living and dining rooms as well as guest bedrooms and the kitchen. A private elevator rose from a 71st Street entrance to the fifth floor.

The biggest eyesore in the neighborhood was a large decrepit building only a block away on the opposite side of the street. It filled the remainder of the block not occupied by the church. Ben had briefly looked at the building, but it was far too large for their needs. He admired its massing and declared that it had "good bones," but the intricate detailing was seriously deteriorated and the upper floors were covered deeply in shit from birds who had entered through several broken windows.

He felt sad for the building. It would probably end up being demolished and replaced with a far less interesting building, something glassy and anonymous. It would take someone with a lot of vision and a lot of money to take on a restoration. He thought of Marcel, but doubted that he would be interested in a large mansion on Madison Avenue. Marcel had a smallish office in the Chrysler building that housed his U.S. sales and finance groups, as well as Pascal's New York offices. He didn't need another New York home since he already had an apartment at the Essex House. The Rhinelander mansion had to face its fate without Ben's intervention, as alone as it had been for a very long time.

230

THE SNOW WAS falling lightly on Madison Avenue. Ben sat in the bentwood rocking chair, Daniel gurgling at Ben's towel-draped shoulder. Ben wasn't looking for gurgling, he was hoping for a good belch from his young son, but the baby's happy sounds and the snow early on a Sunday morning gave the day a peaceful feeling.

Peace seemed like a ludicrous dream right now. The Vietnam war dragged on despite Richard Nixon's proclamation that "the end is in sight." Marcel's aircraft parts division which manufactured electrical harnesses for the Mirage fighter suffered strikes from unions that the French and American governments claimed were led by Communists. The American economy was slipping into a deepening recession. Both of the New York buildings that Ben was working on were put on hold. The office might have closed except for a commission to design the U.S. headquarters for a Canadian insurance company.

Claudine's business seemed to be miraculously untouched by the recession. Her showings of fall designs were mounted in both Paris and New York for the first time. She had been approached by a conglomerate of department stores to design a ready-to-wear line, and she was considering a new show during Paris haute-couture week.

As soon as Nanette, Daniel's nanny, walked into the room, Daniel belched and dribbled small amounts of food and drool onto the towel. Ben smiled at Nanette, partly because her appearance often resulted in an obedient burping from his son, and partly because he was still amused by the thought of "Nanette the nanny." Claudine thought he was too easily amused and objected to his oft-repeated introduction of her as "Nanette the Nanny."

After Nanette took Daniel to have his morning bath and change of clothes, Ben started his Sunday morning ritual of dissecting the newspapers into separate piles: to read; maybe to read; to throw out without reading. He lit the fireplace, got his first cup of coffee, tuned the stereo to a Sunday morning jazz station and lifted the first section from the "to read" pile. He noticed that the snow had become quite heavy. Peacefulness settled like a blanket about him.

By eleven o'clock, a fourth pile of newspapers—the "save for Claudine" pile—had formed and the "throw-out" pile had grown.

The telephone rang twice and was picked up in the middle of the third ring. Nanette appeared a few moments later and announced that it was a Captain Meehan of the State Police in Topsfield.

"Topsfield, New York?" Ben wasn't sure there even was a Topsfield, New York.

"I don't know...he just said Topsfield."

Ben picked up the receiver and punched the blinking button. "This is Ben Holt."

"Ben, Mike Meehan...*Captain* Mike Meehan now. Massachusetts State Police, Topsfield barracks. We went to high school together."

"Hi, Mike...*Captain*. Of course, I remember you."

"Mike is fine. We've got your brother, Don, here. We brought him in last night. He'd been in a fight."

"Don't tell me he killed someone."

"If he did, we didn't find them. We found him unconscious next to his car. His face was a mess, but that's not why we brought him in. He was drunk as a skunk and we brought him in for his own protection."

"So you'll be releasing him this morning?"

"No, that's why I'm calling you. We found your business card among his possessions and I wanted to let his family know. You know, old school ties and all."

"Thanks, but why are you holding him?"

"The night sergeant ran a check, SOP, and found there are five outstanding warrants for him. Most of them were minor stuff... misdemeanors...but one was serious...grand larceny, a felony. We need to hold him for arraignment in the morning. Normally a magistrate might set bail, but it's Sunday."

"Of course."

"Thing is, he's screaming bloody blue murder, wanting to get out. Says you can get him out and he wants to talk to you. I wanted to give you a head's up and lay out the situation for you."

"Thanks, Mike. I'm inclined to leave him where he is. I'm not sure that anything good will come from his being out and I can't be there to keep an eye on him. I'm in New York."

"He won't be happy about that."

"No, I don't suppose he will."

BEN CALLED HIS mother and told her about Don's situation and about his decision to leave Don in the Topsfield cell. She became frantic, alternately cajoling Ben and screaming her demand that Ben get Don released. Ben refused. He promised to get his brother a good attorney and to cover his bail, but Don would have to stay in custody until the next morning. When Ben hung up, his mother was crying.

Ben's next call was to Blair Winston, Pascal's New York-based attorney. He called Blair's office number and left a message. He had the attorney's home number, but decided not to call it until the afternoon. As he was hanging up, Ben noticed the button for the next line flashing and hit the button to answer the line. "Ben Holt."

"Mike Meehan told me he called you. You can't leave me here. I'm going fucking crazy."

"Don, listen to me…"

"No. No, I'm not fucking listening. *You* fucking listen. I want out. I'm not staying here."

"Don, you *are* staying there."

"I'll call Ma."

"Mom can't do anything for you."

"*You* can. *You* can get me out of here. I can't stay here. Get me the fuck out of here."

"Don, it's Sunday, and even if by some miracle I *could* get you out, it wouldn't be the smart thing to do."

"What do you know about fucking smart? Did you get eight-hundred's on the fucking college boards?"

Ben ignored his brother's ranting. There had been a time when his brother's superior academic performance would have hurt. Now it didn't seem to mean much of anything. ' I've called a lawyer for you. We'll arrange representation at the arraignment. I assume the lawyer will come to see you before you go into court, probably in a holding cell at the courthouse."

"I don't need your fucking 'representation'...I can represent myself. Fuck off."

"What is this grand larceny thing about?"

"I snagged some TV's that they said were worth three hundred bucks each. They fell off of a truck."

"Sure...probably with a little help."

"Maybe..."

"I'll try to get the lawyer to come check on you this afternoon. That's the best I can do."

Ben didn't wait for a response, but could hear Don's angry ranting as he placed the handset in its cradle.

No sooner had he hung up when the phone rang again. He considered ignoring it, but before he decided to pick it up the light glowed solidly, then flashed, and Nanette appeared in the doorway announcing it was Blair Winston's secretary. The secretary, Marjorie, reported to Ben that she was in the office cleaning up some work and had just checked the messages. She'd called Mr. Winston at home. Ben should expect a call back early in the afternoon.

Ben went back to the papers. After reading the books section, he noticed that the snow had piled up quite a bit. He decided to go for a short walk before Bertha arrived to make Sunday brunch. He decided not to mention any of the morning goings-on to Claudine.

Blair Winston was Marcel's corporate attorney in New York. Ben had designed the offices for Winston's firm in New York, DC, and Boston, so he knew that Crump Winston etc. had a criminal defense practice that primarily handled financial industry cases. When he called Blair Winston, he assumed the lawyer would give him the name of someone who would handle petty cases in Boston. Thinking about Don and his troubles, he mused that petty cases were those that didn't involve you or someone close to you. Winston surprised Ben by promising to have an associate from the Boston office visit Don that afternoon.

"Thanks, Blair."

"No problem. If it gets bigger than it should, I'll have a partner supervise it, but we'll go this route for now. Sometimes getting a partner involved too early just makes a small situation much bigger."

"Whatever you think."

"By the way, I was planning to give you a call anyway. We represent New England Merchants Bank in the America's Park project and they are about to pull the plug. I recalled that you had had something to do with it."

"Yeah, well, I wasn't much more than a glorified night watchman and I'm not so sure about the *glorified* part. That was a long time ago."

"Hmmm. Do you think that Marcel could use part of the property? I think they used to bring some good-sized ships in there, didn't they?"

"They brought in coal for an old power plant. I'm not sure what condition the channel is in. They haven't used it for larger ships in a long time. The plan was to build a new neighborhood there, with housing, offices and stores."

"Well, it probably would have died anyway. You know what they say about 'Lynn, Lynn, the city of sin'."

"Not my favorite saying."

"That's not what killed the deal anyway. The power company has been holding them up over the burying of the power lines, dragging their feet and demanding ridiculous compensation."

"I'd hate to see an industrial use like one of Marcel's car parts plants there, but I'd have to admit that the city could use the jobs. They've been cutting a lot of workers at General Electric. The site is spectacular though...nearly five thousand feet of shoreline looking south towards downtown Boston. Can the developer get another lender?"

"Maybe, but it's not a good time to find money for big projects like this. Urban renewal is all but gone and the feds aren't offering guarantees like they used to. They've got to pay the war bill, you know. I wanted to see if you had any insights on it."

"Yeah, we'll check the channel issue."

"Shall I tell Marcel that you think it's a good site?"

"I guess. Like I said, it'd be a tragedy to have the area be industrial, but maybe that's what it has to be. It does have good access to the sea, if the channel is clear, and to Logan for air freight, and when the inner belt's finished it'll have good road access also. Just hurts though."

"We have to be pragmatic. That, by the way, applies to Don, as well."

"I know."

"I hope he does. I'll have the associate give you a call to introduce himself after he visits Don."

"Thanks, Blair."

36

"MR. HOLT, YOU HAVE A VISITOR."

Don looked up from his lunch—McDonald's—as the trooper slid open the door to the small, gray cell. The woman who stood behind and to the left of the trooper was nearly as tall as—and substantially more attractive than—the officer. Don noticed that the trooper's grizzled hair glistened and appeared to have been recently brushed. The distinctive scent of Old Spice wafted towards him, tickling his nostrils so that he brushed his nose with the back of his hand to stifle a sneeze. The woman stepped around the trooper, entered the cell, and laid a black briefcase on the bed before speaking.

"I'm attorney Casey. I'll be representing you." She offered Don a card and turned to the trooper. "I'll be speaking with my client, officer."

The trooper stood, unmoving, at the cell door.

"Alone."

The trooper left the door open and reluctantly moved away. When the door to the small cellblock clicked shut, the lawyer turned back to Don who was staring at the card.

"You can read, I assume."

"S-i-o-b-h-a-n? Are you Jewish?"

It's pronounced 'Shi-vahn' and it's Irish."

"Then why does it say See-ob-han?"

"That's how Siobhan is spelled."

"Then you'd better change your name. No judge is going to like this."

237

Siobhan Casey's face turned a deep, hot red that came close to matching her hair and made her eyes—one green, one gray—stand out like sunspots.

"I...am...not...here...to...discuss...the...pronunciation... of...my...name."

"Just saying, that's all."

"Do you want to discuss your case or do you want another attorney?"

"You'll do."

Casey opened her briefcase and removed a yellow legal pad and a Mont Blanc pen. Don noticed an expensive-looking watch on her right wrist and was surprised when she sat on the bed and took the pen in her right hand, not her left.

"Why do you wear your watch on your right arm, if you're right-handed?"

"Why does it matter to you?"

"Just wondering. Most righties wear their watch on the left wrist."

"And judges get irritated if the attorneys look at their left wrist to check the time."

"Where did you go to school?"

"Harvard."

"No, I mean high school."

"Why does it matter to you? I'm your lawyer, not a pickup."

"Well, you're interested...*definitely* attracted."

"Why did the cops pick you up?"

"I was driving up route one and got tired, so I pulled over to take a nap. They found me napping next to my car."

"Had you been drinking?"

"Sure, but I wasn't drunk or anything."

"Then why did they pick you up?"

"There was a bit of a fight in a bar and I took off when the local cops arrived. They must have phoned in the license plate on my car."

"There was no mention of assault and battery or disorderly conduct on the booking sheet."

"Okay. That might be something."

"What about the grand larceny charge?"

238

"A friend who works at Zayre's gave me a TV. For some reason they think it was stolen."

"Did the friend who 'gave' you the TV pay for it?"

"How should I know?"

"Why would he give you a TV?"

"Actually, he gave me ten TV's."

"What? The guy just gives you ten TV's out of the blue?"

"He owed me."

"I don't think I want to know what he owed you for."

"Sports bet."

"Don't tell me anything more about that. I'll just assume that it was a friendly bet."

"Not *that* friendly, as it turned out."

"Enough!"

"That's what the fight was about. You can't have a guy welch on his bets."

"Why do you keep telling me all of this?"

"I want us to start out right. I don't want any secrets between us."

Casey paused, put her pad and pen back in her brief case and closed it. "Academy of our Lady of Nazareth."

"What?"

"My high school. Just wanted you to know so you wouldn't continue with your fantasy of getting into my pants."

"No fantasy. Just the facts, ma'am." Don did his best Seargeant Friday imitation.

"See you in the morning."

Casey walked from his cell, down the short corridor, and slapped her palm on the cell block door.

BEN SAT AT his usual table at Le Saint-Germaine drinking his *allongé*, nibbling on his tartine, waiting for Pascal. The sun was rising just enough so that the awning was beginning to shade Ben's eyes and the bustling forms around him were beginning to sprout faces with distinguishable features—eyes, noses and lips. It was unusual for Pascal to want to meet this early, but he had insisted on eight a.m.. It was now eight fifteen.

There was a time when Ben would have worried about the urgency and secrecy that attended Pascal's call. He made Ben promise to tell no one. It had seemed like an odd request, but Ben had become so comfortable in his relationship with Pascal and confident in his own work that if there was any moment of concern, it passed instantly. He had kept his promise to Pascal and hadn't even told Claudine.

Claudine. Just the thought of her spread a deep and comfortable warmth through his entire being. Ben had been thinking recently about how they had started out together, young and carefree—about how they'd gotten pregnant, married, had Daniel, and acted like real parents without really having thought any of it through. It had not been rational. It had been a lark. Now, after almost four years of being together, they were becoming married, becoming real parents, and Ben liked it. They had been lovers; now they were becoming much more, and it was fearsome and wonderful to Ben. They had broken through the cloudy veil that had made a life this rich incomprehensible to most. Ben closed his eyes and drank in the warm richness of his reverie.

"BONJOUR, MON AMI."

"Good morning, Pascal."

Pascal sat, arranged his napkin and took the last piece of Ben's tartine. "I am so hungry this morning, Ben. Won't you have a real breakfast with me?"

"I could do some eggs and ham, maybe some *fromage blanc* and berries...sure."

"In American diners that would be the 'number one,' would it not?"

"Delete the *fromage blanc* and add home fries, bacon, toast and jam, and you'd be right."

"How can you people eat that way?"

"I believe that it's an overwhelming desire to die young and obese."

"How are Claudine and Daniel? I haven't spoken to Claudine in a while and Marcel hasn't spoken to her in almost a month."

"Bernadine talks to Claudine every other day. Claudine is surprised that Marcel has been incommunicado. They are well, Claudine and Daniel."

"When are you flying back?"

"Tomorrow night. We are driving to Vermont on Friday afternoon. We'll be spending the weekend looking at land in Woodstock."

"Where the infamous rock concert was?"

"No, that's New York. Woodstock, Vermont."

"Ahhh. You know that Marcel and Bernadine are disappointed that you're not looking near them in Cape Neddick."

"Yes. We'll still visit them there, but Claudine is very taken with the peacefulness of Woodstock...especially South Woodstock near the Green Mountain Horse Association. You know how much she loves horses."

"And just far enough away from Maine that Bernadine won't just stop by some Saturday afternoon."

"We'll have to make sure that we keep enough trees to avoid having a convenient helicopter landing," Ben laughed, "but that is probably not why you wanted to meet this early."

"No. That's most serious."

"Oh."

"You've been the manager of the New York office for almost three years now. I know that it hasn't always been easy. You had to manage during a downturn and I wasn't giving you much support because of the troubles here."

"Yes, but we're starting to see a bit of improvement now and I have some initiatives that I'd like to review with you."

"That's my concern. I know that you worked hard to turn New York around and I respect that, but I don't have the skills to manage the business from Paris."

"Then what do we do? Certainly you don't want to throw away the investment you've made in the New York office, in the U.S. operations."

"No, I don't. I am honest enough with myself to know that we can't continue this way, so..."

The blood was rushing to Ben's ears, and the roar of the waterfall within made it hard to hear Pascal. He had worked hard to build the New York office and it was beginning to bear fruit. New York was becoming an important part of his family's life and he didn't want to see it cut off now.

"Ben, did you hear me? Are you happy about this?"

"Happy?"

"I know it's a big step, both personally and professionally, but you're ready for it."

"I don't know what to say. I..."

"We will change the name of all of the U.S. operations to Satart Holt, of course. I hope you'll say yes."

Ben shot back in his chair and almost fell against the glass of the café's facade.

"Yes."

Pascal reached into his shoulder bag and withdrew a sheaf of papers, which he handed to Ben. "Marcel's attorneys have reviewed these. You can get your personal attorney to review them if you like. Marcel will finance the new partnership."

"Is that why he's been avoiding Claudine?"

"It is. He knew that if he talked to her he'd not be able to keep his secret. We Frenchmen understand our weaknesses."

"I assume Bernadine doesn't know."

"No. That's the delicate part. Marcel would like you and I to join him in his office this morning, and together the three of us will call Bernadine and Claudine to tell them."

"So you two assumed then that I'd say yes?"

"We did. Why would you not?"

Ben thought for a moment, then shrugged. "What about the Paris and Milan offices?"

"They will be separate, but also will be renamed Satart Holt. You and I will be the senior partners in New York, with Jared and Paul as junior partners with ten percent interests each. In Paris, I will be the majority partner with you having a twenty-five percent interest and three of the more senior staff each having a ten percent interest. Your interest in the European operations will increase by five percent per year until I retire or…" Pascal smiled, "you fire me."

They stood to leave and Pascal raised his right hand and waved. His driver walked to the table with two boxes that were obviously hat boxes. The driver opened one box, Pascal the other. They each withdrew a black beaver fur cowboy hat. Pascal handed the one in his hand to Ben and took the other hat from the driver. He put his on, motioned to Ben to do the same, and extended his right hand. As Ben took the hand, Pascal pulled him close and hugged him.

"*Pahdnah.*"

"Do me one favor, Pascal?"

"Of course."

"Never try to speak Texan again."

"*D'accord.*"

37

April 1973

D O MOTHS COMPREHEND THE DANGER THAT attends their attraction to the flame?

Siobhan considered this as she looked in the mirror. She liked her face, the symmetry of its parts, the color of the skin on her tight cheeks, the shape of her lips. It was her eyes that bothered her. Not the difference in the color between them—that had always made her unique, a one-off. It was not how they were seen, but what they saw that bothered her now.

DON'S TRIAL HAD gone well. At the end of the prosecution's presentation of its case she had made her perfunctory motion for dismissal and was so surprised at the judge's proclamation—"motion granted"—that she had to ask him to repeat it. She was proud of her cross-examination of the prosecution's witnesses. She thought she had shown them to be less than truthful, but she had planned to use that testimony to contrast to Don's testimony, which she had hoped would look as truthful in the prosecutor's cross as it had in their practice sessions.

The prosecutor was visibly, and too vocally, upset and had been ordered into the judge's chambers. She couldn't blame him—it had been a stunning verdict. She had to wonder whether there had been external factors. Don had worked on the judge's campaign when he had run for district attorney. He had lost the campaign, but had won the southeastern Essex County cities and towns handily, the areas that Don had worked hard for him. Don had promised her that he had not spoken to, nor attempted to speak to, the judge, nor had he asked others to approach the judge.

She had expected the prosecution to ask the judge to recuse himself during the pretrial, but that motion never came. Don had told her that the judge had gone to high school with Ben, but he didn't think they'd been very close. She'd become uncomfortable when a commotion arose in the gallery just before the court was called to order and Don had whispered excitedly to her that Ben had just arrived at the trial. She'd turned to see a tall, handsome man in an exquisite suit accompanied by a stunning woman in an equally stunning pantsuit. Flanking her was a shorter, silver-haired man who looked fairly familiar, but she couldn't quite recall why. The commotion had subsided when the clerk had called for order and announced the case. Siobhan felt upset and angry at Ben for having caused the disturbance. She would tell him so later; for now, she wanted a dull, straightforward case.

After the dismissal, the courtroom erupted. Siobhan wouldn't have heard the prosecutor's vocal tirade if he hadn't been standing right beside her. When the judge left, followed closely by the prosecutor, she turned to Don, accepted his hug, and deflected his kiss.

"Not here. Not now."

"I want to *take* you in this courtroom, on this table."

She grabbed his elbow and moved him ahead of her towards the gallery. A dense circle was surrounding Ben and his wife. Siobhan recognized at least two Boston TV reporters. She wondered what they were doing here. Who had tipped them off?

As her anger flared, the man who'd been with Ben and his wife emerged from the throng and smiled at Siobhan. She knew that she knew that face from somewhere—and thought she was close to remembering how—when he offered his hand to Don.

"Congratulations, young man," he said, then turned to Siobhan. "I was very impressed, Siobhan. I hope you approve of the attention you'll be getting from the press. Good for you, and good for our firm."

A light switched on and Siobhan remembered—it was Blair Winston. His portrait hung in the main conference room at Crump Winston's Boston office. The blood rushed to her head and she almost fainted. Instead she sat herself on the railing that separated the gallery from the dock.

SIOBHAN SPLASHED WATER on her face and dried it, covering her face with the towel. When she removed it, the reflection in the mirror remained unchanged and that disappointed her. She went back into her bedroom and slipped beneath the sheets made warm by Don's body. Without speaking, he slipped his arm around her and drew her to him. She didn't resist and they made love for the third time since having dinner with Ben and Claudine the evening before.

Siobhan had found it hard not to like Claudine. She was charming and "real." She may have come from money, but she worked hard to be successful in her own right, and she was comfortable and easy to talk to, even with her French-accented British English. Only once or twice had she spoken to Ben in French and those words appeared to be private instructions, because afterwards, Ben had ordered more butter for Siobhan's lobster and another beer for Don.

Ben had been fairly quiet; Don had been more loquacious. Ben gave a perfunctory report when Don asked what he was working on. Don had barely let Ben start speaking anyway before launching into his own "I've got plans" speech. Ben listened quietly to Don's rambling soliloquy. Ben's one flourish of excitement came when Claudine mentioned that they'd found a beautiful piece of land in South Woodstock, Vermont and that she was pregnant with their second child. Siobhan thought she noticed Ben's eyes dance when Claudine spoke of her pregnancy. That made her love Ben and made her think this crazy thing with Don just might work out, after all.

As they were walking from the restaurant, Don asked whether Ben had heard about the demise of America's Park. "Tell me about it."

Siobhan couldn't tell whether Ben had already heard about it or not, but somehow she expected he had, perhaps from Blair Winston.

If she had become more comfortable with her relationship with Don after their dinner with Ben and Claudine, her nagging doubts soon returned. It wasn't one big incident that brought them raging back, but a series of jabs and blows.

THE SUN HAD barely cracked an opening in the gloomy morning sky. Don sat on the edge of the bed, motionless, unblinking. In the opening moments of the day he would retreat to his safe world. Here he spoke Russian like a native, though he'd never taken a Russian language lesson before. Here he transported himself from place to place magically, painlessly, though he'd never considered how that could be done. It just happened. He'd barely wake up and would appear at work—no need to nurse his car to life to drive to Wonderland, to take the crowded Blue Line to Bowdoin and cross Cambridge Street to the garage under the State Office complex.

Siobhan stirred, sensed that Don was in his usual morning reverie, and slipped back into her dreams.

DON AND SIOBHAN sat next to each other on the clammy seat. The morning was already warm despite the heavy clouds, and Siobhan felt a trickle of sweat run down her spine. No one who didn't see them together each morning could have guessed they were coupled. Siobhan wore a crisp, gray suit with a well-starched white blouse, her hair up and pinned neatly in the back. Her stockings were gray, her shoes black with a modest heel. Don wore a T-shirt under his gray State Office Center uniform shirt with darker gray trousers, a brown belt, and well-worn work shoes. His hair was short—a wiffle—and he hadn't shaved since last night. He hated shaving in the morning—he hated mornings generally—so he'd shaved the n.ght before to prepare for the following day.

Don read the *Record American*, folding it in half vertically. Today's newspaper carried several stories that upset Don, stories about the new governor, about the uprising in the state house that threatened to replace Sam McGonigle as speaker. Don had worked hard for McGonigle and his job had come at the Speaker's behest after Tony had cut him loose. In two years, he had risen from gatekeeper to garage maintenance. He had done some carpentry work when the project was too small to bring in a contractor. He had been hoping to get on a maintenance crew in one of the office towers. He ran a small sports book on the side, so everyone knew him. That had worked in his favor when he'd showed up in Judge Blaisdell's courtroom. The judge was one of his more frequent customers and Don often advised the judge against making a bad bet against the spread. He calculated that he had saved the judge thousands of dollars in bad bets.

Maybe the judge could get him a job in the Courts building, he thought. Siobhan might like that. He looked across at her and smiled.

"What's that for?" She barely looked up from her papers.

"I'm planning a surprise."

38

June 1981

"**P**ULL OVER AT THE NEXT CORNER."

Ben, Marcel and Claudine were touring several locations in the city to scout out potential sites and buildings for a Boston office for Satart Holt. Marcel was in Boston to meet with some of the bankers who were financing one of the bidders for his U.S. auto parts operations.

The limo stopped in front of an ornate Art Deco mansion at the corner of Commonwealth Avenue and Hereford Street. Marcel briefly looked out the window of the car, then burst through the door before the driver could make his way to the curb.

"*Amazing.* It's *wonderful.*"

The broker was standing by the walkway to the front door and moved towards Marcel with his hand outstretched.

Marcel didn't notice the hand—or the man, but looked up at the roof line and the gargoyles that rimmed the parapet. "Ben," he said. "You *must* have this." He walked past the broker to the front door, but found it locked. Claudine and Ben emerged from the limo and greeted the broker, shaking hands and exchanging business cards.

"Shall we go in?" The broker motioned up the walk.

"Yes, lets…before he breaks in," Ben laughed.

The mansion was a bone-white, three-story pile of limestone under a mansard roof that fronted a fourth floor. Its facade was populated with scores of figures—dragons, gargoyles, gryphons, cherubs, chimeras, and grotesques, as well as several faces of lions, eagles, and demons. There was a double bay facing Commonwealth that flanked the arch of the entry porch and a heavily-figured bronze grillwork over the glass door. It was spectacular and so different from Ben's work as to be a counterpoint to his designs.

Ben liked the building because the hidden proportions of the massing were comfortable and reflected his own, more obvious, massing of elements. He had already spent considerable time studying the facade, applying the Golden Mean, and enjoying the results of his analysis confirming the connection between great design over the ages.

While Ben and Claudine stood in the long vestibule, taking in the intricate detailing that carried into the interiors of the great house, Marcel was off wandering the four floors and the basement, trailed by the broker, desperately trying to keep up, apparently worried that Marcel might steal the place and spirit it back to Paris piece by piece. There was a protocol to follow, and this crazy Frenchman wasn't playing.

"How much do they want? Give me the real number...I don't want to bargain...just a number." Marcel had pushed the broker against the stairs. One more step back, and the poor man would topple.

"It doesn't work that way." Before Marcel could grab the man, Ben had moved between them. "It's a *bid*, Marcel. The building is owned by the BIA. We need to submit a written proposal and a bid. They are as interested in what we would do with the building as much as what we would pay."

"Nonsense."

"Besides, I have to talk to Pascal about it. The Lewis Wharf property was interesting as well, and we could develop the property around it for a good profit."

"I'll take care of Pascal. You went to the BIA before you came to Paris, did you not? You must know someone."

"I do, but we must respect the process."

"No. You must make the process *yours*. Now where is this BIA?"

Claudine grabbed her father by the elbow and turned him away from Ben and the broker. She spoke sternly, but quietly, in French until Marcel finally nodded.

"My father will respect the process, for the time being."

Ben smiled. He felt he knew exactly what Marcel intended to do. Claudine frowned at him, chastising him for the smile, but knew what Ben was thinking and conceded that he was probably right. They said goodbye to the broker and returned to the limo.

"So, Marcel, what night do you want to have dinner with Angelo Pescara?"

Claudine glared at Ben.

THE LIMO DROPPED Ben and Claudine at the Parker House. They had lunch in the main restaurant on the first floor sitting in winged armchairs at a table in the far corner of the dining room. After lunch they took a nap, then Claudine packed a suitcase for Ben to take back to New York.

AFTER MARCEL LEFT Claudine and Ben at the Parker House, he had the limo drive him to the Boston Federal Reserve building on Franklin Street. He had lunch with the president of the Boston Fed, the French consul in Boston, and several of the Boston Fed board members. The Boston Fed President spoke of Boston's financial community and noted that Russell Higgins, the CEO of the investment group which was the lead bidder for the stake in Marcel's U.S. auto parts operations was a member of the Boston Fed board, although he recused himself from this lunch because of his status as lead bidder.

"Excuse me, but that is foolish. I am here to to arrange a marriage, and the bride is missing."

The Boston Fed President spoke quietly to an aide. Ten minutes later, Higgins walked into the room and took his empty seat.

"Excuse me, Mr. Aubrey, for being late. I am Russ Higgins."

"Ah, the *betrothed*."

AFTER A LONG afternoon of meetings with Higgins' partners and banks, Marcel declined to meet with Higgins' lawyers.

"I see no use in meeting the lawyers."

Higgins was taken aback. "I thought that we were close to a deal. I'm surprised that..."

"The marriage will take place. I don't need to meet the priest."

"Okay, then."

"Tell me one thing though."

"Yes, of course."

"Who designs your offices?"

"Mo Sather of Campbell, Brown and Sather. They are one of the top firms in Boston, even in the country. Do you need an architect? We can certainly introduce them to you. They are an excellent firm. I play squash with Sather."

"No need. Just wondered. My son-in-law is Ben Holt of Satart Holt. They are one of the top firms in Paris, Milan, London, New York, even in the world. They will open a Boston office soon."

"Perhaps we should meet him."

"Perhaps."

AFTER BEN DELIVERED Claudine to her plane at Logan Airport, he returned to the Parker House. As he walked to the elevators, a bellman scooted across the lobby with a piece of paper in his extended hand.

"A message for you, sir."

"Thank you."

Ben tipped the bellman and read the note. It was from Marcel. He had been called at Higgins' office by an auto dealer by the name of Bob Malaczyk who'd said he owned several large parcels of land on a highway in Lynn that might be good for warehousing and manufacturing parts. It was close to the airport and had a wharf on a deep water channel. Marcel wanted Ben to look at it with him that evening if he was free.

Ben walked to a lobby phone, asked the operator for an outside line, and dialed Marcel's hotel. The call was routed through to Marcel's room and he answered.

"*Bonjour.*"

"Marcel, it's Ben. I know the land well. Pick me up and we'll go to see it. There is something else I want to show you nearby."

"*D'accord.* Fifteen minutes."

"Marcel..."

"Yes?"

"Don't write a check for it yet."

"Hmmm...*D'accord.*"

THE DAY WAS almost over for Don—just one more call to cover, a complaint about an overturned trash barrel on the second level. Don grabbed a broom and an old coal shovel and headed for the location indicated on the hand-written note. Usually the complaints were typewritten, but this call had come in late, and Betty, the maintenance director's secretary, had already left.

The barrel was next to an exit stairway and its strewn contents had fallen in front of the door. Often people used the stairway instead of waiting for an elevator and Don saw that they had walked over and through the trash.

"What pigs!"

Then he noticed movement in the trash—ants attracted to the leftover scraps of what had been a Table Talk cherry pie. How he hated ants; more than mice, more than rats, almost as much as maggots.

He returned to the maintenance shop and grabbed the gas can, shaking it to see if any gas remained from the last time he'd used the small chainsaw to cut up fallen branches from the trees on the Plaza. There wasn't much, but it should be enough to do the job.

He ran back up to the second floor, using the stairway closest to the trash. The ants were still thronging at the scraps of pie, but as he poured the gasoline on them, several that were untouched scurried away. He poured the remainder of the gas on the fleeing ants, stepped back, lit the book of matches with one hand and threw it onto the gasoline. The flare up surprised him and he jumped back, dropping the gas can into the flames. Afraid that it might explode, he ducked behind a car and peered at the can through the window of the passenger compartment. The fire alarms started screaming and lights flashed. Before he could grab a fire extinguisher cart from near a column and drag it to the fire, the sprinklers let go. Water spread over the flaming gasoline for a few moments, and the fire died out.

It was then that he heard the sirens. Moments later, firemen, fully dressed in gear and breathing apparatus, appeared at the opposite stairwell door.

It seemed to Don as if an hour had passed before the sprinklers were turned off. Don looked at his watch. The entire episode had taken less than half an hour. At least he wouldn't be late meeting Siobhan.

BEN REPLACED THE handset and rose from his chair as the bellman hurried towards him again.

"Another message, sir."

Ben looked at the note and saw that it was from Beth, the receptionist at Satart Holt's Manhattan office. Ben looked at his watch—it was just before seven—and wondered briefly why Beth would be in the office at that hour. He folded the note and slipped it into his jacket pocket, making a mental note to call her in the morning. He slipped through the revolving doors and out onto School Street looking for Marcel's car, which was just pulling around the corner at that very moment.

The driver headed onto the Central Artery north and over the Mystic River Bridge. As they exited onto the Revere Beach Parkway and passed the old shopping center, Ben's thoughts turned to Annie, to the deep and unabiding depression he had felt and the tears he had shed in that place. It felt like a lifetime ago and yet it saddened him again. He wondered where she was and what her life was like now. He loved Claudine and Daniel and the baby still to come. He loved his life, Marcel, Pascal, and all the things large and small that had come his way. Yet, somehow it did not surprise him that he still loved Annie.

"Ben?"

"Yes, Marcel."

"A memory?"

"Yes, Marcel."

"Hold them close…memories are gifts that remind us of who we are."

"Yes, Marcel, they do. They do."

AS THEY DROVE over the General Edwards Bridge, Ben pointed to the power lines that paralleled the waterfront and directed Marcel's driver to a dirt road that ran under them. The turn onto the road was to the right and 180° from the highway, so the limo made a wide counter-clockwise circle through a hotel parking lot and looped around to access the dirt road. The driver reached beside his seat and flipped the safety off on his automatic pistol. He instinctively felt in the dark for the handle of the parking brake and clicked its release button to make sure it felt loose. He was ready for the tour.

The road quickly turned to the left and Ben pointed out that the water to their right was the Saugus River and that the land on the far bank was Point of Pines, a part of Revere. They continued to another left turn and Ben had the driver stop some two hundred feet after the turn, then gestured across the water to point out Revere Beach, the buildings of Boston in the distance, and the Nahant Peninsula that had once been a couple of islands, but were now connected by a causeway. To the left were the backs of warehouses and small manufacturing plants, and beyond them, toward the Lynnway, the bright lights of auto dealerships, including those of Bob Malaczyk.

They continued further and arrived at the old construction trailer. Several pieces of construction equipment stood rusting where workers had ended their workday more than a year earlier. Here the land was more open, and they could see the remains of the foundations of buildings that had been put down for America's Park. A huge mound of earth arose beyond the flattened landscape.

"Is that soil that was brought in for this construction project?"

"No, Marcel, that's the remains of an old dump that will have to be relocated."

"For what?"

"We'll talk about that later, but I want you to see the rest."

They drove on and stopped at the base of the huge crane that ran on tracks. Ben got out of the car. The driver immediately stepped out of the driver's seat, grabbed the gun, and using the door of the limo as a shield, swept a 360° swath for signs of anything or anyone moving. Marcel followed Ben, who led him to the edge of the wood plank wharf.

"My brothers and I spent a lot of time fishing here."

"Did you catch anything?"

"Mostly crabs that would steal your bait and hang on to the line until you almost got them up. They'd drop back into the water with a loud splash. To this day I could recognize that splash blindfolded."

"I would often fish with my father off of the wharves where he worked in Marseille. It was before the Germans came. It is the smell of that water that I recall. Not a nice smell, but a fond friend in my memories."

It had gotten rather dark, but the two men remained, standing silently, looking out at the water. Marcel swung his arm over Ben's shoulder and together they watched the now-quiet harbor as the moon rose before them, silhouetting the hulls of the boats.

"Marcel, I want to build a city here."

39

THE PHONE NEXT TO BEN'S BED RANG. HE LIFTED his head, looked at the blinking light, looked at the time on the clock radio, and decided that five thirty a.m. was too early to talk to anyone. He laid his head back down on the pillow, and the ringing stopped. Moments later, the phone rang again. He lifted himself to his elbows. It wouldn't be Claudine—they had an emergency signal: two rings, hang up, call back—because Claudine was terrible about answering phone calls. The ringing stopped and then started again after a few more moments.

"Holt."

"Ben, it's Josep. Why didn't you answer the phone?"

"Because it's five thirty here," Ben barked into the phone.

"Ah, I understand."

"What's wrong?"

"Nothing is wrong. It's great news. We won the La Defense commission...*you* won the La Defense commission. They announce it at a lunch at noon. Pascal's there."

"They bought the whole design? The four blocks?"

"We don't know the details. Pascal got a call. This is all a secret...we are not supposed to know."

"Who did the call come from?"

"Bill Button."

"The *dog*!"

"Bill Button?"

"No, someone else I spent much of yesterday with. Someone who had to know whether Bill Button knew, and who said nothing."

"Ah, I understand."

"COME IN AND close the door."

Peter Harrington was in charge of all the state office buildings and was the Deputy Commissioner of the State Building Authority. Don had applied for an open job as the superintendent of the two office towers that sat above the garage where he worked. When Sam McGonigle had lost his bid to be reelected as Speaker of the House in the Massachusetts legislature, Don thought his chances for the job had been lost, as well. It was then that he'd started doing favors for the new Speaker, giving his staff, friends, and visitors preferred spaces near the elevators or the garage entry. He made sure that the Speaker's car was washed at least once a week. Now his extra attention had paid off. He sat in the chair in front of Harrington's desk.

"Please have a seat." Harrington's tone was surprisingly sarcastic.

"Thanks."

"I'm suspending you for three days without pay."

Don thought that he must have misheard Harrington. The follicles of his hair tingled. "What?"

"You almost burned this place down."

"What? Who told you that? Yeah, we had some water, but *no way* was it close to burning the place down. It really wasn't even much of a fire…just some dead ants is all."

"And water damage and three fire trucks here and more on the way before the firefighters called them off."

"They overreacted."

"You showed terrible judgment and this wasn't the first time."

"What does that mean?"

"You didn't think I'd find out about the favors you'd been doing for the Speaker? You got away with that for a long time with

McGonigle, but Speaker Warren is a reformer and his Chief of Staff—*his chief of staff*—called to complain about the favors. They ran on reform and the *Globe* called them to ask why they were still getting preferential treatment in the garage."

"*Fuckers!*"

"Warren's Chief of Staff was just doing his job, which is more than I can say for you."

"No, not him...the *Globe*."

"They were just doing their job, too."

"I gave them *good* spaces, too..."

Harrington shook his head and laughed. "When you get back, there will be a grievance hearing about your job."

"Why would there be a grievance hearing?"

"We'll be firing you." Harrington touched the intercom button on his phone. "You may want to get a lawyer."

"You fucker." Don lunged over the desk towards Harrington, who stood and then fell back into his chair, which then crashed into the credenza against the wall. Harrington's office door opened and two very large state troopers moved quickly, one grabbing Don by his right arm, the other wrapping a hold around Don's neck. Ben realized then that Harrington had *expected* him to explode.

"You fucker. I'll be back for you."

"Shut up, Don." It was the trooper with the arm around his neck. Don knew him; he was a regular in Don's sports book.

BY THE TIME Don met Siobhan that evening for their usual journey home, he was thoroughly drunk. As Siobhan came around the corner from State Street, she knew by his posture—excessively upright—that he had been drinking for a long time. He stared directly at her, but his eyes were black, his pupils filling the center of his reddened eyes.

"Hi, Siobhan."

She walked right past him. As she did, she was immediately enveloped by a perfume of alcohol so strong it took her breath away.

"*Wait.*"

"No," she said. "Come on. We're going to eat before we go home. Something to sop up that alcohol. And don't come too close to me...I can't breathe with all that alcohol you're exhaling."

Don obeyed and followed her along the edge of City Hall Plaza to Washington Place, around the Old State House and onto Washington Street. He was five or six steps behind her, catching up only when she held open the door to Burger King. She motioned to a table in the corner and he staggered past the few people sitting at tables, people who looked up at him as he passed, then got up and moved to other tables farther away.

It seemed to Don like a long time before Siobhan returned with french fries, two plain cheeseburgers and a huge Coke. "Drink some of the Coke first...it'll help settle your stomach before you eat the grease." She pushed the Coke and all of the food towards Don.

"Aren't you gonna eat?"

"No."

"A french fry?"

Don smiled a thin smile at Siobhan.

"Don't talk to me right now."

Don drank three big swallows of the Coke. The cool liquid soothed the fire in his belly. He ate a handful of fries and savored the salt, even as it stung his sore lips.

"Tell me *why*." Her voice was dry and toneless.

"I thought you didn't want me to talk to you right now?" He smiled at her.

She stared him down.

"I got suspended."

"For what?"

"For three days."

"No," Siobhan shook her head. "*Why* did they suspend you?"

Don told her the story of the ants and the gasoline, the water and the firemen. "And Harrington said that they would fire me when I get back. There'll be a grievance hearing. He told me to get a lawyer."

"The union will provide you with a lawyer."

"I don't want a lawyer. I'm just telling you what he said."

"Call the union tomorrow. When they tell you who the lawyer is, call me and I'll talk to him."

"Thanks."

"I can't have you drinking like this. I know you still drink even though you said you would stop. I can't go back to drinking like we did, and if *you* do, *I* will."

"It's just this one time, Siobhan, really."

"I'll help you, but you have to help me, too. I can't slip back into that hole."

"I know...I won't."

She shook her head slowly. "Go to the bathroom and get some of that alcohol out of your stomach. I'll meet you across the street in front of the drugstore."

She stood and left the table, walking out into the street. Don sat for a few minutes, then stood with some effort, cleared the table, dumped the wrappers and cup into the trash barrel, and wobbled to the men's room.

40

A FTER SCANNING THE HEADLINES ON THE TOP HALF
of the front page, Annie unfolded the *Boston Globe*. The picture
of Ben in the lower left corner took her breath away. The adjacent
headline read "Local Architect Crosses Atlantic" over a smaller headline "Born in Boston, to Design Paris Landmark." She felt lighthead-
ed as she read the story. Ben had been selected to design a complex
of buildings in a new area of Paris called "La Defense" which was
named for a statue commemorating the Franco-Prussian war. It went
on to say that his firm was also designing the expansion of the U.S.
headquarters for a Canadian insurance company in Wellesley and that
the firm "with offices in Paris, Milan and New York is rumored to be
considering a Back Bay landmark for its Boston operations."

Annie sat back in her chair and sipped a long sip of her tea. So
her mother had been wrong about Ben. She longed to call Ben and
laugh about it with him. She longed to hold him again. Then she
thought of Harold and the kids, her job and her life. It might not be
Paris, but it was all she had ever wanted.

She picked up the paper and read the last paragraph again, noting
"Paris, Milan and New York." At the bottom of the column she read
"architect, page 6" and turned to page 6. It was what she read there
that bothered her most. "Holt is married to noted fashion designer
Claudine Aubrey. She is the daughter of French industrialist and finan-
cier Marcel Aubrey. Claudine and Ben have homes in Paris, Cannes,

New York and St. Bart's and recently bought a large tract of land on Morgan Hill in South Woodstock, Vermont. They have two children."

Annie knew that her feelings of jealousy were irrational. She had chosen Harold and Harold had chosen her. It was true that marriage was extremely different from courtship. Harold thought her attempts to renew the early excitement of their relationship had been funny and even charming for a while, but he had grown tired of the magazine articles and books she'd left out for him to read. Leaving a book among the *Readers Digests* next to the hopper *had* been a bit much, she thought. She'd known by the laughter coming from the bathroom that it wasn't "Reignite the Flame: Renew Desire" that Harold was reading in there.

The wall phone in the kitchen rang. Annie got up and crossed the room to answer it.

"Annie, did you see the *Globe* today?"

"Yes, Diane, I did. I'm glad for him."

"Makes me wish I *did* chase him when you were done with him."

"Why didn't you?"

"Loyalty, I guess. Pride maybe. I probably didn't want your leftovers."

"And you'd never hear the end of it from my mother if you brought him to my house."

"No, she wasn't much of a fan, was she?"

"I don't think it had anything to do with him. It was where he came from. I can still hear her say 'fruit from a bad tree'."

"Yeah, I remember. Well, who knows anyway. If you hadn't dumped him, he might've dumped you for his model wife, anyway."

"Designer."

"What?"

"She's a designer, not a model."

"Well, I saw her picture once in one of my magazines...*Vogue*, I think. She certainly *looks* like a model."

"Thanks for that."

"Sorry."

"No you're not. I have to go to work."

"Will I see you this weekend?"

"We'll be there."

"Maybe I'll invite Ben and his *model* wife."

"Screw you." Annie hung up the phone. It had barely settled in the cradle when it rang again. "What *now?*"

"That's not a very lady-like way to answer a phone."

"Sorry, Mom. I thought it was Diane calling me back."

"Did she see the newspaper article?"

"She did."

"I told you that family was no good. Fruit from a bad tree."

"What are you talking about?"

"The article in the *Record* about Don Holt. I thought you said Diane called you about it."

"What about Don Holt?"

"He tried to burn down the state office buildings, then when the state fired him, the union filed a grievance. He lost...thank God... but now he's suing the state for firing him. What is this country coming to? Your father is probably spinning in his grave."

"No, I didn't see that. Diane and I were talking about the article in the *Globe*."

"What was *their* take? They are so liberal they probably think he should have kept his job."

"It wasn't about Don."

"What was it about?"

"Ben."

"What trouble has *he* gotten himself into?"

"I've got to go to work, Mom. I'll leave the paper on the breakfast nook table. You can read it when you bring the kids home from school."

"Can't you just tell me what..."

"Got to go, Mom. Work."

As she hung up the phone, she wished she could be there when her mother read the story. Screw her.

TWO YEARS HAD passed since the front-page article in the *Globe* about Ben's project in Paris. Occasionally Annie would see a mention about Ben in the business section or in Ellsworth Nelson's architecture column, but nothing like this.

The front cover of the *Globe Magazine* was plastered with a picture of Ben and Claudine on the porch of their South Woodstock home. The article inside described the new arts and crafts style home, its barn, guest house, separate studios for Claudine and Ben, as well as Ben's plans to build a school and conference center in the village. There were more photos of the buildings and the gardens and the screened meditation gazebo overlooking a small pond. There was a full-page photo of Ben and Claudine and their two boys, Daniel and Pascal, with a caption noting the boys' polo shirts with the "International School, New York" logo.

Annie felt pains in her stomach. She had spent the last two years fighting off an obsession with Ben—no, more accurately, with *Claudine*. She knew about Claudine's love of horses, about her clothes and hair and dislike of any makeup except for a lightly-colored lip balm that was made especially for her by a French cosmetic company her father owned. She knew about her household staff and the restaurant in Paris owned by her former chef. She knew that Claudine only allowed Ben to cook at the Vermont house and that he was an accomplished cook, but "without a single Michelin star"—a fact she had once used to rib Ben in a Today Show interview.

"I'm working on it," Ben had smiled. Annie could just feel their loving bond through the TV.

Harold never noticed much about her these days, but he did finally notice the growing pile of magazines with articles about Claudine and Annie's new fondness for expensive French cosmetics. He confronted her about it and banned any magazines with Claudine's picture in them from their home, so Annie read them during breaks in the emergency room at Union Hospital.

Then one day, while sitting on the break room sofa, she spotted an article with Ben's picture. The article was about the state of the world economy. She thought it strange that Ben's picture would appear with the article, so she read it carefully, even though it was lengthy and dense. Two thirds of the way through, it mentioned that, due to the state of the French economy, Ben's acclaimed but much delayed office/retail and residential project—the largest project in the new business district of La Defense—had been canceled. A number of Satart Holt projects around the world had been put on hold. Other firms were facing the same fate, and the article projected that some of them might close.

Annie read the article as if it were a death notice. Claudine's storybook life would disappear on the cold wind of the recession, but Annie would still have her work at the hospital and her family. Claudine had flown too close to the sun and would now plummet to earth.

Annie felt her obsession with Claudine melt away. She physically felt it leave her body and imagined it as a puddle on the floor. She stepped out of the puddle and went back to work.

41

IT WAS ALMOST THREE THIRTY IN THE AFTERNOON and Don sat at the kitchen table drinking iced tea. The first three days without a drink had been a horror; the past seven days had been worse. Ten days without a single drink made the alcohol in his mouthwash burn. How he longed to swallow it. The trial was to start in the morning; there was no telling how long it would be before he could have another drink. He had promised Siobhan that he wouldn't drink—not even one—until the trial was over. He thought that this might be the hardest thing he had ever done. His nerves were frazzling; the pain was excruciating. He wanted to scream at Siobhan, at anyone around him, so he took long walks on the beach from Swampscott to Nahant, then back again. He often walked home along the Lynnway and watched the buildings rising along the waterfront. Although they were Ben's, Don felt as if they were his. Ben had abandoned his home; Don had stayed and deserved ownership of those things happening here.

He had doubted whether Ben's plan to build what he called a "new town" was real. No one Don knew ever pulled off anything this big. Ben would probably be able to build a couple of small buildings, then the project would stop and the buildings would rot. That was the destiny of this place—constant, depressing rot that drained the color from your dreams. In the meantime, he might as well get Ben to use his influence to get him a job on the project.

"I will be Clerk of the Works," he said aloud.

SIOBHAN LEFT THE meeting at the state offices with a two-page agreement in her briefcase. She thought about going back to her office to call Don but decided to take the Blue Line to her car parked at Wonderland and drive straight home instead. It was after five-thirty anyway, and the agreement seemed to emit light every time she opened the case to look at it.

Don would get two years' pay, payment for all accrued vacation, sick time, personal days, and comp time. He would also get his pension contributions unless he got a new public job and rolled them over, unlikely even though they'd agreed to expunge the firing from his record. "Voluntary separation," the record would read.

His reprimand for setting the ants on fire would remain, but there would be no mention of the favorable parking arrangements for politicians and reporters. All in all, a very favorable deal for Don. The court case would be dismissed in the morning. Don would need to attend.

Siobhan had dreaded the prospect of Don on the stand. She knew he would be battered by the state's attorney and that he'd want to lash out, his short temper flaring. The fire he set on the ants would pale by comparison. She was happy this was over and that his attendance at the hearing would be perfunctory and silent.

As the old cattle cars of the train rattled her home, she envisioned Don's response to her news. Maybe they'd celebrate with dinner at the Hawthorne and then go home and make love for the first time in months. Don could have a drink or two with dinner and the pins and needles of their recent relationship would disappear. She was proud of Don for keeping to the no alcohol rule. Now he could build on that and live a more sober, fulfilling life. She saw herself and Don and the kids having cookouts in the yard of the house they'd buy in Lynnfield.

ELLSWORTH NELSON CIRCLED the model, notebook in hand, Bic at the ready, occasionally scribbling a terse note. He was mostly ignored by the flow of people in and out of the building through this main lobby. Only one person, an elderly man, stopped to talk to him. The man didn't recognize him but mistook him for a city worker and asked where to go to pay his water bill.

Nelson wanted to say, "don't you know who I am? I'm the foremost architecture critic in Boston and I write for the national magazines. I am Ellsworth Nelson, you dolt." Instead he said, "No, but there is a directory at the top of the stairs."

After another turn around the model, Nelson picked up the manila envelope he had placed atop one corner and headed out the front doors to City Hall Square. He crossed to the far side and peered down Market Street past the crumbling concrete railroad bridge to the open sky beyond. Opening the envelope, he pulled the brochure and the separate pages of drawings out and looked at the site plan. He shuffled the papers and looked at the artist's rendering, noted to have been taken from this viewpoint.

In Ben Holt's design for the huge expanse of Ocean Park, there were only three large plazas: one at the Gateway from the General Edwards Bridge side that opened onto the river as it met the harbor; one that opened onto the Lynnway near the center of the new town's highway frontage and opposite Shepard Street; and one that opened onto the harbor and views towards Nahant. This last plaza lined up just right of the axis with Market Street. The taller buildings on the site were to be located near the plazas, but were separated from the plazas by structures—lower parts of the taller buildings—that would be no more than five stories tall. Along the water the buildings ranged from three to five to seven stories high.

Nelson pulled a chart from the pile and perused it. All of the proposed buildings were odd numbers of stories, not just those along the water. He smiled and envisioned the headline for his article, "The Odd Architect."

"I DON'T THINK that I can *live* in Lynnfield."

Don sat before a plate laden with prime rib, broiled potatoes and carrots, savoring a bottle of Miller and ignoring the empty glass that the waiter had brought for the beer.

"Why don't we just look at a few properties. If you don't like any of them, we'll just drop it."

"When will I get my money?"

"The first payment of thirty-seven five should be issued in the next two or three weeks. Then checks for thirty-seven five on the first of June, December, and June again. Four checks in all, unless you take your pension out...but you don't need to decide that now."

"A lot less than the two million I was gonna get."

"Don, you would never going to get two million dollars."

"Maybe...maybe not."

Siobhan crushed the larger claw of her lobster in her left hand, trying to dissipate the anger that coursed up her spine and lit up her nerves. Why did all clients think they were going to get rich on their suits? She closed her eyes and concentrated on suppressing the energy. Don watched her face, felt a growing fear that she might explode at him, unfolded his arms and leaned toward her to lay his right hand on her left. The oil of the lobster had leaked through her fingers. It repulsed him, but he left his hand on hers anyway.

"Maybe we can look at some houses on Saturday."

"Maybe." Siobhan opened her eyes and started picking at the lobster.

"I'm going to call Ben. I'm going to work on the America's Park project."

"It's *Ocean* Park, now. What job are you looking for there?"

"I'll be Clerk of the Works."

"Oh?"

"He can get me the job."

"Hmmm. Well, they should be starting construction on the Market Street end of the property soon. They've already built the marketing center and a couple of buildings for construction materials and equipment. I'm sure you've seen the frames of some of the new buildings going up. They still have the power lines to bury on the Revere end. At least that's what I hear."

"How come you know so much?"

"We represent the developer and the equity partners."

"Who are they?"

"Some French group. They have offices in New York. I think they're somehow connected to Claudine."

"Maybe *you* could get me the job."

Siobhan loved Don, or at the least she was drawn to him in a way that felt like love. Sometimes the practical side of her, the side that had gotten her through law school and made her a good, no, a great lawyer, told her to run, but the attraction was so strong that she had no choice but to stay. The thought of putting her job on the line to try to get Don this crazy job brought out her practical side.

"I don't really know anyone there. Blair Winston…you met him after your arraignment…is the managing partner who deals with them."

"You could check with him."

"Yes, I'll give him a call."

They both knew that she never would and both silently agreed to leave it there.

"So, a couple of weeks and I get my first check?"

"Should be about that."

"I want to take about five-thousand to bankroll my sports book. I think I can double or triple it. I'll give you most of the rest to put away."

"Do you think that's smart? You've kept your book under the radar."

"Tony's not involved in betting anymore. Those guys are into drugs now. More money in it. The old man never liked drugs, but he's in jail now and everything's changed. The State is trying to make gambling more legit with the proposed lottery, but people still like the sports bet."

"Who's in it now?"

"The only big guy is Clyde Washington, but I've taken him and his brother before. If push comes to shove, I can take them now."

"Do you have to, Don? I don't like it…it worries me."

"Just something small to keep my hand in, that's all."

The voice in her head said, "Run, Siobhan, *run*".

42

'HOW AN ARCHITECT BUYS A REPUTATION' BY Ellsworth Nelson

You, my loyal readers, know that it is in my basic nature to celebrate greatness. These pages have flowed with my paean to the great artists that turn mere bricks, sand and steel into monuments to the human spirit. Conversely, I abhor the waste of God's gifts that crass practitioners visit upon our built environment. To them I reveal the depths of our enmity, for ennui is a mere pass allowing them to continue to foist their feeble work upon us all.

But I have discovered that the world is not merely painted in black and white, good and bad. There is among us a greater danger and a greater sin visited upon God's benevolence. Ben Holt, celebrated in France and the Arabian peninsula, places you might think would have higher standards, has by-passed the hard work that great architects must do to hone their skills. He has found a shorter, less intensive, path to fame: His father-in-law bought it for him, perhaps as a wedding gift.

Now, you, Dear Reader, might be tempted to think that Ben might be that unusual talent, a great designer who sprang whole from the womb. I have it on great authority that this is not so. No less than Munroe Owen Sather has confirmed that Holt was, at best, an incompetent student, perhaps worse. Mo has taught platoons of students the rigors of an examined life in design and they invariably love him for it. When the work got tough for Holt, he disembarked to Paris and became a mere apprentice.

You may appropriately ask what sort of faux accomplishment money will buy you and I am here to provide that answer—a city. Yes, this child has bought his way into the job of creating a new city where accomplished practitioners of the highest stripe have failed. The defunct America's Park site, that drain on the American spirit whose current condition is better described as 'American Stark' is set to rise again, this time under the even more profane moniker, 'Ocean Park.'

I have seen his massing model of the site and have found it profoundly derivative. I will write more on this at a later date if it survives long enough to warrant the expenditure of more valuable newsprint. Sometimes an early death is the most merciful.

DON FOLDED THE *Post* and laid it on the table. "I could kill him and dump his body in the Saugus marshes. Maybe in the trash incinerator. That would be poetic. His body would burn to make electricity. He'd light up Boston." Don laughed at his own joke.

"Don't talk trash. You're not going to do anything to him. You're going to stay far away from him."

Siobhan didn't really think that Don would do anything, but she got worried when he talked like this. She wondered who the real Don was. Was it the kind, generous, attentive Don who brought her seashells and left loving notes in her briefcase? Was it the racist, xenophobic Don who railed against minorities and immigrants getting welfare or job preferences to make up for the prejudices of earlier generations? Was it the first-grader Don who had given a gift to a black child because that child might not receive a single toy for Christmas? Was it the small-time hood who ran his own sports book and physically "discouraged" competition? Was it the smart, well-read, articulate Don who could debate issues with an uncanny clarity and passion? She wondered about her investment in Don and whether it was the volatile combination of all the Dons that made her love him, that made her need him.

278

ANNIE FOLDED THE *Post* and laid it on the table in the break room. She was shaking, angry. Ellsworth Nelson was a pompous ass who had no idea who Ben really was. She wanted to write a letter to the editor, to defend Ben. She took the pen from her pocket and the small notebook sheet used for patient notes. Then she sat there waiting for the words that wouldn't come.

What could she say? That Nelson didn't know Ben? She realized that *she* didn't know Ben either—not this Ben, maybe not the high school Ben either. Who was she to write in his defense? She had dumped him, hadn't she?

The movie played clearly in her head: Ben walking by the car that night in 1967, Ben seeing her and Harold making out, her hand groping Harold's crotch trying to set him free. She saw the car chase through the city, Ben finally turning right when they'd turned left. For the first time, she saw that she hadn't dumped him, but rather he had set her free.

She wrote in her notebook, "Ellsworth Nelson is an ass."

"DID YOU READ Nelson's article?"

"I did."

Ben folded the drawing in half vertically, base to base, then folded the leaves back so that a quarter of each face was now exposed. He then folded it in half horizontally and slipped it into the large white envelope.

"Well, did it piss you off?" Paul was looking for a sign of anger in Ben's face.

"I find Mr. Nelson to be quite humorous."

"MR. HOLT, I wanted to call to apologize."

"For what?"

"For Ellsworth Nelson's article in our paper. The chairman of Post-Media called to complain about the article. He pointed out that your father-in-law is the majority owner of Post-Media which owns our paper. He will be calling Mr. Aubrey personally. I don't usually get involved in editorial content, but given the circumstances..."

Ben interrupted. "What circumstances are those?"

"The article was rather nasty, unnecessarily nasty."

"I didn't notice any factual errors, did you?"

"I don't think..."

"Mr. Spencer, Ellsworth Nelson is a pedant whose articles sell newspapers. Post-Media is in the business of selling newspapers. Marcel...Mr. Aubrey...is in the business of investing in companies that make money. Mr. Nelson mentioned my name several times in the article so I got something out of it, too. So I think everyone is whole. I only ask that you print one correction."

"Yes, of course. What is that?"

"Just a correction saying that Satart Holt is the designer of Ocean Park, not Ben Holt. Nothing more."

"We can do that. I can just imagine your reaction when you read the article."

"Probably not."

"I'm sorry?"

"I laughed."

43

"YOU HAVEN'T COMPLETED THE APPLICATION."

The woman who sat on the other side of the steel desk lowered the sheet of paper to the desktop and slid it towards Don. Her brown hair was tied back, revealing a small brown mole on her earlobe where a diamond stud should be. She wore a beige blouse beneath a dark gray jacket. She was slightly overweight with ample round breasts, the overall effect of which was appealing to Don. He thought he'd be happy to bang her, but he reminded himself he had Siobhan.

"Why don't you take it to the waiting room and finish it?"

"Why don't you read it? You don't need any more than the information written there."

"I'm sorry?"

"Read the name."

"Don Holt?" She didn't bother to look at the paper.

"Yes."

"Should that mean something to me?"

The Ocean Park project was bringing in a lot of people who were new to the area, Don thought. These were people who knew nothing about the real power in the city. "Ben Holt's brother."

"I'm confused. Who is Ben Holt and why should that mean anything to me?"

"The architect, something and Holt."

"Ah, Satart Holt."

"Yes, *that* Holt."

"Did they send you? Were you supposed to see someone specifically?"

"No, I haven't talked to him yet."

"Oh, I see. Well we don't work for the architect. We are doing the hiring for the engineering firm that is managing the contractors. What job are you looking for?"

"I'll be the Clerk of the Works."

"Well, you'll need to finish filling out the form and list your education and experience."

"My experience is that I can make sure you don't have any problems."

"I'm not sure I understand. Did you read the job postings in the waiting area?"

"I don't *need* to read job postings. I'm the guy who can make sure you don't have problems. Understand?"

"What kind of problems?"

"All sorts of problems: deliveries, the union, trash pick-up. I'm sort of an all-around problem solver." Don looked at the nameplate sitting on the desk. "Now listen, Rebecca Hart. There are all sorts of people you will need to take care of on a project like this. I can make sure everything is copacetic."

Rebecca Hart had been shocked and dismayed when the first guy who'd offered to make sure there were "no problems" had showed up in her office. Don was the sixth or seventh—maybe eighth if you counted the guy who'd mumbled so badly you couldn't be sure of what he was saying. After the first two had come in, her boss had worked out a procedure with the local police and the FBI. The "applicant" would be told that they had to come back to meet with someone more "senior." That someone would be an FBI special agent.

"You need to meet with someone more *senior* than me. We'll call you to set it up."

"Can't we set it up now?"

"I don't know his schedule. He should be in tomorrow. We'll call you."

"Maybe I'll stop in tomorrow."

"No need to do that, we'll call *you*."

She got up from her desk, walked to the door, opened it and walked out, leaving Don sitting at the desk. He sat there for a few minutes, wondering if she would return. Finally, he stood, walked to the doorway, looked up and down the row of offices, all with closed doors, and walked out to the waiting area. He stood before the reception desk and waited until the receptionist finished a phone call.

"I was meeting with Ms. Hart. Do you know where she went?"

"She left for the day."

"Odd."

Don exited into a day that had turned gray and walked home along the beach, scheming.

"SATART HOLT"

"Can I speak to Ben?"

"Mr. Holt is away. Can I take a message?"

"It's his brother, Don."

"Yes, Mr. Holt. Mr. Holt is in Paris.'

"Okay, I'll call him there."

Don didn't want to let the receptionist know that he didn't have Ben's Paris phone number, or that he didn't even know how to make a call to Paris. Maybe you could call the operator. No, Siobhan might be able to get the number. She knew how to call foreign places.

He had a couple of hours until she got home. He could stop by the Hi Hat and Tony's and see if he could pick up some bets. Baseball was producing for him. Some guys wanted to bet on the Braves as if they were still in Boston. The young guys never bet the Braves, but the geezers did. As long as they stayed alive and away from Florida, Don made good book.

44

"**D**A-DEE."

Pascha was sitting with Ben in the oversized chair that Ben had designed especially for this room. It was early morning and the sun was just rising over the university buildings east of their Paris home. Ben had designed and built this room atop Claudine's art deco mansion as a square with tall French doors on all sides leading to a walkway that ran around the outside walls. An arbor shaded the walk to the east and south where the mahogany walkway was deepest. Two large rattan chairs sat outside the center doors to the east, separated by a teak table only large enough to hold a couple of cups and two small plates. Ben often started his day in one of those chairs. Today Pascha had joined him and climbed up into the chair so that they could read together.

"Da-dee, can we do *flaneur* today?"

"Pascha, you know that Claudine doesn't like you to mix French and English."

"But Da-dee, I am a mix of French and English, and American, too."

Ben smiled and squeezed Pascha to his chest. "Are we going to invite Claudine and Daniel?"

"Maybe." Pascha thought about the question. "Maybe we should let them sleep."

"It looks like it's going to be a nice Sunday. Let's leave a message for them to meet us at Marché Sainte Catharine."

"Da-dee, can we go to the secret Rose Garden?"

"Yes, of course. Come let's get you dressed."

45

May 1983

DON LAY IN BED STARING AT THE CEILING WITHOUT really seeing it. Siobhan had left for work an hour earlier. As usual she opened the window in the bedroom before she left so that Don could smell the sea air. Her apartment, now *their* apartment, was on Phillips Street, so close to the ocean that you could hear the waves slapping the seawall if there was an offshore storm. There was no storm this morning so the prevalent noise was some traffic on Humphrey Street. Don didn't hear that noise either; it was his trance time—the hour each morning between awaking and arising. Each day this hour was full of silent thought, often daydreams, sometimes leftover arguments to be continued and rejiggered so that they worked out in Don's favor. This morning he was running accounts for his burgeoning sports book and his plans for expansion. His musings finished with feelings of searing anger over his rejection at Ocean Park and Ben's refusal to help his brother.

Even though several months had passed since he'd had lunch with Ben at the Capitol diner, and despite the money he was now making on gambling, Ben's refusal to step in and get Don the clerk job still stung, and Don still ran through imagined scenes of the project's failure and his own triumph during his morning reveries. In each scene, the project would need him, and each time he ran the scene, he would refine the details: They would need Don to crush the union unrest or to deflect threats from mob-controlled subcontractors. They would send

Rebecca Hart to beg for his help and offer herself as part of the deal. He would turn her away, remembering that he loved Siobhan, and demand that Ben himself beseech his aid. Ben was his brother, of course, and Don would not deny Ben his help.

Having finished his reverie to his satisfaction, he arose, showered, and dressed. In the kitchen he found a half-finished bottle of Miller and poured it into a juice glass, draining the contents in two gulps. He belched lightly, grab his jacket with the elastic-bound index cards in the inside pocket, and headed out the door. He was scouting new territory today, driving through the neighborhoods on either side of the Salem line. He would make notes on the bars he found and would plan to return to the promising looking places late that afternoon. That was the best time for sports bets, he thought, before the bars became too busy with the evening rush and you couldn't keep an eye out for cops or Feds or competition. If he had time, he might even drive over near the College in Salem. He hadn't done much book with college students yet, but he thought they might be a natural market—a good fit for his superior intelligence.

BEN FOUND HIMSELF becoming cranky whenever the time for leaving Paris again drew near. Over the past few months he had been spending more time in the New York office and traveling to Boston to supervise the design and construction of Ocean Park. He had also spent a lot of time in Vermont checking on the clearing of the undergrowth on the parcel of land adjacent to their South Woodstock house. He and Claudine had talked about building a studio and school there, but as much as Ben loved South Woodstock, he worried that the new venture would take him from Paris even more.

PASCAL AND BEN spent every other Monday afternoon at their usual café table talking about projects and staff, design issues, engineering issues, client reviews, whether to open an office in Chicago or San Francisco. They had six offices now—Paris, Milan, Beirut, London, New York and Boston—and two large administrative and support staffs in Milan and New York. Pascal headed the Milan, Beirut, and London offices and was traveling often to Buenos Aires to consult on a large project there with a firm headed by a Satart Holt alumnae. Ben had been quietly proud when Pascal has suggested that he take over responsibility for the Paris office and happy that his responsibilities now made his Paris trips more than just a personal matter.

Ben's flights to and from Paris had developed into a routine: taking the latest flight from Boston, sketching and writing notes for the Paris office, taking an early evening flight from Paris, sketching and writing notes for both U.S. offices. Ben's bound notebooks now numbered close to fifty. Each was numbered and dated and stored by the firm's archivist in Paris. While Pascal's notebooks were a small A3 size, Ben's were quite large A6 size—as large as two sheets of standard American paper. Pascal often joked that his notebooks were made for the sensibilities of a Frenchman, while Ben's were big, brash, and American. Ben decided that he liked the description and had small U.S. flag labels attached to the lower right corner of the back cover.

One Monday morning, as they sat over their coffee, Pascal brought up the subject of his notebooks. "I want to ask you how you would feel about donating my sketchbooks to a foundation. Not immediately, of course, but when I have gone."

"Are you ill?"

"No, I am very well, as far as one can know these things. I was in the back stacks with the archivist...Madame Bello, I think...looking for some sketch plans for an article I am writing, and I noticed several shelves of my old old notebooks...and yours, as well."

"What is the name of the foundation?"

"One of my old students approached me with the idea of establishing a foundation which would operate a small school and research library to continue my work. We have been bringing fewer students to work and study in the office...the foundation would take over that responsibility."

"Interesting. Claudine has been talking about starting a school in South Woodstock. She even told the *Globe* about it when they were interviewing us for an article about our new home there."

"Yes, I remember the article. It describes a very idyllic place."

Ben smiled, then continued. "Satart Holt has grown so much that I have much less time to just sit and think. It makes my moods darker and my natural orneriness more mean. She thought that the school might bring me back to my roots...*our* roots really...and make me happier. It seemed to me like just more work, even though it might be work that I'd love."

"Is everything well between you?"

"Yes, yes, of course. I only get dark and cranky when it is time to leave her and the boys."

"And will you start the school?"

"We bought a large piece of land next to the Vermont House. She said we should buy it for the school. I've been clearing some of the underbrush, but I think I have other plans for the land."

"What is that?"

"Walking and riding trails. There are two riding trails through the land right now, but they are narrow and in bad shape. You know how much Claudine loves to ride. The boys...especially Pascha... love to wander with me. It is our favorite alone time."

"Yes, I believe that I've heard Pascha call it 'doing *flaneur*'."

"He does. Some day both of the boys will be grown and on their own and those meanderings will be my fondest memories."

"You must make them now."

"And you must make your foundation. I could not deny others what you have given to me."

Pascal smiled, lifted his cup in salute, then sipped his espresso looking intently at Ben's face. "There is one other request that I must make for the foundation."

"You don't even have to ask. Claudine and I will be major benefactors, of course. You must ask Marcel as well. He will be hurt if you don't."

"It's not that, but thank you. Would you consider donating some of *your* notebooks, as well? I know it is much to ask, especially if you are planning your school, but I have asked all of those who studied with me to donate at least a small piece of their work. The foundation would not be complete without something from you."

"Pascal, I could never deny you anything that you want or need."

46

March 1987

IT TOOK ALMOST FOUR YEARS TO COMPLETE THE FUN-
draising, design and construction of the Satart Foundation Library.
It was built on the old farmstead of Pascal's grandfather's family in
the foothills of the Pyrenees above St. Jean de Luz. Pascal had insisted
that Ben design the library and its gardens, and Marcel, who was the
major benefactor, approved.

Ben had conceived several parts for the library—a barnlike fieldstone structure, a building with a tiled façade that recalled Pascal's
favored material, a rough-formed concrete structure that recalled the
battlements on the nearby Atlantic shore. In the end, it had been a
comment by Daniel as they walked the woods and fields at the site,
that had generated the final design.

"It would almost be a shame to build anything here," Daniel had
said. Young Pascha had simply nodded.

THE FAÇADE OF the building shown like old gold. The soft glow
of the copper screening that covered the façade would turn a soft
green over time, but for now it was burnished by the Aquitaine sun.
Behind the screening, panels of tall sliding glass could be moved
aside and stacked near the middle of each façade, creating large open

expanses from which to view the gardens and woods. Slender steel columns were set back more than five feet from the façade.

On the fourth side, a crisp silver shaft enclosed a single support from which cables radiated for a bridge that crossed the stream at the building's entry and engaged the copper-screened box. Here an inner box was clad with thin translucent marble panels and contained the library stacks as well as conference rooms, work areas, kitchen and toilets and a three-hundred person theater-style seminar room. A thirty-foot-wide overhang of the roof protected the entry which was flanked by low, bench-like elements of slanted steel supported by a steel structure that recalled driftwood. There were three of these—two on one side of the entry bridge, one on the other—and Ben called them "perches," to be leaned against, much like he and his friends had leaned against a low wall in high school.

When Daniel saw the completed building, he squealed with delight. "It is perfect as Pascal's place, Ben!"

Daniel was almost fifteen now and too old for "Da-dee," but Ben knew he could look forward to at least one more year or two of hearing it from Pascha. If Daniel was Ben's child, Pascha was Claudine's. Ben loved watching Daniel and Pascha together, two different personalities, negotiating their relationship. He leaned against one of the perches and watched them explore the space. He began thinking that it might be time to change his relationship with the firm that Pascal Satart had started and grown with Ben's help. This building, this homage to Pascal, might be the catalyst for the change.

"Da-dee?"

"Yes, Pascha?"

"Can we go into the library and see *Oncle's* sketchbooks?"

"Yes, let us." Ben called out, "Daniel!"

"He's already there."

"Well then, let's go join him."

Pascha slipped his hand into Ben's and they headed for the library. Tonight a large crowd would gather for the dedication, but this morning the special place was theirs alone.

"I LIKE WHAT you have done with my father's farm."

"*Merci*, Père Satart...that means much to me."

"I never thought I'd live to see it...a building almost as beautiful as your wife, but alas, even this building must fall short. Your wife is more beautiful still."

"Indeed she is, but you see her through the eyes of a normal man. In eyes colored by love, she is far more beautiful than anything man has ever made."

Pascal's father, now ninety-four, kissed Ben on both cheeks and patted his shoulder. The band had stopped playing, so Ben slipped his hand under the older man's elbow and guided him toward the dais. Claudine was standing with Pascal, Marcel, and Bernadine, and the children were sitting on the edge of the dais, young Pascha dangling his feet over the edge. Père Satart kissed Claudine on both cheeks and whispered in her ear.

The crowd quietened and the speeches began. The Minister of Culture apologized for President d'Estaing's absence due to an appearance at the United Nations in New York and gave a long, convoluted speech about the importance of art to a great society. The mayor of St. Jean de Luz welcomed all of the distinguished visitors and all but begged for them to spend some money in his little town. The director of the library spoke of the great gift that was the library, the great talent that was Pascal's, the great generosity that was Marcel's, and the beauty of the building and grounds. Then Pascal rose to the podium, thanked everyone for their kind words and their attendance, and claimed to be an ineloquent speaker. As he described the place and the history of his family on this land, he looked to his father and became so choked up he could no longer speak.

WHEN BEN ASKED Claudine to join him on the dais, she looked at him quizzically, wondering what he was up to. Although she didn't speak, Ben understood her question. "Come celebrate our friend," he said.

They mounted the dais together and the two boys immediately joined them, young Pascha with one hand in his mother's hand and one hand in his father's. Daniel walked a step to his father's left.

The four stood at the lectern and Ben spoke. "This building rises from the spirit of this place and from the love that Claudine, Daniel, Pascha and I have for our dearest friend. Please enjoy it."

Ben turned towards Claudine, who wrapped her arms around his waist and kissed him warmly. The crowd's applause grew as the kiss persisted. Claudine drew back and looked into Ben's eyes.

"You are an eloquent man."

"It wasn't much of a speech."

"Short perhaps, but so eloquent...like your words to Père Satart."

As they moved towards the side of the dais, Ben noticed the eye-patch in the crowd of faces. At the bottom of the steps, Bill Button grabbed Ben's arm.

"Can I see you before you head back to New York?"

"Tomorrow. Eleven. I'll be in the garden here."

47

B EN SAT IN THE GARDEN AT THE TOP OF THE HILL.
Père Satart struggled up the hill and dropped to the bench, out
of breath. He sat silently for several minutes, then spoke.

"What are you drinking?"

"Just black coffee."

"Ah, your *allongé*."

"Yes."

"Are you expecting someone?"

"Yes, I am."

"Well, they are coming up the path.'

"They? I am expecting only Bill Button."

"Well, *they* are coming up the path."

Père Satart rose stiffly and ambled toward the path that led back
down the hill to the museum. Ben saw him stop at the verge, then
disappear just as Bill Button and Rachel crested the hill from the
opposite path. The sun behind them silhouetted Rachel's attractive
figure. Ben counted the years since he'd last seen her; he thought it
must have been at least six.

"You didn't tell me you were bringing company." Ben stood and
faced Bill, ignoring Rachel.

"Does it matter?" Bill raised his hands to his waist, open palms up.

"No, it's your meeting."

Rachel leered at Ben. "Do you still hate me?"

"I never hated you. I just didn't have much use for you."

"I think I'd rather you hated me."

Ben turned away from Rachel. "Bill, what is this about?"

Bill sat next to Ben while Rachel stood and scanned the garden, then finally sat down next to Bill. Bill swore Ben to secrecy, telling him that what he and Rachel were about to reveal included information important to the security of the United States as well as to its friends, information that might also be of great interest to certain of its enemies.

"Then why are you telling *me?*"

"Because your brother is about to fuck up our operation." Rachel had reached around Bill and was jabbing a finger at Ben.

"Rachel!" Bill pulled Rachel's hand away from Ben's face. She resumed scanning the garden.

"Excuse Rachel's outburst. What she says is true, though we believe his involvement is coincidental."

Bill reported that he had left the cultural attaché position and was now a trade representative. Rachel was still with AID but in an international commerce position.

"If you want me to believe what you're telling me, drop the cover. I know you are both CIA. Hell, everyone knows you are both CIA."

"Rule number one: Never drop your cover."

"Thank you."

Bill resumed his description of the operation that he and Rachel were involved in. He left out names and details, but described a money-laundering operation that involved anti-government factions from France, Germany, Italy and Japan. He and Rachel were following the money to organized crime syndicates in the United States. After the criminal prosecutions of the last several years, the syndicates had broken up into small pieces and new groups had taken over some of the syndicate's former businesses, including bookmaking and prostitution.

"And you think Don's involved in this?"

"Not directly, but he started out with a small sports book which he has been quite aggressively working to grow. This growth has brought him to the attention of another group whose territory he has been invading."

"Don knows his way around...that doesn't sound like something he'd do."

"The word is that this other group is headed by a guy who Don has butted heads with before."

"Name?"

"Clyde Washington."

"Shit. Clyde Washington is a pretender, a small-time tough. Don personally beat the crap out of him thirty years ago. Don worked for Tony Angelo and has a whole slew of political connections...he's *way* out of Clyde Washington's league."

"Not anymore. Clyde got hooked into the money-laundering game and he has flourished. Angelo dumped your brother a long time ago because of his alcohol problem."

"What do you want from me?"

"Don's battle with Clyde is creating a lot of noise. Clyde's on edge and has his antennas up. That's making it hard for us to get on the inside. I'm afraid Rachel's rather indelicate outburst is true. Don is about to fuck up our operation."

"What can I do?"

"Get him to drop out of the business. If our guy can approach Clyde as a broker to an agreement to get Don out of the sports book business, we think Clyde will let our guy in."

"I'm not sure that either Clyde or Don are gentlemen's agreement types."

"We'll take care of Clyde...he'll jump at the chance. Rolf can make it worth his while. You have to convince Don."

"What's in it for him?"

"He gets to live."

Ben stared into Bill's eye. He read the message there.

48

June 1988

T HE WATER IN THE OIL-STAINED MEN'S ROOM SINK
was marbled with the blood from Don's hand. The small finger was
probably broken and all of the knuckles on his right hand were starting
to swell. His jaw was sore, but he was quite sure it was still intact. He
opened and closed it gingerly, but detected no inordinate movement in
the joints as he explored them with the fingers of his left hand.

It would be at least an hour before Siobhan got home. He had
already packed his stuff for the weekend trip to Old Orchard Beach.
She had packed two nights ago and their suitcases, her makeup bag,
and a bag of snacks for the road were sitting near the apartment door.
If he got home first and took the bags downstairs, she might not see
his mangled hand in the dark.

He opened the restroom door and scanned the lighted forecourt
of the gas station. The only car at the pumps was a Toyota Celica
being fueled by a youngish woman. He slid out the door, walked
briskly to his car, got in, depressed the lock, turned the key in the
ignition and drove home.

DON HAD JUST brought the bag of snacks downstairs and set
it atop the suitcases when Siobhan drove up. She was early. As she
emerged from the car, almost before she could even finish standing

up, she turned to find him standing in front of her about to plant a kiss on her lips.

"I've brought the things down. I'll load the car if you want to go upstairs to use the bathroom before we go."

"You seem awfully anxious to get out of here."

"Just excited. We haven't been away in a while and I'd like to hit the road."

"Okay. Just let me check to make sure there isn't anything else I need."

Siobhan walked up the stairs and into the apartment. She looked through the bedroom and her closet, grabbed a white, stretchy top from her dresser drawer and headed for the bathroom where she opened the medicine cabinet, stared at it for a moment, and looked around the sink counter. She'd started to turn for the door when she noticed several bandage wrappers in the trash basket. She took them out, looked at them for a moment, then replaced them. She turned off the bathroom light and headed across the living room and out the door, locking it and then descending the stairs. Don was already sitting in the passenger's seat. Siobhan slipped into the driver's seat and turned to Don.

"You don't want to drive?"

"No, you can...if you're not too tired."

"Did you hurt yourself? I found bandage wrappers in the waste basket."

"God, I was so stupid."

"Pray tell."

Don held up his right hand far enough away so that Siobhan couldn't see it well in the dim light of the car. "I closed my car door on my hand. I was talking to Robbie and not paying attention. There was blood everywhere. I'm so embarrassed."

"Did you break anything?"

"Probably not, but if it's not better Monday I'll stop by the emergency room."

Don had always refused to have a regular doctor even though he was covered on Siobhan's insurance now. Siobhan had given up trying to convince him that the emergency room was not what the insurers meant by "primary care." She could take a look at his hand when they got to the hotel and see if it was all right. She turned the key in the ignition and backed out of the driveway taking care not to hit the black sedan parked on the opposite side of the street.

Stupid driver, she thought. One of the first things her father had taught her about driving was never to park across from a driveway. It had been his pet peeve, and on more than a few occasions he'd approached visitors to their neighbors to inform them of the dangers in so doing. His lectures had embarrassed her as a teenager, but the lesson had stuck.

As she shifted into drive, she noticed that the driver of the sedan was a man with a large round face and a crew cut. He seemed to leer at her as he drove away.

Siobhan drove out to Route 1, picking up the highway just past Goodwin's in Lynnfield. She thought of stopping there knowing how much Don loved their fried clams, but decided that it was too early to stop. Maybe they'd stop in Topsfield or at the Agawam in Rowley. If Don didn't want to stop there, they could stop at the Howard Johnson's at the Portsmouth Circle, but that was a good hour-and-a-half away. In her mind, she settled on the Agawam.

The drive up Route 1 was fairly easy. Don fell asleep in the seat beside her. His head fell over onto her shoulder and she tried to drive with it there, but after a short time her arm began to fall asleep. She gently pushed him off her shoulder and he flopped over to the door side of the seat, his head resting against the hard door pillar. The feeling returned to her arm, but now she felt guilty that his head was knocking against the metal pillar. She looked over to check to see that the door was locked. It was, and she felt a bit better knowing that at least he wouldn't fall out of the car.

As they left Peabody and drove through Danvers, the number of businesses on the road thinned out and the traffic became lighter. She had started out the day tired, and the hum of the tires on the road wasn't helping her alertness. A couple of times she seemed to lose

track of her location and wondered whether she had fallen asleep at
the wheel. She looked at her watch. It had been just over a half-hour
since they'd left home. She thought that they'd be at the diner soon.
The thought had barely formed in her mind when she saw the sign
for Route 133 and knew the Agawam was just ahead.

Don awoke as she turned left into the parking lot. He looked
at the silver façade and immediately knew where he was. "Ah, the
Agawam. Good choice."

They chose a booth along the windows and Don immediately
started flipping through the song lists on the tableside jukebox. He
dropped in his coins and selected three songs including an old song
by the Lettermen which played first, "When I Fall In Love."

Don ordered the meatloaf and Siobhan the egg salad sandwich
and a cup of black coffee. They shared a piece of cherry pie, the kind
with a lattice top—Don's favorite. As he stood at the cashier's counter paying the bill, Siobhan noticed a man with a round face that
looked strikingly similar to the man she had seen in the car at the end
of the driveway. Odd, she thought, but dismissed it as coincidence.
There must be a lot of men who looked that way, not uncommon
among certain European ethnicities. Still, her experience as a criminal defense attorney made her wary of the type.

Don held open the door for her and she walked through it. She
scanned the parking lot for the black sedan, but saw nothing resem-
bling it among two pickup trucks, a stake-body truck and a smattering
of cars—including two VW beetles parked side-by-side, both yellow.

She looked into the diner as she was starting the car. The man
with the round face was still sitting at the counter. She looked again
through the rearview mirror as they waited to drive onto Route 1.
The man was gone. A small panic welled up in her until she detected
him again just inside the door, talking on the pay phone. She relaxed into the seat, hit the accelerator and slipped onto the highway,
but headed south. She drove only a couple hundred feet, pulled into
a parking lot and made the U-turn back onto Route 1 north. As
she drove by the Agawam, she looked across towards the diner. The

headlights of the stake-body truck blinded her for an instant, but as she drove by the entry, she could make out the silhouette of a man on the phone and thought it must be the man with the round face.

The road was mostly empty for the next several miles. Occasionally, a car would enter the road just ahead or just behind them, then turn off onto a side road a half-mile later. A vehicle— probably a truck since his headlights were positioned above that of most cars—was following some distance away, but didn't seem particularly dangerous. It was probably the stake-body truck that had been pulling out of the Agawam lot as Siobhan had driven by the second time.

The traffic grew heavier as they approached Newburyport. Suddenly, in the rear view mirror, Siobhan recognized the stake-body truck in the right lane about ten cars behind her. She wasn't sure why she felt so wary of the truck, but decided to get off at High Street. She didn't use her turn signal, and the car behind her blared its horn, the driver saluting her. When Siobhan saw the stake-body truck continue on past the exit, she breathed more easily. She looked over at Don—he was asleep again, and she began to resent his absence while she worried about their safety. She wound her way through Newburyport and reentered Route 1 at Merrimack Street.

As they crossed the Merrimack River Bridge and entered Salisbury, the traffic became lighter again. Siobhan chided herself for her wariness and vowed to leave her defense attorney antenna at the office in the future. She lightened her grip on the steering wheel and settled back into the seat.

The stretch of road ahead was mostly bordered by businesses that closed at night. With the weekend ahead she didn't expect even late workers to be hanging around. So it didn't surprise her that all the buildings looked dark and the parking lots abandoned.

As she approached a large scrapyard, she saw taillights come on ahead on the right side of the road. Drawing closer, she realized it was the stake-body truck. She depressed the accelerator to pick up speed. She turned to look into the cab of the truck as she passed by and just barely missed a teal blue Toyota pulling out ahead of her. She leaned on her horn as the other car accelerated. The driver slammed on his brakes, and she reacted—pressing her foot to the brake pedal as hard as she could. The car squealed to a stop almost on the Toyota's bumper and then stalled out just as the Toyota burned rubber, fishtailed, and sped away. Siobhan leaned over to turn the key in the ignition, but felt a bump from behind. Looking into the rearview mirror, she realized the stake-body truck had begun pushing her car down the road.

Don was awake now and yelling obscenities at her. They both reached for the keys in the ignition at the same time and the keys fell out onto the floor. Siobhan and Don felt along the mat frantically trying to recover the keys. Siobhan felt them for a moment, but they slipped away. Suddenly, she felt the car tilting onto its side. The truck was pushing them off the road and into a swampy area. The car started rolling side-over-side and the driver's side door pillar slammed into Siobhan's head. As the darkness enclosed her, she felt dizzy and disoriented, then vomited and blacked out.

DON FELT WET, rough grass around him and realized that he had been thrown from the car. He heard low-toned voices and tried to cry out for help, but nothing would come from his mouth. His throat hurt. It was hard to breathe and the pain in his legs was overwhelming. He began to feel the wet trickle from his nose.

Suddenly he felt himself being pulled from the grass. Hands under his arms dragged him up the embankment. He tried to open his eyes, but could barely manage a slit. He made out the silhouettes of two big men standing in the light of the stake-body truck. Including the men dragging him, that amounted to four. He'd taken three men before, but he had never felt hurt this badly.

The men dragging him dropped him on the pavement beside the truck. Don thought this might be his one chance, but immediately felt a huge weight slamming into his chest. Three blows later, his lungs exploded.

Don became serenely calm. A white light around him grew brighter. At first he thought it might be the truck's lights, but this light was whiter, brighter, and it drew towards him until it enveloped him. He felt an urge to move towards the light. He could still hear the men's voices, heard one of them tell the others to drag the woman from the car. He wondered if he should go back for Siobhan, but the draw of the white light was too strong.

49

THE SCANNER CRACKLED, THEN BEEPED THREE tones, and Annie heard Phil Hidcote's voice from the black box. She turned up the volume with her left hand while writing notes with her right.

"White male, mid-forties, head trauma, probable internal bleeding, not breathing, unresponsive, ETA two minutes."

She called Dr. Hawthorne's beeper number and headed towards the emergency room doors, grabbing Suzie McKenzie from a cubicle on her way. She could see through the small glass panes in the double doors that the ambulance had pulled into the parking area and was now backing into the dock. Almost before the ambulance had stopped, the back door flipped open and the new guy on Phil's crew jumped out. He had the stretcher half-way out of the truck before Phil and Sam came from the cab to take the other end.

The new guy rattled off numbers. They were not good. This guy was clinically dead. Dr. Hawthorne ran through the open doors and looked at Annie who had her stethoscope plugged into her ears. She shook her head. Hawthorne looked at the body, noted the color, touched two fingers behind its left ear, and stood back to look at his watch.

"I'm declaring him dead, ten fifty-five p.m., although I'd guess he died before you got him into the ambulance. Better bag him for the coroner."

Annie nodded, then looked at Phil. "Any ID?"

"Yeah. We've got his wallet. Didn't need it anyway. I know him. Don Holt."

Annie turned white. She slumped against the bumper of the ambulance. Phil grabbed her arm to keep her from toppling to the pavement.

"Did anyone contact his family?" she said.

"Yeah. Cops called them. Trooper named Meehan knew his brother. I guess he's some big mucky-muck."

"Ben."

"Yeah. You know him?"

"He was my high school boyfriend."

"Oh."

The new guy spoke. "He's in the magazines all the time. He's married to Claudine Aubrey."

Phil looked surprised. "The fashion designer?"

"You know fashion designers?" It was Annie's turn to be surprised.

"Nah. Wife loves her. Dragged me to a benefit she was at. Must say she's hot. Husband was there, too. Spoke about some building named for a friend of theirs. Guess the husband designed the building."

The new guy was intrigued by the possibility of meeting Claudine. "Maybe she'll show up with him if he actually comes in looking for his brother. He may not know he's dead."

Two state police cruisers with lights flashing but no sirens pulled in front of the ambulance. They were followed by a black Suburban with dark tinted windows, which was in turn followed by two more cruisers. The doors of the Suburban all flew open at the same time. Two men in dark suits emerged and were quickly joined by four troopers from the cruisers. The troopers hesitated for a moment when a man in a suit and shirt but no tie got out of the truck. The man held his hand back into the truck, and a tall slim woman in a dark sheath dress emerged and wrapped her hand around the man's arm.

The gaggle of people moved past the ambulance and into the emergency room. Before they disappeared, Annie and Phil stared at the woman. The man with her caught sight of them and almost smiled. He slipped his hand into the small of the woman's back. She reached up and caressed the back of his neck.

"Ask and you shall receive," said Phil. "Have to call the wife."

"Yeah."

"That Ben?"

"Yeah."

"Sorry you let him go?"

Annie stared toward the emergency room door. "No."

"Right."

HALF AN HOUR later, Claudine walked up to the nurses' station where Annie stood filling out paperwork on a new patient who had just been sent up to Radiology.

"Pardon me, but could I have a glass of ice and some water for my husband?"

"Yes, of course."

Annie walked Claudine into a room behind the nurses' station and filled a glass with ice from a large icemaker. She pointed out a water bubbler in a counter near the waiting area.

"I'm sorry about Don."

"Did you know him well?"

"No, not really...not for a long while anyway."

"Ah. I did not know him well either. We live in Paris and New York much of the time, so we do not get to see him. He was very much part of who my husband is, if you know what I mean."

"Not really, I guess...I was an only child."

"Alas, I too was an only child. It is much different to be from a large family, no? My husband is designing the Ocean Park on the harbor. It is a labor of love for him. He used to fish there with his brothers when they were young. Are you from here, too?"

"Yes, though I never fished from the Gas Wharf, I did hear many stories about it from my high school boyfriend."

"I'll ask my husband to speak with you before we leave. You can share old stories from your boyfriend."

Annie was burning to tell Claudine that Ben *was* her high school boyfriend, but she thought it might make her look like the loser. She was just a nurse; Ben was married to this beautiful, rich, successful woman who had arrived amongst bodyguards and troopers. She watched as Claudine walked back to the cubicle where Don lay waiting for the last of his family to arrive and say goodbye.

Two days later, a large bouquet of flowers arrived in a gorgeous, simple vase. The accompanying card read, "Thank you for your kindness, Nurse Hachette. —Claudine Aubrey Holt."

Annie left the flowers at the nurses' station, but took the card and slipped it onto the shelf in her locker.

The funeral was almost a week later. It had to be delayed for the autopsy and a coroner's inquiry. The police were still searching for Siobhan. They had initially considered her a "person of interest" in Don's death, but after interviewing Blair Winston, her family, court officials, and Ben, they filed a missing person's report. Even with all the testimony in her favor, they still thought that she might somehow have been involved. They started looking into bank accounts, credit card transactions and insurance records.

One morning, the Captain called a meeting of the officers on Don's case. Three suits were at the meeting, obviously Feds. The investigating officers were told that the FBI was taking over the case and were to turn over all of the investigation materials. One of the cops made a stink about being taken off the case and wondered aloud about a cover-up. The senior agent, six-foot-four and about two-hundred and twenty pounds, grabbed him at the collar and pushed him into an office. He told the cop that he was running down the wrong road and to keep his mouth shut or he would shut it. The agent stopped on his way out the office door and turned to the cop.

"She's dead, too, most probably. The killers wanted to send a message with Don. He was found because they wanted the message

to be clear: 'Don't fuck with our business.' This is above your rank…
mine too…I'm just an errand boy in this. I'm no happier than you
are. This is being handled out of Washington. An inter-agency operation. That's all I've got."

50

BEN MET BILL BUTTON FOR BREAKFAST THE morning of Don's funeral and Bill told Ben about the Washington's suspected involvement in Don's death. He recommended that Ben arrange more intense security for himself, Claudine, and the boys. Ben reported that he'd already suspected Washington's involvement and that Marcel had arranged for their security detail to be assigned from his own internal security operation even when they were in the United States. No more rentals.

BEN DID THE eulogy at Don's funeral. His dad and Ron sat silently in the front row flanking his mother. She did not cry, but sat staring at Ben. He knew that nothing he said or did would redeem him in his mother's eyes. He had failed his brother and he knew that she wouldn't be convinced otherwise, so he didn't try. Claudine and the boys sat in the front row on the farthest end from the casket, and Ben, Marcel, and Bernadine sat in the row directly behind them.

The church was crammed with relatives, childhood friends, Don's drinking buddies, neighbors, politicians, old girlfriends, beach people, and, scattered throughout, federal agents. Bill and Rachel were there in the same row with Marcel and Bernadine. Annie and Phil sat near the back.

Ben stood beside the casket, his right hand resting on it, and spoke of his brother. He told childhood stories that made the congregation laugh, cry, and nod their heads, recognizing in Ben's stories the Don they had known.

He told of Old Man Brown showing up at their door to complain about Mr. Holt's hooligan sons. Old Man Brown hadn't seemed surprised that the tall man was wearing an overcoat in the house in the middle of summer, an overcoat that concealed Don on Ben's shoulders, speaking in his lowest voice, promising to discipline his sons. They would have pulled off the ruse had not Mr. Brown encountered their dad just as he'd walked down the driveway to leave. Ben looked to his dad who confirmed the story with a vigorous nod of his head.

Ben told of coming home from school just before Christmas in first grade and informing his mother that he needed to bring a twenty-five cent present to school for Secret Santa. His mother had asked Don if he needed to bring one, too. Don had said that he hadn't heard anything about it, but his mother, assuming Don just hadn't been paying attention, had sent him into school with a gift, as well. Don's class didn't celebrate Christmas, so instead of bringing the gift back home, Don had given it away to a child he thought might get little or nothing for Christmas—a child whose dad was gone and whose mom didn't have a job.

Finally, Ben told the story of their senior year in high school. Don had had American history the period before Ben and had arranged to slip him the answers for the quiz that would be given that day. Ben had distributed the answers to his friends. When the teacher had started reviewing the quiz, he'd quickly realized that the class had been given the answers and asked Ben to stand and list them out loud. Ben had smiled and recited "ABABCDABAB."

Finishing the eulogy, Ben ran his hand along the length of the casket, said "Goodnight, brother" in a low voice, turned, and walked along the face of the row to Claudine and the boys, and embraced them.

51

July 1989

THE DEDICATION AND OPENING OF THE FIRST OF the three Ocean Park villages was held on a hot, sunny day. It was July 10th, a date selected because it fell between Independence Day and Bastille Day, a nod to its French financiers.

The ceremonies opened with a prayer breakfast held in the open-air of the ferry dock, under the huge cantilevered roof of the ferry building. The roof extended more than fifty feet from the two-story glass façade towards the dock and the inner harbor. It was barely a foot and a half tall at its leading-edge, but quickly deepened to more than eight feet where it met the façade. The trusses that were enclosed in the roof extension outside were exposed inside, giving the lobby the feeling of a large, open pavilion. Ben had briefly considered solid walls on the two sides perpendicular to the dock, but had decided instead to continue the truss design of the roof onto those sidewalls. The result was a series of deep, lacy alcoves furnished with seating cubes that could be used by commuters waiting for the ferries north to Salem and south to Boston. A café in the lobby offered coffee, pastries, sandwiches, and other refreshments. During the last days of construction frenzy, the ferry building was jammed with construction workers on break. The construction managers were very upset about the crowded space and blocked off access to the rest rooms. But Ben ordered them reopened. He loved the commotion and the life it brought to his building.

After the prayer breakfast, most of the crowd moved to the dock area. Set in the brick plaza was a brass plaque dedicating the building and dock to Henry Bacon Lovering, the former mayor, State Representative, and Congressman. Back when city representatives had suggested the dedication and the plaque, Ben had realized the glass façade had no place on which to attach such a plaque, nor a place for a cornerstone. One day while walking in the Marais with his sons, he had come across a worn slug of brass set into the sidewalk bearing the name of an intersecting street. Looking at it, he'd realized it was the perfect solution for the ferry building plaque and cornerstone.

BEN FELT A light touch on his right elbow.

"Sir, could I speak to you for a moment?"

Ben looked at the brass name tag on the left breast of the young police officer. He was tall, thin, and crewcut, with lips that seemed to want to smile.

"Officer Gilroy..." Ben said. "Any relation to Jimmy... Jim... James?"

"Jimmy's my dad."

"What can I do for you?"

"There's a group of demonstrators over at the old crane. They're good people. They weren't allowed at or near the dedication. I think it would be good if you would meet with them for a few minutes."

The two large men in dark suits and sunglasses standing behind the officer were shaking their heads vigorously.

"What are they demonstrating about?"

"After Don Holt died, they erected a monument at the base of the crane. For a while it was allowed to remain. Recently the contractor has been removing the flowers and mementos and has moved equipment in to prepare to demolish the crane."

"That's not surprising...the next phase of the project is centered around a village square there. What do they want?"

"If you could just talk to them, sir."

"My security detail here is very much against me going over there. They will go crazy if I just walk into a large, demonstrating crowd. Let me think for a minute. Can you wait right here?"

Ben walked into the ferry building followed by his security detail. In addition to his two bodyguards and the two assigned to Claudine, there was a six-trooper detachment from the State Police inside. He caught Claudine's eye and motioned for her to join him at the café serving area. He asked one of the servers to get a café manager. The small group talked amongst themselves for about twenty minutes, the shaking heads of the security people and the café manager slowly becoming nods. Claudine stood by Ben's side, her hands on his left arm, guiding him with squeezes and slow strokes.

Signaling that he was done with conversation, Ben asked one of the troopers to bring Officer Gilroy in.

"Okay, Officer Gilroy, here's what we're going to do. I will meet with twenty to twenty-five of the demonstrators here in the café at one p.m. They will be offered lunch."

"Yes, sir. Thank you, sir."

"You will personally select the twenty to twenty-five. Anyone you pick must be known to you. You must give the name to Captain Vorias by noon. By twelve-thirty you will be informed as to whether anyone is unacceptable. Everyone must be in and seated by twelve forty-five. No one will be allowed to enter after that time. Are you clear on all of that?"

"Yes, sir. Thank you, sir."

"No, thank *you*, Officer Gilroy. Will your dad be in the group?"

"No sir, my dad died three years ago."

Ben touched the officer's left forearm. "I'm sorry to hear that. I didn't know."

BEN AND CLAUDINE walked crisply into the ferry building, holding hands. They moved to an area along the glass wall that had been selected by security because the light streaming in behind them made them a more difficult target. Ben knew that it also showed off Claudine's figure, a figure that still excited him as it did the day they had met. Claudine was well aware of the effect.

"Good afternoon. I'm Ben Holt, Don's brother...and this is my wife, Claudine Aubrey." Ben scanned the café. He thought a few of the people looked familiar, but he couldn't connect them with names. "We've been told a little bit about your concerns, but we'd like to hear more. Please stand when you talk and give your name. I may know many of you, but it's been a long time. We'll have a couple of breaks to let you get more food and drink and to use the bathrooms, but the security people get a bit freaky if people move around while the discussion is going on, so I ask you to stay seated."

Slowly at first, but picking up frequency and intensity, people rose to make pleas, add comments, ask questions, and complain.

"Why must they remove the monument?"

"Why are you standing in the light? We can't see your faces clearly."

"You may have grown up here but you're not one of us."

"This is just another harebrained scheme, like America's Park, doomed to failure. Then this will be a wasteland again."

"You have a fancy life and a fancy wife, now you want to make this place fancy."

"The prices you are charging will raise property values throughout the city and we'll be forced out."

"Your villages and their shops will destroy all small stores in the city."

"I've researched federal law and you're violating several statutes."

"Why are you trying to destroy the unions?"

"Can we set aside an area for a memorial for Don Holt?"

"People from this city should have preference for jobs and apartments."

"Why should I have to join the union to get a job?"

"The ferry will bring outsiders and our city will change forever."

"Are you going to listen to us or is this all just window dressing?"

Ben ended the meeting after an hour-and-a-half. "We heard a lot from you today. I can tell you that the memorial will remain for now.

You will be notified at least fourteen days before it is removed. Some of the other issues you raised will be considered. Some, frankly, will not. Thank you for coming."

Ben and Claudine were quickly surrounded by state troopers and moved towards the exit. Captain Vorias told the demonstrators to remain seated until they had left. Several in the crowd stood and shuffled in place. City police lined the walls inside and outside the ferry building as the crowd rose and slowly left the building, gathered in noisy clusters outside, and one by one dissipated into the late afternoon. Some of the clusters cackled excitedly about seeing Claudine, about how they loved her dresses, her slacks, blouses, jackets, life. Others complained that it was all a waste; nothing would be done, no one was really listening. Where was the mayor, the state reps, the City Council? One guy was telling anyone who would listen that he'd researched federal law and that the developers were violating several statutes.

A thin, bald man with a sharp nose was writing notes, nodding at each speaker. He could use some of the complaints in a new column. The ones he liked he wrote quickly and intently; the others he ignored. They were all idiots, but he could use them, anyway. His reward would be seeing Ben make changes tied to his criticism; the more involved and expensive, the better. He drew a large tic-tac-toe chart in his notebook and labeled the headings across the top: "Crit," "Change," "Cost." Ellsworth Nelson saw himself as the prime shaper of the new city, and soon everyone else would, as well.

52

KIM DESCENDED THE STAIRS, A HALF-DOZEN magazines in her hand, listening for the familiar sounds of her mother. As she entered the kitchen, she saw Annie sitting in the breakfast nook on the far side of the room. Annie was softly blowing across her bowl of tea. The bowl had once been a large, shallow cup—her favorite—but it had long ago lost its vestigial handle.

"Mom, why do you have so many fashion magazines with Claudine Aubrey on the cover?"

"Maybe I like her clothes..."

"*Maybe* you're still in love with her husband..."

"Kim, you never forget your first love. You remember when love and life was less complicated. It may have been loaded with its own anxieties, but no mortgages, work frustrations...no taxes, no kids. Sorry, Kim. It *was* brutally sweet. Yes, I may still love him, but that doesn't mean I want him now."

"Really?"

"Yes, *really*. You come to realize over time that you want to think they've suddenly grown up one day and finally realized what they have lost..."

"It doesn't look like he thinks he lost too much. Sorry, Mom. Besides, wasn't it *you* who dumped him?"

Annie ignored Kim's last comment. "You never know what really goes on in a marriage," she said.

Kim lowered her eyes, looking at the table just in front of her mother's tea. Her lips quivered, but she squeezed them together to regain control. She flipped a lick of hair from her face and looked up into her mother's eyes. "Mom, I need to stay here for a while."

"What's going on? You're not fighting with Connie and Mac are you?"

"No. Nothing like that."

"What, then?"

"They don't have jobs...not regular jobs, anyway...but they do have lots of money. Then, a while ago ago, Connie came home with a bloody hand. He tried to hide it. He said he wasn't paying attention and slammed the car door on it. Mac seemed a bit surprised by his explanation, but then backed him up. They said that they'd been together."

"Why don't you believe them?"

"At first, I wasn't sure, but then I thought it might be true. They had used a lot of towels to clean up the blood though. It just seemed odd."

"Is that it?"

"No. A few weeks later, I was putting some beach towels in the trunk of Connie's car and I noticed a woman's handbag jammed behind the spare tire. The strap was hanging out."

"Did you ask him about it?"

"He saw me take it out and look at it. He grabbed it...ripped it, really...from my hands. He looked very angry, but then he calmed down and said, 'Damn. I forgot to turn that in. We found it in front of a bar, but the bar was closed so we thought we'd bring it back the next day'."

"Sounds like a reasonable explanation..."

"Mom, I think there was dried blood on it."

"Did you mention that to Connie? Maybe the woman was hurt?"

"No, I didn't say anything about the dried blood, but I did suggest that we open it to see if there was any identification inside. He got angry again, said that we couldn't open a woman's purse and accused me of not trusting him to deal with it. I've never seen him that loud and that angry."

"What did you do?"

"Nothing. I let it go. When we went to the grocery store a week later, he opened the trunk to put the bags in and I noticed that the handbag was gone. When I put one of the bags in the trunk, I slipped my fingers behind the tire to confirm nothing was there."

"Did you ask if he'd returned it?"

"No..."

"Well, you know you can always stay here if you want to, or if you need to. What will you tell Connie and Mac?"

"That I want to spend more time with you."

"In my golden years?" Annie smiled at the thought.

"Come on, Mom...you're not old. And you're as sexy and beautiful as Claudine Aubrey."

"Thank you, Kim."

"Now what do you think their marriage is really like?"

"She probably abuses him and has lots of affairs with gorgeous men...maybe with the male models in her shows."

"Or Warren Beatty."

"Kim, almost every woman in America has had an affair with Warren Beatty, or has at least dreamed of it."

"What about you? Am I your love-child with Warren Beatty?"

"Kim, you will always be my love-child, but no... it was Robert Redford."

The two women looked into each other's faces, their eyes alight, searching for the stories that their faces held. It was Annie who faltered first, dropping her gaze to the table, then moving it back to rest on Kim's eyes.

"Kim, thank you for making me laugh. I'm proud of you—of your judgment, your decision to walk away from a potentially dangerous situation. I'll worry less in the future, but I'll always worry at least a little. You'll understand that some day."

"I know it's different when you're a mom. I hope to understand that...to feel that kind of love. I thought I might have found it with Connie."

Kim's eyes filled, and Annie slipped from her bench around onto Kim's, reached for her hand, and cupped it in her own.

53

September 1989

BEN STOOD BY THE HUGE MODEL, HIS CHIN CUPPED in his hand, the crooked index finger of his right hand caressing his lip. The model makers slipped the newest building into the space that opened from the plaza of the middle Village out to the harbor. When the Plexiglas and bass wood structure had settled into its location and the model maker had withdrawn his hand, a wisp of breath slipped through Ben's lightly closed lips. He looked at the new element for a few moments, then reached over and drew the new structure deeper into the throat of the opening. He pursed his lips, then smiled.

"Thanks, Sam. I believe that is it. Let's cut out the topography and set it in."

"I'll have it done by the end of the day, Ben."

"Thanks."

"Do you want to have it draped?"

"No. Leave the drape for me. I want to show it to Claudine and the boys and to my parents tonight after dinner. I'll drape it before I leave."

DINNER WAS IN an upstairs private room at Anthony's Hawthorne. Ben and Claudine dined on broiled haddock prepared per

Ben's instructions with butter, lemon, and garlic and with long, thin, garlicky green beans on the side. Ben's mom anguished about whether to get the lobster or the prime rib; Ben's father ordered both, barely touching either, but having the remainders packed for upcoming meals. Both of the boys had spaghetti and meatballs, content to be freed from the cook's nightly regimen of healthy meals.

After dinner, they were driven to the development office where Ben ushered them into the two-story lobby and gathered them around the model. He stepped away to the wall and flipped several switches that controlled the lighting. They all stood silently for several moments, then Claudine gasped, "Oh, Ben. Oh, Ben. It's amazing... so amazing. It's *perfect*."

Ben's father shrugged his shoulders. "What? I don't see anything..."

Daniel and Pascha stood staring at the new building.

Pascha reached towards it. "See, here...Can I touch it?"

"Yes, of course."

Pascha ran his index finger over the ridge of the roof. Daniel moved to the harbor side of the model and stooped to bring his eyes level with the plaza. He peered back towards the village square. Claudine draped an arm across Ben's shoulders, around his neck, and pulled him to her and kissed him.

"What is it?" Ben's father asked in a way that made them think of those terrible fifties horror movies. Ben smiled at the memory.

"It's the Don Holt Winter Garden."

"What's a winter garden?" Ben's mother looked confused.

"Essentially, a large greenhouse."

"Wouldn't people understand better if you *called* it a large greenhouse?"

"The Don Holt Large Greenhouse, then."

"*Now* you're making fun of me."

"Yes I am, Mom."

AFTER TWENTY MINUTES or so of looking at the model, everyone knew they were done and silently started to head to the door. Ben asked the boys if they needed to go to the bathroom before they left. They did. Ben's father announced that he was going to "go point Percy against the porcelain" and headed towards the men's room, as well. The two women went to the ladies' room and Ben was left standing alone in the lobby. He flipped the switch for the model's lights and waited. The boys came out and announced that they would wait in the limo. The women emerged a few minutes later and did the same. Ben was about to go into the men's room to check on his father when the older man emerged.

"Thought I fell in, did ya?" he said.

"I wondered..."

"*Hoped*, you mean? No such luck." He turned as if to head from the building, but didn't move. "Listen, I'm a bit short. Can you lend me four hundred bucks?"

"What for?" Ben said.

"General needs," he answered.

Ben looked at his father who still stood facing the door. He thought about demanding that the old man look him in the eye. "Here," Ben said. He reached into his pocket and counted out five hundred dollars in hundreds and twenties. His father barely turned to take the money.

"You know, of course, that this new building doesn't make up for the fact that you were a shitty brother to Don."

"It's not meant to make up for anything."

"Just sayin', that's all."

"Yeah, well, don't."

"Too bad his life ended the way it did."

"Yes, it is."

"And *he* was the smart one, too."

Ben thought to himself, "I just hand this guy five hundred bucks and he tells me that my alcoholic, hoodlum brother was the *smart* one?" He knew that his father was remembering Don from his school years, before alcohol had consumed him. He thought of Don, the funeral, the demonstrators at the crane. He thought maybe the old man had had a point. Although Don may not have had Ben's brand of success, he did have an awful lot of people who loved him. In the Brickyards, friends were worth more than money. "Come on, Dad, let's go."

"What? You got nothin'?"

"I got nothin', Dad."

"Don would've brought somethin'."

"Yes, but then he was the *smart* one."

"He would have had his fists up. He would've brought somethin'."

"Yes, Dad…but if *I* did that, the guys in the black suits next to the Suburban would shoot you." Ben smiled and walked out the door.

54

T HE WINTER FLOPHOUSE, BY ELLSWORTH NELSON
    "Let me first state that I am a fan of the more positive aspects of a measure of ego and greed. Both can be tools that create great art in the hands of a master. History is riven with the wonders that the marriage of ego and greed can create. The Egyptian kings, the Medici's, the railroad and shipping barons—all fostered the creation of works of genius.

Ah, but there, then, is the secret of this successful marriage. Mistress Genius must be present to season the joining lest the marriage be dull and unproductive.

Ben Holt is no genius. His ego and the greed of his financiers have imposed upon a working-class city a development that destroys the traditional working waterfront and creates a new work-less class. No factories, no warehouses are allowed in his vision for Ocean Park. Now he comes and dumps new detritus on the displaced classes. In one strange and inglorious move he seeks to memorialize both the former character of this site and the Holt name. He succeeds instead in demeaning both.

The Holt Winter Garden is a grandiose glass and steel structure that encloses the old crane that had been used in brighter times to unload coal from ships to feed the boilers of the power plants and factories of this once-great waterfront. In making a museum-piece of the crane, Holt mocks it and the values that it represents. As a building, the structure is a non-building. It has no apparent mass, no texture. It is simply a vessel, a large Pyrex dish, signifying its own nothingness.

Holt has said that greenery, seating, and a café would take up residence in its confines. What use, I ask, is greenery to the work-less class? The only green they need is on one side of a dollar bill, a dollar bill that has been ripped from their grasp. Holt's sketches and model show a structure that takes the outline of a traditional European conservatory—a form of structure rooted in aristocracy, not the democracy of the worker. The transgressions against decency pile high, seven stories high, erecting a conservatory when what is needed is a conservation not of trees and plants, but of jobs.

No one knows this better than Holt's own father, Holt père being a local union leader. We are given to understand that Holt's own mother has chided him for his pompous vision and has suggested that the "winter garden" moniker be dropped in favor of "large greenhouse," as she has told many of her friends. Your humble servant opines that it best be known as "the large flophouse"."

LETTER TO THE editor:
I wanted to thank you for allowing Ellsworth Nelson to bring attention to my work.
—Ben Holt

A note appeared at the end of Ellsworth Nelson's column about the Paul Rudolph-designed Lindemann and Hurley centers:
I find that I must respond to Ben Holt's letter. I have tried on many occasions to engage Mr. Holt in a serious discussion about his unfortunate work. He insists on engaging only in persillage.

Letter to the editor:

I wanted to thank you for allowing Ellsworth Nelson to remind us all that persillage does indeed exist.

Everyone at Satart Holt enjoyed a hearty chuckle.

—Ben Holt

55

November 1989

I T WAS JUST AFTER SEVEN-THIRTY AND BEN WAS LATE
for the morning meeting. Doug Strout would already be on his
second cup of coffee and halfway through his appetizer of blueberry
pie. Doug was a big, solid man, slightly shorter than Ben. He had
been a bodyguard for Marine Corps generals and had a way of barking
at people that belied a comfortable gentility.

He was also ex-CIA. That would be a plus in the assignment
which Ben had for him. It might help to pull aside the curtain that
Ben couldn't get through—the curtain that kept Ben from understanding Don's death, Siobhan's disappearance, and the identities of
the perpetrators. Clyde Washington may have been behind the killing, but he had an alibi for his whereabouts that night.

The monthly meetings with Bill and Rachel, attended by a variety of Treasury, Secret Service and FBI officials, produced nothing of
value. Ben was annoyed with himself that it had taken five months of
these meetings to realize he was being stonewalled. His relationship
with Bill had developed an uncomfortable chill, and though Bill had
said nothing, Ben realized his superiors had him on a short leash and
that Rachel had probably been assigned to monitor him.

WHEN BEN ENTERED the Capitol diner, it didn't take long for him to spot Doug. Doug was sitting at the counter listening to Shirley, his fork in mid-air about to deliver a substantial portion of pie to his open mouth. The stools to either side of him were empty, except for a camel-colored canvas coat draped over the stool to his left. Doug saw Ben in the mirrors that lined the diner's walls as he approached, and he reached for the coat.

"Excuse me, Honey. I need to talk with this gentleman."

"Good morning, Ben."

"Good morning, Shirley."

"You having breakfast?" she said.

"Yes, please."

Doug arose from the stools, pie plate in hand, and handed Ben his coat. He grabbed his coffee cup, then moved off to the last booth in the back corner against the windows. He took his coat from Ben and placed it on the table of the booth next to the windows, then took Ben's and placed it atop his own. He slid onto the bench against the back wall. Shirley came over with a cup of black coffee for Ben and a plastic-laminated menu, which he handed to Doug. Doug laid it unopened on the table.

"Honey, do you folks have hash?" Doug said.

"Yes, of course," Shirley said.

"I'd like a double order of hash, then. Set it on the grill, break an egg on top, and just heat it through for a minute."

"Great. More coffee?"

"Yes, please. And Ben will have…?"

"Already got it," Shirley said. She winked at Ben.

No sooner had Shirley spoken when the cook appeared at her right side with three plates. Shirley moved aside and the cook slid the plates onto the table. The larger held a small pile of scrambled eggs as well as triangles and squares of home fries crisped on one side and mixed with raw onions. A second plate held four slices of tomato arranged in a fan-shape and accompanied by eight slices of bacon. A small plate held dry rye toast.

Doug looked at Ben and smiled as Shirley and the cook moved away. "Breakfast is the second most important meal of the day."

"Okay then...what's the most important meal?"

"The next one."

"Is that Marine lore?"

Doug looked up just as Shirley approached their booth and set the plate of hash in front of him. She stepped back and looked as if she were about to speak. Doug shook his head and she turned and walked down the aisle that separated the stools at the counter from the window-side booths.

"Now...where *were* we?" Doug said.

"You were about to tell me what you found out in the last couple of days about my brother," Ben said. "And if it's not everything I need to know, you were going to tell me how much time and how much money it will take to get me there."

"Oh, I thought we were still talking about breakfast," Doug said. "My mistake."

"My usual breakfast is *allongé* and tartine...black coffee and a baguette that has been toasted in the broiler and served with cultured butter. When I was a kid, I was skinny and ate a breakfast like this almost every morning. I like to order the same here when I come."

"Do you mind if we get down to business now?"

Ben looked into Doug's face, snorted, and shook his head. "Sure."

"I don't know how much you know, so bear with me if I repeat things you've already been told."

Doug reported on his preliminary discussions and his review of available reports. Don's murder had probably been a gang hit, planned and executed by a person or persons with some experience, but probably not a professional hit. There had been signs that the primary assailant had had some military training—perhaps Army Ranger—but unlikely Green Beret or Marine advanced reconnaissance.

"Are you sure you can handle this? Some of the details are...let me say, unpleasant."

"Probably no more unpleasant than what I can conjure. Tell me what you've got," Ben said.

"Don died of massive internal injuries. Siobhan is probably dead, but I can't confirm that just yet. It's possible that she led him into the trap, but that theory doesn't quite fit."

"She certainly didn't seem like the type. I spoke to her boss about her. He didn't know her well, but…"

"Stop there!" said Doug. "Let's get something straight. You hired me to investigate Don's death, so let me do my job. I don't need a partner."

Anger welled up in Ben as he glared at Doug.

"That's just the way it needs to be, Ben." Doug's face softened, and he blinked.

Ben let a long breath exhale through pursed lips. His eyes relaxed. "Yes, you're right., Doug. It's hard for me to let someone else do it, but you're right."

"Thank you."

"What are your plans from here on out?"

Doug listed the information he needed: autopsy (it was complete but not released); progress on the search for Siobhan (currently a dead end); background on Siobhan (in progress); status of CIA and Treasury interest in Don and Don's cohorts (treading carefully here); background on Ben, Ben's family, Claudine, and her family (Ben would have to cover all the bases); assembling a list of Don's 'clients'; and assembling a review and investigation of his relationship with Tony Angelo.

"There are an awful lot of bad actors in that group. You're putting yourself in grave danger."

"Yes, you do have to be careful in this business. You have to be aware of possible complications, but mostly it's boring stuff."

"Certainly not like the CIA."

"Actually, very much like that. It's not all car chases, beautiful women, and tuxes."

"What did you do for the CIA?"

"Do you have sufficient clearance to know that?"

"Probably not."

Doug smiled. "I was a trainer on contract. I wasn't an employee."

"Oh, I heard you were ex-CIA."

"When people hear that, they make certain assumptions. I don't go out of my way to correct them."

"Don't tell me you were something like an accounting professor training them how to track financial transactions..."

"No, not exactly."

Ben raised his eyebrows and cocked his head in a gesture that asked, what, then?

"I taught agents how to kill...either with no weapons, or with common objects at hand."

"Very interesting."

Doug looked into Ben's face, trying to read whether Ben was sorry he'd asked the question or disappointed with Doug's answer. What he saw worried him.

56

December 1989

BERNADINE DROVE UP THE DRIVEWAY TO THE VILLA, parked in front of a set of three garage doors, and pressed the button just above the rearview mirror that opened one of the doors. She pulled in and turned off the ignition and sat quietly for a few moments, knowing that the security cameras were watching her. Finally, she opened the car door and swung her long legs from the driver's side, rising in one motion like a bird. She walked through the garage and a short corridor to emerge in the villa's sunlit atrium. As she set her briefcase on a small table near the front door, Pearson James appeared in a double doorway from a large room off the atrium. Bernadine heard a gaggle of voices from the room he had just left. James turned and closed the door behind him.

"*Bonjour, Madame.*"

"Hello, Pearson. What do we have today?"

"A full house, *Madame.*"

Pearson was the CFO of Cambridge Investments and Cambridge Re, the investment and insurance arms of Addison Ltd., the old family-owned companies that had been run and run down by the old men of Bernadine's family. Pearson was a short, balding man whose round face made him look like he should be portly, but whose body was so thin it neared the point of emaciation. He wore a pair of rimless spectacles on his shiny, bald forehead and a surprisingly crisp white shirt and dark suit in the Bermuda humidity. The villa was air-conditioned, of course, but Bernadine had never seen him sweat—even on the streets of Georgetown or at the tiny, stifling office in Hamilton that was the company's official address.

The villa rambled over ten thousand square feet on three and a half acres of land that overlooked Gunners Bay, Saint George channel, and Paget Island beyond. It was less than three miles from the airport near the end of a long dead end road. The owners of the adjacent properties were seldom on the island.

"I assumed that you wanted to see Mr. Clyde first so I put him in the garden with a couple of sitters."

"Well done, Pearson. Would you tell Sheikh Ahmed's party that I will see them in ten minutes?"

Bernadine didn't wait for Pearson's reply. She walked through the glass doors in the center of one wall of glass into a garden that was enclosed on six sides by various wings of the building. Only two of the walls were glass; the rest were solid—two of them with windows that had been blocked up with stucco that matched the adjoining walls. The only hint that windows had once been there was a slight difference of texture in the shape of a tall rectangle, highlighted when the sun hit it just so.

CLYDE STOOD AS Bernadine entered the garden. He took a few limping steps forward. He offered his hand, which Bernadine ignored. She moved to a bench set in front of a fountain and patted the stone beside her. "Sit, Clyde," she said.

Clyde Washington dropped onto the bench, using his palm to break his fall. He stuck his bad right leg straight out. His inability to bend his right knee had been a parting gift from his father when he was five.

"It's a bountiful place that you have here, Mrs. Addison."

"Clyde, what am I going to do with you?"

"I'm sorry, Mrs. A, I don't... I mean, I've been holding up my end... I think we've been straight..."

"Oh, it's not about money, Clyde. You exposed us to some potential problems."

"How? I don't understand."

"You killed…or *had* killed…Don Holt, and, I assume, his girlfriend, Siobhan."

"That boy has been a problem for me and my family all of my life. He was cutting into my business…*our* business…and I won't hold no poaching. He was a sample…a sign…that you can't poach on Clyde."

"That boy was the brother of a close friend, Clyde, and I don't need any complications among my inner circle. His girlfriend was a lawyer in the U.S. law firm of another close friend. There's more heat from this than your local 'hood killing. You let your emotions control you. I want you out of sight until this blows over. That means *way* out of sight. Pearson will have someone meet you at your hotel. I want you in Jamaica tonight, and *don't* be seen until we come to get you."

Clyde was about to object when he looked into Bernadine's face, read the message there, and hesitated. Just then, two of the biggest, blackest men he had ever seen walked through the atrium door straight toward the bench where they were sitting. Bernadine held up her left hand, palm out, and they stopped dead in their tracks. They were clad in black suits and starched white shirts, open at the neck. The cut of the suits seemed to make them look bigger, more muscled. Clyde had no way of knowing they were merely accountants.

"Who did that hit?" continued Bernadine.

"Two guys from Baltimore…brothers, and my brother Woodrow. His friend, Connie, rode with them."

"I need full names." Bernadine pushed a small notebook and pen towards Clyde. He didn't look up, but wrote quickly in the notebook.

"Clyde, my partners and I have made a big investment in you. Don't disappoint me again. Pearson will show you out now."

Pearson appeared at the door and Clyde rose from the bench and hobbled toward him. He kept an eye on the two big, black men who had been standing stoically by a large table some fifteen feet away from the bench. He almost expected them to whack him as he moved uneasily past them. As Pearson stepped aside, Clyde stole one more look at the two men and almost ran into a tall, extraordinarily beautiful woman who was just entering the room. Pearson's hand grabbed his collar and stopped him short. Clyde looked into the woman's eyes and a shiver coursed through his spine. He found himself involuntarily moving back to let her pass. Her scent moved with her and lingered in his nostrils. If it was fear that made him try to suppress the desire to have this woman, it failed. Clyde knew then that this woman would be his quest until he had her—maybe her, and Mrs. Addison, too. He smiled to himself.

BERNADINE MOVED TO the head of the table and Claudine sat to her left. The two big black men sat together to her right and slid file folders that had been sitting on the table across to Bernadine, then one to Claudine, and one each for themselves.

The man closest to Bernadine spoke. "The first report is the financial statement from the Ocean Park group. It is as yet unaudited, but Armando Lowell presented it at the last executive committee meeting so it will be presented to the Board in its current form. There is currently little cash flow so the internal rate of return bears no significance." He paused as Bernadine and Claudine leafed through the papers.

Bernadine closed the file and folded her hands atop it. "Tell me about the financing and the status of debt service."

The second man spoke: "Just under fifteen percent of the financing is from local banks and organizations with about five percent from the trade unions that are included in that number. The rental apartments are funded primarily by a quasi-governmental agency with federal guarantees. The remainder is placed with the international consortium. All are interest-only loans until the condominiums sell, then a portion of each sale will write down the principal. The biggest part of the principle will come due in five years at which time it will probably be refinanced."

"So thirty percent is being invested by Marcel?"

"Yes, unless he has some side investors, but there is no evidence of that and apparently no interest in that until now."

"Why the change?"

The second man spoke again. "The agreement with the lenders states that all increases in cost are to be paid from funds of the developer."

"So Marcel pays?"

"Until now, yes."

"What percentage of Marcel's fund is invested in this project?"

"It's now up to thirteen percent. Lowell has expressed some concern about this and wants Marcel to agree to bring in one or more investors to bring the percentage under ten percent, preferably to about eight percent."

"Hmmm. That seems like an opportunity then." She looked to the first man again. "Mr. Belmont, have you evaluated this?"

"Yes. Most of the factors are positive with one note of caution."

Belmont ran through all of the financials, spoke of the publicity the project was getting—all positive except for one architecture critic in Boston. This seemed to be a fair amount of interest in both the office space and the planned condominiums. The rental market was strong and the marina spaces were already fully reserved. There was some softness regarding the retail space, but much of that was due to Mr. Holt's demands for limitations on the types of retail he would allow in the development.

"Is that the note of caution then, the retail?"

"No. My concern is that there is no definitive exit strategy. The condos will be sold, of course, but the office, retail, and rental apartments will remain with the developer."

"Let's do this: approach them with an offer to invest with the condition that we get to buy out the rental apartments in five years."

"That would create other problems. The Feds have to approve any buyer."

"Okay, so we get Marcel to split off the rental development into a separate company now. Over five years, we get to buy more stock in the company. Will that do it?"

"I'll check with the lawyers, but I think so."

"Okay. Go ahead and invest up to sixty percent of the dollars Marcel and Armando Lowell are looking for."

"Yes, ma'am."

"Give me five minutes with Claudine and fifteen minutes with the Germans, then send Sheikh Ahmed in. I told them ten minutes and it has been forty. They should be sufficiently ripe by now."

Belmont and Leicester took their folders as well as the two folders that Bernadine and Claudine slid to them. They left through the doors they'd come in by. Bernadine turned her attention to Claudine.

"Are you flying back to Paris tonight?"

"I'm actually flying out in an hour. Ben is flying in tomorrow night. Family time."

"Give my best to the boys and to Ben."

"I will. When are you returning?"

"In a couple of days. Marcel is in Brazil until the weekend and I want to see as many investors here as I can on this trip. It's hard to get away when he's in Paris."

"I know. Good luck with the investors."

Claudine rose, bent over and kissed Bernadine on both cheeks, and walked over to the mirrored wall, exiting through a hidden door.

"GENTLEMEN, I HOPE you've been well looked after."

Bernadine greeted the three men at the door. Two were in their late twenties; the third looked much older though Bernadine knew he was in his early thirties. All were German. Despite the nasty reputation of their organization and the terror that they visited upon Western Europe, the three were charming gentleman who cherished the returns that Bernadine's investment house delivered, as well as the status their investment returns conferred upon them amongst their colleagues.

Unknown to the Germans standing before her who represented a left wing cabal, Bernadine and her organization managed investments for a German neo-Nazi group and Red Army associates in

France, Ireland, the Netherlands, Indonesia, Morocco, and Bali. They did the same for several rebel groups in Central America. She advised them on the less violent ways of raising money and invested the proceeds in real estate, insurance and some of the more arcane market instruments as well as a few ventures like Clyde Washington that she thought of as boutique investments. While the returns were well above market, they also had the distinct advantage of being nearly immune to government seizure. In fact, only one of her investments had been seized—a freighter that she had planned as the first of a fleet but that she had foolishly allowed to be connected to the Red Army group—and that was a very small investment and a hard learned lesson. All of her subsequent investments for her more questionable clients were double-blind. Blind to her companies, blind to her investors. More importantly, they were blind to Claudine and Marcel. She may have been able to use her political connections—and protestations of ignorance—to skate through the freighter affair, but she would not get another free ride. That was what scared her most about Clyde Washington.

Bernadine had four more meetings that day, all leftist groups with the exception of the Sheikh, and three more the next day, all rightists. Her staff made sure that the first groups were safely ensconced on cruises before the next set of groups landed in Bermuda. Each of the cruises were bound for different destinations.

Her staff was top notch, well-paid, and exceedingly loyal. Each had attended the best British public schools—most had been Oxford or Cambridge—and several, including Belmont and Leicester, had attended the London School of Economics. She often thought that the City would love to have them, but the City didn't offer the amenities of Bermuda.

57

FOR THE FIRST TIME, BEN HAD BEATEN DOUG STROUT to the Capitol Diner. He was sitting in the last booth with his back to the wall when Doug walked through the door and stopped to flirt with Shirley before heading to Ben's table. Doug took a chair and flipped it around, sitting down in it with the back up against the table. He unzipped his leather jacket and pulled a manila folder from inside, sliding it across the table to Ben. Ben let the folder lie on the table. He stabbed three of the home fries with his fork and raised them to his mouth. Only after he finished them did he look at Strout.

"That's everything I've got. There's a story there...the who, what, when, where, why."

"But you're not satisfied."

Ben stared into Strout's eyes. They didn't blink, they didn't look away.

"Something's missing," Strout said.

"What makes you think so?"

"Clyde Washington is a smalltime hood with a big footprint. It doesn't add up. Someone or someone's behind him and I can't find out who. Blank wall, dead-end."

"The mob?"

"No, if it was I'd find out."

"The Feds? Maybe they set him up as an informant?"

"Actually, yes, they did, but we're talking much bigger money behind Washington. The Feds can give a lot, but they don't have *that* kind of dough. Someone legit, or *almost* legit."

Ben smirked. "Someone looking to make an investment."

"Or launder money…but *there's* the blank wall. If that's the case, they're good. Not a whisper out there. And there's another complication…"

"What's that?"

"Clyde disappeared day before yesterday…no trace."

"Shit!"

"No shit."

"Doesn't that sound like the Feds?"

"It does, but if it *was* the Feds, I'd know it."

"Another blank wall…what happens now?"

"You can take what you have in the folder to your friend at the Staties."

"He's a shift commander. I doubt they'd let him run with it. I'm not saying he's not capable, but wouldn't they kick it over to the investigators?"

"Probably, and it might get buried there. Don was *not* one of their favorite people. They'll have to decide whether to commit the resources to pursue it or not."

"What if they don't?"

"Then you'll have to take it to the Feds."

"What if no one can find him? What if he's gone underground… or he's dead?"

"If he's alive, he'll show up…probably sooner rather than later. They usually do. If he's dead, he'll show up sooner."

"I'll call Mike Meehan. I'm not sure I feel comfortable about it, but unless you have something better…"

"By the way, thanks for the check. You're a stand up guy. Mostly people wait until after they see my report, *then* decide whether they want to pay me or not."

Ben patted the closed folder. "You're welcome."

58

February 1990

IT WAS BARELY EIGHT THIRTY A.M. WHEN BEN WALKED through the courtyard, pausing to smell the perfume of old and new; brown, green, and limestone. He was smitten. He was in Paris with the people he loved and there was nothing more important in the world.

He went straight to the kitchen and turned on the espresso machine. The day's bread was already standing like emerging stalks of asparagus in the tall, narrow basket on the granite island. He withdrew a baguette, cut a third of it off the loaf and split it in half. He set the two pieces under the salamander.

Robert must have brought the bread in. Ben reminded himself to apologize to Robert for not letting him meet him at the airport. He had wanted the time to himself, time to see Paris like an average visitor, time to savor its early-morning mood, to observe the way it worked when it wasn't on stage.

Leaving the tall, steel-framed glass doors open, Ben took his breakfast into the garden. The sun was clipping the tops of the bare Magnolia trees, illuminating them. The breeze was steady but light. Today would be a walking day and he would put off his meeting with Marcel until the evening. He expected that Claudine would need to work. Spring Fashion Week would begin the weekend after next. She had been unusually excited by her work this year and Ben looked forward to seeing all of it.

Ben crossed the garden to the pergola, walking around the small pool with its tiny waterfall that gurgled softly, the water slipping over a stack of stones Claudine had brought back with her from Cannes. He set the timer that controlled the striker on the tall Chinese gong—a device he had built himself—and sat on the granite bench beneath the pergola, calming himself, preparing for twenty minutes of meditation.

It had been a while since he'd meditated. He could prepare himself easily in Vermont or St. Bart's, but he found it difficult in Boston or New York. As he relaxed, the sounds of the courtyard—birds, moving leaves, and an insect grabbed by one of the pond fish—arose, then faded.

Three gongs sounded: one, deep in his consciousness; the final two, audible. During the meditation, a dream had come to him of a pergola in a massive, glass structure populated by massive, muscular shafts of steel. He recognized the structure, withdrew his moleskin sketchbook from his pocket, and quickly drew a small plan and elevation.

In the few minutes it took to do the drawing, Daniel and Pascha had each arisen, dressed, and run to the courtyard knowing that the three peals of the gong meant that Ben was home. Pascha came tearing across the courtyard first.

"Da-dee, Da-dee."

Ben stood to catch Pascha in his arms. Daniel walked towards them, steadily and with a certain dignity that Ben recognized as being Marcel's, and greeted his father, kissing him on both cheeks.

"Good morning, Ben."

Ben smiled. Brothers they were, with shared experiences, shared lives, and yet so different. He thought of Don and Ron and himself. So different, yet brothers still, with the root connection that siblings take for granted if, indeed, they recognize it at all.

CLAUDINE EMERGED FROM the house in her silk pajama bottoms and embroidered camisole top. As she grew closer, Ben saw in the fabric of the pants a faint windowpane-check that matched the pattern in the pajama bottoms she had made for him. The originals of those had been made of black silk with a silvery check, but Ben hadn't liked the lack of structure in the drape of the silk, so she'd had them remade in cotton. He loved them.

"Fall collection?" Ben pointed at the bottoms.

"Ah, yes, it is."

"I like it already."

Claudine grimaced. She was as unfond of casual comments about her work as Ben was about his. Ben knew this, but it never stopped him from making them. She wouldn't exactly forgive him for this, but she let it go knowing that after he'd seen the whole of the collection he would critique it without making allowance for his love. While some thought of fashion design as more frivolous, of less importance than architecture, Ben didn't. He had an expectation that all design should be approached with the same rigor and gave no pass for those who held a belief that there were greater and lesser arts. It may, she thought, be one of the many reasons she loved him so.

As they finished breakfast—folding their napkins and laying them on the table with the precision of a crack drill team—they paused to consider the schedule for their day.

"Will you be going to the d'Orsay for a production meeting?" Ben said.

"Yes. The lighting team will be there already." Claudine looked at her watch. "I'll meet the construction crew about ten, then a parade of florists, PR people and the like, until a run-through of the program at four. What will you do?"

"We'll walk you over, then I'm sure my companions here will want to wander with me."

Pascha erupted in excited clapping, and Daniel smiled; too young, Ben thought, to be so reserved and sophisticated.

"Then I'll meet with Marcel at five," Ben continued. "The boys can stay with Marcel and Bernadine tonight. Shall I plan to meet you for dinner at ten?"

"*D'accord.*"

59

B EN MET MARCEL IN THE BAR AT THE HOTEL PONT
Royale. Marcel was already sitting at a corner table with his
back to the wall. Ben's mind flashed to an image of Doug Strout. He
smiled to himself, thinking of the differences in the two men and the
different venues.

"*Bonjour*, Marcel."

"Hello, Ben. How are you? I heard that you and my grandchildren spent the day wandering. You must take me along one day."

"The boys would love to have you join us. I'd like it, too. As close
as we are, I feel like we don't spend enough time enjoying each other,
except when we are in Cannes."

"Ah. Cannes. Cannes is for enjoying. Paris, for me, is all business.
You must teach me to wander."

"We call it meandering...sort of wandering with a purpose that you
only discover while in the act. We'll make you into a first-class *flaneur*."

"I've taken the liberty of ordering Côtes de Beaune. I think you'll
like this one."

"Thank you, Marcel."

Marcel poured the red wine into a large balloon glass, expertly
wiping the neck of the bottle with a napkin. He watched intently as
Ben raised the glass to his nose and inhaled deeply. Ben canted his
head, nodded once, and pursed his lips.

"Wonderful bouquet. Full of ripe fruit." Ben raised the glass to his lips, sipped lightly, swished the fluid in his mouth, then drew his tongue across the face of his teeth. "Wonderful. Perhaps lighter than I usually like, but delightful."

"Now, we talk a bit of business," Marcel said. "And get it out of the way so we can spend the rest of our time enjoying the wine and each other."

BEN GAVE A progress report on the Ocean Park project, describing the multitude of construction projects underway and the schedule for upcoming work. He talked about the progress of rentals in the first village and, drawing a few sheets of paper from his jacket pocket and handing half of them to Marcel, reviewed the project's financials including a report for projects completed, projects underway, and projects yet to come. The pro formas were strong and the consolidated statement prepared by the accountants tracked the projections well, as far as the original plans were concerned.

Ben paused while Marcel absorbed the numbers. He then started to describe the changes he wanted to make to the plans—more courtyard housing, retail at street level on the road between the villages, the Winter Garden, and a new marina club. He withdrew two more sheets and passed one to Marcel.

"While the new housing and retail shops add to the cost, as does the Marina club," Ben said, "market research indicates that we can increase our sales prices with these improvements and more than cover our standard margin. The development has changed market attitudes about the city. Already investors are looking to develop parcels across the Lynnway."

"And what of the Winter Garden?"

"I won't try to snow you with numbers. The Winter Garden might contribute to the marketability of the development in the future, but for now, it is a personal project."

"How would you propose to pay for it?"

"I could offer to sell some of my shares in the project."

"But?"

"But you would either need to buy them...which only increases your cost and your exposure...or you would need to give me permission to sell them to a third party."

"Hmmm. Ben, my financial people have always been concerned that I...*we* really... have too much exposure in this project. My company's investment portfolio is too heavily committed to it. If I were to advise a friend, I would tell him to reduce his exposure. So maybe this presents an opportunity to reconfigure our investment. What percentage of your stock do you think you'll need to sell to finance the Winter Garden?"

"As you know, I currently hold thirty percent of the stock, Pascal holds five percent, and the unions together hold four percent. You hold the other sixty-one percent. That was done, in part, to assure that you hold control of the development company under Massachusetts law."

"This, I know."

"I would probably need to sell twenty-five percent of my stock, seven-and-a-half percent of the company, to finance the Winter Garden. The rest of the money would come from a loan to a nonprofit company that would run the gardens."

"Okay," Marcel said. "Let's structure a deal like this: each of us will give the other permission to sell stock to a third party. The stock for each will be equal to the number of shares that represents no more than seven-and-a-half percent of the outstanding stock. One restriction I would want is that you can't pledge your remaining stock to guarantee the Winter Garden loan without my permission."

"That's doable. Now there's the question of who we sell to." Ben looked expectantly at Marcel.

"I've been approached several times by investors looking to buy in to Ocean Park. You've done a great job here." Marcel's eyes smiled at Ben. "The development has captured the imagination of the investment community. You must be getting a lot of inquiries at Satart Holt...potential new clients."

"We have. Nothing that's gone ahead yet, but a lot of interest in having us be part of their project team. The funny thing is that every time the *Post* critic, Ellsworth Nelson, slams us, we get new calls."

"I'm not surprised." Marcel laughed, then his face became serious and pensive. "There is one interested investor who might be a good match for us. It's an insurer based in Bermuda who's looking to get into U.S. real estate. They would be a hands-off investor, looking to management to be prudent, but they wouldn't hold enough to be a real disturbance anyway. I'll talk to their representative in New York."

"Great."

"Then, I want to say something to you about the Winter Garden. I know why you want to do it. Claudine approached me about it. While I think it might mean more to you if you financed it yourself, I want to be a part of this. I have watched you grow from an uncertain kid to a man with wisdom greater than his age. I have watched the way that you love my daughter and my grandchildren, and I love you for it."

"Thank you, Marcel. Claudine is a demanding companion and sometimes a difficult partner, but I can't imagine life without her."

Marcel nodded. "Now I must go. My grandchildren await me. Give my best to Pascal."

ALMOST SIX MONTHS had passed since Ben was last in the Paris office, but little had changed. In fact, little had changed since Ben had first stepped into these offices almost fifteen years earlier. Surely the walls had been painted, he thought, as he looked around the space. He noticed the old lithograph of Corbu's Modulor, which hadn't moved since his first visit.

He heard voices coming up the stairs: a woman's voice, young but with an odd timbre, and Pascal's voice, deeper and intertwined with the feminine. Ben opened the door just as they reached it, and Pascal stood before him with his right arm around the shoulder of a woman who was a good six inches taller than him, model-thin, and with high cheekbones. Her dark, curly hair set off a very light complexion.

"Ben, this is Severine. She has joined our little firm."

"Not so little anymore, Pascal. Nice to meet you, Severine. You seem to have a positive effect on Pascal. I have never known him to be so... *boisterous.*"

Severine silently allowed Ben to kissed her on both cheeks.

Pascal said, "Are you jealous that *you* never made me laugh, Ben?"

"Definitely. I can see now that my days are numbered."

"Oh Ben, I could never replace you."

"Thank you, Pascal."

"You own more than half the stock now...it is *you* who must replace me, I'm afraid."

"We'll see. Can I steal you away for a bit? We do need to go over the papers the lawyers prepared."

"No need for you to wait, Severine. We can meet in the morning before our flight to Brazil. We should leave the office by noon."

"Goodnight, Severine."

Severine leaned over and kissed Pascal on the forehead, turned and walked through the door without saying a word.

As soon as Severine had left them, Ben and Pascal hugged. Pascal, expecting that Ben had been surprised by Severine's silence, explained to him she was deaf. Although she could speak, she was uncomfortable with what little sense she had of the sound of her own voice since she heard it only as vibrations in her skull. She was immensely talented though, with a deft hand.

"But you were *talking* to her..."

"She can read lips. Funny though, when I talk to her I speak louder as if she can hear me only then. I'm getting better at it, but I do catch myself falling into a louder voice sometimes."

"You seem to like each other a lot."

"We do, I think...but I'm an old man and she's so young. Let me show you some of her work."

Pascal went back into the studio to the table closest to his own and picked through a pile of drawings, rolling several of them up loosely.

He and Ben went downstairs to the conference room where Pascal unrolled a dozen of Severine's drawings. They were finely-detailed renderings with a placement of soft colors that spoke of buildings in the soft spring light. Ben was instantly smitten with her work and thought briefly of snatching her away to work on the new streetscapes for Ocean Park. He looked into Pascal's eyes and saw that Pascal knew this instantly. Neither man said a word about it. Ben quietly nodded and Pascal nodded with him. In those simple gestures a universe of communication was completed.

Ben lifted a briefcase onto the conference table and, laying it flat with its open mouth towards him, withdrew a bulk of papers. He placed one set beside him and the other one in front of the seat at the end of the table. The two men sat side-by-side, kitty-corner, and read silently. Ben finished first and withdrew a fountain pen from his jacket pocket, signing and dating the last page of the weighty document. He turned to Pascal.

"Are you sure this is what you want to do?"

"It is. I think I knew that this day would come on the day that I met you. You have flourished and so has the firm. It is time that it is yours."

"Do you understand the non-disclosure agreement?"

"Yes, I do. You make it seem like you are doing it for you, but I can see right through it. We never were good at hiding things from each other, were we?" Pascal chuckled warmly.

"No."

"This is the best way to complete my life. I have my work, although I suppose it's *your* work now, and I have my teaching and my writing. That is all I ever wanted. You are better built for more, for all that this has become."

Pascal picked up a biro to sign the papers, but Ben put his hand on Pascal's arm and offered him the fountain pen.

"I am still a simple man." Pascal signed the agreement with the biro.

"Will you marry her?" Ben said.

Pascal looked at Ben, surprised, but his face relaxed and he smiled.

"I love you, Pascal."

60

BEN BARELY SAW CLAUDINE OVER THE NEXT TWO weeks; if he did, it was only for Sunday breakfasts and dinners late each night. Her runway show would be on Tuesday and it was always a good idea to stay out of her way in the run-up to the show. If Ben was eerily relaxed in the days before a major presentation, Claudine was his opposite: tense and intense, worrying over every detail. If Ben's attitude was *"que sera,"* Claudine would fret over the wind, rain, and traffic. So Ben took the boys to school and met them at the end of their day. In between, he went to the office and settled into an empty table in the studio at the far end from Pascal. He went about his work quietly, avoiding interference with the normal rhythm of Pascal's people.

As much as possible, he roamed the neighborhoods, sketching— constantly sketching—observing the idiosyncrasies of each of the *arrondissements*, looking for the personality that made the Fifth different from the Seventh, and the Eleventh from the First. Most of the time, he walked, though when it rained, he rode the Metro like every other damp soul in Paris.

On Sunday he and the boys set off after breakfast to roam the stalls of the market at Neuilly. When the market closed, a bit before two, they roamed the side streets of the suburb, down Madeleine Michellis and École de Mars, along Rue Belanger and Rue Berteaux-Dumas, then back across Charles de Gaulle and over to the Jardin d'Acclimation.

As they crossed Charles de Gaulle, Ben looked toward the arch at La Defense. He would visit another time, alone, before he went back to New York. He felt the need for animosity toward the development and the developers, but he could raise none. His feelings toward the new part of the city were just empty.

CLAUDINE HAD ASKED Ben to sit in the front row at her show. Ben had demurred; he'd felt the front row seats were for fashion editors, movie stars and celebrities. In the early days of their relationship he'd stood in the wings—until the year Claudine had asked him to be an onstage escort for the models. That had lasted for one show—there had been the unfortunate incident with the "bride" who'd kissed the "groom" a bit too passionately—and Ben had spent the intervening years sitting near the back of the hall.

This time, Claudine persisted, Ben would be a star himself, an international architect whose vision for the "new city" was to be celebrated in a forthcoming book and television production. Ben still resisted; the book and the production were yet in the talking stage, a concept pushed by a former associate who was now a producer for American public television. Claudine pressed, and Ben pressed back. Even so, Ben knew he'd be sitting in the front row.

One of Ben's conditions for agreeing to sit in the front row was that he could choose his own wardrobe. That was fine with Claudine, since she didn't think he could go far wrong at a black tie event. When he walked through the stage curtains, she looked up from the clipboard on the backstage lectern, looked him over, and beamed broadly. He wore the cashmere shawl-lapel jacket and the tuxedo pants she had created for him. Beneath the jacket, he wore a crisply-starched white bib-front tuxedo shirt, tieless and open at the collar. A silver silk scarf hung around his shoulders, the tasseled ends kissing his waist. Her smile though was aimed primarily at the hem of his trousers. He wore perfectly black, intricately-tooled Lucchese boots. Perfect, perfect. Ben kissed her on each cheek, "*bisou, bisou*," wished her well, reminded her that he loved her, and kissed her on her forehead. He turned and disappeared back through the curtains. Claudine returned to her clipboard, then went back into the huge dressing room for one last inspection before showtime, encouraging the dressers, fluffing the models' egos, and rallying her own emotions.

Claudine and Ben seldom shared their designs before they were produced, unless one had a difficulty and wanted the other's eye. Strangely enough, given their arts, Ben's work was more intuitive, Claudine's more analytical. She worked in geometry, texture, drape, construction. He worked in space, light and shadow, vista, enclosure and release. Even his interiors, with their programmatic and functional demands, spoke of his sense of progression through space, often using color and texture to map the journey.

The spring collection was stunning: Bright whites overlaid with silver; ecru-tonal changes splashed with bright yellows, printed and appliquéd; pants draped soft and full around the legs; tops defined with fitted bodices and camisoles. The overall effect was sexy, yet demure. Claudine had taken a big chance with the subtlety of her colors, akin to the perfect seasoning of a simple dish. The designs required brilliance and consummate skill and a *soupçon* of confidence.

AS THE PARADE of models ended and the music subsided, Claudine emerged to a thunderous applause. Ben stood, the front row followed, and then the entire crowd. Claudine beamed. Two assistants approached Ben laden with flowers, but with a wave of his hand, he dismissed them. Pulling a robust branch with small long thin leaves and tiny blue flowers from his jacket, he mounted the stage. The twig looked like the offering of a child who had found a flowering weed to offer to his love.

As Ben reached the top of the stairs, Claudine looked at the twig, recognized it, and rushed into his arms. From the motion of her head against his shoulder he knew she was crying. He stood calmly, cradling her against him until she raised her head from his shoulder and he released her. She took a microphone from a model standing behind her.

"This is my husband, Ben, who knows all the small stories of me and celebrates each one." She held up the twig to the audience. "This is rosemary, the herb of memory and one of my favorites from the gardens in Cannes. He brought it to me tonight so that I will remember. Remember love."

The crowd erupted anew. Ben and Claudine walked back the length of the runway hand in hand, exiting through the cluster of models at the end and past the parting curtains. The crowd began to collect belongings and line up to exit through the drapes that enclosed the show space within the d'Orsay's cavernous hall. Ben had arranged for the ushers to hand out sprigs of rosemary, and as the scent of rosemary passed from hand to hand, the ushers took up the chant, "Remember love."

"Remember love."

"Remember love."

THREE WEEKS LATER, the new issue of *Paris Vogue* featured Ben and Claudine on the cover, holding the twig of rosemary over the caption "Remember love."

61

WHEN BEN WAS ON HIS FLIGHT TO PARIS, IT SEEMED to him that three weeks away from the U.S. would make for a long, long sojourn. A week-and-a-half into his stay, however, the three weeks felt like a miniscule blip in the march of time. He had promised Pascal that nothing would change in the operation of Satart Holt, but he found himself scheming to find ways to spend more time in Europe. With Pascal spending so much of his time in Brazil and Argentina, perhaps Ben should spend more time in Paris. Every time he hatched a new scheme, the realities of the U.S. offices intruded. There were more than one hundred employees in New York now and twenty five in Boston. He and Pascal had agreed to open a San Diego office to service a large project under development there, and the Washington DC office with three people would open a month after Ben's return.

It was all getting too big, too complicated, and Ben found himself in too many management meetings that devolved into discussions of how to reduce the number of pencils that were ordered. Other than Ocean Park, much of his design time was spent in review meetings revising the hard work of others and becoming more ornery. Each meeting seemed to be a repeat of the meeting before. One morning while in Paris, he found himself sitting in the pergola sketching organizational charts instead of design ideas. Looking at his two-page sketch showing the number of people he directed, he knew that changes needed to be made. He crossed the courtyard to Claudine's atelier, let himself into her office, and took a new notebook from one of her cabinets. He sat at her desk and sketched drawings in a half-dozen different colors of pencil.

THE WEEKEND BEFORE Ben was to return to the U.S., Claudine, Ben and the boys planned to spend a long four days in Cannes. Ben was dispatched to deal with the headmistress at the boys' school, to inform her that Daniel and Pascha would be out of school on Friday and Monday. Most of the parents avoided informing the head mistress of any variance from the school schedule or standards, fearing her acerbic rebuke. Heads of corporations, used to directing whole populations of staff, deferred to her. Movie stars, pop musicians and television personalities, used to having their peculiar demands met, kept their complaints about teachers and curriculum to themselves.

Whether through ignorance or optimism, Ben waltzed into Camille Nadeau's office on Thursday morning and told her of the family's plans for the weekend. His tone was matter-of-fact and he offered no opportunity for objection. When Madam Nadeau suggested assignments for the children during their recess, Ben waved her off with a sweep of his hand.

"There will be no time for that."

Madame Nadeau's response was equally direct, *"D'accord."*

One of the parents who'd been sitting meekly in the anteroom heard the exchange through the open door. Word spread quickly. Ben became an instant legend. Parents talked about confronting the headmistress themselves, but none ever did.

WHEN THE LONG weekend was over, Ben prepared to return to the U.S. The languid days in the sun at Cannes, reading on the terrace, walking on the beach with Daniel and Pascha before Claudine awoke, and cruising the shops and enjoying long family dinners had refreshed Ben. He'd sketched and written in the notebook he'd taken from Claudine. He was close to devising a plan that would set him free, set Pascal free, and build a new foundation for the office they had built. He was more excited than he'd been in years.

The day before he left for New York, Claudine appeared as he ate lunch at the Paris café with Pascal. Ben rose and hugged her, kissing both cheeks. She beamed as Pascal held the chair for her. Saks had called. They were offering her a place on the third floor at the Fifth Avenue store. Would Ben please go by and look at the space? He *must* design it, of course—no assistants. It must be Ben, himself. She didn't stay to eat, but grabbed a single olive and placed it to her lips. Her tongue flashed and the olive disappeared. She made apologies for interrupting them, but before they could object, she was gone.

62

B EN WAS ONLY IN NEW YORK FOR TWO DAYS BEFORE
he left for Boston. There was much work to do on Ocean Park—
some of it to answer the questions of the contractors—but much of it to
prepare materials for the prospectus for the new investors. Two representatives of the Bermuda-based insurance company, Messers Belmont
and Leicester, would be visiting the site in the middle of the next week.
Armando Lowell had prepared financials for them, which updated
those sent to Bermuda earlier. Ben's staff produced large boards high-
lighting some of the information, information that included photos of
the completed portions of the project, artists' renderings of the work
underway in the second phase, and photos of the work planned for the
third phase. A final board showed the timelines for the project—all
twenty years of it—and highlighted important dates with thumbnail
images related to each of those dates.

On the Monday before the meeting, Ben had the large site
model removed from the City Hall lobby and installed in the Ferry
Building. The largest of the model apartments was spruced up, re-
painted and cleaned, with new furniture installed to await Belmont
and Leicester. Ben wanted control of their entire experience, so he
nixed the idea of them staying in a Boston hotel. They would be met
at the airport, whisked to the East Boston wharf, and ferried directly
to Ocean Park. The only element he couldn't control was the weather.

When he jokingly asked the pastor at St. Mary's to intervene with heaven on his behalf, the priest had simply replied with a smile, "I'm in sales...you need to get in touch with operations."

The day before the presentation, Ben decided to relax by taking a ride up the coast to Rockport along the scenic route that he and Annie had taken a long time ago. He hadn't been to Rockport in almost twenty years and thought that its combination of history and kitsch was just the antidote he needed. The prospect of being driven in a Suburban was unappealing though, and the Jags were parked in the garage at Ocean Park. Without telling anyone, he took the T to Lewis Wharf where the ferry was docked. He hopped on the ferry just as it was leaving the dock and rode it to Lynn under the guise of making a final site visit.

AFTER HALF AN hour spent with the site-work super, Ben walked to the garage and slipped into the XKE. He inserted the key into the ignition, turned it to "accessories," and lowered the top. Then he turned the key in the other direction, started the engine, slipped into gear, and pulled from the garage waving his security card at the automatic gate. Once on the road, he tuned the radio, looking for some oldies 60's station, but settled on NPR. The classical music provided the background chant that relaxed him.

He drove on along the shore, through Swampscott into Marblehead, then up through Salem over the bridge into Beverly, turning off of 1A and onto route 127 for the ride up along the seashore communities. Once he got to Pride's Crossing, he noticed that the roadside landscape seemed unchanged since he'd ridden these roads with Annie. He thought of her briefly and found that the sadness that enveloped his memories of her remained. Not even his love for Claudine and the boys—for his life and his work—could erase the lingering pain in his heart. He smiled, glad that the feeling was still there.

Ben found a parking spot immediately in front of the Madras Shop. He started walking up the same side of the street, looked at the street number of the shop and realized that the address for the photography gallery he'd heard about would be on the other side of the street. He crossed in front of a parked car and peered to the left at a line of cars snaking slowly up the street. He crossed ahead of them and found the address a few doors up.

As soon as he entered the gallery, he was enthralled. There were a few landscapes and seascapes, but most of the paintings were vignettes of gates and doors and windows, intriguingly-colored and exquisitely lit by sunlight. By the time he was ready to leave, he had collected a half-dozen of the doors and a trilogy of photographs of a small town in England called Clovelly. One piece showed the road winding to the left in its approach to the town, one had been taken from under a stone bridge with houses chockablock on either side of a cobbled street, and the third had been taken from the end of the main road across the dock to the sea.

"Will you take a check?"

"Yes, Mr. Holt."

"Do I know you?"

"I doubt it, but I know of you, and I know your work." The photographer pushed a business card toward Ben so that he could write the check.

"Well," Ben said. "David Edward Dempster, now I know *your* work and wonder if you would make photographing my work part of it."

"I don't do contract work."

"I'm not thinking of contract work. You'd be free to photograph what you like, to interpret what you see with your unique eye. There is a narrative in your photographs that intrigues me. Will you think about it?"

"I won't say no…not yet, anyway, but don't count on it."

"I can be very persuasive."

"I imagine so. Thank you for buying my art."

Dempster agreed to ship the framed photographs to Ben's New York office. They shook hands and Ben left the shop, standing at the closed door and scanning up and down the street. He decided to head toward Bearskin Neck. He crossed the street just before the Jag, checked the time on the meter, and topped it off with another dime.

Ben spent an hour cruising the shops, taking in the gaudy, the baudy, and the beautiful. There was a crowd in front of the moccasin shack and smaller groups in front of the lobster shack and the ice cream window. Ben negotiated his way around them all. He stopped at a couple of the small galleries and a silversmith before reaching the end of the jetty. He returned on the other side of the narrow road and stopped in a toy store where he bought a couple of whirligigs for the boys. At the landside end of the road, he turned up Mount Pleasant Street looking for the old art supplies store. It was gone. A one-hour photo shop occupied half of its former space. The other half was empty and "available," according to the sign in the window.

Returning to the car, he placed the bag with the toys behind the passenger side seat, walked around to the driver's side, dropped into the low seat and started the engine. He pulled neatly from the spot and accelerated up Main Street, a pleasant rumbling trailing behind.

DIANE STOOD AT a display at the front of the store looking at brightly-colored Bermuda shorts. She noticed movement near the beautiful car beyond the window and refocused her eyes in the bright light on the beautiful man slipping into it. Her heart skipped a beat when she realized the man was Ben. She stood staring at him until he pulled from the curb and drove away, the rumbling of the car's engine singing to her. She felt a light touch on her shoulder and turned around.

"What are you looking at?"

"Ben...Ben Holt."

"You saw *Ben*?"

"The Jaguar was his."

Diane peered into Annie's face, looking for a reaction. There was a flash of something, but it was gone before she could define it.

"His wife must've bought it for him," Diane said.

"I imagine he has enough money of his own to buy a Jag."

"Yeah, but according to the magazine she makes more and comes from money."

"I'm just saying..."

"You always defended him."

"So?"

"Why didn't you marry him?"

"He wasn't in love with me, he was in love with you."

"Well, that didn't work out for him, did it?"

"Maybe it did. They seem to be happy and they're both certainly successful. You'd probably wear her clothes if you could afford them."

"She's not that hot. Tell me when she's on the third floor at Saks Fifth Avenue."

"A lot of successful designers never make the third floor at Saks."

"The best do."

"And what do you own from one of them?"

"I have my Diane von Furstenberg."

"That you bought at Filene's basement."

"Still..."

63

A S HE CLEARED THE VILLAGE, BEN RAISED THE convertible's top, accelerated and turned on the radio. The station was still tuned to NPR, and Ben was drawn in by the broadcaster's gravelly voice.

"One year ago today a chartered American seven-forty-seven took off from Washington on a flight to London. It never arrived. Just short of two hours into its flight, it plunged into the sea, killing two hundred and fifty people."

Music rose with the soloist singing "Amazing Grace." The music subsided.

"Today, on the National Mall, relatives and friends, coworkers of the crew, investigators and just plain folk gathered for a memorial service."

Music rose again and faded as the song ended.

"Greg Lynch's life changed forever that day. His pregnant wife, Linda, and his two sons, aged three and six, died on that plane. Craig is the former Director of Aviation for the U.S. Border Patrol and is now the owner of an aircraft servicing company, known as an FBO or Fixed Base of Operations, based in Virginia. He says that he came to Washington for the memorial service to remember his family and to see the family members of the other victims who he came to know so well in the days and weeks after the plane was lost.

"Mr. Lynch, thank you for joining us."

"Thank you, Chris."

"It must have been hard for you to come to Washington, to relive those painful days when you were waiting for news about your family, perhaps

hoping that they might be found alive, then the weeks waiting for the recovery of their bodies. Why did you come?"

"We all came to honor the loved ones who we lost and to reconnect with those with whom we shared this tragedy. We share an experience and a relationship that no one who hasn't been through this can truly understand. They might be sympathetic and supportive, but they just can't understand."

"You are a leader of the survivors group and, given your work, more knowledgeable about aircraft than others. Has this helped you deal with the NTSB and other government agencies?"

"Perhaps later in the investigation I could help others understand some of the details. Early on it helped in dealing with the FBI when there was a criminal investigation underway as a result of some reports from commercial fishermen in the area who reported seeing a flash across the sky just before the plane fell."

"They thought it was a missile as I recall."

"Yes."

"When was that theory extinguished?"

"Almost two weeks later, after they lifted the largest pieces of the fuselage from the seabed."

"Did you see that section?"

"I had the opportunity to see the reconstructed aircraft. I looked for a missile hole and there was none. All of the metal was bent outward and was in the area near the center fuel tank. The plane was brought down by bad design, the air conditioning unit adjacent to that tank had heated the fuel and a spark of electricity had ignited it, all exacerbated by the age of the plane."

"The families have filed suit against the airline and the aircraft manufacturer claiming negligence. Wasn't it all just a tragic accident?"

"It was an avoidable event, fueled by negligence and greed. The initial design, with an air-conditioning unit adjacent to the fuel tank contributed. Some executive at the airline chose to make money by flying that aircraft long after its useful life. That aircraft was designed for a lifecycle of sixty thousand hours. It had flown more than a hundred thousand hours before it took off."

"What are you and the other family members seeking?"

"*I can speak for myself, but I think most of the others would agree, that we have an obligation for justice. We have an obligation to our loved ones to make sure that this never happens again.*"

"*Will money do that?*"

"*I think so…we hope so. There are mornings I wake up so angry that I want to find that executive and that designer and kill them, so that they never kill again.*"

"*Do the legal maneuvers of the airline and the manufacturer make you more frustrated and angry?*"

"*It's repugnant to think that they killed my family and so many others, and then, in the days just before the anniversary, they filed a petition claiming the Death on the High Seas Act applies to this case, limiting their financial exposure to compensating the families of victims who were earning a wage. Children, retirees, people like my wife who was a volunteer attorney for the Innocence Project are, they claim, of no monetary value. In their eyes these people are worthless. It's all a feeble attempt to avoid justice.*"

"*Are there people who advise you to give this up, to move on with your life, to close this chapter?*"

"*People talk about closure, sure, but I don't want closure. I want to remember my wife and my sons. Sometimes in a day I'll think that I should play ball with my sons when I get home, then I remember that they won't be there. Sure that makes me sad, but then I smile because I can remember them and that feeling.*"

"*Greg Lynch, thank you for talking with us today.*"

"*Thank you for having me.*"

"*I'm Chris Rollins from Washington. This is APS. We'll be back after this break.*"

ONE PHRASE RETURNED repeatedly to Ben's mind: "Obligation for justice."

64

August 1990

BEN HAD BEEN AT THE CAPITOL DINER FOR TWENTY minutes and had finished his third cup of coffee. It was unusual for Doug Strout to be this late. Ben ordered his usual diner breakfast and resolved to leave after he ate it if Doug hadn't shown up by then.

Shirley was headed up the aisle with his breakfast plate in her left hand and two small plates stacked on her left forearm, when Doug came through the door and followed her up the aisle. Shirley stopped at Ben's table and Doug slipped behind her into the chair opposite Ben.

"Just black coffee and dry toast, Honey."

Shirley looked at Doug quizzically.

"Doc says you're killing me."

Shirley shook her head and walked off. Doug slid his chair around so that he was sitting next to Ben. Shirley arrived and set the coffee on the table.

"Where were you?" Ben said. "I was about to leave."

"You have quite an entourage. I've been watching them."

"Them? The guy in the black Suburban is mine. I went off by myself, driving up to Rockport, left my driver at home. It pissed Claudine off and we had a big argument about it. Now I can drive myself only if I have a tail."

"There are three guys...four actually...but *three* vehicles. *Two* black Chevys and your Suburban."

"I think that makes it three black Chevys."

"Keep screwin' around. These guys are serious."

"So am I."

Doug looked Ben in the eyes. Ben didn't blink. Doug thought about another plea to Ben about acting serious, but knew it would be useless. Underneath the smiles and jokes, Ben had a tempered strength. Ben's jocular personality bothered Doug, but he had learned from his checks on Ben that he could bring the heat when he needed or wanted to. Several contractors attested to that.

"The Suburban...*your* guy...is parked diagonally across the street with a clear view of the door and with that first guy in his sight. That guy is probably Turkish, Ukrainian or Russian." Doug read the question on Ben's face. "He's smoking black Sobranies. At first I thought that the other car was FBI, but they're not...they're Secret Service."

"Why would Secret Service be following *me*?"

"I don't know...yet. Are you printing money in your basement or involved in some international financial scheme?"

"No. And our financial people have been very careful about our reporting, both for my office and for Claudine's. Marcel uses the same people. They're actually Marcel's people."

"What about the financing for Ocean Park?"

"Marcel's investment is from funds generated by his U.S. operations, as is mine, which is relatively small anyway. There are the French and the Spanish banks with sizable investments, but they are in the U.S. with other investments much bigger than ours. I don't know the details of their relationship with the U.S. government, but I expect that they're above-board and experienced with financial transaction reporting."

"Even if they weren't, it wouldn't make sense for the Secret Service to be following you because of them..."

"Did you think of asking them?" Ben smiled.

"Actually I *did* ask them. That's how I found out that they were Secret Service. Guy in the passenger seat flashes his badge and tells me to fuck off."

Ben looked at Doug. Old baseball cap, nylon windbreaker over a polo shirt. Ben assumed that Doug's pants were wrinkled khakis and that he was wearing old Keds. These were Doug's work clothes; they allowed him to disappear like the average geezer on the street. The only striking element of his clothing was the Yankee logo on his cap. Ben had read a novel with a character dressed like Doug in it, an international hit-man with a penchant for assassinations on crowded streets. The only description that witnesses could give was of a guy in a Yankee's cap. Even in Berlin and Rome, they hated the Yankees.

"I'll find out what's going on, but I'm sure you wanted a report on what I found out about Don's murderer."

"I do."

"He's back," Strout said. "Reappeared as instantly as he disappeared, and he's back at the same game. .running a book...but now he's looking to move into drugs. That's a dangerous move. He's looking to move in on some really nasty folk."

"When did he reappear?"

"Yesterday."

"What's his life expectancy?"

"Less than a year, maybe a lot less."

"Good."

"I can understand why you'd want him dead. I'd feel the same way in your shoes."

"I want to kill him."

"I know. No one can blame you for feeling that way."

"No, no. I want to assassinate him. *Myself.* I want you to tell me about how you trained CIA agents. Let's say I'm writing a novel and am doing research."

"No can do."

"Why? You *know* he's scum."

"Yes, and if he killed my brother, *I'd* probably kill him."

"Then why won't you do just this little thing for me? You wouldn't be involved."

"You're a good guy with a good life, a good wife, and a good family. People depend on you. You have something to give to make the world better that others don't have. Don't go off on some 'obligation for justice' thing."

"I've heard that phrase before."

"Obligation for justice?"

"Yes."

"Killing a man face to face requires more than an understanding of technique. I've seen it change strong men: Army Rangers, Navy SEAL's, Special Ops."

"You don't think I have the balls?"

Doug shook his head slowly, pensively. "Listen, don't ask me about this again. I'll assume you were kidding. If you pursue this with me, I'm going to the cops with it. Understood?"

"Understood."

"Now you can buy me a real breakfast. I'm done with this black coffee and dry toast crap. Shirley!"

BEN AWOKE ANGRY, more tired and irritated than he'd been in a long time. He was angry with himself for going to Strout with his intentions. He thought that he could have been more subtle and drawn out the information he needed from Strout in conversation over time, but he didn't *have* time. It was getting late to send out the message that killing Don had created a family obligation. He resisted saying "obligation for justice" again. He wasn't sure how justice played in this case. Clyde had killed family; that was the only point.

Ben would be flying to Paris in two weeks, then on to meet Claudine and the boys in Cannes. He had thought about making the hit the night before he left. The problem now was that he had no plan. He felt he'd been naïve to expect Strout to provide one. There would be no easy way; he had to do this entirely on his own. He wondered if Strout would go to the cops if Clyde Washington's body showed up. He realized that he might suddenly have an interest in keeping Washington alive and healthy. He fell back into an uneasy sleep.

When he opened his eyes again, he stared at the ceiling and played his meeting with Strout over and over in his mind. He was determined to proceed with his plan, then, realizing how foolish the whole enterprise might be, was determined to abandon it. Strout was prob-ably right—he *didn't* have the balls. He *had* said say that, hadn't he?

Ben looked at the clock on the bedside radio. It was almost four a.m. He got up, threw on some sweats, and headed to the kitchen. He poured a glass of milk and took three Club Orange cookies from the refrigerator. He took his snack and went to the bath off the master bedroom. He turned on the tap and let the Jacuzzi fill with water while he went into the library on the other side of the bedroom. He took the hand-colored photo of Don, Ron, Jen and himself and went back into the bath, setting the photo, milk, and cookies on the wood-en surround of the Jacuzzi. As the bath continued to fill, he peeled off the sweats and slid into the tub, pressing the control button that brought a soothing flow of water in a low, bubbling rumble that beat against the muscles in his back.

He was barely in the tub when he arose, stepped out, and, with-out drying himself, crossed to the library again. There, he picked up a framed picture of Claudine, Daniel and Pascha and headed back into the bath.

Ben decided to drive up to the Ocean Park project, then changed his mind and decided that taking the ferry might be a better choice. He liked taking the ferry and liked the different perspective that the ferry gave him of the Ocean Park project. He would walk over to the Capitol diner for breakfast and he might be able to enjoy his day without the Claudine-ordered security tail. Thinking of Claudine raised a hollow feeling in his heart and he longed to be with her, to be with the boys in the Mediterranean sun. He longed for this night-mare starring Clyde Washington to be over.

As the ferry drew around Point of Pines and approached Ocean Park from the southeast, Ben was struck by the way the sunlight hit the completed buildings at the far end of a development, reveal-ing a texture of structures he thought of as "toothiness," much like the texture of a great Côtes de Beaune. He looked at the unfinished portion of the project closest to him and the crystal enclosure of the Winter Garden. The master plan envisioned the unfinished portion to be built in much the same way as the first section—similar massing, similar texture, consistent color. Ben suddenly realized that this would be all wrong. He took his sketchbook from his jacket pocket and started outlining a massing that reflected the way the clouds settled on the panorama.

In the ten minutes that it took for the ferry to make its way to the dock, Ben had completed three sketches that would completely rework the newest and last phase of the development. His mood rose. Long ago he had learned that ideas were often buried deeply, but would emerge into the light in due time. The work of the designer was to unearth them.

He planned to have the Boston staff start work on developing his sketches into construction documents tomorrow. His immediate goal was to have breakfast. After that, he would begin his plan for killing Clyde Washington. The world looked particularly bright this morning.

65

B EN SPENT MUCH OF MONDAY WORKING WITH
Bernie and John on the new designs for phase three of Ocean
Park. They devised a way to keep the same mix of housing units
while reconfiguring the buildings and their massing. The office staff
would prepare drawings for the estimators so that the development
team could determine the impact on the budget. Ben was convinced
that his new plan, which placed more building mass and more housing units directly on the water, would bring in more revenue to offset
any additional costs. The designs would go to the marketing people
as soon as the estimators and development managers could determine
a per unit cost.

By three p.m., Ben was done with his meetings and went to his
office to call his parents. He had a surprise for them. He was going to
fly them to Cannes for a visit with Claudine and the boys. As an added incentive, he promised his father a three-day side trip to England
and Ireland to play golf. They would leave in nine days if their pass-
ports were up-to-date. His father jumped at the opportunity for golf;
his mother just wanted to spend time with her grandchildren. Ben
promised to have someone take care of the house and the cat while
they were away.

Early that evening, while the sun was slowly descending behind the used auto parts lot, Ben drove one of the Ocean Park

Volkswagens down Alley Street. It was too early for much activity to be in evidence at Clyde's childhood home-turned-headquarters, but Ben knew the building, anyway. He peered beyond the house at the elevated track bed of the B&M Railroad and remembered the long summer days playing along the tracks with his brothers and friends. The girl he liked in sixth grade had lived two houses down from the Washington's and he had stopped along the track bed from time to time to watch her and her sister in the yard until the taunts from his friends had drawn him away.

"Knit one, purl two..."

Ben made a mental note to return and walk the tracks for a surveillance from that vantage point. He wondered if the old switch house was still standing over on Commercial Street. He yearned to write his thoughts and his plan in his notebook, but knew that would be a mistake. No notes.

FOUR DAYS LATER, in a light drizzle, Ben walked the tracks in old, brown Oshkosh overalls and an old, faded, cotton shirt over a V-neck T-shirt. The boots he'd borrowed from the maintenance locker room at Ocean Park were a size too small, and his feet hurt. He logged another mental note: boots too small. They altered his normal gait.

When he came to the rear corner of Clyde's headquarters, he pulled a large wrench from the long pocket along his pant leg, bent over, and pretended to check a bolt. He proceeded down the track, repeating his actions every four feet or so while taking in the house, its doors, windows, parked cars, and a picnic table near the back door.

Ben decided he would need at least one more visit, a late-night one, before he could execute his plan—and Clyde. Time was running short. His parents would leave on Wednesday, Clyde would die Thursday night, and Ben would be in Cannes a week from tomorrow. He would have preferred to do his late night recon on the same night of the week as the night of the hit, but there was no time for that. He decided that Tuesday night was too close to D-night, and he might need Tuesday for one last visit. Sunday might be an off-night, so it could only be Monday night for the next visit.

Late Sunday morning, Ben went to his parents' house, knowing that his mother would be in church and his father would be at the golf course. He brought with him a new black suitcase for his father and the three-piece luggage ensemble with flowers printed in the fabric for his mother. He found the key to the front door under the doormat.

Entering through the vestibule to the living room, he called out to his mother to make sure no one else was in the house. Getting no reply, he set down the luggage and headed up the stairs to his parents' bedroom. He crossed immediately to his father's closet, its door open as usual, and reached into the back right corner of the top shelf, feeling for the hard, steel handle of the gun and noting its orientation before he withdrew it. He was glad to see that it was as shiny as the day he'd first seen it some thirty years earlier, probably as shiny as it had been the day it had been issued to his father before boarding the B-24 on his first training flight. He released the clip and saw it was fully loaded. Thankfully, for his current purposes anyway, his father didn't believe in unloaded guns.

He withdrew a similar gun from underneath his jacket. Ben had bought the gun at an auction. It was registered; his father's gun was not. He compared the two guns. They were identical in Ben's eyes. He knew his father would be able to tell the difference between them, if he knew there was one. In that case, Ben counted on the fact that no one would listen to the old coot anyway.

Ben wiped his father's gun, replaced it exactly as he had found it, and left the bedroom. He went downstairs and out the front door. He was headed for the car when he remembered that the key was still in his pocket. He went back up the front stairs, replaced the key, and turned back down to the sidewalk and the waiting Suburban.

His driver, Charles—because Thomas was off on Sundays—opened the door for Ben.

"Thanks, Charles."

Ben realized he still needed to work out a car plan for the coming week. Taking one of Ocean Park's cars would be a problem, emblazoned as they were with the "O," stylized with an ocean wave across it. He briefly considered the auto junkyard, but gave that up as too risky, given the guard dogs and night watchman. He put the problem aside, like he often did with difficult problems, knowing that the solution would come to him in due time. Time though, was not a currently bountiful commodity.

Eureka!

"I'll be going to the office, Charles. You can leave me there and go on home. I'll be staying at the apartment tonight, then driving to Woodstock in the morning."

"Yes, sir. How long will you be away? They told Thomas to expect to take you to the airport at the end of the week."

"I'll be back by Thursday…Friday at the latest."

"Yes, sir."

"Oh, and can you arrange to have my parents driven to the airport on Wednesday?"

"Yes, sir."

The thought of Vermont, which came to him as Charles had slipped into the driver's seat of the Suburban, made him smile. There was an old stake-body truck in the barn that was only used for moving hay from the fields. He had thought of junking it for a while; now he had the perfect use for it, and the junkyard off of Shepard Street was about to get an unsolicited donation.

THE OLD MAN wore a ratty red bandana over his head, tied at the nape of his neck. It was covered by an even more ratty straw hat with several of the straw weavings tattering at the edge of the uneven brim. Attached to the front was a huge, green plastic badge that read "John Deere" with a tractor on a field of wheat behind the words. He wore a T-shirt under his old long-sleeved chambray work shirt, its sleeves buttoned at the wrist, despite the warmth of the day. He drove with the windows open, his elbow resting on the sill and the cigar stuck between his fingers. The back of the old stake-body truck was empty, except for a few blades of straw, which would occasionally take flight as the wind picked up. Stopping for gas, he handed the gas station attendant a ten-dollar bill for nine dollars worth of gas and slowly pulled out onto the country road. A BMW headed south stopped just short of him and the driver blared his horn, yelling and gesturing while the old man returned friendly waves, noting the New York plates.

The old truck and the old man traveled together down Route 5, across the Massachusetts border to Route 2. They then headed east all the way to Route 128, turning north until coming to Route 129 in Lynnfield. They stopped at Perley Gilbert's service station for gas, then again a minute later at Goodwin's for a grilled cheese and tomato sandwich.

When the counter girl asked what he wanted to drink, the old man asked how much it would be for water. She told him water was free. He told her it would be water then. He took two folded one dollar bills from his billfold and counted the correct change from an oblong plastic purse that opened when he squeezed its sides. The counter girl looked at him sympathetically. She noticed he was actually quite handsome under his growth of scraggly whiskers. She told him to go to the next window to pick up his order.

As the old man turned from the window, he noticed that a short line had formed behind him. A middle-aged couple was first in line. They had waited some five feet behind him and backed away as he turned so that they bumped into the young couple behind them, almost knocking a pregnant woman over and setting off a small melee of angry shouts and proffered apologies.

Happily for the occupants of the line, the old man's order arrived quickly and they didn't need to spend much time shuttling from foot to foot waiting for their food in his company. The old man hobbled away toward the old truck, opened the loudly creaking door, lifted himself inside, and ate his sandwich, wiping his whiskers with the back of his left hand each time he drank from the paper cup.

"Probably spiked with cheap whiskey," the male of the pregnant couple offered, loudly enough to be sure the old man could hear.

Because he'd gone to Woodstock, Ben had missed his Monday night reconnaissance, but figured the trade-off was worth it. It was dark when he parked in the elementary school lot. He made a quick change before heading up the hill to his parents' house. Moving quickly, he retrieved the key and, without turning on any lights, headed up to his father's closet and exchanged the guns. He was out of the house and back down the hill to the truck in under fifteen minutes. He didn't think anyone had seen him. He probably hadn't needed to have changed before heading to the house, but he hadn't wanted any neighbors to see the old man at his parents' house. He settled into the truck, took a deep breath, and let it out slowly. Moving to the passenger side, he changed back into the old man's clothes. Tonight his obligation to Don would be met.

66

A S BEN DROVE DOWN SHEPARD STREET AND
approached the railroad bridge, he saw two black cars parked
a block ahead near the auto junkyard. Official cars. Fords. The headlights were off, but the dome light in one of the cars was on, and the
two men in the front seat were turned toward the back seat, apparently talking to someone there Ben couldn't see. He peered at the
license plate of the closest car: New York plates. So they weren't state
or local undercover. Feds, maybe. Dumb Feds with the dome light
on. Ben shook his head. What were they doing?

Then a man in a dark suit walked from Alley Street, turning away
from Ben, and hurried to the waiting cars. The guy walked like a
Fed—heel, toe, heel, toe. He walked to the driver's side of the car
closest to Ben and got into the back seat. The dome light went out.

Headlights behind Ben cast a shaft of light through the small
rear window of the stake-body truck. There was a lot more activity
for this hour than Ben had anticipated. He thought of driving on,
but the headlights turned into an alley behind him. The Ford with
the four men moved toward Ben, its headlights still off, then turned
down Alley Street, leaving the second, empty Ford behind. A gold
Cadillac pulled onto Shepard street from the Lynnway, slowed as it
passed the Ford, then turned down Alley Street, too.

For the moment the street was quiet, and Ben took the opportunity to hobble from the truck and slip through a gap in the fence

that secured, more or less, the railroad tracks. He climbed up the embankment to the track bed and walked toward his planned post behind Clyde Washington's headquarters. Halfway there, he heard furtive voices in the tall weeds beside the tracks, followed by low and intermittent moans. He smiled: Kids having sex in the weeds.

He moved on, wishing he had a silencer for the gun. He had thought of ordering one, but discarded the idea. He wanted to leave no trails.

He reached the spot he had selected from which to watch the picnic table in Clyde's backyard. There was a hole in the fence adjacent to it, so the line of attack and the line of retreat would be convenient and swift—swift being an important virtue. Ben took off the too-small boots and laid them next to his feet. He'd worn no socks; he would attack barefoot. Hobbling might disguise his gait, but disguise was not important now. Quite the contrary. He wanted Clyde to know who it was, wanted Clyde to know that justice had come upon him and that Ben had satisfied his obligation.

Over the next hour-and-a-quarter, Ben watched the floodlit picnic table. Visitors would arrive singly or in pairs, sit at the table with Clyde, slide fat envelopes across the table, envelopes which Clyde would not pick up, but would instead cover with his left hand and slide from the table to a waiting gym bag. He never took his eyes from his visitors, never lifted his right hand to the table.

Ben surmised that there must be a gun, either in Clyde's waistband, on the bench, or in the gym bag. A complication, perhaps, but one that Ben had considered. He knew that the floodlight would be his cover, that Clyde's eyes wouldn't be able to see far into the dark yard. Ben had to be committed, to be ready and willing to fire as soon as he stepped into the pool of light. He could, of course, fire from the safety of the dark, but Clyde wouldn't know it had been Ben who'd come for him. A split second in the pool of light would be enough. There would be three to five minutes between visitors—more than enough for Ben's attack.

At twelve fifteen, Ben decided the time had come. He would move in as soon as the next visitor got up to leave, using the activity to cover his own movement. The next twelve minutes seemed like twelve hours—time slowing to an excruciating crawl. Finally, the big man sitting in front of Clyde rose from the bench, and Ben moved to the hole in the fence.

The hole was tighter than he thought it would be and the chain-link must have grabbed him, because he somehow couldn't move through into the yard. A bug bit him on the neck and he instinctively reached up to swat it, but his fingers hit something distinctively metallic. He was suddenly falling to his knees, a dark unconsciousness closing in on him. He fought it, but failed to hold it back. A light arose, and he was visited by Claudine and Daniel, Pascha and Don, and finally, by a darkened face with an eyepatch.

The dream came to an abrupt end. Ben's nostrils filled with a salty liquid. He realized he couldn't breathe. He *had* to breathe. Desperately he opened his mouth and gasped for air. A heavy liquid choked him, and he began to cough uncontrollably. He gasped again, and air—cool, salty, heavenly air—filled his lungs. He forced his eyes open and realized it was not dark at all. It was bright and sunny.

His head was resting on a towel, a wet towel that he soon realized was soaked with his own drool. He decided he needed to try to sit up and was surprised to find that he could do so with relative ease. He was groggy and sleepy, but more alert than he'd expected. He glanced at the towel and noticed the logo, a logo which he himself had designed, the logo of the Ocean Park sports club.

Ben looked around and smiled. He knew exactly where he was. Even the smell was familiar. He was face-down on the floor of the trailer that he had once lived in at the America's Park—now Ocean Park—site. It was still sitting on the land that would become the third phase of Ocean Park, now surrounded by weeds and trash, but soon, gloriously soon, it would be a part of his completed masterwork.

BEN WALKED ACROSS the stretch of land between the old trailer and the construction office at Ocean Park. He always kept two changes of clothes there, a suit and jeans. People would see him entering the building and he would need to get someone to let him into the locker room, but he didn't care.

Old Henry was at the security desk. He didn't even raise an eyebrow when he saw Ben. Henry kept to himself, Ben's mother would say. He had retired from life as a dairy farmer in Benedicta, Maine, and was a distant cousin—his second cousin or something like that. Henry had moved to Massachusetts to be near his daughters and their children.

"Man was in to see you yesterday," Henry said.

"Who was it?"

"Don't know, wouldn't say."

"I see."

"Had an eyepatch though and dressed real nice."

"Thanks, Henry." Ben started to walked away, but stopped and turned. "Henry, what day is it?"

"Saturday."

"Thanks, Henry."

There were many things Ben needed to understand, but right now he had things to do. He showered and changed into jeans. He said goodbye to Henry, who barely nodded back at him. He walked to the water taxi dock and waited while a captain and a mate brought a boat around for the unscheduled trip.

BEN THANKED THE captain and mate as he jumped from the boat to the dock, not waiting for the gang plank to be set. He walked up Atlantic Avenue, cut up State, across Tremont and the Common, through the Public Garden, up Commonwealth into the office and his apartment at Hereford Street. He didn't need to pack since he had plenty of clothes at the Cannes house, but there were his notebooks and some gifts he had bought to bring to Claudine, the boys, Marcel, Bernadine and his parents.

He went to his office and read the mail and a pile of memos on his desk. He wrote notes in his own special blue-black ink on the memos and left the reduced pile on the upper right corner of his desk to be taken away Monday morning.

By the time he finished, it was almost four p.m. He looked out the window onto Commonwealth Avenue and saw Charles waiting. Ben grabbed the black leather bag that held the notebooks and gifts and headed out through the office, down the grand staircase, and out to the waiting Suburban.

An hour-and-a-half later, he was seated in the first-class cabin, a glass of red wine in hand. A bottle of sparkling water stood nearby, and a stewardess with a warm towel in hand was at his side.

"Do you have today's Boston and New York papers on board?"

"Yes, Mr. Holt. I'll bring them right over."

"No particular hurry. Thanks."

Ben closed his eyes, but didn't sleep. After the plane took off and reached cruising altitude, he took one of the notebooks from his bag. He opened the newspapers—the *Herald* first, then the *Globe* and the *Post*, then the *Times*—and read them. The story of Clyde Washington's death was on the front page of the *Herald*. It was buried deep in the second section of the *Globe* and in a small sidebar item in the *Times*. None of the stories included much detail.

Like it or not, he would call Doug Strout when he got to Cannes.

67

PEOPLE OFTEN ASKED BEN IF HE LOVED BEING AN ARchitect. Early in his career the answer would've been a resounding "yes," he couldn't dream of doing anything else. There was an intrinsic sensuality to creating massing and space, assembling color, texture and detail. There was a powerful egotism in creating a physical presence that would immediately become part of the history, the symbology of a place.

Music and writing, painting and dance were all arts that Ben admired. All, except for the work of very few artists, were ephemeral. Even when architecture was bad or banal, it became an immediate presence. Ben believed that good architecture influenced people in a way that other arts could not. Architecture was a constant: people moved to it, moved into and out of it, danced along its edges, peered at its canvas. Architecture established the patterns of their lives.

Ben thought of the question again as he sat on the terrace at the Cannes house, drinking his morning coffee and a freshly squeezed orange juice. Like a longtime relationship that starts as a torrid love affair, the fire of passion had subsided and been replaced by a comfortable presence that was constant. Ben mused that architecture was like a favorite old shirt.

Ben loved Claudine with a passion that only grew. She had fascinated him when they'd met, when she'd made him her lover and taught him the pleasures of a fulfilled life. That might have been enough, but

Ben was finding that time burnished his love for her. Their love was not shining brighter, but deeper. He loved Daniel and Pascha, Pascal and Marcel. It was in all of them that his love alighted.

No, he didn't still have a passion for architecture, but as he fingered the buttons of his linen shirt he knew that he could never cast her away.

DOUG STROUT CALLED just after one in the afternoon, making apologies for calling so early. Ben had explained the time difference many times, but Strout didn't seem to comprehend the concept. He had gotten the same reaction in dealing with his parents when he'd called them in Lynn from Paris or Cannes.

Strout wanted to meet. He had asked when Ben would be back in the U.S. When Ben told him it would be at least several more weeks, Strout was silent. After several moments, he asked if Ben could make a special trip. He had some important, very important, news that couldn't be reported over the phone and couldn't wait.

Ben suggested that Strout fly to Cannes and stay for a few days. Strout immediately refused and fell silent again.

"Why won't you come to Cannes? You surely can't be afraid of flying."

"I can't tell you why over the phone."

"I'll meet you in Paris then."

"No. Not Paris, London."

"Okay, London then. This better be good."

"No, it's not good. It's very, very bad."

"When do you want to meet?"

"The day after tomorrow at ten a.m. at Kensington Park on the High Street side. We can walk somewhere and have breakfast."

"No way."

"What?"

"I hate English breakfasts."

"Kensington Park. We'll skip the breakfast."

BERNADINE HAD BEEN planning an opera dinner for several weeks. It was to be the night of the same day that Ben had promised to meet Strout in London. If he took the :et, he could spend a couple of hours with Strout and still be back in Cannes long before the dinner.

Ben paid the attendant two pounds for two chairs. He sat himself under a massive old English oak near the walk that paralleled Kensington High Street. He had placed the two chairs facing each other, carefully placing the second chair so that there would be no glare from the sunlight behind it. He wanted to see Strout's face clearly. There had been an urgency in his voice which Ben wanted to see.

Strout was late, even for Strout. Ben waited half an hour, then decided that Strout was not going to show. As he started to rise from his chair, an old man approached him and held his hand out. He asked whether Ben could help out an old veteran and his dog. The dog, an English springer spaniel, stepped out from behind the man's legs as if on cue. Ben reached into his pocket and found a half dozen coins amounting to a bit over two pounds and placed them in the man's hand.

"Thank you, kind gentleman. May I sit here for a while? My dog and I are quite tired."

"Sure. I was leaving anyway."

"Oh, don't leave. I have so much to tell you."

Ben looked past the scruffy beard and into the man's eyes. There, he found Strout. "Where did you get the dog?"

"Belongs to a friend who lives just off the High Street."

"Great get-up."

"Friend's father lived in the apartment until he died two months ago. She hasn't had the heart to throw him out."

"Well you look great in a dead man's clothes."

"I don't want to see *you* in a dead man's clothes, so listen up. There's a storm growing around you and your family. The hit on Clyde has stirred a maelstrom."

"I didn't kill Clyde."

"I know you didn't, you damned fool "

"Were you the guy who knocked me out?"

"No."

"Do you know who did?"

"Bernadine."

"What?"

"More accurately, Bernadine's man."

Ben remembered the image of the eyepatch as he had lost consciousness that night at the fence. "Bill Button?"

"The same."

"But he's CIA. Aren't they proscribed from assassinations after Gerald Ford's order?"

"Executive order 11905. Yes. But he's not CIA anymore. Got a better offer from Bernadine. Anyway, he was there, but didn't make the actual hit."

"I'm flabbergasted. Bernadine is basically a wealthy housewife. I know that she owns some kind of boutique insurance company in Bermuda, but I don't even think she's active in day-to-day operations. It's an investment vehicle that she and a bunch of her wealthy housewife friends used to invest their extra household allowance. They specialize in high risks that others won't cover and get a high premium for the chances they take. I think they do pretty well, but their pool is quite small..."

"In the last few years they expanded their pool and broadened their investor profile."

"What does that mean?"

Strout described Bernadine's company and its line of business. He explained that they ensured security and construction companies doing business in war zones, small independent oil companies wildcatting wells in lucrative but dangerous areas and small technology and research companies with military potential.

Only about ten percent of the companies they insured survived more than three years, but the ones that did—and stayed current with their premiums—paid off well. Of the companies that didn't survive, about half filed for bankruptcy and often left substantial amounts on their premiums due.

Bernadine's "book" was divided into discrete "pools," with some of the higher-risk pools returning as much as forty percent after it met administrative expenses. Bernadine had only small amounts invested in any of the pools but took thirty percent off the top to cover those administrative expenses, including her profit. The insurance operation was above board and meticulously followed accounting and industry standards.

About seven years ago, Bernadine learned that one of her investors was the front man for an Italian terrorist organization, the Red Brigade. For some reason—maybe fear, maybe greed—she didn't report the investment to authorities. In fact, she used her newfound knowledge to expand her involvement with similar organizations, eventually taking on all comers including competing organizations that were deadly enemies. This had been possible because most of those organizations had evolved from political zealots into well-managed operations with sophisticated management.

Over the last few years it had become increasingly difficult to maintain her returns at the same time that government pressure was causing the arrest and prosecution of many of the leaders of those organizations. As they aged, many of these leaders were looking to cash out and walk away. Bernadine started taking on riskier investments, many unrelated to insurance, and bringing on less sophisticated investors. This is where Clyde Washington came in.

One of Bernadine's new lines of business was making loans to organized crime. She would finance drug deals, the takeover of previously legitimate businesses, and bookmaking. Bookmaking had turned out to be more of a headache than she'd thought it would. The big boys followed the big money—drugs, trash collection, construction—leaving bookmaking to the smaller, less sophisticated hoods. Bernadine was ill-equipped to deal with this culture and found the Clyde Washingtons to be unmanageable.

This is where William Button came into it. Bill had been in Ops for the CIA for several years, working on a joint task force with Treasury and the FBI looking for Commie's hidden in supposedly legitimate businesses. One of the biggest and most diverse of those businesses was Ben's father-in-law's conglomerate. Because of their diversity and management structure, they quickly became a target for the joint task forces interest. The JTF spent years searching out Communists first, then left-wingers, with almost no success. Their only "find" was a couple of janitors who had connections to a socialist political party. Eventually the JTF was disbanded, but not before Button had made the connection to Bernadine's less than legitimate investors and learned that at least part of her business was no more than a money-laundering operation.

Button wanted to use Bernadine and her business to keep tabs on her investors, but no one at the CIA was interested. He never took it to Treasury, though he may have told his wife, Rachel, about it. She had been on the JTF until Treasury found out that she and Button were married and transferred her back to a U.S. desk job. She lasted three weeks, then quit. A month later, she was hired to head up the compliance unit in Bernadine's company. Just over a year later, Button quit and became a freelance "consultant," a problem solver. He worked for a number of interests, including, at one point or another, a major clinical organization, several Fortune 100 companies, and political candidates in the city of Boston.

"Now, here's where you and your brother come in. Don has had a running feud with Clyde Washington for years, but you know that. Don worked for Tony Angelo before Angelo had to turn him loose because of his alcoholism. Don kicks around, working political campaigns for local pols, and runs a small but profitable sports book on the side. He meets Siobhan and starts to turn his life around. Rumors are that he considers dropping the sports book. Too late though. His book is cutting into Washington's business. Washington's newfound friends, Bernadine & Co., pump up his ego and, unbeknownst to her, he decides to play mob boss. He calls in some help from a cousin in Atlanta and orders a hit on Don. Four guys, two from Atlanta and two locals, make the hit.

"Rachel hears that Washington ordered the hit, passes that info onto Bernadine, who calls Washington on the carpet, but is less than impressed with Washington's response. For his part, Washington doesn't *like* being bossed by a woman. Anyway, Bernadine orders the removal of Washington and tells Rachel to take care of it personally."

"Let me guess…Rachel hits Washington and Button drugs me and dumps me at the old construction trailer?"

"Half right. Rachel hits Washington, Button runs cover, drugs you, and leaves you by the fence to take the heat for the hit. *I* dragged you to the construction trailer."

Ben smiled. Strout didn't.

"So what happens from here?"

"Not sure. There was a bit of a complication. Washington didn't die immediately. Tough prick was so stupid that the shot to the back of his head didn't hit anything. The next numbers runner finds him at the picnic table and rushes him to the hospital. Ten minutes in the emergency room and he dies. Nurse says that he said one thing before he died, "Holt." She calls a state cop she knows, Meehan. Meehan calls the Feds who pull the covers over everything."

"Why would they do that?"

"Now you're getting into an area I don't know. When they pull the covers, it gets really dark. They can't keep it dark long, so my guess is that something is going to come down soon."

"How soon?"

"Two days? Two weeks? Probably not more than that."

"Any ideas?"

"I think they were looking for a way to take Bernadine down. They couldn't use the tax route because her companies are based in Bermuda. The hit on Washington may have been her first misstep. They always get careless."

"Shit. This is going to be one fucking mess. Claudine, Marcel, Pascal, the kids. Their world is about to turn inside out."

"Sorry. I know it doesn't count for much, but I *am* sorry."

"She didn't need the money."

"Need is an odd concept, especially when it comes to money."

"I need to get back to Cannes."

"For the opera party?"

Of course Strout would know about the opera party, Ben thought. "No, I need to be with my family."

"Of course."

"By the way, just out of curiosity, what was the nurse's name?"

"Annie something. I can check my notes."

"No need."

68

"CAN I HITCH A RIDE WITH YOU TO CANNES?"
The voice came from behind Ben.

The co-pilot who had been stooping to pick up Ben's shopping bags stood up, and Ben saw the reflection of the eyepatch in the co-pilot's sunglasses.

"Will your wife be joining us?" Ben asked, without turning around.

"*Ex*-wife. No, Rachel is in Cannes already, preparing to fly your mother-in-law to Morocco."

"I didn't know she was a pilot."

"Feds trained her. Helicopters, jets. Anything up to a 727."

"Handy. Sure, you can fly with us. I want to talk to you anyway."

"Are you sure you do? I know you talked to Strout. What he told you is hearsay. Anything more and..."

"I'm not interested in history. I want to offer you a job."

WHEN THE LEARJET reached cruising altitude, the steward brought sparkling water, a plate of hard-boiled eggs, and a small bowl of caviar in a larger bowl of finely crushed ice. He set it on the table between Ben and Bill Button.

"So, Bernadine and Rachel are flying to Morocco. Insurance business? Client meeting?"

"Probably not. She called me at the hotel this morning and asked me to come to Cannes to pick up our daughter. She told me you were meeting Strout in London and that I could probably hitch a ride with you. She said she had to fly Bernadine to Morocco today."

"You have a daughter?"

"Yes. Why...are you surprised?"

"I didn't think people like you and Rachel were *allowed* to procreate."

"I don't think that's very funny."

"It wasn't meant to be funny. They're not flying to Morocco, are they?"

"Probably not."

"Are you going to try to stop them?"

"No. I'm assuming that there will be some kind of a malfunction in the transponder, that radar will show they drifted off course, that the control tower repeatedly tried to contact them without success. Last known position, somewhere off the Canary Islands. Wreckage never found. Something like that."

"Sounds like a plausible scenario."

"The Feds won't buy it, of course...they'll keep trying to find them. In the old days, a couple of skeletons would eventually be found to match their general physique. Then they'd be homefree. Now there's DNA testing."

"Why?"

"What do you mean, why?"

"Why now? What spooked her all of a sudden? It couldn't have been the hit on Washington."

"An old friend of Marcel's at the Finance Ministry tipped him off about Bernadine's business dealings and to the developing criminal case against her. Marcel confronted Bernadine. After the hit, the FBI agent she's been having an affair with told her that Clyde Washington was an FBI informant and had been supplying valuable information on Bernadine's activities. Supposedly the agent didn't know that Rachel made the hit. That's all I know. I can imagine what happened from there, but it would all be conjecture."

"Hmmmm."

"You seem very calm about all of this..."

"It actually solves a big problem for me. The thought of a protracted public battle, disgrace for Marcel, confusion for my sons, pain for Claudine...this simplifies everything, there will be a period of grief, of course, but we can handle that."

"That's an interesting take."

"You seem pretty calm, yourself."

"In this business you always need an exit strategy. This one is a bit obvious, but I think they may be able to pull it off."

"That's why I want to hire you."

"Oh?"

"I want you to work with Marcel. Kill the investigation. Black hole it. That way, if Bernadine and Rachel pull off the disappearance at sea, there's no collateral damage for my family. That's the way I want it to go down."

"You've come a long way from that kid that I first met twenty years ago. Plucked from the Brickyards and plopped down in Paris."

"No. No, I haven't at all."

69

June 1st, 1991

IT WAS DON'S BIRTHDAY. CLAUDINE AND THE BOYS hadn't been back to the U.S. since Bernadine's disappearance. There had been a memorial service, and the U.S. official delegation had been headed by former president Jimmy Carter. There had been no service for Rachel. Button had declared it inappropriate to memorialize an exit strategy and their daughter was too young to understand a memorial service, anyway.

This coming summer, just after Bastille Day, Claudine and the boys would come to spend the summer in South Woodstock. Claudine was pregnant again, very pregnant, and was due in a week. The baby was going to be a girl, Emma, and the boys were thrilled.

Ben had been working long hours and traveling between the U.S. offices and Paris more frequently than his body liked. He would wrap up work today and fly to Paris tonight, staying with Claudine and the boys through Emma's birth, returning with them for the long, languid summer that lie ahead.

Just before four, he asked Thomas to bring the car around. He wanted to go to Ocean Park to see how the last phase was progressing and to make one other stop before heading to the airport.

After a short tour of the Ocean Park site, Ben pulled the pad of gridded paper from his briefcase and quickly drew a map. On it, he marked out thirteen milestones: "Ocean Park—Lynnway—Market

Street—City Hall Square—Franklin Street—Boston Street—Sallie's." Then he handed Thomas the piece of paper.

It was a good day for a Miller.

Acknowledgements

THE OLDER SIBLINGS IN MY FAMILY – BOB, JOHN AND I – were very competitive growing up. We played as many sports as we could and were rather vicious with each other. When we looked for another sport to compete in we would often look through the Encyclopedia of Sports that someone had given me and plotted to try them. I have to admit that we were stymied by Jai Alai.

The competition between us didn't end at sports, though. I included books, and magazines and newspapers – anything that we could read. I think that it was that competition that instilled in me the love of words. For that, I thank them.

I want to thank Tim Huggins and Rebecca Boyd for their kind words and their strong hand. They made this book much better. I also want to thank Jackie Young for reminding me that characters are not only for delivering dialog, they need to be loved and hated and embued with all the emotions that we bring to our lives each day.

I need to thank Diana Beuudoin, Eliza Brown, Isabelle Deschamps Fontaine, JJ and Joanne Green, Christine Jellow, Klaudia Mally, Rosie Niland, Stephanie O'Connell, Tim Morris and Simi Raaven, Matt and Meiling Morris and many others for reading my work.

Finally, to all the students at Grub Street, the second largest independent center for creative writing in the United States, whose hard work and perseverence is an inspiration.

About the Author

GLENN MORRIS IS AN ARCHITECT WHO LIVES JUST A short trip down the Massachusetts Turnpike from Boston. When he's in Boston, he dreams of being in Paris again. When he's in Paris, he dreams of being in Paris again.

His next novel, *Saving Angel*, is due out later this year.

www.ingramcontent.com/pod-product-compliance
Lightning Source LLC
Chambersburg PA
CBHW050859250626
47155CB00001B/27